Love Never Fails

Love Never Fails

When Love is Questioned, When Lies & Betrayal Are Revealed, Take Everything Away But Self & God And True Love will Prevail

Donna Christopher

Love Never Fails

BlackDiamond Publications Inc.

Dedications

I dedicate this book to my loving husband & wonderful children.

To my wonderful loving husband, I love you from my soul, deep within my spirit, with every breathe I take and with all of my heart. I thank God for you, for blessing me with a wonderful husband and making you perfect in his image just for me. To love and care for, laugh with, relax with and smile with. You are my happiness, you are my soul mate, and you are my forever true love! Thank you for your support and believing in me and my dreams. Thanks for having my back and loving me unconditionally.

For my beautiful children created through me, given to me as one of God's greatest blessings. Jameela, Nneka, Asha, Oronde, Adia, Braylon & Bailey, I am so thankful that God loved me enough to bless me with each of you, to love and care for and to embrace me with your love in return, surrounding me with seven great joys of life. Giving me enough patience and love to pour out to you all. Your lives are proof that God is so amazing. You have made me very proud to be your mother. You are my strength, my motivation, my joy, my reason. I appreciate your uniqueness, greatness and your beautiful spirits. Your character and your spirits reflect kindness, love, brilliance and beauty. Greatness is destined for you all! I love each of you to infinity and beyond, from the depths of my soul, with all of my heart!

Atlantis and Malachi, I may not have been the vessel used to give you both life but you are still a beautiful blessing to me. I thank God for sending me your father and giving me two more reasons to love harder. I am proud to be a part of your life and I am proud that you are a part of mine. Thank you for allowing me to embrace you with love. I Love you both very much!

Always remember your future is in your hands to create and make your dreams a reality. With God first, faith and family by your side, your masterpiece will be painted! #LivingIt

Acknowledgements

To all my family and friends, thank you for the encouragement, motivation and patience you have given me. Every reminder to stay focused, every 'I am proud of you', every call, text and e-mail to check on my progress and motivate me through to the end has been appreciated and I love you all forever for your loyalty and love you give back in return.

I heard someone say if you are not a doer of that 'thing' you call yourself, you can't say that you are that 'thing'. Those words turned into motivation. We say we are designers, writers, mothers, father's even friends. But what do we do in life to live up to and wear our titles. It gave me an entire different view on prioritizing my goals and putting my words to reality to align with my dream. I am very thankful for those words!

My siblings Alanna, Ben, Joseph and Janelle, I love you to the moon and back. Thank you for supporting and believing in my dreams!

For my girls who read my story before print Monique, Nneka, Asha and Desiree I thank you for your opinions, thoughts, advise and for helping and reassuring me. You are priceless to me. I am forever grateful and appreciative of you all!

Janelle, my sister and my best friend! You are my number one fan and I thank you for your support and believing in your sister. You are surrounded by people waiting for the next release and your voice for me speaks belief, confidence and reassurance of me as more than just your sister but as a great writer. You are beautiful inside and out and I thank God for allowing you to be my beautiful loving sister and my best friend.

Chris my love I thank you for believing in me, for walking with me, for listening to me and never giving up on me. Your love, patience and support mean the world to me! I love you forever!

My dearest son Oronde, the day you gave me that motivational speech about following your dreams to listen to spoke volumes to me. To know that my son believed in his mother and my dreams enough to give me that extra push means the world. My eyes were opened, my gift was being acknowledged by my children and I knew that it was time to spread my wings God gave me and allow my gifts to be a blessing to others. You are a Prince, brilliant, thoughtful, kind, a doer, a go getter and you are my son! God showed out when he created you and gave you to me. I am so grateful to have you in my life. I am proud as your mother. A son's love for his mother is priceless and I cherish our bond, our time and our relationship. You are a perfect creation from God and you make us all proud! I know you will one day touch and save lives and God himself is smiling down proud! My first born son ~ You are a King!

Tim Dawson, my friend. Thank you for my amazing cover design. But most of all thank you for your friendship! Your advice, patience with me and your friendship has been priceless. Thanks for using your talents to create what I envisioned. I wouldn't be a friend if I didn't share your talents with the world. Tim Dawson (www.incredible-tech.com).

Mark Rankins, thank you for my author photo. Thank you for motivating and believing in me, reminding me of God's gifts and his perfect timing.

To all the dreamers, if you can dream it you can do it. Believe in yourself and love YOU enough to make your dreams a reality. Research, plan and work hard, taking it one step at a time. Put God first and surround yourself with people who love and support you!

I am who I say I am. ~ Thank you Dr. Eric Thomas for your motivational speeches. My son at the age of fifteen introduced me to you. Thank you for reminding me, pushing me and being a blessing to many just like me. ~ You are born to be great! ET The Hip Hop Preacher or best yet, Dr. Eric Thomas. Dreams come true when your grind is greater than your dream. Eric Thomas you are great!

Momma I love you and will always cherish you in my heart. You are gone but never forgotten. I thank God for you and for allowing me to be created beautifully through you. Rest peacefully my dearest mother.

1 Corinthians 13:4-8

4 Love is patient, love is kind. It does not envy, it does not boast, it is not proud. 5 It does not dishonor others, it is not self-seeking, it is not easily angered, it keeps no record of wrongs. 6 Love does not delight in evil but rejoices with the truth. 7 It always protects, always trust, always hopes, always perseveres. 8 Love never fails......

Love Never Fails

CHAPTER 1
~AMEILA~
GIFTS THROWN AWAY

Ameila Churchwell was in the nursery laying her sleeping baby girl in her crib. She cringed at the sound of her husband's cell phone ringing in fear of waking the baby. She needed to finish getting ready so she could take their daughter to her doctor appointment. Her husband refused to help. She quietly tiptoed out of the room closing the door behind her. She paused hearing her husband answer his phone as he quickly walked away.

"Charles Churchwell." He said answering the phone. "Oh hey hold on let me walk into my office." He said filling the home with silence and the sound of hurried footsteps traveling through the home. He walked into his office pushing the door closed behind him. He didn't want his wife to hear his conversation but didn't want that fact to be obvious.

In a whispering voice he continues his private but yet revealing conversation. "Okay I'm back baby. Yeah, she's still here. They will be leaving shortly." He said waiting on a response. But what he didn't know was the door was cracked and his wife could hear his every word. "No I haven't told her yet. I'll tell her tonight... No she doesn't have a clue, but then again I really don't care... I know. I'm handling everything she has no choice but to leave, this is my house. I pay all the bills here... The kids will be ok, she can figure it out. I really don't care. That baby cries all day and night, drives me insane. I already emptied the savings account in case she tried to go to the bank. I will pay child support if I have to when she takes me to court. Until then it will be me and you making love all over this house. Me making you scream every time I make you cum.

You like that huh. I need you to be here as soon as she leaves so I can fuck you how you like it. I can't wait to feel your insides pulsating baby."

Ameila was standing beside the door listening to her husband talk to another woman about her and about what he would do to the woman who was not his wife. She suspected him of cheating, even seen pictures in his phone of different women. She had to deal with women calling their home and hanging up when she answered. When she was eight months pregnant she stopped having sex with him when he gave her an STD. He stopped initiating sex or even touching her after she confronted him about his infidelity. He didn't seem to care one bit. Working late nights, smelling like perfume and after-sex became his norm. At that point she knew he was involved with another woman. She wanted to fight to save her family for the kid's sake and she continued taking care of them while having to deal with his lies and disloyalty praying he would change. She even put her writing career on hold for the sake of being his wife helping him grow his magazine business. When he was making what he thought was good money he started feeling himself and forgetting about everything she did to help him get there. Enough was enough. Her prayers were not being answered or at least not in the way she wanted them to be.

"Are your panties wet for me baby?" He said continuing his conversation not realizing his wife was now standing behind him. His legs were opened and his pants undone exposing his erection. Legs opened wide he was stroking his manhood, sitting in the chair behind his desk with his back turned facing the window. "You got my dick hard as bricks baby."

He jumped at the sound of his wife's voice. "You bastard! Wet panties and hard dicks huh? I see she has your little dick excited." Standing behind him with her hands on her hips, she was furious and hurt.

Jumping up from his seat he reacts, guilty and shocked. "What the hell are you doing in my office?" He said putting the phone down from his ear and pulling up his pants.

"The better question is who the hell are you talking to on the phone? Because your wife is standing in front of you." With tears in her eyes she reaches for the phone in his hands hanging it up as she fought to retrieve it from him.

He managed to keep the phone and after ensuring the call had ended he yelled back angrily at his wife. "You don't need to worry about that. But while we are talking about my phone call, you do need to worry about finding another place to live. I'm leaving you. And we will be getting a divorce to erase your wife title. I am in love with someone else. Whatever we had is now and has been over. So don't worry about who the hell I am talking to. That's none of your business."

"In love with another woman? You think these women want you? They want the dream of what they think you can give them. They want the thrill of having another woman's man, take his money and give him back."

"I am not your man and it is my money I can do what I want with it."

"So you're just going to leave your family for something that is fun and easy to you? How long you think that will last? I know about all of your affairs! Melissa, Tina, April, the list goes on!"

"That's because your ass is nosey, going through my phone and my personal shit."

"You gave me a STD when I was pregnant with our child. That's how I know. They call here and hang up, that's how I know. You don't even initiate sex with me, that's how I know."

"Well I had to get sex from somewhere you weren't giving it to me, what did you expect me to do?"

"I expected you to love your pregnant wife. At least respect me enough to wear a damn condom with all those hoes you were with. I expected you not to cheat. I'm your wife. I had so many problems with the pregnancy and you knew that."

"Well it doesn't matter now. I'm in love with someone else so you and the kids can find somewhere else to live. She is moving in with me."

"Are you serious right now? Do you hear yourself? You are going to put me and our kids out of our home? What kind of man puts his kids out for another woman? Where are we to go? I have no family here and you know that." She said with frustration all over her face and tears in her eyes. She was standing in the middle of his office and the sounds of their baby crying filled the air. For a moment he looked remorseful.

"You're a smart girl, you can figure it out." He said as he went to stand behind his desk.

Furious, hurt and in disbelief she started yelling. "Figure it out? I do not believe your ass right now. Fucking bastard! All the shit I did to help you start your business and you get the fucking big head think you King Tut or some damn body."

"I am the mastermind behind my business. Your help didn't start my business my money and commitment did. Your Dear Ameila column was good but it didn't make my magazine so don't get it twisted sweetheart."

"You are the one that has it twisted. I don't have time for this, I'm late! We will talk about this when I get back from Darla's doctor appointment. You are stupid you know that. A little dick having stupid ass fool, that's what you are." She turned to walk away heading for the door when she felt her husband pull at her arm swinging her around and smacking her across the face knocking her to the floor.

"There is no later, you getting your ass out right now." His ego was bruised by the way she was talking to him. Even though he was cheating and wanted her gone he didn't like her snapping back talking down to him. He stood over her looking as she held her face. She looked up at him with fear and disgust in her eyes. He stepped over her frazzled and stunned body leaving out the room enraged.

Still holding her face she watches as he walks out the door. She can't believe he just hit her. She gets up off the floor grabs their crying baby from the crib and walk toward the living room. She observes him grabbing her purse and shoes and heads for the front door. "What are you doing?" She asked him with panic in her voice. Reality of him putting her out was starting to sink in fast. She held their crying daughter close to her chest trying to comfort her.

Their son was looking up at his dad not understanding what was going on. "All you're getting is your purse and shoes now get the hell out." He dumped the contents of her purse out into the grass and stomped on everything he could. His anger was fueling his actions. Their son following his dad was now outside with him, standing there confused as his dad headed back into the house full of rage.

Ameila had their crying baby in her arms unable to calm her. She tried to diffuse the situation by talking calm to her husband. "Can you please stop? We can talk about this, work this out. Please you are frightening the children."

He grabbed the baby car seat and threw it outside as well not realizing his son was standing in the path of his throw. "You and that crying baby get out. Get out now!" He stood in the door way holding the door open. His anger was deeper than the words she spoke to him and his family was feeling the wrath of whatever underlying issue he had. Even though he missed his son with the car seat the thought of his daddy being angry and throwing stuff towards him frightened him and he started to cry. The sight of his children crying didn't even move him. His heart was cold and uncaring at that moment. His first born son was witnessing his dad be cruel to the people who loved him most in this world.

Ameila heard their son crying as he stood motionless in the yard and that guided her outside. She grabbed her son and pulled him close, within a second Ameila turned to the sound of the door slamming shut locking quickly. Sitting there trying not to cry she picked up the contents of her purse with her three year old son helping. She was glad her car keys were in there but sadden that her disk with all her writing material was now broken. All she was leaving with was her car, her kids and the clothes on their back.

She placed the kids in their car seats strapping them in and checked her husband's car for money hidden or items she could hold onto to sell later just in case he wouldn't let them back in. All she found was some change and a few bills tucked in an envelope with some lottery tickets he purchased. She took the entire envelope hoping at least one ticket was a winner. She noticed a jewelry box tucked under the seat opening it to see a beautiful diamond ring fit for an engagement. She closed the box and took it and everything else with her. A ring, a few winning tickets and a five hundred dollar scratch off was her luck.

Day after day she tried to get back in the house with no sympathy from her husband. He wouldn't even give her access to the children's clothes. She had nothing and he didn't care one way or another.

When she would call the house women would answer the phone telling her to stop calling their house and laughing before slamming the phone down. Her money was running low staying in hotels trying to survive. She cashed in the lottery tickets and pawned the ring to pay for the rooms, food and clothes. She had no family to turn to for help. She started sleeping in her car with the kids. At that point she realized her marriage was really over. She was feeling the pain of having nothing and no one to turn to. At her darkest moment she did what she knew best to do and turned to God. That gave her peace, praying for him to make a way out of no way she could see, to give her the strength to keep pushing for her children and for herself until that day comes.

Being away from her husband was a curse and a blessing. She was just not in any state of mind to believe the blessing to be true. For every problem that occurs, God has already provided the answer. She gave up on trying to get back into their home, but still wanted one thing that was in that house, her backup hard drive and would keep trying until she got it back. We often ignore God's signs to walk away. When we do, God sometimes take away the people and things you think that you need to survive, that you think are good for you but they really are not good for you to give you something greater and better for your happiness.

CHAPTER 2
~BRIELLE~
EVERYDAY STRUGGLES

In a Deep sleep and all Brielle Summers hear are the same screams playing over and over in her dreams loudly reminding her of the danger she was once in as if it was happening at that very moment. The constant nightmares feel too real awakening her startled and covered in fear. With every bad dream the fear remains, keeping her in constant prayer for the ability to let go and move on with her life.

"Oh no not again, Lord please no. What did I do this time? I scream as he comes closer to me with his fist raised. S*top, please stop, I won't do it again. Whatever I did I won't do it again. Please stop, you're hurting me."*

I continue to scream out from the pain of him hitting me. My screams and pleads for him to stop are feeding his rage. I beg him to stop. *"I'm sorry, please no more. Please I'm begging you."* I am on the floor, crawling backwards trying to get away from him. I can see it so clearly. My heart is racing as if it is happening all over again.

He lashes out with harsh words to intimidate me, letting me know he has power over me. *"Shut up I run you. You think you gonna leave this house looking like that? Are you trying to pick up a man? What you think you gonna cut your eyes at me, disrespect me, and get away with it. Are you trying to impress somebody? Huh? Bitch don't no body want you."* He continues to verbally abuse me as he hits me and I continue to scream. He stands over me with his hands balled up into fists. An image I could never forget. A man who says that he loves a woman but at the same time his actions show his hate. He spits in my face as he continues to scream curse words at me, degrading me. *"You're worthless to me. You are going to do what I tell you when I tell you. Do you hear me?"* His words cut deep through my soul. Did he really say that to me? I am worthless to him. Me? The mother of his children. Worthless?

I was living with Greg, the father of my three beautiful children. We moved in together when I was an adult but yet still a young little girl. I didn't listen to my parents. He filled my head with all the sweet things a naïve little girl loves to hear. Promised to always take care of me and give me the world. Promised to love me with all his heart. Then three kids later he changed. He began cheating on me with different women. He would leave me and the kids at home alone while he went out to party, returning home at five in the morning drunk. His words became harsh towards us. Then the drugs. At that point I had enough. The day I told him I wanted to leave was the day he started hitting me. Once he started he couldn't stop. That control he had over me was the only way I stayed. I was afraid. Especially afraid of him taking my kids away from me; they are my life, my everything. I was afraid of him coming after me. Afraid he would make good on his promise to kill me.

I tried to get up. But he continued towards me with swinging arms knocking me back to the floor. With his tennis shoes on, he kicks me repeatedly in my ribs, my stomach and anywhere else his foot landed. He grabs me by the hair making me move to the bed. He plans to have his way with me and forcefully he does, even as I scream for mercy, begging him not to hurt me anymore. I could tell he was high on something. With blood dripping from my face, my left eye is bruised and swelling fast. My nose feels broken. My lip is swelling. And he is raping me. All I could do was pray for survival.

He has beaten me up before but never this bad. After the beating he would always have sex with me as if it was his way of apologizing. This wasn't any fight and make up session to me. This was abuse and rape. I had no energy and would just lay there until he was done. Once he passed out from exhaustion or from being drunk and high, I would clean myself up and try to cover up the bruises. I didn't want anyone else to know he beat me. The kids saw some of the abuse and knew something was going on. But I always made excuses for anything that I couldn't cover up; typical defense from a victim of abuse.

This time, just when I thought it was almost over, I look up and see the kids. As they stand in the doorway of the bedroom seeing what was happening to me, my heart ached even more than my body. Knowing my kids were witnessing the brutal attack on me by their own father, I knew I had to do something more.

"Daddy stop hurting momma, stop it daddy, please stop it you're hurting mommy." I could hear my oldest daughter Olivia screaming out through her tears. My baby girl was crying and looked terrified. The kids have been around their dad before when he has hit me and their screams and pleads would never seem to matter. But this time was different, it was worse as if his goal was to kill. The kids see me defenseless, begging for forgiveness for something I didn't do. Begging for him to stop hurting me. Begging for him not to continue having sex with me in front of our kids. This time it was more blood and more swelling. This time I was fighting for my life. Our son stood there in shock frozen in place. A protecting rage came over him wanting to protect his mother from his dad. Not a stranger but his dad. What was he supposed to do? His dad should be protecting his children and me. But instead I lay here defenseless against Greg, his father, who is high, drunk and very abusive. No child should ever be a witness to what was happening at that moment to me, their mother.

I didn't want the kids to see him rape me. I tried to find some strength to make him stop, which only made him angrier. *"No, no, stop it please stop it. The kids are in here stop it please."* I was pleading and begging some more but it was all in vain. I pulled at my clothes trying to stop him. I couldn't fight him off. He wouldn't stop. Nothing I did or said seemed to matter. He didn't care about the kids. He didn't care about me. I tried to get the kids to leave the room but the fear and rage was over them.

My son wants to protect me and starts screaming at his dad to stop. All of a sudden I see him screaming and running. He runs over full of anger as he is witnessing his dad swing at me. He grabs his dad by the arm pulling at him screaming for him to stop and he starts beating him in his back. Greg swings hitting our son in the face throwing him across the room. His dad screams at him *"you think you are a man boy."* He leaves me, pulling his pants up as he walks over to our son and starts kicking him. He grabbed him by his neck squeezing blocking his air flow.

"No, not my baby. Not my baby." I try to fight back keeping him focused on me but he is too strong. He let his neck go and started punching and kicking our son more punching him repeatedly before he turned back to me. He hits me harder punching me in my face over and over again. The girls are screaming as their mom is nearly unconscious and brother lays unconscious on the floor…

Beep beep beep beep beep, sounds roaring through the room from the alarm clock going off on Brielle's dresser waking her from her nightmare, reliving that tragic day. Somehow it always seems to happen that way; something awakens her in the midst of the horrific dreams. She stays in prayer to God that one day these nightmares will end and she will have complete peace in her life.

She hits snooze on the alarm clock. Sweat is dripping from Brielle's body. She sits straight up in the bed with her arms shielding her face. Her eyes are full of tears and her heart pounding rapidly. Brielle sat there looking around, crying sobs of tears as she begins to pray out loud through her tears.

"Oh thank you Jesus. Thank you Jesus! Lord, please clear my mind and take over my dreams erasing these horrible thoughts and nightmares. Thank you for bringing me out of a bad situation and starting my life anew Lord. Thank you for waking me up yet another day, and allowing the reality of that day be merely a bad dream that one day will not exist. Keep me Lord in my right mind and at peace with my life. Despite the nightmares, despite my past, I know that you love me and you are my protector from all the evils in the world Lord. And I know that no weapon formed against me shall prosper, in Jesus name. Lord, I thank you for my three beautiful children; Olivia, Carter, and Jayla. And for my mom and dad who are always supportive of me and so loving to us all. And thank you Lord for my brother Isaiah being a big part of my life as well. Lord I know one day these nightmares will cease. Please help me Lord where I fall weak and help me to maintain strength in you Lord. Bless me and my children with your riches pure and genuine in love, happiness, health and wealth. In Jesus name and in your name Heavenly Father I do so humbly pray, thanking you for every blessing along the way, Amen."

No woman ever deserves a man putting his hands on her period!

Reaching over to the dresser Brielle turned the alarm off as she wiped tears from her eyes. Looking at the time, she realized she was about to be late for work. Quickly she jumps up, hurrying into the bathroom to shower, rushing to get ready so she won't be late for her morning meeting. She heads to the children's room to wake them, helping her sleepy kids get ready. Every morning while the kids were on their break from school, Brielle takes them to her mom's house until she get off work. They all stand in the bathroom together brushing their teeth. That's just one of many things they do together. Her kids are everything to her, they are the reason she push forward to make it in life so that she can provide the very best for them.

When they finished getting ready, Brielle grabbed the kid's bag full of items they use or could need during the day and they headed out the door. They hopped on the elevator headed to the secure parking lot of her condo. They jumped in the car and buckled up. Same ritual every day, the children fall asleep in the back seat and Brielle wakes them up all over again when they get to her mom's house. She stopped and grabbed breakfast on her way there for the kids and her mom. Normally her mom cooks breakfast but some days Brielle wanted her to have a break.

On her way to her moms, Olivia woke up. She was looking out the window and spotted a lady and her crying child. "Momma what is wrong with that lady and her baby?" She asked.

Looking out the window, Brielle's heart started to ache for the lady. She seemed ill and possibly hungry. "I am not sure sweetheart they may be hungry. Would you mind if granny cooked for you all today and I give them the McDonalds I bought?"

"Yes that would be okay momma. We wouldn't mind. They could be hungry." Olivia said.

Pulling up closer Brielle wrote a note on a piece of paper and placed it in the bag. She rolled the window down to speak with the lady. When she got her attention she spoke kindly, "Excuse me ma'am, I have food for you and your babies. I just bought it for my children but we don't mind sharing. If it's okay we would love for you and your children to have it."

"You are too kind. Yes thank you so much. God is answering prayers. Thank you pretty lady! God bless you!" The lady said grateful for the food.

"God bless you and your babies." Brielle said before driving away. She looked at Olivia in the rear view mirror still watching the lady through the window. She knew that this would be a life lesson for her daughter. It broke her heart that she was not able to do more for her, she vowed one day to be a blessing for those in need and to be able to do more. Her daughter made her proud knowing she was willing to give. Brielle would be sure to keep the lady and her children in her prayers.

Pulling up at her mom's home, Brielle gave the kids kisses, telling them all good-bye, even her mom before heading out the door to work. Her mom Mrs. Marcella Summers is her rock. She's a retired Nurse and stays home while her husband, Brielle's dad, Mr. Mitchell Summers and Brielle's brother Isaiah get up and go to work. The kids keep her company, giving her something to do. It has always been just the four of them growing up. As time passed and the kids started their own lives the everyday rituals at home stopped. So having Brielle's kids there was a blessing for everyone. They provided so much happiness and additional love within the family.

Downtown Nashville was busy as usual. People were crossing the street in front of cars trying to get to their destination quicker. Officers were directing traffic as frustrated drivers sounded their horns, and care free pedestrians were everywhere. Traffic was thick. And the crowd of walkers was even thicker. Traffic was always like this during morning and afternoon rush hour in the city. But Brielle managed to get through the thick traffic and park.

Walking into the office, Brielle barely made it on time for her morning meeting. These meetings were full of boring discussions that mainly pertain to the VP's and Directors except for about ten percent of the discussion. But showing up late was not an option. Brielle sat there zoned thinking about her dream and how pitiful her love life is because of her fear of dealing with men. For a while now she has been a single woman with three kids and no man. Her kid's father is in jail for domestic violence, assault on a minor, child abuse, child neglect and rape. And she hopes he never gets out. Although she knows she could be in denial, she wonders if fear is keeping her from moving forward. She stays so busy with work, looking after her parents and doing for her kids, that she does not make time for much of a social life. She has faith and prays that she will find her protector, lover and friend one day soon when God is ready for them to meet. She told herself to always keep her heart open to receive love when God presents it to her. And she prays for God to help her do so.

My dream seemed so real. I was actually soaked with sweat. I know God will take those memories and fears away from me, give me peace. I will keep my faith and believe in Him that it is already done. I need to think of positive stuff, like Carter telling me a funny joke. As Brielle was thinking of the joke she snickered and she quickly snapped out of the daze realizing that was an out loud laugh. *Shoot I'm about to get in trouble.* Several people turned to look at her as if she was crazy.

"Miss Summers, do you want to share something with the rest of us?" Her boss calmly put her on the spot and everyone turned looking in her direction. Brielle starts to fidget with her hair as if she was clueless to what her boss has insinuated. If she was any lighter her face would be red from embarrassment.

Shrugging her shoulders she tells him, "No sir, I'm sorry I had something in my throat." *Lord Jesus, please clear my thoughts and let me pay attention and get unwanted attention off me.* Brielle just smiled and bit her bottom lip as she always does when she was nervous. The meeting was long. Brielle tried her best to pay attention and keep her mind on what her boss was talking about and not on her dreams and personal issues.

Brielle was a Financial Accounts Analyst with an annual income of forty-seven thousand dollars. Monday through Friday working eight to five she was a dedicated employee even with the stress of the job. She thought she should be paid more but working with her best friend Chantae makes the job easier to deal with. And fun. She gets the chance to keep up with all the excitement that goes on in her fabulous interesting life on a day to day basis. Chantae always knows what is going on and seems to be the first to know everyone else's business before anyone else knew.

"Hey girl, what you doing for lunch today?" Chantae whispers into Brielle's cube. Their desks were right next to one another.

"I have a grilled chicken salad from home. I can't keep spending my money in that cafeteria. I added it up and I was spending about forty dollars a week on average. I could be paying my water bill with that or put gas in my car. So leftovers it is unless someone else is buying. You want to take me to lunch today girl?" Brielle said being sarcastic. Chantae never has to pay for lunch. Sometimes she even gets Brielle free lunch. One of the many things she always gets free. Good looks and a big booty often come with privileges.

"No, not today girl, I have a lunch date and I didn't want to leave you solo but you know your girl got to take advantage of free lunch at a five star restaurant. And you know I love eating good food." Chantae was smiling feeling good about her date.

"Girl you stupid with who Johnny Phelps in IT?" She said jokingly. He was Chantae's secret admirer except everyone knew about it, and it was only a secret to him.

Chantae was now standing up out of her seat and inside Brielle's cube. "No seriously I met this real cutie Saturday night at the club and he got money too girl. He drives this nice Porsche and was buying drinks for his boys that were with him. So you know I'm trying to let him wine and dine me. Besides once I put this big bootylicious thang all up on him he couldn't help but be mesmerized and want me." She began imitating how she was dancing on the guy.

Brielle was laughing at Chantae's demonstration. "I hope you are talking about dancing and nothing more." She tapped her on her thigh as she continued dancing. "Stop girl you look silly up in here dancing like that, people are looking at you." Brielle whispered. She grabbed at Chantae's hand trying to get her to stop moving and swaying her hips mimicking her dance moves from the night before.

"Girl that ain't nothing new. They look at this big booty every time I walk by. They can't help it, especially the Directors here. I walk pass the conference room while they are in their Directors meeting every week and you can hear the pause in their discussion to all turn and look. They undercover hoes and wish they could touch, taste or even tickle this good stuff. But you know that ain't happening. So they go home and dream about all this goodness when they doing it to their little itty bitty no shape wives who done got comfortable and only eat lettuce and carrots." Chantae laughed at her thoughts and Brielle snickered a little too thinking she was probably half way right.

Chantae is a pretty girl with a big booty, small waist, with a B cup breast size. Her voluptuous booty made up for lack in cup size. She had long hair flowing down her back and kept it laid. She dressed in the latest fashion but everything was always tight fitting in the thighs. Her butt was so big it was hard for her to find clothes that fit the way she like. The attention she got from men when she wore clothing that showed off her curves was flattering but often not wanted. She didn't complain instead it motivated her to follow her dream of starting her own clothing line for full figured curvatious and big booty women. Brielle always encouraged her and had faith her friend would make those dreams come true.

Brielle is a stunning and beautiful woman herself. She is a sensual and classy lady. She didn't wear the tight clothing; instead she tried to conceal her sexiness. She left everything to the imagination and still always looked professional, classy and sexy. She was known for her sophisticated look and being a sharp dresser. After getting out of her abusive relationship with her ex, she treated herself to a complete makeover. She didn't want to show off her bodacious booty and large breast so she made sure her clothes covered her assets. Her waist is small, no rolls or fat any place on her body. And her legs are long and flawless, simply gorgeous. She is a size eight and worked out to keep her body firm and toned. She is very graceful and lady like with a great personality.

Brielle was sweet and liked by everyone who met her. She had a demeanor about herself that intimidated men from approaching her. She was the too fine, nothing hoochie about her and nothing easy about her type of girl. She was the type of woman that men thought of as 'should be treated as a queen, put on a pedestal, wifey material'. It didn't bother her that men didn't have enough courage to speak to her. She knew what she wanted in a man and she knew God would send him to her. All she needed was faith and to hold on to what she trusted and believed in God for to deliver when it was her time. If a man was too afraid to approach her then he wasn't the man that God had ordained to be in her life. One thing he had to have was confidence. But she was by no means searching.

After work Brielle was on her way to pick up her refill prescriptions for her migraine headaches she has often, especially lately. The Dr. told her to try not to stress and relax as much as she could but it was hard when you worked pay check to pay check trying to pay bills and maintain good credit. On top of financial stability she had to deal with the nightmares of her ex haunting her. That alone was stressful. Every time she had a nightmare her migraines would return. So her Dr. gave her a prescription to help with the pain and to help her sleep.

Brielle wants to buy a house and move out of her expensive condo. She knew that paying her own mortgage would be cheaper than her rent. It sounded good but she just couldn't get her head above water financially. Her ex had an expensive lifestyle that she too became accustom with. She tried to stay in the same upscale area and not change the way she lived, but maintaining the bills on her own was not easy when she instantly became a single parent. The expensive lifestyle had to be tamed and some bills eliminated. She knew that a little downsizing needed to be done. You can't get child support from a man who is in jail. The tradeoff was far greater as she was better off without him in her life. As far as she was concerned he didn't exist anymore. The kids don't ask about him. They try to erase the terrifying memories of their last abusive encounter with their dad. And that was that.

As Brielle was driving, she received a phone call adding to her stress.

"Hello."

"Hi Miss Summers, this is Caroline with Direct TV calling to inform you that you have a past due balance of ninety eight dollars and twenty four cents and a total bill of one hundred eighty seven dollars and thirty three cents and…"

Brielle politely cut her off and spoke, "Yes ma'am I am aware of that. I'm going to pay the past due on Friday when I get paid."

"You will be making a payment on Friday January 30th and ma'am how do you plan to pay the ninety eight dollars and twenty four cents? By check, over the phone, by credit card or…."

Brielle cut her off again, "I will be paying from my bank debit card online."

"Okay thank you Miss Summers. I want to remind you that if payment is not received in our office the service will be interrupted and a reconnect fee may be charged to restore service."

"Okay thank you."

"Thank you Miss Summers you have a great day."

Brielle was stressing all over again and could feel her headache coming on stronger. Her bills seem to always come due before she was paid and she seems to never be able to catch up. If it wasn't for the kid's joy of Disney channel and her past time for her favorite shows, cable would be cut off completely. She pulls into a parking spot at the pharmacy and dials her mom's number before getting out of the car.

"Hello." Brielle's four year old daughter Jayla answered the phone. Her daughter Olivia was seven and her son Carter was nine.

"Hey momma's baby what you doing answering the phone?" She was so delighted to hear her daughter's voice.

"Hi mommy when you getting off work and coming to get me?"

"Mommy on her way okay sweetheart?"

"Okay here goes granny, love you mommy." She handed the phone to her grandmother very quickly. All she wanted was to hear that mommy was on her way.

"Hey Brielle how was work today?" Brielle's mother was a very loving mother to her children and grandchildren.

"Hey momma, it was okay. Just an ordinary day. How was your day with Jayla?" Gathering her purse, Brielle was making sure she was bundled up good from the cold weather before getting out of the car to head into the pharmacy.

"Me and Jay-Jay be having fun hanging out all day. She reminds me so much of you when you were this age. Full of life and very intrigued with everything. I had all my grandbabies sitting here reading to me. And you know she has to be dramatic when she reads and bring the characters to life through her words." Her mother laughed a little as the kids were talking about it in the background.

As Brielle was walking into the store another man was right behind her almost running her over to get passed her. "Oh I am so sorry ma'am. So sorry." He said to her as he passed her still in a rush but trying to reach out and make sure she was okay.

With the phone away from her ear and gathering herself from the bump she said, "That's okay sir, I'm alright." She placed the phone back to her ear and could hear the kids in the background. She picked right back up where the conversation left off. "They love to read ma. And little Miss Jayla gets it honest from me. I remember doing that when I was a kid and that's how I read to them now."

"Brie, you okay? You sound like something is wrong." Brie was Brielle's nickname her mother gave her growing up.

"I'm okay ma! My head is starting to hurt again. I stay stressed out about these bills. I don't make enough money to keep my head above water. It seems like every time I turn around something is due or should I say past due and I try not to stress but I just can't help it. I want to move out of that expensive condo and buy a house but I can't right now. I wish I had a husband who could help me ma, like you have daddy. I have been having nightmares again too." Brielle was standing in line at the pickup counter behind the man that almost ran her over coming into the store.

"It will get better baby I know it will you are too good of a person for things not to turn around for you and forget about you know who. Try to erase those thoughts from your mind" Mrs. Summers was whispering into the phone so the kids couldn't hear. "Nothing good will ever come to him for what he did. But you are blessed and God is not done with you yet. Keep on having faith baby girl, God is your answer to everything. And I mean everything. You have an innocent pure heart. I see that and God sees that. Brie you have favor over your life sweetheart."

"I know ma, I just got a call from the cable people wanting their money, I hate being broke all the time and I want to be able to do nice things for you and the kids when I want to and to get us out of that condo into a new home. And let's not talk about my car." Brielle was trying to talk as quiet as she could, standing next to people she didn't know.

"I know baby. It will get better and you will be able to soon enough. Right now we are all content with you giving of yourself. God has given you a gift of kind heartedness and the genuine love you give from your heart. And you do them both so well. That is worth more than anything else you could possible give to us."

"Thank you ma. You always know how to make me feel better. I will be there as soon as I pick up my prescription."

"Okay baby, take your time. Love you." All the kids were in the back ground screaming I love you momma.

"I love you too momma and tell my babies I love them too. I will be there shortly." She was smiling as she hung up the phone. She enjoyed being a mother. She could hear that there was a problem at the counter with the gentleman in front of her. She stepped over to the next available lady.

"May I help you?" she said.

"Yes I need to pick up my prescription. Brielle Summers." The lady turned to go find her prescription. She couldn't help but to hear what was going on next to her.

"Sir I understand but there is a co-payment due on this prescription and I can't just give it to you that would be illegal."

"Look I do understand can I give you a credit card number I left my entire wallet at the airport with my wife and kids and my son is very sick and we need the medication before we get on this flight. We are on our way out of town to see my father who is dying and if I go all the way back I won't have enough time. Please is there something I can do?"

"Sir you will have to pay the Twenty two dollars and seventy four cents, I can let you speak to the pharmacist...."

Brielle cut the lady off as she was reaching into her purse she said, "Here is the money for his medicine, this is twenty two dollars and I have the change right here." She handed the lady behind the counter the money for the man's medicine.

As the cashier was ringing the man up he stared speechless at Brielle and thought to himself, *'Wow God does still have his angels here on earth. This is the same lady I nearly ran over and she still has a heart of pure gold to help me out in need. Here I am a very wealthy man and she was just talking on the phone about stressing over how to pay her bills and was still able to give from her heart. "WOW."* He spoke to Brielle as he kept his eyes on her amazed. "I promise I will pay you back plus interest. Thank you so much. You can't imagine what this means to me. What is your name?" He reached both of his hands out to embrace her hand in his, wanting to show his gratitude.

"Brielle Summers and sir please don't worry about it." She said as she was reaching out to shake his awaiting hand. She had a half smile trying to not show the pain she was feeling from the pounding of her head. "Sometimes things just happen. It's okay." She turned back to the lady behind the counter. She glanced back at the man and smiled, noticing he was still looking at her.

The lady who was serving her asked for her address. "Ok Brielle Summers and what is your address?"

"Yes my address is four seven four one True Crossing Brentwood three seven zero two seven."

The lady rung her up and handed her the prescription. She didn't have the money to be giving away like that but she felt bad for the man. And she knew her mother was right. Eventually things would turn around.

"Thank you again Miss Summers so much!" He made a mental note of her address he overheard her tell to the cashier. As he walked out of the store he wrote it down in the car to repay her when he got back from his visit.

You never know when you might meet an angel from God. And on this day, one of God's angels appeared witnessing to those around that kindness do still exist. Brielle always tried to do the right thing and had a soft spot in her heart for genuine people in need.

CHAPTER 3
~BRYSON~
LOVING HIS FIANCÉE

Bryson Mathews is a very powerful wealthy man who is respected as a businessman and as a man who has status of money, power and great character. He's the founder and owner of three major Enterprises. Cole Estates Hotel, which is a five star hotel, Cole Estates Financial is a high status well known financial firm and Cole Estates Entertainment and Publishing Production Company. All three companies are very lucrative businesses Bryson started from the ground up. Money was one thing he never had to worry about. He had enough money to take care of everyone in his family and then some. Whatever he wanted he could have at any moment. They say money changes people and brings out a person's true identity, well it does. But Bryson never changed or treated people any different. His money was just what it was, money that comes and goes. The one thing his money could not buy was true love. This was something he had to find all on his own.

Bryson is one of the wealthiest men in the world and is also one of the sexiest bachelor's yet to be tied down. Women throw themselves at his feet. He has a body that would make you melt like chocolate on a hot day; quiver as if an ice cold breeze came over your bare skin. Make your bottom jaw drop and drool as if all control was gone. He stands six feet four inches tall, and his legs built up firmly with just the right thickness. Bryson has a sexy basketball player's build. His arms are built up nice and strong, cutup and very defined with tone and definition in his muscular form. And the thickness of his neck makes a woman daydream of biting him gently there. Smooth and sexy caramel milk chocolate colored skin. And his teeth are so pretty and white. His eyes seducing make any woman become moist with one glance. Yes this sexy brother was straight from a GQ magazine fine.

He was not only very handsome but a multi-millionaire as well. Ladies flock to him because they recognize him as a man of money, power and good looks. But they see his pockets and status first then his looks. He never knew if a woman was truly interested in him or his bank account.

Finding true love has always been difficult for Bryson until he met Jewel Taylor. He proposed to her after being together for a year and a half. At the age of thirty four Bryson was ready to start a family. He wanted to slow down from being the front man in his business. He was preparing his self to be a family man first and tending to his business as needed. There were many people within his company he trusts enough to run the business so that he could take a back seat and work normal hours. He was hoping Jewel would be his reason for doing just that.

The wedding was in a few weeks and tonight Bryson was planning to take his fiancée Jewel out for a night on the town to enjoy a stress free evening and fun weekend with just the two of them. He decided to finish up his work in the office so he could head home to surprise her. Just then he receives a knock at the door. "Come in." He says as he continues looking down at his computer.

"Hey man you want to go grab something to eat and have a couple of drinks before you head home? This has been a long week for the both of us." Kenneth Cartwright was Bryson's best friend since high school and his business partner. He was doing his own thing when Bryson was starting his Enterprise and couldn't physically help him start the business up. So Kenneth helped Bryson out by lending him some money. Instead of paying the money back, Kenneth just told Bryson to make him a partner in the company. He now owns thirty percent of the shares with Bryson owning seventy percent.

"Hey Kenny man come in let me talk to you for a second." Kenny was a nickname that Bryson called Kenneth since they met in high school. Kenneth walked in and sat in the chair in front of Bryson's desk across from him. "I'm surprising Jewel tonight with a weekend getaway. We will be spending the weekend together away from everything, including business. So dinner and drinks will have to be another time."

"That's cool. You look like you have something more on your mind though so talk to me." Kenneth looked at Bryson concerned.

"This wedding stuff has me shook somewhat man. I know I love Jewel but sometimes I doubt myself, wondering if I'm making the right decision. It feels like something is missing at times." Bryson was now leaning back in his seat.

"Brys man you just have the wedding jitters is all. The nervousness is kicking in." Kenneth laughs out loud, "You have a beautiful woman who loves you man. You deserve to be happy. You will be okay." Kenneth nods his head agreeing with what he just said.

Bryson still had a worried look on his face and was deep in thought. He pauses for a few more moments before speaking. "I guess you're right man. They say all men go through something like this. That's what it is. I guess I doubt myself too much at times. I have always had women fall in love with my money and never knew one hundred percent if they were in love with the money or in love with me. Sometimes I wish I could just meet a woman who didn't know how much I was worth and see if she would love me for me. The money is a bonus. Cause my wife will never want for anything. As long as she loves me as her husband and take care of our kids, she can have whatever whenever and have all of my love in return."

"Wow, yeah I feel you. Okay, so now I see why you say you are having doubts. Do you think Jewel would love you any less if you were broke? Are you making her sign a prenuptial?"

"I haven't said anything about it but I think I might consider it. But I don't know man. I don't want to feel like I have to do anything like that. I wanted to take her out and spend some quality time with her this weekend just to make sure I am doing the right thing. Make sure we are on the same page. I work so much and only see her briefly in the evenings and this will give us time to talk about our future together. So I'm going to surprise her and enjoy the weekend with just the two of us. Get inside her head some more. Its Friday, nothing should come up this weekend that you can't handle yourself. And of course you know if it's an emergency just give me a call. You know how to get in touch with me after hours when I'm in hiding." Bryson looked at his friend with raised eyebrows.

"Yeah aight I got you man. You enjoy your weekend and get your mind right with your lady. I can handle anything that comes up."

Kenneth stood up to head out of the office with Bryson right behind him.

Mrs. Jackie Rowland is Bryson's personal assistant. She acts like a mother to him at times but she always has his back and does an outstanding job for him. He wouldn't trade her for anyone. She was loyal to Bryson no matter what. He stopped by her desk on his way out. "Jackie I am leaving for the day and for the weekend. If something should come up you know to contact Kenneth and he will handle it. If it's an emergency he will get in touch with me. I may be in a little late on Monday so hold it down for me okay."

"Yes sir. As always you know I got this. You enjoy yourself this weekend. Here is your itinerary for your weekend getaway with your fiancée. She should fall in love all over again. This is a nice way to start the beginning of the rest of your lives together. You are a good man Mr. Matthews." She handed him the paperwork for his trip. She had scheduled and made all the plans for him just as he requested.

"Thank you Jackie. I appreciate you. I hope she enjoys it as much as you say she will. I am looking forward to a nice fun relaxing weekend with her." He started to walk away from her headed to the elevator with Kenneth right beside him and turned back and said, "You have a great weekend yourself Jackie."

"Thank you sir. See you Monday."

"She is awesome man. I lucked up when I found her."

"Yeah you did. I wish I would have found her first. My assistants I have had…. Man I don't even want to think about them. Let's just say they don't compare to Mrs. Jackie. We need to let her put together a training course and teach these other assistants how to be on point. Little Miss Jackie's in training." Laughter filled the elevator as Bryson knew what type of people Kenneth has dealt with in the past.

"Now Raquel is a whole different story. I still can't believe we hired her." Bryson said.

"I know. She creep me out when she stares us down as we leave. Like a vulture salivating and watching her prey before she attacks." They both were laughing as the elevator door opened trying to keep their composure.

Walking through the lobby, they both looked in the direction of Raquel the very ghetto fabulous lobby receptionist. She wore the loud dye in her hair and her speech at times didn't seem like correct

English but she kept people in check when they came in the building. The only reason Bryson kept her around is because Jewel knew her and begged him to give her the job. All his important clients came up from the VIP entrance so he was okay with her working in the lobby. He made her do some training on how to be a professional so she is better now than when she first started.

"You have a good weekend Raquel." Bryson said as him and Kenneth both waved good bye to her as they passed still trying to hold in their laughter.

"Goodnight gentleman." She said in her best professional voice. She stared at them until she couldn't see them anymore out the door.

"Um Um they are some good eye candy." She said as she picked up the phone dialing a number. "Hey girl Mr. Mathews just left the building, him and his fine friend. Girl they are some yummy looking men. Oh I'm sorry my bad girl, chill out. You got plans for the weekend girl? Dang rush me off the phone why don't you. Hello, hello. Oh no that heffa didn't hang up on me." Her professional training only went so far.

Bryson picked up his phone in the car to call his fiancée Jewel. "Hey baby I got a surprise for you. Get dressed in one of your sexy dresses and I will meet you at the house in about 30 minutes. Okay baby I will see you soon. Love you." Bryson was smiling after hearing her voice. He doesn't know why he was tripping or doubting himself about marrying Jewel. He was in love with a beautiful, sexy woman. His soon to be wife. He drove home to meet his beautiful bride to be for a weekend of romance and passion.

Before exiting the car he called his brother who stayed at his house more often as a resident than a house guest. His voicemail picked up. "Hey Bradon, I need you to do me a favor. Jewel and I are going out of town on a little weekend vacation and I have the security people coming to upgrade my system. I need you to give them access when they arrive. It will be a guy by the name of Ron Greer and a few people that will be working with him. He knows what to do. Please do that for me. They will be at the house about eight in the morning so make sure you don't party too hard tonight. Love you bro. Enjoy the house to yourself."

Greeting him at the door, Jewel jumped up in Bryson's arms wrapping her legs around his waist and kissing him passionately. Flames were flaring, sparks were flying. As bad as he wanted her they had an agenda he wanted to stick to and needed to get ready.

"Umm, you taste so good sweetheart. As bad as I want to make love to your body at this very moment we have to hurry. We will have plenty of time for love making. But I have to shower and change quickly. We have a car waiting for us outside. And we don't want to miss our flight." Bryson said undoing his tie on the way to the bedroom.

"Miss our flight? Baby where are we going?" She asked following him to the bedroom with a smile on her face.

"It's a surprise, you will see. We will be gone for the weekend just the two of us." He said as he went into the bathroom to shower.

Smiling from ear to ear, Jewel watched as he walked his sexy handsome body into the bathroom undressing on his way. "Babe I don't have any clothes packed. It's going to take me at least thirty minutes to pack."

"No need to pack, we will buy what we need once we get there. Just grab a few basic things you may need." He screamed out through the closed door.

She was hoping this trip would include some shopping and she got her confirmation. While Bryson was in the shower Jewel went to her phone to send out a text.

> *5:45pm*
> *I won't be able to kick it this weekend MY FIANCE' is taking me on a romantic weekend getaway. Not sure where just yet but I won't be taking my phone. Powering my phone off, talk to you when I return.*
> *#HisPricelessJewel*

She shut her phone off before receiving a reply and placed it in the drawer beside the bed. She gathered a few personal items to put in a carry along bag just in case.

During the trip, Bryson was the perfect gentleman from holding the door open for Jewel, feeding her strawberries as they sipped on champagne, to rubbing her feet as they were in the limo on their way to their first destination. Things even got a little hot and steamy between the two of them, kissing and grabbing, hands inside clothing caressing the smoothness of their skin. Their hearts were racing with excitement as Bryson's nature was rising and Jewel's intimate pleasure was pulsating. Her inner thighs heated up as honey started to flow. Things would have become X-rated in the backseat of the limo but the driver announced they were less than a minute away from their destination.

They arrived at a private location and boarded their flight where they would be taking off on their journey to Miami in Bryson's personal private jet. He had his jet on standby at all times in case he needed it for business or personal use. Once on the plane, they had a personal chef and server who made a special dinner for the two to enjoy. Garlic Rosemary chicken wrapped in ham and stuffed with cheese, creamy potatoes mixed with a secret ingredient to give it an Italian flavor with a creaminess that melts in your mouth topped with grilled mushrooms seasoned to perfection with asparagus marinated and smoked superbly. The both of them enjoyed all the delicious mouthwatering food with a bottle of red wine to wash it down.

The wine had them feeling mellow and adventurous. As they stared into each other's eyes while talking the feeling from the limo was quickly back. Jewel was quick to get up from her seat and straddle Bryson in his seat. The passion in their kisses was turning Bryson on. He wanted to be professional around people who worked for him and at any moment one of the workers could walk in. But he kissed his fiancée and forgot all about who could be watching when she fell to her knees and quickly had his hard erection in her mouth.

He saw the waiter coming and signaled for him to stop. The waiter knew exactly what that meant and kept the staff from entering. Jewel had skills with her mouth and pleased her man well. Bryson enjoyed every bit of her pleasing him. She quickly got up and had no panties on under her dress and straddled him again. Allowing the hardness of his manhood to penetrate deep with her warm honey pot and she started to ride him forcing the friction of her g-spot. With every in and out motion she squeezed her vaginal muscles tight around Bryson's hardness and he met her movements pushing deeper inside her. He stood up in one motion with Jewel still straddled around his waist and turned her around over the seat so he could hit it from the back. Jewel arched her back positioning herself to take all of Bryson's big, long, thickness hitting her g-spot so that she could cum back to back. Bryson knew how she liked it and how he was going to give it to her. Long fast deep strokes showing no mercy until she screamed out in ecstasy cumming all over him. Bryson knew where Jewel spots were and how she loved to be pleased. He wanted to be sure to always leave his wife satisfied. Although sex was not the key to a happy marriage it surely did play an important part to add to the happiness.

The sex was great between them and was always long winded. Jewel never seemed to get enough. After the sex-escapade ended they composed themselves and picked back up on their conversation smiling from the satisfaction. Dinner gave Bryson some one on one time to talk with Jewel about their wedding plans and their life together in the future. The after dinner sex was an added bonus and added more excitement to how their future sex life would be. Next thing you know the time had flown by and they had arrived in Miami. Bryson wined and dined Jewel all weekend partying, shopping, touring the city and enjoying the romantic time between the two of them. They made love in the morning, afternoon, and evening, every chance alone they had they were all over one another. This trip was just what Bryson needed to help knock the edge off the wedding jitters he was experiencing. The next couple of weeks he would be so committed to work before he took off for the wedding and honeymoon so he wanted to give them both a relaxing trip together to enjoy each other.

Paying attention to his fiancée's every move and expression, Bryson's doubt had decreased a bit. He studied her eyes, asked her questions about 'what ifs' and wanted to see how she reacted. One thing she did mention that caught and kept his attention was she wanted to have kids but just not right now. Bryson thought, she didn't have to establish a career, she didn't have to impress anyone else, and she has all of the time in the world to be a mommy and raise their children. He was confused as to why but didn't press the issue. Once the love making started with no protection he knew the babies would come. Bryson put his mind at ease and accepted the fact that he was about to be a married man. They enjoyed the rest of their weekend getaway together before heading back home to the chaos of the next few weeks in preparation of their wedding day.

Back at home late Sunday night all Bryson wanted to do was rest. Jewel decided she would stay up for a little while and let him rest. She retrieved her cell phone from the bedroom and kissed her man goodnight. She grabbed her computer from the dining room table and powered on her phone and uploaded her e-mail to do some social catching up.

Monday morning will be back to business as usual and Bryson knew that he would hardly see Jewel until he was coming in to get some rest. Before the trip he wanted to ask her about a prenuptial but he decided to dismiss the thought all together. If he had to ask for a prenuptial then he doubted their forever. He wanted his wife to have what he had freely with no worries. Bryson still could not shake his jittery feelings about getting married. He even thought about postponing the wedding, making up an excuse concerning work or something. But he didn't think it would be fair to Jewel just because he was scared. He worked hard to get to where he was in life. He trusted Jewel. She never complained about him working and always pleased him in the bedroom. He tried to dismiss the doubts and focus on the rest of his happy life with Jewel.

CHAPTER 4
~JEWEL~
AT THE GYM

Tuesday and Thursday afternoons are Jewel's scheduled days to work out at the gym with her personal trainer. Her wedding day is in a few weeks and she wants to make sure her body is flawless when she walks down the aisle. As she enters the gym dressed in her tight fitting workout clothes, she gains a lot of attention from the men. All eyes on Jewel, that's the attention she strives for. When she accomplishes her goal of gaining their attention, at that point she knows the bait has been set and her womanly curves are speaking volumes as she move around watching the men follow. She know she is a sexy lady and she enjoys the attention.

Jewel is a big flirt. Her looks and her body are all she has going for her. That's how she landed Bryson as her man, that and her charm. Attention from the men does not stop her from working hard to maintain and improve her perfect shape. She loves to feel the burn and break a good sweat. The end results were all worth it to her and her man. He was happy so she kept making him happy keeping her twice a week appointments with her trainer. She smiles and speaks to the men she pass on her way to meet her trainer. He gave her a good program to follow when she was away from him but she wasn't discipline enough at home so that was her excuse to meet with him twice a week.

Michael Anderson was a certified Grade A trainer with very high end clientele. His prices were ridiculously expensive and his schedule was booked out a year in advance. He was that good at his job and he was in high demand for his services. His clients were loaded with money and they wanted to pay for the best. Since Jewel was marrying Bryson she was marrying money, and she had money to afford his services. He provided his fiancée with a black card, free to spend as she needed too. Even with a solid booked schedule Michael could not say no to Jewel. She was a gorgeous woman, long sexy legs and caramel chocolate smooth skin. She wore a long weave that looked like her natural hair. And her curves were perfect with perky breast that were well-proportioned for her tiny frame.

When she approached him for his services a few months back, she knew she had to come correct if she was going to get him to squeeze her into his schedule. She wore a very sexy tight fitting short red dress that accentuated her curves and showed off her sexy long legs. He stopped dead in his tracks and was drooling at the mouth saying yes to her every want. He realized afterwards that he would have some mad clients having to readjust their schedule for Jewel. But he was mesmerized by her beauty and would deal with whatever the circumstance was just to be in her presence.

Jewel got to know her trainer well and was very comfortable with him, as he was with her. He would help her with weight lifting standing behind her, touching her body in ways that if her husband walked in he would question his motive with his fiancée. Sometimes he was so close she could feel his breath on the back of her neck. She never corrected him and he never stopped. He didn't even respect the fact that she had a fiancé. He was very hands on helping his clients stay fit, but Jewel was extra special to him. His clients didn't mind his hands on them at all due to him being so fine himself. He was six foot three inches tall, milk chocolate smooth like baby skin, his muscles were cut in places that seemed impossible and his chest and abs were rock solid hard and ripped. The ladies thought he was very good looking eye candy.

During one of her training sessions their conversation escalated a bit causing their relationship to become a bit more personal.

She took a break from her workout when Bryson called. Jewel dried her face with a towel and answered her phone. "Hey baby."

Bryson enjoyed hearing her voice. She had him smiling on the other end. "How is my precious Jewel? Are you done working out?"

"I'm good and tired. I'm almost done with my session. Just taking a quick break. Babe do you have to work late tonight?" Jewel said in a sweet pouty voice.

"Yes, it's Tuesday and we are still working on these deals so I will be home late baby, sorry about that."

"It's okay baby. I will find something to do like always. I may go hang out and go to dinner with the girls or something." She looked up at her trainer sensing he was ready to start again.

"Okay well be ready for me when I get in okay. Wear something sexy that you know I like okay."

"Anything for you daddy. I gotta go the trainer is waiting for me. Love you, see you tonight." She had her back turned to Michael.

"Love you too sweet lips. See you later tonight."

As she continues with her workout routine, her trainer whispers in her ear, "So your fiancé is working late again huh?"

"You have some very good ears I see. He works late every Tuesday and Thursday night, it's a part of his job. Why? Do you want to keep me busy while he is working?" She was flirting and joking with her trainer. She could not resist and was not blind to how fine he was.

"That doesn't sound like a bad idea. How about I take you to dinner instead of your girlfriends?"

"You and me, dinner?" She said in between a squat with weights.

"Yes. You and me. What's wrong with that? We are friends right? I can either pick you up or you can meet me there. We both have to eat, why not together and enjoy the company while doing so. Call it a nutrition session, part of your training."

Jewel paused for a moment and looked at him in the mirror in front of her as he stood behind her holding on to the weights. She could see his muscles flexing and the sweat making his skin glisten. She knew that if she was alone with this man it would not be good. But thought if she met him there it would be harmless and he would have on more clothes. "Okay we can meet at six tonight. You pick the place since you will be paying and make sure its somewhere nice. You know I have expensive taste." She looked at him and smiled.

"I know the perfect place. I will text you the information where to meet me. It's a date among friends." He had a smirk on his face that signaled he had a little more planned than dinner.

"Okay, dinner with a friend is what we are calling it, not a date. I'll be there. Make sure the place matches my style of dress. I see you looking at me when I walk in here dressed in my before workout clothes." They both giggled and continued the training session. At that moment their friendship went beyond the gym and beyond him just being her personal trainer. A friendship that Bryson was unaware of.

CHAPTER 5
~BRADON~
LIVING THE SINGLE LIFE

Bradon has always been known as Bryson's little brother. He looked up to his big brother and knew, just like everyone else knew, his brother was destined for greatness. Bradon on the other hand took the slower road. He went through school to become an Architectural Designer and even studied up under some of the greatest Designers ever known. He knew he didn't want to work for anyone else and he was such an amazing Designer that he didn't have to. He wanted to be a businessman just like his brother. Procrastination kept him from starting his business and the fact that his older brother had plenty of money that he shared with him freely. Bradon was young and having fun.

Being a man who lives under the shadow of your wealthy brother was a good thing at times, and very humbling as well. But for Bradon, it was mostly a good thing. He didn't have to rush to start his business. His biggest reason for taking it slow was fear of failing. But he knew he could still live a wealthy lifestyle. Bryson's home was Bradon's home and he had access to his brother's money freely. Bradon was able to live as his brother did. Buying clothes and simple things was easy. But buying larger extravagant items like cars an expensive diamonds, he would have to go through his brother.

Bryson didn't mind giving Bradon anything, but he didn't want him to use him as a crutch to fail in life. He wanted him to complete his goals of becoming the greatest Architectural Designer and the major competitor everyone else in the business would fear.

He wanted him to follow through with his goals in life, to pursue his dreams.

Bradon was comfortable for the moment. Living life, partying and being single. He didn't have any responsibilities but himself. He went out every weekend and every night during the week if something was going on. His habits were an attempt to cover up his fear that he would not be as successful as his brother. He had the same successful genes but being the little brother of a multimillionaire was intimidating. Especially knowing that everyone was watching to see what your next move was going to be. So he partied to pass time by until he was ready to take his business to the next level.

Bryson never mentioned anything to him or pressured his brother to do anything. Even gave him his own room and space in his home. Material things were not high priority in Bryson's life. They were nice but not a necessity to live in this world to him. So sharing his space with his brother was easy for Bryson. He enjoyed having him around and Bradon was able to enjoy the space while his brother was working or out of town on business.

Bryson's house was huge. Forty thousand plus square feet. Two kitchens. An enormous master bed room on the main level and another on the second level. This house even had a movie theater, two entertainment rooms, indoor pool, workout room and a bowling alley. It was more than Bryson would ever want but since he gave full control of building his home to his little brother, this is what he got. The house was designed amazingly and was known as one of the best designed homes in the state. Bryson was so impressed that he wanted to start the business for his brother but Bradon was simply not ready. So he told him the offer stood when he was ready to move forward.

Saturday Morning, Bradon, his brother and their friends were all at the gym ready to play a game of basketball. Every Saturday morning at six they all met to play ball and talk about what was going on in their lives. This was their getaway from all the stress that life brought their way. Have fun amongst good company, get some cardio in and catch up on what's happening in each other's life. The good and the bad.

Bryson was engaged to Jewel. They would be married in a couple weeks. He was never the type to date a lot of women. Always wanted a family. He was the loving family type.

Kenneth is Bryson's best friend. He was more private about all of his relationships. He didn't want people associating him with any female unless he was planning to marry her. But he loved women. He dated them long enough to see if they could be Mrs. Right. If not he had fun and cut them loose.

Bradon was single and liked to party. He didn't make any commitments with any one girl. He likes the challenge of finding the finest girl to take home or go home with and using his favorite line when he was done. "I'll call you". But everyone knew Bradon would one day sooner than later meet his match. That it would take a special woman to settle him down.

Andre was Bradon's friend. He had a few girlfriends. One main girl, a couple string along girls and the one night stands. He was a ladies man who loved to play the field and never got caught. He was a smooth talker with the ladies. He would talk his way out of any lie he was caught in between his women. But he kept them all happy and no one complained about anything.

Sitting on the bleachers lacing up their shoes Bryson and Bradon had a moment to talk alone. "You talk to your people who installed the security system last weekend? I let them in and knowing you trusted the man so I watched a movie in the movie room while they worked." Bradon said to his brother. He hadn't talked to Bryson during the week with him working a lot and Bradon partying as usual.

"Yeah he got the job done. Thanks for doing that for me." Bryson said.

"No problem bro, that was easy. You know I got your back. That was high tech stuff they installed, spy shit."

"Yeah, with your wild parties and late nights and all the craziness in the world these days, I just wanted to make sure we were covered." Bryson said.

"Cool. That's what I'm talking about." Bradon said as he stood grabbing his ball heading towards Kenneth and Andre.

"What we playing today fellas, brothers against friends or friends against friends?" Bryson asked approaching the court in his black Nike basketball shorts with a white and black Nike shirt cut at the sleeves.

"Naw we not doing the brothers teaming up against friends. You two have been playing together since y'all were kids and you are not going to embarrass us again in front of the ladies." Andre said.

"Bradon is on my team and you can keep Kenneth on your team. Let's keep it interesting and fair like we always have. Last week was a setup." Andre said shaking his head.

Andre and Kenneth thought they would take on Bryson and Bradon last time they played and didn't realize how well the two of them played together. It was like playing street ball with Michael Jordan and LeBron James on the same team against some college rookies. They took them to school on the court, showing no mercy for their friends.

Bryson and Bradon laughed knowing they beat them pretty bad last week. They embarrassed them in front of the beautiful ladies and spectators who were there to watch.

Kenneth said, "I know how they use to play but I didn't think they still had the skills since they are old men now." He laughed.

"Who you calling old Kenny? I am younger than you and matter of fact I am younger than all of you." Bradon said.

"You are only younger than me by a few months Bradon. It's your brother and Kenny that are old. My stamina is still strong and my stroke is still long and lasting." The guys laughed at Andre's cockiness. He loved women but loved himself even more.

"There is nothing wrong with my stamina or my stroke. I puts it down every morning and night. I don't hit the gym daily for nothing. I want to stay looking young, feeling young and performing like I'm young." Bryson commented.

"You better with that young girl you about to marry. Women out last men with their sex drive." Andre said.

"Yeah that's what I read. Men stop working out and let themselves go and lose their stamina. But women, even if they let themselves go their sex drive can still be high." Bradon said.

"Jewel doesn't complain. I keep her satisfied. She will be the one telling me she is tired." Bryson said. "I told y'all, I feel and perform like I am young. I am only in my thirties and there is nothing old about thirties."

Kenneth looked at the guys and said "No, thirties are not old. But people tend to get in the same routine of doing things when they start to get older. The key is to keep your love life interesting and change it up. Do something different that your woman doesn't expect. You have to have more skills than just keeping your stamina up and working out. Good sex does nothing when it becomes habit. But great sex is an art and a skill that only a few of us good men have." Kenneth grabbed the basketball and shot a jump shot.

"Look at my team mate spitting knowledge to you so called young boys." Bryson laughed. "You need to listen and learn so you will know how to maintain when you both get to that age you call older. This living the single player life will get old quick when you realize you are alone. Then what?"

"I have been enjoying the single life and all the lovely ladies that come along with it. But if the right girl come along that keeps me interested I will be sure to snatch her up and become a one woman man." Bradon said with a laugh. "But until then, I'm going to keep doing what I do best. Make the honeys crave my pleasure and put it down."

"You do that Bradon. You become a one woman man. Do it for me and you. I will keep my main chick and keep my chicks on the side. Until it all catches up with me, I am having fun and enjoying myself. If in a few years I feel different then I will handle business then. If it's too late I am willing to live with that. Tomorrow is not promised anyways so I might as well have fun doing what I enjoy. And I enjoy sex." Andre said.

"You say that now. But if you lose the best thing that ever happened to you, then you will be singing a sad love song depressed in your man cave all alone. You and your right and left hand." Kenneth said and everyone started laughing.

"Do you even have a woman? Date anyone? Or have one night stands Kenny?" Bradon asked. "I mean because you have a lot to say but who you picking up?"

"Yeah, how you talking this BS about how to have great sex when we never see you with a woman or hear about you dating anyone?" Andre added.

"Just because I don't broadcast my business doesn't mean I'm not handling my business. When I meet a woman worthy enough to hold on to and call my own, you fellas will be the first to meet her. I'm not trying to be associated with no random girl who I don't plan to spend the rest of my life with. I have to be sure she is about me and not the money." Kenneth said.

"I feel you on that. How do we really ever know if a woman wants us for who we are as a person or how many zeroes are in our bank account? I mean do we ever really know?" Bryson asked.

"Yeah I see your point." Andre said with Bradon agreeing with him.

Bryson was pondering on that thought. How does he know he is marrying a woman who truly loves him or does his money have anything to do with it at all? He tried to focus and get his mind ready to play a game of basketball, trying to shake the same reoccurring thoughts.

The game started. The guys talked mess to each other throughout the entire game. Sweat was dripping, muscles was glistening. They were very delicious eye candy to the ladies that were there walking the above track. When the guys saw them they had to put their serious game face on and stop talking about girls. It was then time to show up and show off their basketball skills. Flex their muscles and show off their sexiness.

After the game they sat around in the floor resting, wiping their sweat away with towels and drinking sports drinks and water to replenish their body's deficiencies. Andre had his eyes on one of the ladies walking the track. He made his way over to talk to her as she was leaving. He followed her out the gym door. Bryson, Bradon and Kenneth sat there a little longer to talk a bit more.

"Bradon man, are you any closer to starting that business?" Kenneth asked.

"I think about it a lot. Thinking about making it happen this year. I do a lot of pieces on the side so the passion is still burning." Bradon replied.

"That's good. You know we have your back when you are ready. We are always looking for business deals. I see you making a lot of money doing what you do so you can definitely count on me as an investor." Kenneth said as he downed his energy drink. "Besides we are brothers too."

"He knows that man. He just needs to put his plans into action. He know we have his back. One morning he will wake up and realize today is the day." Bryson said gathering his items getting ready to leave.

"Yeah you right bro. One day soon. I have to make a stop so I will catch up with you all later. Thanks for letting us add another win to our winning record. We will take it easy on the old guys next time." Bradon said.

"Whatever. Meet me in the weight room and challenge me there." Kenneth challenged Bradon.

"Naw you too damn strong for me. That's because you not getting any." Bradon laughed as he headed for the door.

"Boy if you only knew. I could teach you a thing or two about women, how to get them, love them with no strings attached and maintain being single with no drama. You just break hearts and create stalkers." Kenneth and Bryson laughed.

"Okay you got jokes. How about we go out tonight and I can see you in action. Bryson you can come too if Jewel lets you out of the house."

"Okay it's on. I will meet you out tonight. I can't believe I'm letting you talk me into this, but ok." Kenneth said. "You two can have the club scene. Not for me. But you know the spot where you need to be, so make it happen and check on things while you're there." Bryson replied speaking of one of his spots he owns. An upscale spot where all the business ballers frequent and the classy about her business women attended.

The guys left the gym with plans made for the evening. Bradon told Andre the plans for Kenneth to go out with them later that night. He too was surprised and had to see it to believe it. Although they went out the night before and had plans to attend a party Sunday night as well, this was the norm for them both. Partying was a part of what they did at least four nights out of the week.

Later that night Kenneth kept his word. Bradon planned to show Kenneth how he handled the ladies but instead of his plan being followed through, Bradon ended up meeting a woman that had him mesmerized by her beauty and her smile. This girl made his heart skip a beat. It was a feeling that he had never felt before. He could not stop staring at her. Every time she turned around he was looking at her and it made her smile even more. Kenneth and Andre were both shocked at how he was acting. But Bradon was having a moment he never expected. The girl was dancing on the dance floor and he was in love with her beauty, her smile and her body. Meeting her was the only thing he wanted at that moment. The way she kept turning and smiling at him, he knew his chances were good.

Kenneth and Andre let him be and decided to mingle and meet the ladies. Kenneth was definitely the man he said he was. Women were all over him, smiling and giving up their number. He was smooth and Andre was taking notes and trying out the same moves. Andre was enjoying the success he was having with the ladies. Kenneth just gave him the tools he needed to improve his game.

"I don't know if this is a good thing for you or not. I may have created a monster out of you, giving you ammunition to win over more victims." Kenneth said to Andre.

"And I thank you for that! You are definitely the man Kenny!" Andre said.

Bradon walked over to where the young lady was standing when she finished her dance and introduced his self.

"Hey Beautiful." He said in a sexy tone with a smile on his face.

"Hello there. So you think I'm beautiful?" The young lady smiled as she looked up to his broad chest, tall frame and up to his beautiful hazel brown eyes.

"Absolutely I do. And your smile is beautiful as well. I'm Bradon, what's your name?" He extended his hand to her seeing that he made her blush.

"Chantae. Very nice to meet you Bradon." She put her hand in his and with his soft moist lips he kissed the back of her hand never taking his eyes from her face. She quivered all over and the excitement of this man ran through her inner body. She only wished he was kissing her lips instead of her hand at that moment.

"You smell like you taste so sweet." He watched as her smile grew and she was now blushing even more. He wanted her to take that however she wanted to but did not want to disrespect her or imply anything sexual so quickly. So far he liked this girl and something was telling him she was a keeper. At this point he wanted to treat her like a priceless diamond, rare and perfect.

"You have me blushing. So tell me what do I smell like Mr. Bradon?" She was smiling from ear to ear.

"You smell fresh and fruity. Almost like the sweetness of fruit loops mixed with a pack of now and laters." He watched as she was tickled by his response. Now he knew she was also interested. If she wasn't, she would not have been entertaining his humor or lack of.

"Okay fruit loops and now and laters. I will take that as a compliment since I like both. So what's your favorite flavor of now and laters?" She was amazed at this fine man standing in front of her.

Bradon never took his eyes from her. He stared at her lips like he wanted to feast and indulge in her kisses. He was making her flutter inside with excitement. One thing she loved to do was kiss, so just the thought of him kissing her was making her panties moist.

"I like most of them except for banana and chocolate. What's your favorite Beautiful?" Again the more he complimented her the more she blushed.

"Well." She paused for a moment and looked at him still smiling and enjoying how good he looked. "Pineapple and Strawberry are my favorite. And my favorite fruits as well." She was turning flips on the inside. Bradon kept his eyes on her.

"Where are my manners? I am so mesmerized by your beauty I didn't offer to buy you a drink. What are you drinking tonight?" He placed his hand in the small of her back as he guided her to the bar.

"Okay. Well. This is not a line but, I like to drink the same drink all night long and not mix it up so..." she paused for a moment and looked at him with a grin on her face and a sexy look in her eyes. "Sex on the beach is what I'm having tonight. But I like to give special instructions for them to make it with extra pineapple and extra cherries." She couldn't wait to hear his response. She was very bold in her sexuality but didn't come off as an easy lay.

He raised his eyebrows and licked his lips, not really sure where to go with his response. His nature was starting to rise quickly. Could she possibly be a sweet innocent girl who is an undercover freak and just as freaky as he was? He brushed a piece of her hair back from her face, smiled at her as her eyes followed his hands then back to his lips moving replying, "If sex on the beach is what you want beautiful then that's what you will have as long as you want tonight, on me. All night long." He stretches the words in a sexy low voice. He stares into her eyes raising his hand to signal the bartender.

"What can I get you sir?" She asks. The bartender eyes were wide admiring Bradon's handsome sexy swag. She too started to blush trying to be professional. Bradon was very handsome just like his brother. Their strong presence demanded attention the moment they stepped in any room.

Staring at Chantae he says, "Yes let me have 'sex on the beach' with extra pineapple and extra cherries. And give me silver eighteen hundred with pineapple juice." He smiled at Chantae wanting her to know that he was not afraid or intimidated but enjoyed a challenge.

"I am impressed. Thank you in advance for my sex on the beach. I am sure I will enjoy every drop of it as much as I am anticipating." She spoke in a sensual tone. She is giving him subtle hints to hold his interest and keep him wondering if she is talking about the drink or having sex.

Bradon doesn't know what to think at this point. Not sure if she is giving him hints that she will have sex with him or if she is really talking about her drink and finding it funny. "You are more than welcome pretty lady. You are intriguing to me. I don't want to be that guy who buys you a drink and stick around unwanted if you know what I mean, but I would like to stay for a while and talk with you more if you would have me. Get to know you a little better and admire your beauty a bit more. If that's ok?"

"I would absolutely love that." She glanced in the direction of her girlfriend as Bradon followed her eyes. She held her phone up to signal for her friend to check her phone. She typed a text message to her.

11:02 pm
U see this cutie here with me well I think I'm in love, lol don't wait on me I'm sure I'm in good hands. If something happens to where I need u I will call or text, and if I don't have a ride I will catch a cab. Love you sis. Be safe when you leave.
#SmartBeautifulCurvy

"Your friend good?" Bradon asked observing what just transpired between Chantae and her friend.

"Yes of course, just letting her know I am in good hands. I am in good hands right?" She looked up at Bradon.

"You are definitely in good hands sweetheart." He met her gaze until she softened her stare all the way to a timid blush.

Chantae's phone buzzed with a message back from her friend.

11:03 pm
Girllllll he is finnnnneeee!!!!!! Okay you be good and have fun and I will catch you tomorrow. Call me if you need me. Love you back. Be safe but have fun.
#GotMyLifeTogether

Chantae was all smiles now that she had her friend's official approval.

Receiving her drink from the bartender Bradon began to pass it to her when someone bumped him from behind. Nothing was intentional and the guy apologized but he noticed he spilled drink onto Chantae's arm. "Oh I am so sorry." As he reached for a napkin he paused, noticing her biting on her bottom lip with a sexy grin looking down at her arm. Instead of wiping it with a napkin he used his finger and trailed her arm where the drink was running and brought his wet finger to his mouth tasting the sweetness of her soft smooth skin. He then leaned over and in a seductive sucking motion he used his tongue to wipe away the drink from her shoulder. Then he wiped the excess away with the napkin. "Did I miss anything?" He looked up at her with a grin on his face licking his lips.

With one finger in her mouth biting down, Chantae snapped back to reality and responded, "Oh, yes I think you got it all. And I think you are trying to seduce me in this club." She said as she started to fan her face with her hand.

"Is that right? Well is it working?" Smiling back at her he grinned showing all of his pretty white teeth.

"Yes, I think it is. You get an A plus for licking my shoulder really well and my skin thanks you too." They both laughed and eased the sexual tension that was building between them. From that moment they both had a feeling they had met their match. Based on words unspoken and the feelings that were now flaming between them, Bradon and Chantae both knew that sexing each other would be a must sometime in the very near future.

From that point forward her attention belonged to Bradon.

Chantae captured Bradon's attention and held it all night. They sat there at the bar talking and drinking, smiling and laughing. Not realizing how much she was drinking Chantae attempted to get up to use the ladies room and wobbled a bit. Bradon escorted her there and waited until she was done. When she was done Bradon was in the same spot waiting on her outside the ladies room. She wanted to dance to try to sober up a bit. Her head was spinning and she knew her tolerable limit was maxed. She was a light weight drinker. Swaying her hips made Bradon excited and his nature was rising. He took another drink from his beer, left it on a nearby table and pulled Chantae to the dance floor.

After about thirty minutes of dancing, the club was winding down. Bradon's boys were long gone and Chantae's friends had left as well. The two of them had enjoyed a night of conversation and each other's company. Being as drunk as she was, Bradon asked if she needed a ride home. She told him she would call a cab hoping he would insist on taking her home.

"No way will I let that happen. I am responsible for you and your safety at this point and I will make sure you get home safe and unharmed I promise." He wouldn't allow her to take a cab. She held on tight to him as they left the club and Bradon put her in his car. Once he was in the car he looked over at Chantae admiring her beauty, knowing he was to blame for how intoxicated she was.

Bradon asked where she lived with no response. The alcohol had consumed her body and her mind. Chantae could do nothing but fall into a deep intoxicated sleep. That was all right with Bradon. He was not ready for her to be away from him. Feeling something special about her he knew he had to take care of her. He took her back to his home. Not his typical evening after a night out at a club but one he would enjoy all the same.

CHAPTER 6
~CHANTAE~
WAKING IN HIS ARMS

Ummm, this feels so good. Wait. What tha... Where am I? Who is this holding me in their arms so tight? Whose clothes do I have on? Oh no, I was so drunk last night. Lord no. I know I did not come home with that fine ass man. Chantae paused for a moment and squeezed the strong arms wrapped around her. *Damn his arms are nice. Did we?*

Chantae was wrapped up tight not knowing for sure who's bed she was in. She didn't remember anything about last night past the dance floor. She wasn't even for sure if she was with Bradon. She only hoped it was him.

I just hope it's the cutie from last night at least. I can't believe I am in a stranger's bed. Did I sleep with him? Well of course I'm sleeping with him. Think Chantae. If you would have had sex surely you would have remembered. I don't feel like anyone has entered my loveliness. Okay. I was at the bar, got up to go to the ladies room and then Bradon and I were on the dance floor. Okay then what, think Chantae you have to remember. That's right. Cutie asked me if he could take me home, to my house not his. Although this place is nice, but it surely is not mine.

Oh my God is that what I think it is on my back. Chantae moves her butt just a little to see if she gets a response. *Yes, that is definitely his penis on my back and it seems to be extra-large. I want to touch it but I better not. Surely I would still be throbbing from that so we couldn't have had sex. But why and how the hell do I have on different clothes.*

Chantae tried to ease out of Bradon's arms. When she moved he pulled her closer to him. Although she loved the feeling she had to know what and how. She tried a little harder to remove his hold but her movement wakes him.

"Hey beautiful, you feeling better this morning." He asked in his sexy sleepy voice.

Sexy body and sexy morning voice, Chantae was surely turned on. "Well I'm not sure of what happened last night after the dancing or how I got here. You care to share what I don't remember past the dance floor?" She looks at him with a smile on her face anticipating any embarrassing stories or out of her character things she may have done.

"You even smile in the mornings when you wake up. Simply beautiful." He was mesmerized and didn't answer her question.

"Come on now, tell me. Did we do, you know?" She looked at her clothes she was in and noticed it was one of his shirts. She made a mental note to be sure to take it home with her. It was nice and oversized and would make a good lounge around the house and sleep shirt. Plus it smelled of Bradon.

"Well to ease your mind a bit, no we didn't have sex." You were so wasted that you passed out as soon as I put you in my car. I didn't even get your address to take you home. I enjoyed your company so much that I had to take care of you beautiful. So I hope you don't mind that I brought you here to my home." He rubbed his hand across her face moving her hair back a bit.

"So we didn't have sex. Well explain how and why I am in these clothes."

Lying back in the bed with a smile on his face he grinned looking up at her. "Well beautiful, when I carried you in the house you woke long enough to ask where the bathroom was and you puked all over the floor and your clothes. I cleaned you up and put you into something clean and dry. Although nothing happened sexually, I did enjoy undressing you. But I didn't touch you inappropriately." He threw his hands up in defense.

With a grin on her face she looked at him with devious eyes. "I bet you did enjoy it. Sorry about this. I probably ruined your night and messed up your bathroom. Is there a mess for me to clean up in there?"

Seeming as if she was a bit embarrassed, he eased her mind. "Actually, my house keeper stays here during the weekend and she heard the noise, came rushing in and she actually cleaned you up and dressed you, not me. Although I did watch and was pleasantly enjoying the beautifulness of your body. She ended up putting me out until she was done." He smiled looking at her. "She also cleaned the mess. And you made my night a wonderful night. The best part was being able to lay here holding you in my arms all night beautiful."

Saying all the right things Chantae was blushing with butterfly feelings in her stomach. Could he be her prince charming? She just met this handsome man and she was already burning with desire for him. Not having sex last night was the best part of it all. He held her all night in his arms and woke up holding her tight without even trying to wake her to have sex. Although, the morning was still young she thought. "Thank you." Chantae was nervous and smiling back at Bradon.

Caught up in her smile once more, Bradon knew he had to snap out of it before he put his tongue down her throat. "Can I make you breakfast?" Looking away from her he stands sliding into his house shoes and walks around to the side of the bed where she was sitting.

"You can cook too?" She said with raised eyebrows

"Yes indeed and very well I must say. "

"I am hungry considering." She looks up briefly feeling a little embarrassed to have barfed in the man's home. "Let's see what skills you have in the kitchen." She stands, following him into the kitchen to watch him work his magic.

"Baby girl I am a master with these hands in all things I do." He realized that his comment could have been interpreted as sexual. It was definitely on his mind, but he made the comment more so to reference his cooking and craftsmanship with design. "This home is one of my master pieces. I am an Architect Engineer. Sometimes I design pieces of furniture for fun but my true passion is building design. I use my hands for some amazing creations and make a lot of people happy when I do."

"Oh. I thought you were referring to using your hands on a woman but I am impressed with your explanation as well." She looks into his eyes with an exotic grin on her face. Letting Bradon know with a lick of her lips, holding on to her bottom lip with her teeth for seconds longer, that she is very interested in seeing how his hands perform with her. She was intrigued at how well he was maintaining his composure around her as most men can't take their lustful eyes off her and can't wait for the opportunity to have their way. But then again he was looking at her body last night when she was lethargic and under the influence. Maybe that was his reason for putting her in his big shirt and shorts. Her body was very well concealed.

"Is that right beautiful? I did say in all things that I do. No exceptions." He watches as she starts to smile even harder trying to conceal it but she could not. "Are you allergic to anything? I'm preparing a vegetable omelet with shrimp and ham and grilled raisin toast. Fresh squeezed orange juice"

"Oh that sounds interesting and delicious. Shrimp in an omelet is new to me. What vegetables are you adding?" Chantae was sitting at the bar that separated the kitchen from the dining watching as Bradon came alive in the kitchen. He moved with so much confidence and sexiness causing her waterfall of love to be turned on awakening her inner sexual desires. She could not deny the powerful connection she was feeling but knew she had to conceal it the best way she could to prevent from giving it up within the first twenty-four hours. She might not live by a ninety day rule but she surely wasn't a one night stand girl.

"Let's see, we have some peppers, broccoli and spinach. We have some tomatoes going in last to prevent the juices from forming. Mushrooms and onions. And then of course the ham, shrimp and cheese. You will love it I promise." He noticed her face frowning regarding the different ingredients.

"Broccoli in an omelet for breakfast is new to me but so is shrimp. But I'm sure if you say it is good, I will love it." She rested her chin in her hands leaning forward watching his every move. They engaged in simple chatter never missing a beat in their conversation until he was finished preparing their breakfast.

When he was done preparing her plate he feed her the first bite of her omelet even blowing it to cool it first. After a moment he asked, "Now, how do you like that?" He leaned in very close to her face.

"Umm that is very good. I'm impressed with your skills. Are you this dedicated to perfection in all that you do?" She started blushing as she looked up seeing that he was staring at her with a sexy grin. His eyes glowing with affection.

"Are you testing me woman." He said in his deep sexy voice.

Chantae chuckled, "I just asked a simple question is all Mr. Wonderful." She said with a smile.

"Yes I aim for perfection. I am very dedicated in making sure my outcomes are simply pleasurable to me and those who are affected by my skills. But I only show my skills to those who are worthy and you are worthy pretty lady." He smiled and raised his eyebrows at her.

Chantae started choking on her food, trying to swallow after his response. He patted her back asking if she was okay the entire time smiling. He knew she was turned on just as much as he was and they both were trying hard not to move too fast. Bradon knew that Chantae was only there because she passed out and he didn't know where she lived. He wanted to make love to her body but wanted her to come to his place willingly on her own terms or invite him to her place. Today was not the day even if she was willing.

Looking him in the eyes, Chantae could not believe how sweet this man has been to her. She was use to men always trying to take her home and trying to get in her pants. This experience was different for her. She had a sense of belonging with Bradon. The attraction was so powerful and being with him was so easy and felt normal. She attempted to speak when Bradon leaned in to kiss her with his eyes never leaving her eyes. Closing her eyes, her breathing became heavy as her heart was pounding fast. Bradon first kissed her lips gently and fully pressed together. Then whispered as he planted kisses on the side of her lips, "Do you mind if I kiss you for a few moments?"

Chantae opened her eyes and softly and sweetly said, "Not at all."

He grabbed the back of her head with one hand and lifted her chin before moving back in to kiss her. Bradon traced his tongue around her top lip and then traced his tongue around her bottom lip. He kissed her on her top lip, then kissed her bottom lip before kissing each corner of her lips. He pulled her bottom lip into his mouth. His tongue pierced her lips open as she welcomed him inside her mouth. Their tongues entangled together, dancing around in each other's mouth. He gently bit her bottom lip, sucking on it before indulging the inside of her mouth again. He kissed her so romantically with such passion and feeling. It was magical. Sucking on her tongue as it entered his mouth. He kissed her sweetly, passionately and seductively. Chantae's breathing was increased and her arms were now around Bradon's back holding onto his shoulders.

The passion that she felt for Bradon was all new to her. She had never been kissed this way before. She knew that this was special. Her mom always told her you can tell a lot about a kiss. And she was right. This was a man who she could fall in love with.

Bradon kissed her for what felt like an eternity of blissful orgasmic pleasure. She did not want him to stop. At that moment she wanted him to take her in his arms, carry her to the bedroom and make love to every inch of her body. He kissed her eyes. He kissed her nose. He kissed her all over her face. Chantae moaned with every touch of his lips. The more she moaned the more aggressively he kissed her. Tracing the length of her neck with his tongue he gently bit her all the way back up. She was in paradise. He came back to her lips, his tongue finding the inside of her mouth once again. He kissed her aggressively, letting her know that he wanted all of her. She returned the feeling through her acceptance and receptive passion she gave back to him.

Bradon pulled back from her, looking in her eyes. "Your kisses are so sweet. I could kiss you all day but I better let you finish your omelet."

"WOW. What are you trying to do to me? You hold me all night taking care of me. Then you feed me. And then you kiss me so passionately, so wonderfully. I must be dreaming I'm in a fairytale."

"No dream. This is a fairytale come true Princess Chantae. And I am your prince charming." He had a sexy grin on his face as he moved away from Chantae to prepare his omelet. He had to control his urge to put her up on the counter and make love to her there.

"You are amazing Bradon you know that." She looked up from her plate glancing at Bradon whose eyes were still on her.

"You haven't seen anything yet. Do you have plans today?"

"Yes. I go to church every Sunday and today I have to pick my mom up. After church we are heading back to her house for Sunday dinner. My family comes over to my mom's every third Sunday of the month for Sunday dinner. So I really should be getting home."

"Oh no problem. I will take you home after you finish your omelet. I hope this is not the last time I will see you."

"Of course not. I would love to see you again. We must exchange numbers before I leave."

"Yes. That we must do pretty lady."

After a morning of blissful happiness together, Chantae and Bradon both were on cloud nine.

Chantae was so happy. She hoped that this was the beginning of a promising relationship with Bradon. She knew that men often sold women a dream with intentions of sleeping with them but he had several opportunities and he didn't try. She was hoping he was feeling exactly what she was feeling. After breakfast, Bradon took her home and walked her to the door where he kissed her again goodbye for now.

CHAPTER 7
~BRYSON~
IS SHE CHEATING

Its early Monday morning and Bryson is up getting ready for a busy day at the office. His body and his mindset wouldn't allow him to sleep in, even after a long weekend of mixing pleasure and relaxation with working and a late night with Jewel. This was a habit that would be hard to break and something he would have to work on once he was married. Jewel was fast asleep on the other side of the bed. He leans over and kisses the back of her neck. He walks to the bathroom and his briefs are standing at full attention with the thickness of his bulge stretching to maximum expansion. This happens in the mornings and doesn't go down until after his morning release in the bathroom. He stands there stroking every inch of himself trying to aim towards the rim. With one hand on the wall he leans over a little tilting forward so he can aim straight. Yes this brother is packing a very lovely thick and long package. Bryson was blessed with good looks, good skin, good height and good thickness in all the right places.

After washing his hands he heads toward the kitchen for some juice grabbing his phone on the way to call his Kenneth.

"Talk to me." Kenneth answered in a groggy voice yawning.

"Yo Kenny, you up dawg?" He said as he heard the sleepiness in his voice.

"I am now man where are you? What time is it?" Kenneth was reaching for his watch on the night stand beside his bed, wiping at his eyes to focus on the time.

Bryson was in the living room of his luxury mansion and turned the TV on to watch the morning news. "It's a few minutes before six man. We have that big meeting today with Warner Productions you have your presentation ready? We need six solid productions for them. I have seven, but you know how hard they can be to please and make these motion pictures."

"Yeah I have my stuff ready I have eight myself so out of our, what is that, fifteen? They got to love at least six." Kenneth said stretching.

"Aight well I'm about to jump in the shower and head to the office." He paused for a moment noticing his fiancée purse sitting on the table and her phone buzzing from a pending text message flashing urgent. He picks the phone up and was about to clear the message from beeping when he saw the name 'Boo Thang' flash across the screen. "What the fuc... man I'll hit you back." Curiosity always winning, he reads the text message as he hung up his own cell phone.

Boo Thang
2:45am
Hey baby girl I e-mailed you and you didn't e-mail me back you must be sleep or either faking the funk again all hugged up with that nigga. You betta not be giving him none of my good sweet..... Make sure you are there tonight at seven. I love making love to you in your 'soon to be husband' hotel. LOL!!! I booked the room. Meet me in room 279 at the Presidential Suites level. We have almost reached the top floor. See you tonight sweet lips for dinner & dessert. Umm guess what I'm imagining....
#MissingMySweetLips

Boo Thang
2:53am
Jewel you still up baby girl....
#StillMissingMySweetLips

Boo Thang
2:57am
Call me in the morning when you wake sweet lips... Good night pretty lady.....

By the time Bryson was done reading, he was fuming. In an attempt to calm down and think rational, Bryson thinks for a moment, *how I know this isn't someone playing on the phone hoping I would see this message just to get a rise out of me in hopes of messing up our relationship.* He needed more evidence that she is cheating before he jumped to conclusions. But his blood was definitely boiling with anger. He makes a quick call to a friend who is a private detective. Someone who can find out what this was all about. He jots down the number of the person who texted and gives it to the detective.

"I wish I could get into her e-mail. Wait a minute she was on my computer at work I bet I can look in archives for her password. It keeps screen shots of everything typed." Speaking out loud Bryson hurries to get dressed so he can get to the office. Once in the car he would be sure to call Kenneth back to try to make some sense of this situation.

Hoping this was all a joke, Bryson's heart races and his blood was still boiling trying to think of who this man could be. How he could not know they were messing around with his fiancée right under his nose, in his hotel that he owns. After the wonderful weekend they had last week, he refused to believe this to be true. He calls Kenneth back to talk to him about it. He is his best friend so he has nothing to hide from him. He trusted him with his life.

"Talk to me baby, I'm on my way into the office." Kenneth said sounding fully awake and energetic.

"Kenny man I found a text message on Jewel phone from some nigga she has saved as Boo Thang."

"What? It's got to be a mistake or something. Jewel wouldn't be talking to another man, she loves you too much. What did the text say?"

"Man, first I thought it could be somebody playing a joke but she has the number saved in her phone. More and more I think about it the more my blood boils." You could see Bryson's temples swelling from the anger he was feeling.

"She had it saved so yeah she knows the nigga. What did it say man?"

"Something about, he e-mailed her and she didn't hit him back, asking what she doing faking again hugged up with her nigga, something about she better not be giving her goods away to me and that they be fucking in my hotel that I mother fuckin own. They supposed to be meeting there tonight at seven in the Presidential Suite's room 279 even said they have fucked in almost all the rooms in my hotel. And he called her sweet lips. Man that's my pet name for her in the bedroom and I know the reason I gave her the name and this nigga calling her that." Bryson was so upset and with every word you could tell how angry he was. I'm supposed to be marrying this girl in a couple weeks and if this is true...." He stopped, unable to finish his sentence. The thought of betrayal from a woman who he was in love with was hurting him deep.

"Damn man yeah you pissed off and I see why. I hate to say this man but you know it's not impossible and she could be cheating. With your busy schedule she has so much free time unaccounted for. Although I never thought of her cheating on you or doing you wrong in any kind of way. You know what they say; an idle mind is a devil's playground. I'm pulling into the parking lot now I'll pull the hotel records for repeat visits from her and see who has that room booked for tonight."

"Yeah thanks man, do that for me."

"Brys man I hope this is a joke or a misunderstanding because you don't deserve this. But you got to put this to the side for a couple hours until we get through this meeting today. We are talking close to a half billion dollars here. And I need you to be able to concentrate. Your happiness is worth more than any amount of money but I know you feel me on this. Now I am going to handle some things for you on this matter and we will discuss after the meeting alright man?"

"Yeah you right. It could be nothing. I'm going to get through this meeting but you know everything else will be postponed after that. So tell Jackie to reschedule the other meetings pending a day and time. Man this is Jewel calling me right now." Looking at his incoming call on his other cell.

"Don't answer it. She probably got the text message and wants to make sure you didn't see it. Just play it off and act like nothing's wrong. Still treat her the same way you have been in case you need to creep up on her you feel me." Kenneth knew that was easier said than done.

"Yeah I feel you. Aight man I will see you in a minute thanks for listening and giving your boy advice." Bryson ends the call on his business phone and called his fiancée back on his personal phone. He inhaled and tried to clear his thoughts and make himself smile before talking to her.

"Hey baby girl, I was on a business call, I see you're up early." He was trying hard to fake a smile, gritting his teeth after his words. His heart was broken and shattering in a million more pieces as his thoughts revolved around what she has possibly been doing when he wasn't around her.

"Yeah I've been up for a few minutes. I just wanted to call and tell you I love you and hope your big meeting goes okay this morning." She was stretching and yawning wiping the sleep from her eyes as she was looking through her phone. She was wondering if Bryson had gone through her phone. By his tone she assumed she was in the clear.

"Thank you baby, yeah I'm trying to gather my thoughts before the meeting but I think we got it together and everything should go great. What are your plans for the day?"

"I don't know baby I'm going back to sleep for a little while and I don't know after that. I am hanging with the girls later on. I think somebody playing on my phone. I got a crazy text message. I might stop by the phone company." She paused seeing what his next words would be still wondering if he saw it.

He thought for a minute wondering if it could have been someone playing or if she was trying to see if he saw it. He made sure to mark the text as unread and put the phone back in her purse. He hoped that it was a joke but deep down he knew this was real. He thought about his doubt and realized that sometimes when you don't see something God has placed in front of you he brings it to you in a different way. Even if it hurts. "Playing on your phone? Saying what? Who is it?" He hoped she would give him some kind of explanation to help ease his pain.

"I don't know, if they keep on I will just get my number changed its nothing." She thought she was off the hook and was sure he knew nothing of it. "Aight baby I love you, I will call you later okay."

"Okay, love you too." He hung up still feeling convinced but hoping his sweet little angel was as innocent as he imagined. He was hoping this was a joke. After the meeting he should hear back from the investigator and should know something more once he check the archives to obtain her password to her e-mail. He might need to have the investigator look through those while he is in his meeting in case she decides to cover her tracks and delete some stuff. So he called to have him meet in his office before the meeting.

"So what do you think? Out of the fifteen story lines' you think they will choose at least six for the motion pictures and sign the contract with Cole Estates Enterprise?" After the meeting Kenneth and Bryson sat in Bryson's office and although Kenneth knew Bryson had something else on his mind he tried to break the ice talking about business first.

"We had some really great ideas. And I think we touched on a lot of what they were looking for so I think yes. They will take six to make motion pictures and those are the six we are banking on. They will take another six to make a movie to send directly to DVD and cable and then we will work on stage two and come up with seven authors who can write the book for the movies. So be thinking about that coming up. I know four of the fifteen we just presented are for sure deals for motion pictures. You could tell by their reactions and eye contact with each other." Bryson got up and walked towards the window looking out into the city view. He was deep in thought about his fiancée.

"Yeah I saw their reactions on four of them for sure. We will know their decision in about a week. Hey man, I know you have other issue's pressing on your mind. I had Jackie reschedule your day and..... Well I found out who has the room booked for tonight. And honestly, I hate to say this but he has a room booked here every Monday and Thursday. I found nothing in Jewel's name. His name is Michael Anderson." Looking at the reaction on Bryson's face Kenneth asked, "Does that name sound familiar?"

"Michael Anderson? Why does that name sound so familiar to me?" He sat there thinking pondering the name over and over in his head when his phone buzzed breaking his concentration. "Yes Jackie."

"Sir, there is a Rodger Maxx here to see you."

"Please send him in Jackie. Thank you!"

"Who is Rodger Maxx?" Kenneth asked knowing that Bryson had every connection to get anything done he wanted.

"He is the private investigator I have helping me figure this out. I need to know what's going on for real and right now. He is the best." Bryson had a look of anticipation on his face, knowing he was about to hear the truth.

"Hi Rodger, how are you man?" Bryson met him at the door shaking his hand as he entered his office.

"What's going on man?" Kenneth reached out to shake his hand as well.

"This is my best friend and partner Kenneth Cartwright. He knows about everything so feel free to talk in front of him." Bryson offered him a seat. He could tell that this was not about to be good looking at the stack of papers and photos in his hand.

"Bryson let me just get straight to what you pay me for. This is going to sting but I don't have any other way of putting this. She is definitely seeing someone. I was able to pull e-mails from your computer and even gained access to her e-mail. Apparently she uses your computer more often than you think."

"Well, my home computer is tied directly to this one." Bryson said with intensity in his voice.

"Oh okay well that explains it then. Apparently they have great pleasure at e-mailing back and forth and having online sexual conversations. They plan to meet twice every week in your hotel on every Monday and Thursday, those apparently being your busy late days. They have a twisted sick game going where they plan to have sex in every room of your hotel. She's definitely cheating and thinks that it is a fun little game that she will never get caught at. I have shots from the surveillances that show them both going into different rooms over the last month and they always meet at seven in the evening and typically leave out by eight thirty."

"Damn! She knows I usually work until ten here in the office on Monday's and Thursday's. What else you got." Bryson's voice was cracking. He was trying not to break down in front of them both from the hurt and pain he was feeling.

"In the e-mails, and I will leave these with you if you like, it talks in great detail about what they do from the time they walk through the door until the time they leave. Apparently they go straight to showering and having sex upon entering the room and then showering and getting dressed to leave right after their encounter together. They meet in other places like movie theaters or have dinner together even work out at the same gym. And…."

"That's where I saw the name before. I went to surprise her one day at the gym and now I know exactly who this man is. He was touching on her and I was a little upset. When I confronted him and her she said he was her personal trainer helping her get her body in shape for me, she was getting ready to walk down the aisle. I am so stupid. I should have known what was up then." He turned and walked toward the window. "So how do I catch them together? I want you to find them together and call me so I can be there too. I need to see with my own eyes, catch her in the act so there will be no excuse or confusion between either of us why we will no longer be together. I am sure she will have an excuse for that too."

"They are meeting tonight and from the looks of things they are pretty consistent with sticking to the plans. The way I see it, you own the hotel and have access to any key you want without any questions. You can have the bar lock taken off just in case they use it and then you will have complete access to the room. I would say about seven thirty tonight you should be able to catch them right in the act. There will be no excuse at that point. I can follow her and let you know when she arrives and then the rest is up to you at that point."

"This relationship is over. I want to make sure she knows I know and give that bastard something to think about." You could see his temple's pulsating and his jaws clutching together, but looking at Bryson you could really tell that he was a man who was hurting deeply from the betrayal of a woman who he loved. "Yes Rodger, call me when she arrives at the hotel to meet him. I want to know as soon as you know."

"As soon as she arrives I will give you a call. And if for some reason she doesn't I will still give you a call." Rodger said standing to his feet.

"Bryson man whatever you need me for you know I am here no matter what." Kenneth felt bad for his best friend who was also like a brother to him. He knew he didn't deserve this one bit.

"Thanks man I appreciate that Kenny. Rodger, I thank you for your time and your help on such short notice. I will be expecting your call this evening one way or the other." He reached into the inside of his desk and retrieved an envelope of cash and handed it to Rodger, payment for his services. "I will call you if I need anything further." He shook his hand knowing that this was the beginning of what was to come.

"Thanks Bryson, and again I am sorry for the bad news. I will be in touch with you soon. Mr. Cartwright it was good meeting you." He reached out to shake Kenneth's hand.

"Thanks man, take care." Shaking his hand Kenneth walked him to the door and closed it behind him. "So what's next man? What now?"

"This hurts Kenny. How could I be so blind, how did I not know? Why me? I have money, I'm good looking and the loving is out of this world, I know I be putting it down. I am so good to that girl. Gave her everything a woman could want. I guess me working so much was a problem." He sat there with his face in his hands. Tears were rolling down his face. He was hurting and angry at the same time.

"Man this is a messed up situation and I know it hurts but don't kick yourself and blame yourself for this. There is no excuse for cheating. None! If she couldn't handle your work hours she should have bounced. She knew if she cheated she wouldn't have all of the luxuries you give her. I am sure the guy she is seeing is broke compared to what she is accustomed to with you. Her loss, she doesn't deserve you." Kenneth sat down in the seat across from Bryson's desk.

"Yeah you right. She surely has put up a big front. What a man got to do to find real love. Everyone loves the money part of me but that's not who I am. I don't flash my money to get things. I don't go overboard with buying things. I just have it and don't mind sharing it with the woman who will be my everything, my wife. But I don't want anyone trying to get over either and use me for that. Maybe I need to live life as a normal man and hide that side of me when I meet people. Live as an average hard working man in average clothing."

"Man you know you wouldn't know how to do that as GQ as you dress. You could make clothes from Wal-Mart look like Kenneth Cole himself designed and put them together." Kenneth chuckled a little.

"Yeah I guess you are right. I would have to borrow some from a homeless man or get somebody else to dress me huh. Why don't I just pretend to be homeless and see if I could meet people? You think I would be believable? We could see how people treat me if they thought I didn't have any money. Huh that would be a good story. Bryson Mathews living his life as a homeless man, I can see the headlines now."

"No way! You wouldn't last a day. Besides you wouldn't meet any women that way only hateful greedy people. But it would make for a good storyline to see how people treat you. One of the richest men around appearing to be homeless. People don't realize who they are meeting. That's why it pays to always be nice. Jesus himself could be here in rags and people would pass him by not knowing who HE was!"

"It's crazy man. I'm just glad I didn't marry her without a prenuptial and she take half of what I have once I found out. It would have eventually come to light if not now. It always does."

"Yeah you right. What's done in the dark will come to light eventually. If you go through with it tonight I will be right with you. You will probably need a drink after that."

"Cool. I guess that means I have to talk to her for the rest of the day as if nothing is wrong. I think I need a drink now."

"Or you could just ignore her all day."

"She typically calls me every day just to see how late I will be working. Huh, and now I see why. Yeah, ignore her all day is my best bet if I want to catch her tonight. I will tell Jackie to inform anyone who calls that I am still in meetings. That way if she calls and can't get me she will think I am still in my very important meeting."

"Brys, what if you don't catch her? She could be suspicious and try not to show up. Then what? Is the wedding still on? Does she get off the hook? Man I know you love her, I am just trying to see where your head is." Kenneth said.

"This is the ultimate betrayal and even without catching her in the act it is most definitely over between us. I still have the proof. And no man can just up and get over what I just found out. You don't get over something like this and keep any plans, definitely not wedding plans." Bryson was sitting at his desk stretched back in his oversized leather chair.

"Aight, you deserve better than that is all I am saying." Both men were quiet for a brief moment before Kenneth spoke again. "You want to go get some lunch?"

"Yeah let's get out of here. I'll let you pay today." Bryson said to Kenneth, knowing that Kenneth's tab was really his tab. Kenneth has a company expense card just as Bryson to pick up their lunch and dinner expenses that revolve around business. This was no exception. No matter what the occasion work always come up at some point so it would be a legitimate business write off.

"I got this." They both headed out of Bryson's office straight to the private elevator to leave for lunch. They didn't want anyone to see them leaving just in case Jewel had someone watching them. The less he saw of her the better.

CHAPTER 8
~JEWEL~
JEWEL'S SNEAKY WAYS

Bryson left for work early Monday morning. Knowing that he had left the house, Jewel woke up looking for her cell phone. She always waited until he was gone so she could plan her day. Most of the time in planning her day, she was always up to something sneaky. She was a different person when she wasn't with Bryson. Sneaky became her middle name. It's funny how money can change the way you act to play a part, perfect fiancée. Little did Bryson not know before was that little 'Miss Perfect Jewel' was not as perfect as he thought.

She went to the living room to retrieve her purse and her phone. She saw several new messages that read from Boo Thang. She was hoping Bryson did not to see it flashing across her screen. She decided to call him knowing he was on his way in to work. "Humph, no answer." She decided to call Raquel who worked the front desk in Bryson's building. Jewel knew her from the hood where they grew up. She knew Raquel had potential to be a professional, but also knew she had no common sense about simple things. So she used her indirectly to spy on Bryson. "Hey girl you working hard?" She said as Raquel answered the phone.

"My morning hasn't started jumping off yet girl. Not too many people get up this early and get started. While I got you on the phone you hung up on me Friday and I don't appreciate that." Raquel hands were on her hips and her finger was twirling as she was speaking.

"My bad girl I didn't mean to. My phone died on me and I had to charge it up. I meant to call you back." She said lying through her teeth.

"Ah okay, I'm sorry girl. I am going off on you for nothing then. You know you my girl. What you up so early for? Your man ain't got in yet." She simply answered the first part of Jewel's question without her even asking.

"Girl I know. I didn't want to bother him I just wanted to make sure he got to work okay is all. He hasn't been sleeping much. Can you call me when he gets there so I will feel better? I know he is tired. You know men don't like women worrying about them so remember don't tell him. I am trying to be a good fiancée soon to be wife to him."

"Girl I feel you. I got you, I always do. I will call you back." She said before hanging up. Not realizing she was being used.

And just like that, Jewel had her spy to let her know Bryson's comings and goings. She decided to go in and take a shower and just before she jumped in the phone rang. It was Bryson calling her back. She tried to play it off about her cell phone. She just needed to make sure he didn't see it. Once she was good thinking he didn't, she was back up to no good.

After showering she put on some very kinky lingerie. A black see through baby doll lace top with a crotch-less bottom panties for easy access. She put on all her smell goods, and lotion. Then she waited for her call that Bryson was at work as she pranced around admiring her curvaceous body. Jewel was a perfect size eight without an ounce of body fat. To her, she was the perfect size woman. She stayed in shape thanks to her genetics and personal trainer. Raquel called her back to announce Bryson's arrival at work. She then quickly dialed a number and proceeded to touch herself. She was having phone sex with another man besides her fiancé.

"Hey daddy you got a few moments to make momma cum." She spoke into the other end of the phone.

"Damn girl you sound so good. You know I'm at work and can't talk long." The man spoke into the phone in a quiet tone.

"I know daddy, go sneak off somewhere so you can play with my clit through the phone. It's all wet for you, needing to be licked by your flickering thick tongue. Don't you want to taste my juices baby? This honey is flowing just for you." She said in her soft sexy voice.

"Oh girl you gonna make me tear your ass up when I see you this evening." He said as he was walking to the bathroom checking the stalls making sure no one was there.

"I wish you were here right now. I have on some sexy lingerie just for you. The white teddy laced in baby blue your favorite color." She was stroking in between her legs moaning in the phone. She told him she had on something different than the black lace teddy just to play the role with him.

"You want daddy to come fuck you my precious Jewel. You got daddy hard as a rock. I'm going to get all up in between them thighs, deep inside your warm wet pussy when daddy sees you tonight."

"You know I like it rough daddy. What else are you going to do to me?" Jewel was rubbing her clit faster at the sound of his voice.

"I'm going to stick big daddy anaconda in your mouth and watch you deep throat him trying to suck the cum out. Can you do that for me sweet lips? Nobody has ever sucked daddy like you do." He entered the bathroom stall locking the door behind him as he started to undo his pants.

"Umm I got you daddy. I need you here right now. I'm about to explode and I want to cum all in your mouth and all over big daddy anaconda." Jewel was really into touching herself at this point, almost reaching her climax.

"Girl you got me stroking myself here at work." He was now in the stall jacking off.

"You gon make me cum daddy? I'm touching my clit baby. Stroking this kitty imagining it is your tongue licking all this overflowing honey from my lips." She was moaning some more.

"Oh girl oh ahhgghgg." He said something like that as he was cummin all over the toilet seat.

"Baby you cummin without me. You suppose to wait for momma." Jewel was pouting.

"Daddy on the clock baby. I couldn't help it, you sound so good." He said as he was cleaning up the white mess he just made. He was now rushing her off the phone so he could get back to work.

"I have to finish by myself now." She sat there on the bed with her legs open and her hands still in place rubbing as she was pouting.

Washing his hands at the sink and trying to compose himself he told her, "You know I will make it up to you when I see you. We need to meet before tonight baby. Hey man how you doing." He spoke as another gentleman walked into the bathroom. "Baby I gotta get back to work, the boss coming. But thank you for the excitement. Talk to you soon." And just like that his selfishness didn't care about her momentary needs.

"But but......" she heard the click of the phone hanging up on the other end. She was upset that she didn't get the same enjoyment and wasn't able to cum as quick as he did. She was thinking of a sneaky plan. As soon as she hung up she was still feeling herself, wanting to cum over and over with more than the masturbation of her hands. Her hormones were raging and the pulsations between her legs were increasing.

I will prance my way into Bradon's room and he will probably think I'm one of his flunkies he always bringing home. I just hope no one is in there with him now. I heard him come in and I know he was extremely drunk passed out so he should be still semi there. Jewel thought.

She got up and pranced her way through the house to the other master bedroom.

Cracking the door she could tell that Bradon was sleeping well. She tiptoed in and closed the door back so he couldn't see her face in the dark room. She thought, *all he will think is that I must be someone he brought home with him last night. Bradon brings women home from the club all the time when he is drunk, he won't know the difference.* As he slept, she slid up under the covers covering his limp magic stick with her mouth. She had a skill with her lips and her tongue that could bring any man to full attention.

He started to moan and move and wanted to aggressively make love to this woman. He grabbed at her hair to try to see if he could figure out who she was as she worked her lips around his manhood magically. As soon as she had him where she wanted him she was straddled across his waist so fast, placing him inside her wet loveliness of honey. She was horny and he was going to fulfill her desires. She rocked her hips back and forth as she kissed on his chest and his neck. She was driving him crazy with every thrust. He grabbed her by her head several times trying to see if he could figure out who she was. But her thrust was too much pleasure for him that he would let go and hold on for the climaxing ride. He was now holding on to her waist and thrusting himself inside her harder and harder. Her breasts were bouncing as he grabbed her at the high end of her thigh. She was moaning, a voice he didn't recognize as familiar. She was cummin all over him as he thrust harder and harder inside her. Her moan was louder turning him on as he was on the verge of cummin himself. She knew it and she grabbed a hold of him thrusting her hips harder. He started moaning at the start of his massive orgasm. At the same time he pulled Jewel up and started cummin all over her pretty lingerie.

"Umm you were better than I thought you would be." She said whispering in his ear as she kissed the side of his face.

He immediately jumped, throwing her off of him onto the bed and went straight for the light. His heart was now beating extremely fast. He knew this could not be who he thought it was. Lights on, the inevitable was confirmed. "What the hell Jewel? Why are you... What did you just do? Ah hell naw!" With his hands on his head covering his face he couldn't believe what just happened. "Aauugghhhh". He screamed.

"You mean what did we just do?" She said as she was looking down at the cum all over her lingerie. "Don't worry I won't tell your brother and neither will you. Big brother doesn't need to know anything about this love affair we have going." She looked at him through her sneaky conniving eyes.

"What the fuck you mean love affair? There is no love affair. Why did you come in here like that? I thought you were some hoochie from the club. I can't believe this shit. Ah damn my brother is going to kill me." He had his hands over his face. "I'm having a nightmare that's it. I am having a fuckin nightmare. This shit isn't happening for real."

"Calm down and your brother won't know a thing about this, are we clear?" She had her hands on her hips.

"What do you mean won't know? I can't let you marry him after this stunt you just pulled. He loves you. How could you be so fucking scandalous? This is fucked up Jewel." Bradon was pacing back and forth beating himself up. He just had sex and enjoyed it with his brother's fiancée.

"If you say one word I will scream rape." She threatened.

"Rape?" Bradon said loudly.

"That's right rape. I have the evidence all over me. It is your word against mine. I have the loose tracks in my hair that prove you pulled my weave, pulling my hair as I was fighting with you. And I can fabricate some bruises to add to the ones you just made on my thighs Mr. Rough daddy. And I doubt I need to mention your DNA all over me. So are we clear." She looked him stern in the eyes.

"Damn. Scandalous skank. You wouldn't. That would never work you came into my room." He stood there looking her in the eye, standing firm and fuming from her words.

"Oh it will work and I will be marrying your brother without him knowing a peep about this. I surely will let them know I didn't say anything about it because you threatened me, to take my happiness away. So like I said Mr. Rough Daddy, you better not say a word. I'm Miss Perfect remember." She walked out of the room grabbing a freezer Ziploc bag on her way to her room. She placed the lingerie in it for safe keepings just in case she may need it. She got out her camera and took some pictures of her bruised legs. She loved the roughness but she would use this to her advantage.

Jewel loved Bryson at least his money had her thinking she did. She fell in love with his money and the idea of never having to work. Then she fell in love with Bryson enough to marry him. She wanted to have her cake and eat as much of it as she wanted. Marrying Bryson was her gold mine, her very rich future. She had an afterthought that she shouldn't have had sex with his brother but she was caught up in the moment. Her sexual desires took over her mind and there was no changing what was done. Now she had to cover her tracks and hope Bradon was scared enough to keep his mouth shut.

CHAPTER 9
~BRIELLE~
GOOD DEED BLESSINGS

Saturday morning and Brielle was up early doing her T25 workout. She likes to start her morning with some juice or a smoothie for energy. Then one of her workout videos followed by a light jog on the treadmill. She loved to work out and work up a good sweat. Not only did she want to keep her body in shape and looking good for herself and her one day husband, it helped relieve sexual tension and stress. Once her workout was complete she showers, dresses and heads in the kitchen to cook the kid's breakfast.

Brielle's baby girl wakes up and comes into the kitchen. She sits in her favorite seat at the table. With sleep in her eyes she asks, "Mommy what's for breakfast."

Brielle looks at her baby girl, smiles with a warm heart and replies, "Momma has made your favorite sweetie, heart shaped blueberry pancakes, turkey bacon and scrambled eggs with cheese."

"Umm that smell so good mommy. I will get the syrup for you. You want me to help with the eggs?" Jayla placed the syrup on the table and walked over to where her mom was cooking waiting for her to find something else she could do.

"Baby girl you set the table and give everyone a napkin while I finish cooking breakfast. Momma doesn't want you to burn yourself sweetheart." She handed her the forks and placed the plates, cups and napkins on the table for her.

One by one, all three children were awakened by the smell of momma's cooking. She made them all a plate. Sitting at the table, everyone was eating their breakfast, being so kind to one another and enjoying their Saturday morning together.

"Are we feeding the ducks today at the park? It's a pretty day and I know there will be plenty of hungry ducks coming around." Brielle asked the kids. They go to the park often to feed the ducks and enjoy the lake. During the warm months they play in the water and have picnics with a basket full of food, blankets and all.

"Yes ma'am." They all said in unison.

"Momma can I make peanut butter and jelly sandwiches for us today? You said we could have them next time we went to the park. Please." Her oldest daughter Olivia asked.

"Yes baby I'm sure they will be delicious. What else do we want to pack for our picnic?"

"Apples and pickles and some crunch n munch popcorn and and and I don't know what else." Jayla was smiling and trying to hide her face realizing that everyone was watching her go on and on in her cute little voice.

"Yeah let's pack all that stuff" Brielle said.

"Momma that sounds good." Carter said to his mom. "I will get them out of the cabinet and put them in the basket."

"I'll go get the basket momma, I know where it is." Little Jayla said turning to get down from the table.

"Hold on lil momma finish your food first. We still have to get you all cleaned up and I have a few house choirs I need you all to help me finish before we go to the park, ok?"

"Okay momma." Jayla said.

Looking around to the other children they all said okay and finished their food. They were a loving family and very kind hearted to one another and to other people. Brielle's children are very respectful just as she was.

After cleaning the house and completing all of the chores, a couple hours had passed. The children were now getting ready for the park. Taking baths. The girls getting their hair done. Making sandwiches and gathering the items for the picnic. Everyone was now ready for the park. They loved going to the park with their mom. It was like an adventure and something exciting always happened. It gave them a chance to have peace and enjoy the fresh air and all of God's creations. Playing in the water was always fun during the warm months. Making fishing poles out of sticks and string and walking in the water barefoot with their pants rolled up to their knees or higher. Their bond was unbreakable. Brielle made sure that her kids were first priority no matter what. They were the most important thing to her. So family time was very important.

When they returned home from the park the kids all ran to the mailbox to get the mail. Jayla carried the mail to her mom. When they entered the house the children all were tired and collapsed in the living room on the floor pretending to be so exhausted they couldn't stand up. Brielle walked over to the end of the sofa and started going through the mail. Carter started tickling his baby sister who was now pretending to be asleep. Laughter roared through the living room. The kids were happy and loving to each other which made their mom happy. As they played Brielle continued going through the mail.

Brielle had a funny look on her face when she saw a personal letter from a Doctor addressed to her. "What in the world is this? Who is this?" She said aloud to herself. Opening the mail she found a letter and a smaller envelope inside.

Miss. Summers,

First let me say to you, thank you so much for the kindness in your heart and the generosity and favor you showed to me when I was in need. You are proof that there is a God and He still has his angels here on earth working in His Will. You can't possibly imagine what it meant to me, my wife and my son when you gave me the money to pay for his prescription.

She paused for a moment realizing it was the man from the pharmacy. *Ah okay it's the man from the pharmacy but how in the world did he get my address I wonder. Surely they wouldn't have given that information out at the pharmacy.* She thought on that for a brief second and continued reading the letter.

My father was very sick, was on his death bed and my son who is three years old had been running a fever having a respiratory infection. We rushed to catch the first flight out when we got the call about my father being sick. Everything happened so fast we left my sons medicine at home realizing this after an hour and a half drive to the airport. My son started running a fever during the first part of our flight. Well I guess you can imagine, I had his doctor call in another prescription to the nearest Walgreens during our hour layover and there I met you. He is doing just fine now.

It's been about a month and I promised I would pay you back with interest. I heard you on the phone talking about your struggle paying your bills so I thought I would be a blessing to you and send you a little extra interest. I am honored to be able to help you as you cannot imagine how much you helped us. Your good deed service was priceless. But I do hope that this will be a blessing to you and your family and can help relieve some financial struggles.

I wrote your address down when I heard you telling the pharmacist upon receiving your prescription. Sorry it took me so long. My father passed away the next day after we arrived so we have been in mourning. But I know God is amazing and he is no longer in pain. I feel so blessed to have met you. I almost knocked you down when I was rushing through the store and you had every right to want to be evil towards me but instead you showed a heart as pure as snow. You are my angel, you are my sons' angel and I know God has great things ahead for you. Thank you a million times more for your kind hearted deed.

Please don't hesitate to call me if you need anything at all. My business card is enclosed with this letter. You are truly an Angel of God. Please accept this gift from us and I hope it will be of use to you in helping your family get ahead. May God bless you and your family always!

Sincerely Yours,
Dr. Michael Greenbrier

Brielle now had tears in her eyes realizing that this was the man she helped in the pharmacy a little over a month ago. She realized that what she did was so simple to her but meant the world to someone else. It was sad to hear about his father passing as she couldn't imagine the pain. She realized how grateful she was to still have both her parents. She was over whelmed with joy to hear that his son was well and that she was able to be a blessing to them. She picked up the phone to call her dad to tell him she loved him but before she could even dial the number, she opened the smaller envelope realizing now that it was a check for money and her eyes were so wide when she saw what the numbers were.

Brielle started crying really hard covering her mouth in shock. She fell to the floor on bended knees, held the check to her chest and started shouting, "Thank you Jesus, Thank you Jesus! Lord you have never failed me but have always been so wonderful to me. Thank you for favor! Lord you are awesome and you have a plan for my life I know. Lord Jesus I thank you, thank you!" She praised the Lord on her knees crying with so much joy and gratefulness in her heart. Her kids stopped playing and were standing around her looking and trying to comfort her. They didn't know what was going on.

"Momma what's wrong, why you crying?" Jayla said as she placed her arm around her mother's neck to hug her. She didn't like to see her mom hurting, none of the kids did.

"Momma is wonderful baby girl. God is so good to us. We are so blessed." She picked Jayla up in the air and swung her around. All the kids then knew those were tears of joy and momma was indeed happy this time. Brielle went on to tell the kids about her wonderful letter and money she received. She called her parents to tell them how much she loves them and told them about the wonderful news as well.

"Well baby, what are you going to do first with the money?" Her mom asked.

"First, I'm going to the bank to cash the check. It won't be absolutely believable until I see the money in my hands." Brielle said with a smile on her face. "Mom you know I have to give you and dad something you both have been so wonderful to me during my hard times. You both have helped me so much."

"Now you know your father is not going to take any money from you child. We are family and that's what family do. We are there for one another through the good and the not so good. You use that money for you and those kids. You have wanted a new car so go ahead get you a new car. Pay off your bills and take care of you for a change. God has blessed you and He knows and we all know that your heart is so big and generous but this time you need to think about you and those kids. Don't tell anyone else you have this money because you know how people are, gimme gimme gimme." Brielle's mom was proud of her. And you could hear it through her voice.

"You right mom. But you know whose daughter I am and besides God bless people to allow them to be a blessing to others. I love you and dad so much mom."

"We love y'all too granny." The kids shouted through the phone.

"Tell my babies we love them too." Brielle's mom loved the way her grandbabies showed them so much love.

"Granny said they love y'all too." Brielle was grinning seeing the kids jump up and down with excitement saying what they are going do with the money.

"I'm gonna buy a pony and some dolls." Jayla said.

"I'm going to get me a bike and some roller blades and I'm going to get me a cell phone." Olivia said.

"I'm going to get momma something really nice then I'm gonna get me some new Jordan's, and then I might buy me a car if momma let me for when I turn sixteen." Carter said.

Brielle was too tickled listening to her children go on and on. "Momma we will be over there soon. We're going to stop by the bank and cash this check so I can deposit the money in my account before they close. I will bring dinner with me okay."

"Okay baby I will see you soon. Y'all be careful okay."

"Okay momma." Brielle made sure to put the business card in her purse so she could call the Doctor to say thank you.

Brielle gathered the kids, who were seconds ago exhausted and now full of energy, and headed to the bank. "I want to cash this please. I would actually like to have a cashier's check for the amount of one hundred seventeen thousand and eight thousand in cash please. Any denomination of bills would be fine." Brielle said to the bank teller after she passed her the check and her ID.

"Yes ma'am, let me verify funds and I will be right back okay." The bank teller walked away to her superior and Brielle saw that they were making a phone call. She figured they were verifying with the good ole Dr. first.

She came back to the desk and said, "Miss. Summers here is your ID back." She counted out the eight thousand dollars to Brielle. Another gentleman walked over and handed the teller the cashier's check. "And here is your check. Dr. Greenbrier asked us to tell you thank you once again. He wanted us to verify when you came in to make sure he sent the check to the right address. You have a great evening."

"Thank you so much! You have a wonderful evening yourself!" Brielle said placing the money in her purse with a big smile on her face.

After depositing the cashier check into her account she stopped and got her mom and dad a gift and a card and enclosed five thousand dollars. That left her plenty of money to put towards a new car and a down payment on a home. She could now be comfortable for a while and start pulling herself out of debt.

Brielle and the kids stopped and got Chinese food and headed to her mom's house. While in the car the kids were asking her questions and asking what they were going to do with the money. They put in all of their requests which were doable in Brielle's mind. Brielle had some really great kids who deserved nothing but the best.

She thought she would get some extra money out beside what she gave her mom so that she and the kids could blow it on themselves. She would get their entire list of requests and more.

Once at her mom's, the kids ran in the house and gave their grandparents hugs and kisses. "Granny, Grand Pa, we got you something."

"The kids were excited as if it was Christmas."

"You did huh. Brielle what did you do. I told you we didn't need anything." Her mom said to her.

"Oh I'm sure it's nothing too much, besides my grand babies are excited and we love gifts from them so we are appreciative of whatever you all got us." Her dad said as he took the bags of food from Brielle hands. "Hey baby girl." He greeted her with a kiss to her cheek.

"Thanks dad. Well now I feel bad because it's just a card." Brielle said with a smile on her face.

Everyone laughed to ease the suspicion about the gift. Brielle was looking at the kids with squinted eyes telling them to hush. She wanted to give them the gift without making a big deal about it. She knew they did not want to accept any money from her. "Mom I'll leave it on your bed and you and dad can look at it later." She said as she headed to their bedroom just up the steps. She placed the card and the gift cards she purchased for them on her parents bed.

Whispering to her husband Mitchell Summers, Mrs. Summers told him, "You know she has money in that card, she couldn't help herself. I know Brielle all too well."

"I know and we both know she doesn't like being put on the spot so just accept it from her and hold on to it in case she need something one day. It says in the bible the one who blesses others is abundantly blessed. We taught her well. Besides you can go out and do something nice for yourself. Maybe we can take a romantic rendezvous getaway trip." He said kissing her on her cheek standing behind her. The kids were looking at them giggling as they knew their grand pa was being affectionate with their granny.

Marcella Summers was grinning from ear to ear. She loved when her husband showed affection and didn't mind the kids seeing. The kids headed to wash their hands at their granny's request and they all sat down to eat with Mr. Summers blessing the food.

CHAPTER 10
~BRADON~
THIS IS SOME BULL.....

Bradon sat in his room beating himself up about what just happened with Jewel. How could he not turn on the lights to see who he was having sex with? The power that women have is exactly that, powerful. He didn't even wear a condom and that is a no-no at all times no matter who the woman is or how good it feels. He was in shock. He jumped up off the bed and locked his bedroom door. He started taking his clothes off so he could jump in the shower to wash Jewel off his skin. Yes she was a very beautiful woman but she was off limits to him. She was his brother's fiancée and he would never do anything to hurt him. Being with his girl has never crossed his mind. But he now knew why his brother was always sexually pleased. Bradon's heart was heavy knowing he has committed the ultimate betrayal between brothers.

That little skank, who would have thought she would do anything like this. My brother thinks she can do no wrong. She is his precious Jewel, his little angel. How am I going to tell him what just happened? And he probably won't believe me after she tells him her story, or her lie. Ah man rape? For real? I don't have to rape anyone as fine as I am. Ah man, Bryson bro I am so sorry. I don't know how to tell you this but even if you stay mad at me forever I can't let you marry her. There is no telling what else she has done or what else she would do.

As he stood in the shower letting the water run down his face, his mind was racing. Now he's thinking about the times he brought girls home and they both were drunk. Wondering, what if this is not the first time Jewel has come into his room and seduced him. He wasn't the smarter of the two but he was no dummy either. He knew this was not the first time Jewel has cheated on his brother. He was always suspicious of women coming after his brother. Although he was a great catch, he knew that one of the reasons women flocked to his brother was for his money. Bryson was a good man and Bradon wanted nothing but happiness for him. Bryson gave him the world and has not once complained about anything he does for him.

The one thing Bryson requested of his brother was for him to get an education, stay out of trouble and off drugs. He granted his request and graduated with his MBA in Business management and Architectural Design. Street smart wasn't the only thing he had. Bradon dressed quickly, grabbed some items and left the house. Jewel was standing in the kitchen watching him as he left. As the door closed she hollered out to him, "Remember what I said." Bradon called up his boy as soon as he reached the car. He could see Jewel looking out of the window with a frown on her face. She may have threatened him but he also knew she was scared he was going to tell Bryson about the incident as well. He sped down the long driveway as his friend was answering the phone. With his blue tooth in and both hands on the wheel he began to ask his friend for advice.

"What's up man what you doing this morning?" Bradon asked Andre.

"Nothing man I'm just now getting up, we kicked it hard last night for real. I can't believe yo ass up before me. Oh snap I got a hot sexy chick in my bed. Man I don't even remember… oh wait a minute yeah its coming back to me I remember that tattoo right there. Um um um." He was lifting the covers up to see the young lady's entire naked body lying there next to him revealing a butterfly tattoo spread across the small of her back.

"She going to scream when she wake up to see you lying next to her." Bradon said. He managed to half way smile. He was not in a laughing mood but was trying to ease his way in to telling his friend what happened.

"Real funny, I see you got jokes." Andre said.

"You know I'm playing man. Listen I have a question. Would you believe me if I told you that I was asleep and a girl came in my room started putting it down on a brother, literally, waking me up. And it was so dark in the room that I didn't know who it was until it was over and she said something in my ear? Would you believe that?"

"Yeah I guess it's believable. Why what's up? I have a feeling its more to it." Andre was no longer laughing sensing something was bothering Bradon.

"Okay what if I was asleep at your house and it was your girl who came in the room I was sleeping in and did that? Would you believe me then?" Bradon said sounding nervous.

"B man, are you trying to tell me something about my girl and you. Don't be calling me telling me about you and my girl done….."

"Andre man no. I ain't been with your girl and you know that."

"Well damn man where is this coming from? What done happened to you? I can tell by your voice it wasn't something pleasant. Well at least not the who it was part. So what's up?" Andre knew Bradon all too well.

"Who said it happened? I was just asking giving you a scenario. Why it gotta be true and why it gotta be me?"

"Come on man we been friends since kindergarten we go way back like cracker jacks. Wait a minute, hold up, ah man it was Jewel? Tell me it wasn't Jewel man. Ah man it was Jewel wasn't it. B talk to me man was it Jewel?" Andre was shaking his head hoping that it wasn't Jewel but he already knew it was true.

"Damn man I can't believe it either and I can't believe I didn't turn on the lights and see who the hell was putting they lips on my man."

"She did all that?"

"Yeah I was sleep and thought I was dreaming and I was still tipsy from last night. I kept grabbing her by the hair pulling her head towards me to see who the heck it was because I couldn't remember bringing anyone home with me. And she kept doing this thing where she would tighten up around my man and pulling or some trick and I was losing my mind. So it wasn't until after I was cummin and she said something to me that I realized who it was."

"Damn she was doing some tricks huh." He said enjoying the story.

"Andre man seriously."

"Sorry, what did she say to you?"

"She moaned and said 'you were better than I thought you would be'. Afterwards I wondered if she has ever come in before when I was drunk and pulled her scandalous trick."

"Well this probably was her first time coming in there if she said that. That would make me think that she didn't know what it was gone be like, meaning her first time, so it probably was but it's still bad." Andre was standing butt naked in his kitchen with the refrigerator door open pouring him some orange juice.

"The first and the last. But get this. I didn't use a condom and you know I never forget to use a condom but she hopped on so fast and I was sleep and still drunk. But I pulled her off of me before I came and it got on her clothes. She had on some lingerie and I was a little rough grabbing on her leaving markings on her upper thighs."

"Dang man this is messed up, you did your brothers fiancée and you didn't wear a condom and you left markings on her. He is not going to believe a word you say if you tell him and you know she is not going to tell him. He can't marry her now she probably out there fucking anybody and everything behind his back."

"Exactly what I said. I don't have to worry about her saying anything because she wants to marry my brother's money. But check this, she threatened me not to say anything, said she will scream rape and she's saving the lingerie with my cum all over it and taking pictures of the bruises. She said she would fabricate some more if she needed to. That it was her word over mine. You know how everyone thinks she is so perfect. Now I see why my mom's don't care for her."

"Damn, you remember they had that case on the news about the young black brother in college who was falsely accused of rape. All it takes is for her to get all emotional and have her story straight and people start believing the shit and feeling sorry for her ass."

"Yeah that's what has me scared. I remember that, but I might not get so lucky if she tries to accuse me of rape. This is awful."

"Man you never know who a person really is for sure. She is showing out on some crazy shit for real. That's one psycho bitch. You got to tell your brother though man everything. He might be mad and he might not believe you at first but the truth will come out. He will see her true colors. You are blood and you two have a bond so thick."

"Yeah you right, I know I have to tell him. I just need to figure out how. I have to do it before the wedding."

"Man this is some wild shit right here. You let me know how things are going when you tell him. I hope he don't kill your ass. You know he is one strong cocky dude." They both laughed.

Bradon hung up the phone as he pulled into the gym. He needed some quite time to think this all through. He went in to workout and think about what happened. He could feel the mountain weighing heavily on his shoulders. If he knew about the discovery his brother had this morning this may not seem so hard for him. But this was the beginning of the end of Bryson's life with Jewel and Bradon didn't want to see his brother hurt.

CHAPTER 11
~BRYSON~
CAUGHT IN THE ACT

Bryson and Kenneth were still hanging out and the time was approaching seven o' clock. Kenneth was trying to keep Bryson occupied to keep his mind off his fiancée and her cheating ways. You could tell his heart was breaking into a million pieces. Bryson has been dating Jewel for almost two years. They were sitting at a local bar not far from the hotel when Bryson received the call from the investigator confirming the arrival of his fiancée and the man she's cheating with. Kenneth looks at his face and realizes that the moment had arrived.

"She's there Kenny, you rolling with me right? I might need you to pull me off somebody if things get ugly."

"I'm right behind you man. You sure you want to go through with this and see her like this?" Grabbing Bryson by the wrist, Kenneth looks his broken hearted friend in the eyes and wonders how much more he can take. No man wants to catch his woman with another man.

"Yes I'm sure. I want to get this over with and behind me. Seeing the look on her face knowing that she was the one that messed up what we had will be what I need to help me completely get through this and over this relationship. Let's go." Bryson turned to walk out the door with Kenneth right on his heels.

Kenneth drove knowing that Bryson would not be in his right mind behind the wheel. They headed a couple blocks over to his hotel for the revealing of the madness taken place within his enterprise walls. Shaking his head on the way there, Bryson felt so betrayed and deceived.

"How could I be so blind to not even notice this was happening? Nothing good will ever come to her. Nothing!" Bryson was venting his anger and Kenneth knew it. The few beers he had at the bar helped calm his mind some. But the beer made him have a little more attitude and boldness. Some would call it liquid courage to say and do what you normally wouldn't do with a sober rational mind.

Walking into the hotel, Bryson walked toward the front desk and Kenneth stopped him. Kenneth thought he should get the key and Bryson could wait for the investigator. He spotted Rodger Maxx in the lobby and went up to greet him.

"Hey Rodger, is she still here?" With a somber look on his face Bryson looked at Rodger with his hands in his pocket.

"Yes. She has been up stairs with the gentleman for about 15 minutes now. I have snap shots here as you can see the two of them greeting in the door way with a kiss all the way in nonstop until the door shuts." Rodger was scrolling through the pictures for Bryson and now Kenneth who joined them to view as Rodger spoke about the beginning of Jewels night of reveal. "I apologize for speaking so bluntly about the situation but you know that this is my job and my heart goes out to you Bryson. We have been friends far beyond business and I'm truly sorry this is happening to you. I am sure once you walk through that door you will see what any man hopes he never see from the woman he loves."

Stunned with what is now reality for Bryson he stands there with a blank look on his face. His eyes were glistening, appearing to be holding back tears. Anger is written all over his face. He nods his head as he backs up away from the huddle the men were in and heads toward the elevator.

Kenneth follows behind Bryson yelling back toward Rodger. "Thanks man. We will call you if we need you." Hopping on the elevator he looks at Bryson. There is a look he has that Kenneth has never before seen in his friend. "You aight Bryson? Are you sure you want to go through with this? We can leave right now if you want it's not too late." Making gestures with his hands he reaches for the down button.

"I'm good man just in shock about the entire thing. She comes home kissing me after being with another man. Huh. That's funny right there. Why do good men finish last always! One day, one day." The elevator stops and with key in hand they head for the door. "Do

not disturb sign, well I imagine so but today that will be happening."
Bryson grabs the sign, throwing it to the floor.

"Wow." Was all Kenneth could say.

Opening the door and turning on the lights, Bryson walks in further to the room. "Room service." Sounds of shock from the invasion roar through the air as they both reach for the cover to shield their naked bodies from the invaders on looking eyes. Music is playing in the background muffling the sound of the door opening. "Surprise surprise fucking surprise. What do we have here?" Bryson's eyes fell right upon his naked fiancée's body. The same body that he caresses and holds every night in his arms.

As Jewel pulled the covers up over her body she looked Bryson in his eyes and tears started to form. "Oh my God, oh my God, Bryson baby it's not what you think. Baby I'm so sorry." She was reaching for her clothes trying to put them on quickly.

"I wouldn't go there if I was you." Kenneth stated as he was coming through the door witnessing the look on Michael Anderson's face. He was looking at Bryson as if he was about to try to step to him. Kenneth revealed the piece he had on his hip. No intentions of using it because either one of them alone could take this brother down by themselves. Even with his muscular body frame he was no match for either of them. But just in case he pulled out a weapon on them, Kenneth was prepared.

"Bryson baby please can we go somewhere and talk. Baby I promise I didn't want to do this, I promise baby I only love you. This is nothing to me. Baby please say something to me." Putting on the last of her clothing and grabbing her shoes she approaches Bryson attempting to grab his hands and hold on to him.

He doesn't respond but stands there firmly looking at her beg. After a few more seconds of her insisting she was sorry saying it would never happen again, listening to her attempts at reasoning her wrong doings, Bryson grabs her by her face firmly applying pressure out of anger to her jaw area and her neck. Her hands are now wrapped around his big hands from the pain she's now feeling. "Was it good to you Jewel? Did this man fulfill all of your desires sweet lips? You have been sharing with this nigga what we share together? Is this what you want to spend the rest of your life with?" Bryson was tightening his grip out of anger and jaws clenching tight when Kenneth steps up towards him to intervene.

"Bryson man let her go she's not worth it. Let her go man." Kenneth places his hands on Bryson's shoulder. He was hoping he would not have to intervene and keep his friend from choking Jewel to death, ruining his very own life. "She is not worth it man, no woman is worth giving up your life over because of something they did to hurt you. Brys man let go." When Kenneth reached in to grab his hands, Bryson released. He had to snap back to his senses and realize what he was doing, or what he could have done to Jewel and his very own life.

When Bryson let her go, she fell backwards onto the bed and Michael ran to her side to make sure she was alright. She tries to push him away as she holds on to her face and neck trying to regain her voice. "Don't touch me." She pushes his hand away. "Bryson baby please don't do this I love you. We are getting married in a couple weeks. Baby I love you so much please it will never happen again." Sitting up on the edge of the bed crying she falls to her knees in front of Bryson still begging for forgiveness.

"You finally said something I agree with. You are right. This will never happen again, at least not to me. You made your bed with this man now lie in it and let him marry you. We are over and done. Don't worry about coming back to my house. Your clothes are being shipped to goodwill as we speak. You have nothing with me anymore. Oh and that car of yours is in my name say bye bye to that too." He grabbed her keys he saw laying in the opening of her purse and credit cards that belonged to him. He wanted to leave her with everything she came with, including her last name.

She started screaming louder, crying for forgiveness and mercy for what she done to him. She knew the beginning of her forever with all the fortune and fame with this man was now simply a fantasy.

Some women, and men, don't realize when they have a good man or woman right in front of them. They go mess around and do stupid things like cheating. Jewel received a rude awakening. She made her choices thinking she could get away with it or that her sexy body, pretty face would get her out of whatever she was caught doing. But not this time. She was caught in the act and there was no way Bryson could forgive what he saw.

As Bryson and Kenneth turned to leave the room, Michael got up as if he was about to jump on Bryson when he turned his back.

Jewel was in the background screaming don't touch him, still begging for forgiveness. Facing him face to face Michael looked Bryson in the eyes and said. "You let another man catch you slipping and now you mad. I'm glad you found out Mr. Big shot. Now I don't have to sneak around anymore and we can openly make love in every room of your hotel that we haven't already made passionate love in." With a smirk on his face, he looks Bryson up and down. When his eyes came back up to meet Bryson's there was only stars left to be seen.

Boom!!! Bryson punched him so hard knocking him back across the floor. It happened so fast, Michael didn't even see it coming. Kenneth stepped back in and grabbed Bryson so they could leave before it got any uglier than it already was. Knowing that Kenneth had the gun on his side Michael did not move from the floor where he fell. He still had a smirk on his face as he wiped the blood from his mouth. You could hear Jewel screaming and playing out her dramatic performance.

Looking at Jewel with disgust in his eyes Bryson said his final words to her. "I loved you whole heartedly. You remember that, cause now that love has died and over time the memories of you will as well. Have a good life Jewel. The wedding is off!"

Both men were walking out the door and Kenneth turned back just before leaving their sight and said to Jewel, "Some jewel you are."

Jewel stood there in the middle of the floor crying and Michael sat there wiping blood from his mouth.

Once in the car Bryson rested his head on the back of the seat. Kenneth was driving away and they could see Rodger standing in the distance by his car getting in. He knew by the look on his face that Bryson no longer needed his services, at least for now. Kenneth stopped at a red light looked over at his friend who had tears running from his eyes. "Damn, man I'm sorry about all of this. You deserve so much better. You know I am here if you want to vent, yell, cry or whatever man. I know you can't see the silver lining but I feel in my heart that this was all God's way of setting you up for something better in life." Kenneth was driving Bryson home as he knew he was not in any condition to drive his self. "If it's okay with you I will hang out for a while at your crib just in case you need anything."

"Yeah that would be cool man." Bryson reached for his cell phone. He called a friend who worked for a tow company to come pick up his car from the hotel. He then dialed his favorite person in the whole wide world, his mom. "Hey momma how you doing? Did I wake you?"

Bryson's mother Mrs. Brenda Mathew's answered the phone sounding half a sleep. She was an early riser and went to bed early but she always had time for her children. And they loved their momma. "No baby you didn't wake me. Are you okay. Is everything alright?"

"Everything is okay momma. I miss you. Why don't you come visit me for a couple days you can stay at the house you and dad. I would love having both of you around me for a few days." Trying not to sound too down and out he was crying out for help. His mom was about two hours away and he knew he didn't need to be driving in his state of mind.

"Oh baby I don't think it would be a good idea with me staying in the house with your fiancée there. I love you to death son and will do anything for you but I don't know about her. So to keep peace amongst us all I will come and try to get your father to as well and we will just stay at a hotel close by. How does that sound?" He could hear his mom waking his dad telling him they were going to visit Bryson tomorrow for a couple days.

"Mom I want you and dad to stay with me at the house. Jewel is gone and the wedding is off. So you will be here tomorrow? I will send a car for you in the morning and I will get anything you both need. Just let me know what time." His voice was screaming he needed his parents.

Mrs. Mathews knew her son and he sounded like he wanted to cry like a baby. "We will be there son. We will be ready by 6 in the morning. We will talk tomorrow okay baby."

"Okay momma, I love you both and thank you." Tears were falling from Bryson's eyes as he tried to hold them back.

"We love you too son, we will see you in the morning."

Kenneth knew he was taking this hard. He pulled into Bryson's driveway stopping at the gate and buzzed in with the code driving up to the front of his home. He sat there in the car quietly waiting on Bryson to speak first.

"You think you know somebody and then you realize you don't. I wonder where I would be with love right now if the world viewed me as an average man with no money. You try to be honest with people when you meet them and it's like they can smell money all over you. I should have listened to my mom when she kept saying she didn't know about Jewel. You know moms love everyone but her spirit just would not let her get close to Jewel. How could I not see?" He placed his face in his hands.

"Man sometimes you get caught up in what a person is saying to you and you just believe them. She put on a good show cause she had me fooled as well. Money can make a person greedy even in love and sex man. God will send you the woman who is right for you and when you meet her you will know. Your heart won't beat for lust but it will beat for love. True love that is and not one based on money. I know it will take time for your wounds to heal but don't close your heart just yet man. Pray about it and ask God to show you the way and build you up, prepare you for when your true queen come along so you will have room in your heart to accept her and give her the love you want to pour out to your queen. Shoot if I was a woman not saying I would won't you and I know this might sound like some gay shit but you my boy and you know better than that but look at you. You are handsome your physique alone screams security and you know how to treat a woman. You are funny and can charm the panties off any woman if you wanted to. You know how to have a good time so we know you are fun to be with. You love to cater to your woman and not just with material things. Shoot I remember the college days how the women use to fight over you." Kenneth laughed. "Do you remember when you got busted when all three of the women you were dating showed up at the crib unannounced at the same time?"

Bryson laughed a little, "Yeah I remember that. You saved my butt that day shoot I would have been dead if you weren't there. They were fighting each other and the both of us. Me for dating all three and you for always lying to them."

Kenneth felt better he got Bryson to laugh and relax a little. "Man I have an idea, you can give me all of your money and then you can be an average man and go out and find you someone based on you. Get her to buy you dinner and take care of you. But if you give me the money you can't take it back."

Bryson opened the door looking back at Kenneth, "Man what you over there smoking. Give you my money boy you got more money than me you don't need my money. I'm just gone go live my life as a bum for a while and pretend like I don't have money."

They both walked into the house. Kenneth knew his friend was going to be alright and Bryson knew it would all get better. Once he had his mom there he knew things would be better. He saw his little brother Bradon sitting on the sofa as he jumped up when he noticed he was home.

"Hey bro what's up Kenny." Bradon wanted to say something but his brother spoke briefly and went on in to his bedroom.

"Hey Bradon, you not out partying tonight?" Kenneth said trying to avoid the questions he knew Bradon wanted to ask.

"I'm about to go hang out with one of my boys, I was hoping to talk to Brys before I left. Is he okay?"

"He will be in time. I will have to let him tell you details."

"Understandable." Bradon was wondering if Jewel had mentioned what happened earlier that morning. "Where is Jewel? I saw housekeeping packing up her belongings."

"Well let's just say she won't be coming back."

"Oh wow, I see." Hearing the shower going in the bedroom Bradon says, "Tell Brys I will be back in the morning, hopefully he will be up to talking then." Bradon headed towards the door grabbing his coat on the way out.

"Will do man. You be careful out there. Oh hey your mom and dad are coming down in the morning you know she will be cooking once she get here so don't miss that. I know I will be here." Kenneth was rubbing his belly.

"Cool I will be here early then. Are you staying the night?" Bradon asked standing in the doorway.

"Yeah I will be here with your brother for a while."

"Thanks man for taking care of him. You are a great friend." Bradon left the house but planned to talk to his brother sooner than later.

Bryson spending time with his parents is just what he needed. Especially time with his mom. He enjoyed her cooking and their company. The good vibes that his parents brought to his home was a wonderful feeling. It reminded him of home when he was growing up. His heart was breaking and he needed his mom to make it all better.

Early that morning Bryson's parents had arrived and his mom immediately went into the kitchen to cook breakfast. Kenneth,

Bradon and Mr. Mathews all sat down to enjoy their meal while Bryson was still closed up in his room. When he did not appear for breakfast Mrs. Mathews decided to go in to check on him. He was curled up in the bed appearing to be sleep.

She made him get up so they could talk. As she was talking to Bryson he was quiet at first. It wasn't too long after that the tears started to flow and he cried like a baby in her arms. Love hurts and his mom knew her baby was hurting.

"Mom I found out Jewel was cheating on me and has been for a while. I walked in on them in the act of... you know. I hired a private investigator and he found out where they meet and when." Bryson was shaking his head remembering the scene.

Bryson's mom was rubbing her son's shoulders. She was a size ten woman about five foot seven. She was a beautiful woman with beautiful caramel colored skin and dark long thick hair. She stayed in shape maintaining her health and to occupy her time since she didn't have to work. She loved her children dearly and never wanted to see them hurting the way her son was at that moment. She tried to warn him about Jewel without totally isolating herself from her son and his new love. Mothers have a way of just knowing things.

"Momma they were cheating in my hotel and I gave Jewel access to the hotel, no boundaries. I loved her momma whole heartedly, gave her the world and I can't believe she did this to me." He laid his head on her shoulders and his mom held on tight to him.

"Well baby, you know your momma has a sermon behind this and a few words of comfort for you. I know you didn't send for me just to have me cook and hold you. I knew you needed me here to help make sense of all of this. But baby let me tell you. I prayed for you all last night and this morning all the way to your front porch. And son, God has a much greater plan for you. He has blessings far and beyond what you can even imagine. Blessings for you that money cannot buy. You may be feeling down and out and hurting over a love that you thought you had but when God created Adam he created him an Eve. Flesh of his flesh bone of his bone. And your Eve will be here right on time when you don't even expect it. Not in your time, not when you think she should or should have been here, but in God's time. He had to get rid of the mess that was in the way of your true blessings. This did not happen by chance. God was giving you signs from the very beginning but he needed a bigger distraction for you to see what he wanted you to see. To prepare you for the ultimate blessing of love that he has for you. You are being prepared in a way to receive the best blessing he can give you besides life and family. The blessing of true genuine love from someone who will give the same back to you. All things happen for a reason and your next actions will be preparing you for the rest of your life. So be prepared and get ready for it son. You keep your faith and you keep believing and don't close your heart to love."

"Thank you mom, you always know what to say." Laying his head on his mom's shoulder and hugging her tight. His thoughts were reflecting around her words.

"Baby your heart will heal quickly and you will be able to see clearly the mistake that was about to be made. Your true love will find you in your rarest form and will fall in love with you, Bryson the man not the money or the fame but with whom God created you to be. You will know her when you see her. You won't be turned on by lust, her beauty will intrigue you. Not just the outer beauty but the inner beauty as well." She sat there for a moment holding on to her son who was still holding on to her. "So, I have been cooking since I got here, breakfast and lunch so now I am going to let you take me and your dad out to dinner tonight. After that I think me and your dad are going to head back home so we can get to church early in the morning. I have a feeling you will be alright after today."

"Dinner will be my pleasure and I know just the spot you both will enjoy. Thanks mom for coming. You can't imagine what you mean to me and how much I needed you to be here." As they both stood from the bed Bryson hugged his mom tight picking her up off her feet. "I am going to clean myself up and make reservations for dinner and then I will be out. I love you mom." Kissing her forehead before he released her.

"I love you too Bryson. You take your time son. I am going in here to wake your father so we can freshen up ourselves. I know he done laid down by now. He loves his mid-day naps." She left her son alone so he could freshen up to join her and the family to partake in the meal she had prepared.

CHAPTER 12
~BRIELLE~
GETTING HER HOME

Early Monday morning Brielle decided to take off work for the first part of the morning to take care of some business. She wanted to get the process started in order to get her and the kids a new home. Buying a car was a must as well and she wanted something reliable for her and the kids. It felt good to be able to pay cash for a car and she couldn't wait to have the title in her hands.

She met with the loan department of her bank to file all the paperwork for a home loan. After pulling her credit report and looking at her annual income they preapproved her on the spot letting her know she should have no problems being financed for a new home. Now she would have to wait for the final paperwork to be completed leaving her with the task of finding a house she could call her home. Before leaving the building, she contacted a Realtor the bank referred her to and set up a meeting that evening.

On her way to her car she called her father to meet her at the car lot to help her with buying a car. She knew he was off that day and would meet her in a flash. She headed to a lot in the downtown area near her job to look at a car she had been eyeing for a while. She knew exactly what she wanted, a newer model Nissan Altima. That was a very nice car. Her dad met her at the car lot and talked them down on the price almost twelve thousand dollars to drive off the lot at that moment paid in full with cash. She was excited to get a great car at a great price thanks to her dad. He has always had a way with people and a way with words.

Things were looking up for Brielle and she knew this was all God's blessings pouring down on her and her family. She stood next to her new car with keys in hand standing next to her dad. She was so excited she didn't want to go back to work but she knew she had too. Her thoughts were reflecting on the kids and how excited they were going to be as well.

"Baby girl you have a really great car. Now you and the kids can be safe on the road in all weather conditions. The tires are brand new, everything is new and all you need to do is maintain it to stay in excellent condition. And you have a five year warranty. You bring it by the house every now and then and your brother and I will make sure everything is good on it for you." Her father said.

"Thanks dad for being here and for loving me like you do. We are so lucky to have you in our lives."

"Me and your mom are the lucky ones, more so blessed. God blessed us with some wonderful beautiful kids and grand babies." He leaned over and hugged his daughter kissing her on the forehead. Brielle squeezed her dad back and kissed his cheek. They said their good byes and her dad made sure she drove off ok before turning to leave himself.

Brielle headed to work. As soon as she got there she had an e-mail from the realtor already based on the conversation they had over the phone. She had sent her some listing of homes that met her criteria. This was so exciting looking through the list of her potential homes. She minimized the e-mail so she could print it off later. She had to catch up on work before she did anything extra. It was eleven o'clock when she got there so she had a little making up to do.

Chantae was at her desk so enthralled in her work she didn't even pay attention that Brielle had walked in. "Hey girl when did you get in?"

"Hey Chantae girl, I just sat down about five minutes ago. You must be busy. You didn't even look up from the screen."

"Yeah girl Craig just gave me a stack of work. They just fired three people who were embezzling money from the company so I have to fix what they messed up. So get ready cause I am sure they have been waiting on you to get here as well. I tell you what they don't pay us enough cause this right here is some bull. But I guess I need to be thankful I have a job during this recession we in. Plus I heard they are giving us a bonus. So Thank You Jesus!"

"Dang fired three people for real girl who? I wasn't gone that long and done missed out on a lot."

"Well stand up and look around and you will see the three empty desks. But I will say this, they not Black, Latino or Hispanic so you figure it out. They had the police up in here and everything girl escorting them out in handcuffs." Chantae was typing away at her computer trying to keep her voice down to a whisper. She had so much work she had to gossip and work at the same time.

"Here comes boss man now. Good morning Mr. Moore. How are you this morning?" Brielle said as she stood to greet him coming to her desk.

"Good morning Brielle glad you came back a little earlier than you had planned. Do you have a moment to meet me in my office please?"

"Yes sir, right behind you." She stepped out of her cube and followed him into his office to talk in private.

"Come on in and shut the door." The office windows had blinds that stayed open at all times due to sexual harassment policies. No door should be left closed and concealed. "Well we had to let three people go this morning and they have been arrested for embezzlement. The company is pressing charges. This has caused us to have double workloads for the remaining employees in the department for a little while. We are not asking anyone to work over but we will have to double up on workloads and not waste any time. We are giving the four people remaining seven thousand five hundred dollar bonus check on the next pay period after Friday because of this need. The company wants to make sure we get the work done without over working you all and to pay you for any inconvenience. This is also a way to give an incentive for working hard and no playing around. Meaning limit coffee breaks, smoke breaks, socializing that kind of stuff. Taking a thirty minute lunch instead of an hour. We can't close business down and we can't hire and train anyone this quick. This will be for a couple of weeks, three at the most."

"Okay yes sir I understand." She was still somewhat confused.

"Brielle you are and have been the best worker here in this office. We were in the process of making you an offer for a management position when all of this happened but we still want to offer this to you but won't be able to start you in the new position until after the other positions are filled. We plan to fill them quickly.

So therefore we want you to train the new people as they come in to pave the way on how to do the job right for the new comers. Here are the papers for what we are proposing with the salary amount. You don't have to answer at this time take it and look over everything and we will discuss next week. Your pay will increase upon you signing even before you start in your new role."

Brielle was excited about the new position and the raise with that and the bonus for working double. Things are definitely looking up for her. She was just not looking forward to working nonstop catching up on everyone else's work until they get someone in to fill the now vacant positions.

"Sorry to cut the meeting short but there is a lot of work that needs catching up on. So back to work it is for us all. We will talk more next week." They shook hands and Brielle left his office thanking him.

"Chantae now I see why you were so consumed at your desk. But you were right, they are paying us a bonus." Brielle whispered in Chantae's ear passing her with a smile on her face looking back at Chantae.

"Girl for real, so I was right. How much is it did he tell you?" Chantae was all ears.

"Seventy-five Hundred dollars. But it will be based on your performance to get all this work caught up over the next couple of weeks. It will be all or none. But keep this to yourself no one is supposed to know." She knew she was stretching this but she knew Chantae had a tendency to slack and she didn't want to have to cover for her. She also knew that she had a gossip bone that couldn't resist spreading good information. This way she knew it would pass around that bonus was based on performance and every one would be working exceptionally hard to get the large sum. She was already going to be on overload with her workload and training new hire's coming in.

"That is what's up. I surely could use that money. How you know that information?"

"I will tell you later about that girl. We will meet during our brief lunch." They both chuckled as they knew they would probably only be eating for about fifteen minutes maybe twenty.

After work Brielle headed to her mom's house. She printed out the home listings so her and the kids could look them over with her mom and dad to narrow the list down to a few homes. They would be looking at some with the realtor that evening. Brielle found what seem like the perfect house on paper and it wasn't too far from her parents. She and the kids were excited to go see it. She called the realtor and gave her the four houses she wanted to look at. They rode around town looking at the first three before riding to the fourth. Brielle saved the best one for last and everyone fell in love with it.

She told the Realtor to write up the contract she didn't want to look anymore. The house was in foreclosure and the Realtor did all the paperwork right there in the empty house Brielle was ready to call home. The kids were roaming around claiming their rooms. It was a three bedroom two bath with a bonus room. Carter wanted the bonus room to be his room even if it didn't have a door. He didn't care this was going to be off limits to the girls except for his mom of course.

Brielle called her mom as she knew she was a prayer warrior and told her and her father to pray that they win the bid on the house she was standing inside.

CHAPTER 13
~BRYSON~
WEDDING DAY
TWO WEEKS AWAY

Bryson's wedding date was just two weeks away. He sat in his office leaning back in his chair with a heart full of pain and sadness. Two weeks from the day he was supposed to be beginning the rest of his life with Jewel. Everything has now come crashing to an end. 'Time would heal all wounds' is the saying, but finding out your soon to be wife had been cheating on you was weighing him down. Tears fell from his face as he quickly wiped them away. He didn't want anyone seeing him cry. Not a man who was as powerful as he was. Society has its way of making someone of his status feel as if they have no right to express any emotions or to have any feelings beyond business. So he let it out behind closed and locked doors.

He sat there wondering how someone he gave the world to could hurt him the way Jewel did. He was in love with her and he thought she was in love with him. Messages were left on his work voicemail, his home answering machine as well as his cell phone which included text messages and voicemail. Jewel was trying to get him to answer at least one. She would wait for him in the lobby hoping to catch him coming or going but he was taking the VIP entrance coming and going, parking in his private garage. Not too many people knew about it and only one other person had access to it. Security would not let her up into his office knowing that she was banned from all Cole Enterprise establishments thanks to Kenneth.

Listening to his messages, Bryson was deleting them as he went as soon as he heard it was her. He decided to play at least one voicemail from her to see what she was talking about.

"Baby please answer the phone. I need you. I'm so sick without you in my life. Bryson please baby I'm so sorry. I never meant to hurt you. I have a problem and I was trying to get help for it. We are supposed to love each other through the good and the bad and this is the bad and I need you right now. You told me you would stick beside me through anything and you promised. And we both know that you always keep your promises, that's just who you are. You deserve to be loved and I know I messed up, but baby please let me make this right. I don't love Michael I love you very much. I can't do anything without you please call me back and let me come home, to our home. You don't know what I have been through and I should have told you baby. But I was scared too. You know what, I am going to keep planning this wedding. I am not canceling it. You show up okay. You know you love me too. We are good for each other, we're perfect together. Baby please, I didn't mean to hurt you, baby I'm so sorry please call me back we can get through this together. Please don't end us I need you. You know you need me too. What will the public say about your relationship if they found out we weren't together. Think about it, you know you have an image and we don't want to mess that up either. Baby please I love you, please be there at our wedding so we can still spend the rest of our lives together." Beep. Bryson thought about what she was saying and knew that his business was going to be put in the media if they didn't get married. He knew he was taking a chance and possibly could lose a deal or two if he was blasted in the media. He has a very large contract in the negotiating process and was hoping he could get around the publicity piece. He made himself a mental note to call his publicist Sharese McGill to fix this for him in case the media got a hold to the story and blew it up, twisting it around for their amusement. As of now everything was still quiet and no one was aware of the drama.

While listening to the voicemails he also had one from Sharese. "Brys sweetie, hey I talked with Kenny about what is going on with everything and you know I am already on it making sure you don't look bad in all of this. You let me know if you need anything at all from me. I am here for you as always. I will handle the media and you call me when you are ready to get together and talk. I will hit you back if I need you before then. And Bryson you are too good of a man to be going through this. Please know that God has a greater plan for you and a better person already lined up ready and waiting for you. I will talk with you soon." Beep.

Bryson was happy to know that Kenneth had already explained everything to her so he wouldn't have to. Sharese was good at what she does and she was also a genuine friend to Bryson. His mother had just said to him that God has a greater plan for him. He was going to hold on to that and have faith and believe it to be true.

He had a call from his brother to meet him for lunch today. He had something really important to talk to him about. He sounded concerned so Bryson knew he needed to meet with his brother to make sure he was alright. Interrupting his thoughts Jacqueline buzzed in letting him know he had a visitor in the lobby. It was a representative from the production company he met with last week.

"Thanks Jackie I will be right there." Closing his cell he would check his messages later. Bryson hung up and buzzed Kenneth to meet him in the hallway to meet with them both. This was the news he has been waiting on. He had to get his self together and get his mind right so nothing would appear to be a distraction. He composed his self as best as he could. He forced a smile before he left his office and headed towards the lobby. There was a long hair long legged woman in a red dress beautiful skin smiling in his direction. He was wowed at how beautiful she was. Kenneth saw exactly what he saw and the two men were walking toward her mesmerized by her beauty. They assumed she had to be the representative as no one else was in the lobby. Jacqueline was pointing in her direction but she could tell they were paying her no attention. Bryson and Kenneth bumped into each other and it broke the trance. She giggled realizing the affect she was having knowing this happens to her occasionally.

Reaching out to both of the men to shake their hands she greeted them with a friendly smile. "My name is Consuela McBride. I am the Relationship and Contract Coordinator with Ming Production. How do you do?" She was still smiling at both of the men noticing their attraction to her.

Trying to get it together they looked at each other clearing their throats and greeting her back.

Embracing her hand he introduces them both. "Bryson Mathews and this is Kenneth Cartwright. Please follow me to my office where we can talk. How are you today?" Bryson asked.

"I am wonderful thank you for asking. You have a very lovely building here Mr. Mathews." Walking into his office she sat down at Bryson's direction. "And a very lovely office. I like your decorating taste."

"Thank you very much. Kenneth and myself actually decorated the entire space."

"Wow. You both have really good taste. You seem very well put together, very professional. I see why the Ming's were so excited to do business with you." Pulling out her portfolio she knew that bit of information would excite the gentleman.

Bryson and Kenneth looked at each other with a rush of excitement on their face. Bryson knew they accepted at least three of the contracts but was hoping that they accepted the six they were looking to sign. "So we will take that as good news and hope that you have more for us." Bryson was looking directly at her with anticipation in his eyes.

"Yes I have good news for you." Pulling out a contract document she handed a copy to Bryson before continuing. "So to answer your question quickly they have accepted five of your ideas. They like some of the others and want to make films that will go directly to DVD for Redbox and a couple to be TV series. They were very impressed with you both and look forward to working with you. Although the contract was not for anything else more than six films for the theatre they would like to keep the others to use for the purpose I just stated with negotiated compensation of course. Everything is included in the contract with the new dollar figures in which I think you will be very impressed with on page eleven." She paused for a moment. She observed Bryson and Kenneth's face as their eyes widened looking at each other with a smile. That was her confirmation that they were pleased and she continued.

"There is just one thing they are asking of you." They both looked up in her direction still holding the contract in hand. "They are asking for the sixth film to be giving to them within 2 weeks. That does not give you much time but they have confidence in you to deliver. Do you think that will be a problem?"

"Not a problem at all. We are confident we can pull it off."
Kenneth looked at Bryson for reassurance.

"I don't believe it will be a problem at all." Bryson had a look
on his face confirming he had a thought that was a for sure winner.
"Let us review the contract and get with our lawyers and we will
schedule a meeting for mid next week to discuss our ideas and the
contract further."

"That sounds great, I will deliver the message. Please review
the contract thoroughly with your lawyers and we will convene next
week to discuss further. And gentleman it was a pleasure meeting you
both. I look forward to working with you in the near future."
Reaching into her brief case she pulled out two business cards. "Here
is my card, please don't hesitate to call if you have any questions
concerning the contract at all."

Bryson and Kenneth reached out to shake her hand again
thanking her for her time. Kenneth walked her to the door and left
Bryson there looking at the contract. Kenneth could not resist a fine
woman. Bryson looked up and glanced in her direction one more time
before she walked completely out of sight. She just helped his heart
mend a little more. He knew that Jewel was not the last woman in the
world who could make him happy, he just needed to find her. He
knew that God would one day send Miss Right to him and he would
be ready, keeping his heart open to receive her.

Bryson and Kenneth both were now back in Bryson's office.
Bryson had a serious look on his face and Kenneth knew his mind was
fast at work. "Okay I know that look you must share with me. I know
it has something to do with the last deal concerning the contract. So
what's on your mind Brys? Lay it on me." Kenneth sat down on the
edge of Bryson's desk as Bryson stood in front of the windows.

"Okay what do you think about me using myself and my life
as a storyline?

"What I don't understand. Use your life? You not talking
about Jewel are you?"

"No. I don't want to have anything more to do with her." He
stood there looking at Kenneth sitting there with a look of confusion.
"You know how I have been saying that if I was an average man
people would probably treat me differently? "

"Okay and what about that? You want to do a story on that?"

"No. Okay hear me out. I have always been treated like, let's say royalty. People know me as a very wealthy and powerful man who could probably have any woman in the world. What happens if you take all of this away from me and I have nothing to offer the world but the man God made? No money, no assets, no home, no car, nothing at all but me and the clothes on my back. Camera crew and close by security teams can monitor me as the life of a wealthy man living in a simple man shoes basically in a homeless man's world. Can I find genuine friendships, genuine kindness, and possibly genuine love as Bryson the man? In a world as simple as can be where no one knows who I am or what I have. I'm talking about living as if I have been homeless for a while as if that is my life style. The funk, the look, the living arrangements and all."

"Wow is all I can say Bryson man. Are you sure you want to do this? I mean breaking up with Jewel is one thing but letting it drive you to an ultimate low point where you don't have to be is another."

"Kenneth, I am a man just like you are, just like the men on the corner collecting change, just like the man who can't find a decent job in this economy or the man working hard laboring a nine to five. What makes me any different in the way people treat me just because I have a wealthy status with so much money my great, great grandchildren will not want for anything? What makes me different? Yes, I am hurt by what Jewel has done to me. Every man rich or poor deserves to be loved genuinely for who they are and not for their money. But I live this life every day where people treat me like I am God and I am not. I don't abuse anyone and yes I enjoy having the life style that I have, but I want to know how the world would see me in a different light. You know be careful how you treat people you never know who you may be meeting type of light. How would people treat me as a homeless man who stinks not knowing that I am probably one of the richest men in the world? I am not trying to be Jesus but look at who he was and how people treated him when they thought he was nothing. This world is messed up in how we treat each other and how we love one another. And most cruel people choose to be that way towards others based on the status of who they are."

"Aight I'm feeling this. If you're serious I think this will be huge. I think they will want this to be at the top of their list. Let's write it up and I will back you every step of the way. You know they are going to make you sign a two to three month deal or something like that. They have to make sure you stay committed and they get enough footage." Kenneth has a look of shock and disbelief on his face but no matter what he is backing his friend one hundred percent.

"Yeah but of course I have to add my stipulations up front. I have to still run the business with your help. I can't be missing in action 100% of the time. I have to still maintain my life, so when this journey is over I am still maintaining and not catching up or readjusting in our business you know." Bryson looks at Kenneth with a look of confusion on his face. He thought about the idea before really thinking about the idea from a day to day, week to week, month to month point of view.

"Let's write it up and present it to them and see what they say about our terms. I talked to Sharese about everything that was going on so we will need to develop a plan so when the movie comes out people will understand reasoning. We don't want people thinking you dumped Jewel. We want them to know the truth and to anticipate the movie. We will let Sharese handle the publicity part."

"Yeah she called me and left me a message. Thanks for giving her the heads up for me man. Kenny you are a great friend to me. I love you like you are my blood brother." Bryson and Kenneth gave a handshake half hug like men do without showing too much affection.

"Man you trying to make me tear up in here. You know I have a sensitive side. You are my brother and the love is returned. Aight enough of this. Jewel done drove you to be a homeless man and emotional. Ugh." Kenneth shook as if he had chills all over. Both men erupted in laughter.

"You crazy man. But seriously thanks for being here for me. Business and personal."

"I'm your boy that's what I do. I'm about to go and grab some lunch you want to join me?" Kenneth got up and was heading towards the door.

"Naw, I'm about to call Bradon and have lunch with him. He needs to talk to me and it sounds serious so I need to see where he's at. I'll talk to you later this afternoon man and we will go over the details." Bryson walked to his desk reaching for the phone.

"Aight cool. See ya later man." Kenneth left the office and headed to lunch. Leaving out of the front door he walked right into none other than Jewel herself. The looks he gave her spoke volumes.

She knew Kenneth was not the one to mess with and entering the building was a no go. She felt his silent threat enough so that she turned her back towards Kenneth facing the building in search of Bryson to come walking through the door behind him. After a few exchanged words with Jewel, Kenneth looked at the security guard, then at Jewel and back at the security guard. Once he received confirmation that he knew she was not to enter he turned and went on his way. He knew Bryson was not coming through the front door.

CHAPTER 14
~JEWEL~
LIFE CHANGES

Jewel had been staying in hotels with Michael hounding and sniffing up behind her every day. She didn't want to be bothered although she enjoyed the sex part. After she got what she wanted she wanted him to leave. He put up a fight and out of defeated frustration would leave. Michael had always thought that if Bryson was out of the picture he would have Jewel all to himself. He was shocked it took Bryson this long to find out about Jewel cheating. It was his idea to meet in Bryson's hotel. He hoped that it would be easier for him to find out about the affair. Little did he know Jewel used him to help fulfill her sexual desires only.

Jewel called Bryson every day at his office, home and on his cell. She tried everything. He cut her off from all access to him. She kept her car only because of the spare key Bryson didn't find in her purse. She was going crazy with no money and no anytime loving. She had an addiction with sex and although she didn't go crazy with sleeping with a bunch of men, she still craved sex constantly. She made sure she had a man that she could live with and have it anytime she wanted as well as a couple of anytime men she could call on when she needed more than just her toys. Bryson satisfied her sexual standards but her addiction made her desire sex constantly even after hours of great sex she was never satisfied. But she wanted to make sure Bryson was happy and didn't know of her addiction. He had the lifestyle she loved and desired to have and more money than she could ever spend. She hoped she would be able to control her addiction and eventually only needed Bryson. But that obviously wasn't the case.

Did she love him? Yes. But not enough to face her problem and make him her one and only. She got away with it for so long that she kept on doing it. It became her drug of choice. Knowing that his brother would have been a low blow she snuck in and seduced him anyways. Her hormones were taking over her mind and if Bradon didn't want to keep something going after he realized it was her she would blackmail him to cover it up. She thought he might like it as much as she would. What man wouldn't want to be with her as fine as she is and as adventurous as she was in bed. But when he completely rejected her once he realized it was her, her life with Bryson flashed to an end and the only defense she had was to threaten Bradon. She thought blackmailing him would keep him from ruining her chances with Bryson.

Standing outside his office building, she waited for Bryson to walk through those doors. She knew that she would catch him coming out sooner or later. She dialed the number for the front desk inside of the building.

"Hello?" Raquel answered seeing Jewel's number pop up on the screen.

"Raquel have you seen Bryson come in today?" She was pacing back and forth in front of the building.

"I have not seen him girl but I know he is here. What are you doing? Why are you outside walking back and forth? Why don't you just come in? Don't you have your badge?"

"No I don't have it and security won't let me in. I need to talk to Bryson ASAP and he is not answering his phone can you transfer me up without the number showing?"

"No it doesn't work like that and you know it. Miss Jackie takes all of his calls and they have to be identified. What's wrong are y'all fighting?" Raquel was being nosey and all in her business. She thought if she is asking her questions she would pump her for information as well.

"We just had a little disagreement and he mad at me right now. We are fine girl. Call me when you see him coming okay?"

"Umm umm ummm. Okay girl. His fine friend is about to walk out the door right now." She watched his every stride until he left her site.

"Okay girl I got to go. And thank you Raquel!" She was panicking seeing Kenneth approach her not knowing if he would cause a scene or what he would say.

He walked past her looked her up and down and gave her a look of disgust. "What are you doing here Jewel you are banned from this building and all the other Enterprises. He doesn't want to see you so just give it up and leave."

With her back now turned to Kenneth she holds back her emotions to keep from crying. "Kenny you don't know anything about me and Bryson okay so just keep walking and leave me the hell alone alright." Jewel said with her hands on her hips.

After a brief pause Kenneth responded, "Whatever. No need for me to waste my breath on you." Kenneth looked at security confirming they were not to let her in before turning and walking away.

"Go to hell Kenny." Frustrated she turned back to the door with tears in her eyes. She knew if Kenneth felt that way about her Bryson had nothing good to say either. Her arms now crossed in front of her chest, she stood there looking inside the building hoping that she would see Bryson coming. After a few more moments she turned to walk back towards her hotel which was not too far from Bryson's work place. Her funds were very low and the reality of her life as of right now was starting to kick in.

On her way back to her hotel room she calls up Bradon. She was determined she was going to get to Bryson one way or another. She wanted to marry Bryson and get her rich and famous life back and he could make that happen. His little brother was his life and he could influence him into forgiving her and marrying her. So she thought.

"Talk to me." The voice on the other end spoke. Bradon was already seated at the restaurant where Bryson was meeting him.

"Bradon it's me."

"What tha, Jewel?" He had a look of disgust and shock on his face. "What do you want and how did you get this number?"

"You know why I'm calling you. Your brother and I had a bit of a misunderstanding and I am sure you have heard about it by now."

"I'm not surprised. There is no telling what else you have done, but I have not heard of any misunderstanding. What do you want? Trying to blackmail me some more?"

"Look, your brother called the wedding off but it is so not off. You know what the deal is between me and you and you better make sure he is at the altar ready to marry me in two weeks. I am still planning this wedding and if I am left standing there by myself or if something happen to where this wedding does not you can kiss your precious life good bye baby boy. You will become some jail house ass. Do I make myself clear? And don't mess with me Bradon. You know I can make your life hell."

Bradon sat there listening to her not knowing what happened with his brother or if he found out about what Jewel did. His heart was pounding and he didn't know what to expect when Bryson walked through the door. As he looked up he saw him walking his way. He quickly answered Jewel. "Yeah I hear you." And without another word he ended the call.

Jewel was smiling. She knew she had Bradon scared. She also was not afraid to pull the evil card to get what she wanted. She was outside of her hotel headed in with her head held high thinking of all the remaining planning she had left for her beautiful wedding day. True she didn't have any money but Bryson had already paid for services up front with all the vendors. All she had to do was put everything in motion. He even paid for hotel room in advance without knowing he did. One of her benefits of having free access to his black card. When he took that he took away her financial freedom.

Jewel was grinning from ear to ear thinking about her plan. Now she had to figure out how to get help for her sexual addiction. She wanted to make sure she could prove to him that she was getting help once he took her back and took her hand in marriage. She turned on the computer in her hotel room and started searching for Sexaholic therapy. She figured that was the first step.

Just then her phone rung and it was none other than Michael. Just reading about what was considered a sexaholic addiction was getting her aroused so she told him to get there fast to satisfy her desire as she pulled out her sex toys to start. This was going to be a long journey for her to get control of her addiction. The wedding was two weeks away and she had a lot of work ahead of her.

CHAPTER 15
~BRADON~
CONFESSION OF JEWEL

Bryson walked toward his brother Bradon who was already seated at a table. Bradon stands to welcome him with intentions of a quick brotherly embrace. He was reading his face and his body language to see how he was feeling towards him. He wasn't sure if he knew about what Jewel did or if she blamed him and told his brother. He wasn't sure if Bryson was going to punch him or hug him. When he approached he hugged him instead and Bradon was relieved.

"Hey Bradon how are you bro?" Bryson said as he hugged his brother just before taking his seat.

"I'm good I guess." Bradon had a confused look on his face. Jewel said his brother was mad at her but Bryson showed no sign of anger or that something was bothering him. "Okay I am not good. I probably should have told you this last week when it happened and I am sorry I didn't." He paused as the waiter walked up to them to take their drink orders.

"Welcome to the Heart and Soul of Atlantis where our job is to make sure your dining experience is always a pleasure. My name is John and I will be serving you today. May I start you out with something to drink?"

"I will have water." Bryson said.

Bradon thinking that he will need something a bit stronger than water ordered a drink for himself and one for Bryson. "I will take two separate shots of 1800 and a glass of water." Bradon looked over at Bryson who was looking at him with his eyes opened wide. "Believe me you are going to want this shot after I tell you what I have to tell you."

The waiter walked away from their table to place their drink order.

"Believe me bro, my life is already messed up. There is nothing you can tell me that will make me want to drink. I had my time of drinking last week and this weekend. I needed to tell you anyhow that the wedding is off and Jewel and I are no longer together. I know this has happened all of a sudden and very quickly but it's completely over with her. No going back"

"Wow man I didn't know that. But I can't say that I am not happy to hear that. She is so foul. And although you two are separated now it still does not make what I have to say any easier." He put his head down in his hands wiping his face and then looked Bryson in the eyes.

"Just say it man what's up?" Bryson was calm looking his brother in the eyes with his hands folded in front of him on the table.

"Alright I am just going to say it. I went out Sunday night and of course I was partying hard and was sloppy drunk. Drinking like that is over by the way. Well I was still out of it somewhat the next morning and was sleep in my bed when Jewel came into my room. I didn't even know someone was in there until she woke me up but when she woke me up she was already on top of me naked having sex with me." He looked over at Bryson who lowered his eyes and sat back in his chair. "That's not it. I didn't know it was her because it was dark in my room and I was thinking it was some girl I brought home from the club. I was interacting with her still trying to figure out who she was. I didn't have on a condom or anything so you know I was caught off guard and caught up in the moment. I pulled her off of me before I came and...." He paused for a moment as the waiter approached with their drinks.

Bryson took one of the shots immediately and Bradon took the other. Bradon ordered for the both of them as he knew what his brother already wanted. The waiter looked at Bryson and could tell he was bothered by something that must have been said so he quickly wrapped it up and turned away to leave them to their conversation.

"You were already gone for work. I didn't know it was her until after it was over and she whispered in my ear and I recognized her voice. I immediately jumped up threw her off of me and turned on the light. I had a few choice words for her asking her what the hell she was doing in my room. Well she threatened me not to tell you.

Her clothes had my cum on them and her sides had scratches from me. She said she would scream rape if I said anything to you. I promise man this is the truth. I didn't know it was her and would never in a million years betray you like that."

Bryson gathered his words before he spoke to Bradon. "I'm not mad at you Bradon and I do believe you. I caught Jewel in the act cheating on me. I found evidence on her phone the same morning she apparently came in and seduced you. So I called Rodger and had him investigate her. He found out she had been having an affair with this man for a while now right under my nose. And there is no telling how many others she has been with since we have been together. She left a message on my voicemail saying she has an addiction to sex and that it's some kind of real illness."

"So she is sick. I have heard of people like that but I thought it was just an excuse. So right before you came in just now she called me. I don't know how she got my number either because I just got it changed from being harassed by some groupies. But she is threatening me that she will cry rape and that she still has all the evidence from that night and she will play victim if you are not standing at the altar in 2 weeks on your wedding day. Brys you got to get your little brother out of this. You know I would never do anything to hurt you and never anything like this intentionally. You heard what happened to the young brother who was falsely accused of rape and wasted two years of his life messing up his football career over some lies."

"Don't worry about it. Do you remember when I had you to let the security guy in for me while we were gone?"

"Yeah. Why?"

"Well I had him install cameras that are continuously recording and sent to archive just for you. You go out kicking it so much and bring home these different girls I wanted to make sure you were protected. So I had them install cameras throughout the house especially in your room. So we can just pull them and use them as evidence to clear your name."

The waiter approached with their food and quickly placed their food and made sure they were ok before leaving the table.

"Wow so I can go back and watch me stumbling in and everything huh?"

"Yes sir."

"Bro, I am sorry all of this is happening to you. You don't deserve this. Something like this should be happening to me not you. Are you okay?"

"I will be. I will be." Pausing for a moment he had a thought pop in his mind. "I just had a thought but I want to run it by Sharese first. I'm possibly doing a documentary about my life. It's a lot more to it but this will be a good piece to add. This will make the publisher want the story even more and it will clear your name and Jewel will know it's cleared."

"Okay talk to me." Bradon was all ears.

"Let's eat our lunch and go view the tapes first. I am going to take off for the rest of the day."

Bryson and Bradon ate their lunch and headed home to view the recording from that morning. On the way to the house Bryson makes a call to his publicist telling her what he wants to happen. She states it will be a risk but she will work it out for him. He had to view the tapes and make sure everything was good. He believed every word Bradon said but wanted to make sure the footage was clear cut and in favor of Bradon.

At the house the men pull up the taping from that morning to view. Bradon looked at his brother and asked if he was sure he wanted to see what was on the tape. "Are you sure you are up to seeing this?"

"I had to see her in the actual act with her lover bro I can handle this. I'm cool. I am not mad at you at all and I know what you said to me is what I am about to see so it's okay. I have come to terms with knowing how she was or should I say is. I'm just glad I found out before the wedding and not after."

"Aight then roll camera." Bradon and Bryson sat there watching from the moment Bradon walked in drunk staggering. It was hilarious to them watching him take off his clothes, falling because he couldn't keep his balance. He was staggering to the bathroom inside his master suite. Aiming he missed, peeing all over the seat and trying to clean it up at the same time. He was washing his hands and trying to wash his legs from the drippings and gave up heading back to bed. He managed to at least pull the covers back before falling like a ton of bricks to the bed with one leg in and the other hanging towards the floor. Within seconds he was knocked out snoring from all the alcohol consumptions that night.

After laughing for a moment Bryson started fast forwarding to the beginning of when Jewel walked in. He witnessed her phone sex with Michael just before she headed to Bradon's room. Before he got to that part Bradon started having a moment.

"Man seeing this makes me want to stop drinking all together or at least limit my drinks to one or two. That was funny but I was really not in my right mind. Something bad could happen to me while I am out in those clubs. Even though I have a bodyguard and know you have people looking out for me. What if for a moment no one was there. That's so scary. From this moment on I am vowing to be more responsible."

Just then Bradon looked up and Bryson had stopped the tape where Jewel walked into the room. They watched in silence for the majority of the scene until Bryson out of curiosity asked, "What are you doing when you pull her head up bro?"

Bradon was shocked he was asking him that and immediately answered clearing his throat first. "Oh I was trying to figure out who she was. I couldn't remember bringing anyone home with me so I was trying to remember but didn't want to mess up the moment. Not that I was enjoying it, well I didn't of course know it was Jewel so, yeah okay." Bradon closed his mouth not knowing how what he was saying would affect Bryson.

"Here you see bro where I didn't know it was her and she is threatening me." Bradon was pointing at the screen glad that his brother had this all on tape to clear his name and so he would believe him. He was also glad that he went ahead and told him before he saw it himself.

"Okay so I called Sharese while we were on our way here and told her of my plan. You call Jewel and tell her you talked to me and the wedding is on. Tell her I am not ready to talk to her yet that I am going to use this time to gather myself and get over being hurt, that I will meet her at the altar. Tell her to go ahead with her plans. Let her know that I am still hurt but as a man we need time to heal and that between working long hours and taking time for me that I will need these two weeks and we can work on getting counseling when we get married. You are smart so fill in the gaps with whatever questions she asks."

"You are not going to marry her are you?" Bradon looked confused.

"No never in a million years do I plan on marrying her. She and the world are going to see what she did to me and to you. That's if you are okay with me revealing the video at the wedding and in my documentary."

"Oh okay I get it. Hell yeah you can use it, whatever you need to do bro. I see the big picture now." Bradon was smiling thinking of how brilliant his brother was. He liked the idea of exploiting Jewel for the snake that she was. "But what if she try to sue you for showing this?"

Bryson laughed out loud. "I make anyone that comes into my home sign a waiver and an agreement stating that stepping foot onto and into my property gives me the right to record and publish any part of the footage taken or events that take place. And it states I am not liable for any damage caused to anyone while they are present on and in my property. It was a joke at first but then I started taking it serious and had everyone sign it. So there you have it." Bryson was smiling.

"Brilliant idea bro. You are not only book smart but street smart too I see. Aight. I trust your judgment and I know you have my back."

"Always."

"So you know you will soon have to fill me in on this documentary."

"In due time I will. It's not final yet" Bryson said.

"Cool. Ok well I will handle informing Jewel about the wedding plans still moving forward."

"Thanks for telling me Bradon and I am sorry this happened to you."

"I'm just glad you believed me and had those cameras."

"We are brothers and we have never had a reason to lie to one another."

"Yeah, I know. Glad women don't come in between us messing up our judgment."

"Speaking of women, who was the chic you cooked breakfast for? You never cook breakfast they are always gone just as quick as you bring them home." Bryson asked.

"Yeah she was special. I like her a lot too."

They hung out together for the remaining of the evening talking about the wedding plans and the documentary plans, and

Bradon's new friend Chantae. Bradon was glad this was off his chest and that Bryson was not going to marry Jewel.

CHAPTER 16
~BRIELLE~
HEALING SOULS

"In life you meet all kinds of people. Rich, poor, kind, sweet, nice, mean, ugly, spirited, joyful and so on. You meet people of all shades of color. Black, white, ivory, brown, tan, caramel, chocolate. You meet people of all types of character, all types of nationalities and backgrounds. How they look on the outside will automatically give the people they meet a first impression of them. People will assume all types of things. Oh, he must be poor, look at his shoes. Or she must be poor, her hair is all over her head she need a perm. He looks like he got money; look at the nice car he driving. She might be too uppity for me she turning her nose already and I haven't even said hi. I bet she's a gold digger. And then as soon as they open their mouth and speak you automatically assume and form another opinion about them. Praise the Lord how are you. Oh they must be a religious freak. Or Yo yo what's up dawg. One word. Ghetto. Good day sir or ma'am. You see where I am going with this church. So by their tone of what they say, how they say it and what they say you will form your own opinion which may or may not be the correct opinion. But don't be so quick to judge." Pastor Malone continued his sermon on that Sunday morning.

"You may think they are too passive, a push over or that their attitude stinks. They don't have an education or maybe too much education. We form our opinions about people based on their outer shell. Until we know their story we don't know who they are and our opinions are typically always wrong. You never know what someone is going through and what they have been through. We cover up our problems with smiles, make-up and with the clothes we wear. In public, people tend to pretend that everything about their life is wonderful. Most don't want a pity party or handouts from people when they are trying to portray a better image for themselves. I bet we have amongst us right now couples who were fighting this morning before coming to church and now they are sitting here like nothing is wrong. That is until they get back to the car. Or somebody who cursed out the cars in front of them because they were going too slow or didn't turn when you thought they should turn. And now they sit in here saying hallelujah, thank you Jesus. Or what about the mother who was up worried about her child in the streets and she doesn't know where they are. Trying to hide her pain and hold back her tears. Or the Woman who is in an abusive relationship causing her self-esteem to be low but don't know how to get out or ask for help because she is so called in love or even too scared to leave."

The Pastor was standing in front of the congregation preaching to the people. Brielle was sitting close to the front with her children and her mom, father and brother all sitting together. People were nodding and agreeing and saying Amen and preach Pastor. Brielle reflected on her life and how every Sunday the Pastor seemed to be talking to her and about her life in some kind of way. Her soul was truly fed every Sunday.

"Everyone has a story, a story about where they have been, what they went through, how they overcame it or are still overcoming it, and where they plan to be in the future. Your life could be worse than what it is now. Don't judge people or form an opinion about someone until you ask them their story. On judgment day God is the only judge. We all have to answer to our Father in the same manner. God will look at your heart. He will know how you treated people and how you pass judgment. Try this. Next time you meet someone new or even people you see every day now because some of them you still don't know. Ask them to sum up their life; the past, the present and their future in three minutes. You will be surprised how much you can learn from people. But don't pass judgment. Listen with an open, kind and concerned heart. You never know who you may meet in life or who you may need. Always be kind and treat people how you would want them to treat you. Remind yourself what your very own story is in life. Think about Jesus. What would be His story?"

Brielle looked over at her kids and saw they were paying attention. Olivia was taking notes writing stuff down that the Pastor was saying. Brielle felt proud and smiled giving her approval as her daughter looked up at her. As the Pastor ended his sermon everyone stood all over the church holding hands as he prayed for them. The choir sung and everyone was dismissed to partake in Sunday dinner with the Pastor. Once a month the mothers of the church would get together and prepare a meal for everyone so they all could eat together as one big happy family.

Pastor took his seat right next to Brielle. And she knew she would be getting an additional message from him before dinner was over. After the food was blessed everyone was eating and enjoying their meal. Brielle announced to her family good news that she has been holding on to.

"Mom, dad, everyone guess what? We won the bid on the house and we close in a few weeks. Me and the kids are so excited."

You could hear the kids saying yes and jumping in their seats. Her mom, dad and her brother were all congratulating her and expressing their happiness for her as well. Her brother was joking with the kids telling them somebody had to share rooms because he was getting a room in the new house too.

At that moment, the Pastor turned to Brielle as he was finishing up his food to have a heartwarming discussion with her about her life. Having knowledge of her past and what she went through with her children's father. He felt moved in his spirit to give her a word from God about completely letting go of her past, forgiving and moving forward in life.

"Brielle, I am so proud of you and how you are overcoming all past obstacles in your life. Congratulations on your new home."

"Thank you Pastor." She said.

"God is going to bless you far and beyond this new home, you just be patient and keep on believing in him for great things. Keep your faith strong. So tell me, how are those awful nightmares? Have they stopped?" Knowing the answer before she even replied he reached for her hand and squeezed it tight.

"Well no, they have not stopped. I still have them every now and then. They're not as bad as they use to be but yes sir I still have them. I pray constantly for God to remove those thoughts and nightmares. Sometimes it's hard to forget about it though."

Pastor was getting his thoughts together and she knew it was going to be powerful. "Brielle, let me ask you, first have you forgiven yourself? Then I want to ask you have you forgiven him for what he did to you? You don't have to answer me out loud just answer yourself. You have to first forgive yourself and don't blame yourself for anything that happened to you or your children. God gave them a wonderful beautiful mother who is strong indeed. You are not to blame for anything and you must forgive those who do wrong to you so that God can purify your heart. Forgiveness is freedom for your spirit so that you can move forward in your own life. It releases the hold he or anyone else has over you. Now you will never be able to forget about what happened but you can let it go and completely turn it over to God. Close that chapter in your life. Close the door all the way and lock it throwing away the key so you don't go back there, not even for a visit. Release that hold that he has over you, your children and you heart. Set your spirit free from bondage from this man. Trust in God that He is powerful in all things and He is a deliverer of his word. He said if you ask in Jesus name it will and shall be done according to His Will. Have faith and believe that it is already done."

Brielle sat there with her head down listening to the Pastor as he spoke to her heart and her soul. A tear fell from her eye rolling down her cheek. The Pastor reached over for her hand and held onto it tight. There were conversations going on around them. Everyone was loud and not really paying them any attention except for Brielle's family. Her baby girl Jayla came over and sat in her lap laying her head on her momma's chest. Brielle heard every word the Pastor was saying and knew that he was right.

"Brielle I am about to pray for you right now." Her family bowed there head with them in prayer. "Heavenly Father most Gracious Father we come to you right now with our minds clear and our hearts open to be filled with your goodness, mercy and pure love. Lord you are an awesome God, most powerful God and through you all things are possible. Lord we know that what we ask through you will and shall be done according to your Will. Lord asking that you keep Sister Brielle's heart purified and show her the way of forgiveness through you Heavenly Father. Help her Lord, touch her right now Lord, her heart and her mind. Let her walk the way you desire for her to walk. Let her talk the way you desire her to talk. Let her think the way you desire for her to think. And let her forgive the way you desire for her to forgive. Lord we know that no weapon formed against us shall prosper that you are our Lord and Savior over our lives. You are our protector. Protect Brielle and her family from the demons of the world. Cover them with your blood, with your never ending protection, letting her know that no one will ever hurt her or her children again. Release all anger remaining that is hidden Lord within her heart and her mind. Release all hatred remaining that is hidden Lord and remove all of the nightmares lingering. Give Brielle a renewed spirit. You are blessing her right now Lord I know as we speak these words and I ask for continuing blessings in her finances, I ask for continuing blessings in her heart, I ask that you place her in the right place at the right time to meet her mate that you have created especially for her Lord that you have ordained for her Lord. Let your blessings flow upon her and through her and to all those she provides for around her. Lord we love you and we thank you for all blessings and we ask these things and all things in your precious son Jesus' name Lord. We thank you for all things Lord and no one blessing is too big or too small. In your name Heavenly Father we pray. Amen."

Brielle could feel a much needed relief come over her as if all remaining burdens were lifted and her spirit was renewing. Her eyes were full of tears and her mom was emotional praising God. Ushers that were still there had tissue ready for them both. Brielle's brother had taken the kids to go for dessert.

Brielle turned to the Pastor after drying her eyes to thank him. "Thank you so much for that Pastor. I really needed and appreciate you for that."

"You are welcome dear. Now, what I want you to do when the opportunity presents itself is to make friends with someone, a male in particular and find out his story and just see and feel your reactions. You must be able to look at a man other than your family and church members where you always feel safe and know that you will be able to open up your heart and not miss what God has for you. You shouldn't go through life thinking that every man is or will be like your ex. You shouldn't feel threatened by man and risk missing Love Ordained for you my child. God has something far greater for you."

"I will do that. It's amazing how you speak directly to my spirit knowing exactly where I am and what I need."

"I do it all through God who directs me and speaks through me. You are about to experience some life changing happiness my dear and this is God speaking through me."

You could hear Brielle's mother Marcella praising God for the good news. She knows what that means even if her daughter doesn't. When praises go up blessings come down.

Brielle needed that word from God. Her Pastor couldn't have delivered it better. She gathered her children hugging them all as they were preparing to leave. She wanted her family to go see the new house she would soon be calling home and had them all follow her there. The realtor met them there greeting them with a smile on her face. Brielle was thrilled and couldn't wait for her family to see the inside of the house. They went through the house ohhing and ahhing with happiness in their face and joy in their hearts. Their Sunday was full of happiness, joy and family love.

CHAPTER 17
~BRYSON~
SWEET REVENGE

Today was the wedding day for Bryson and Jewel to be married. Neither of them has spoken to or seen the other in the two weeks leading up to this day. Jewel has only spoken briefly with Bradon. He confirmed with her that Bryson would be standing at the altar as planned. Since everything was already paid for in advance Jewel went on planning as scheduled. She had her twenty thousand dollar wedding gown, all the decorations for the church, the photographer, videographer, the wedding coordinator, all the catering and setup for the reception. She had everything going according to plans. This was one of the best and most beautiful weddings ever. She wanted it to be huge and Bryson allowed her to have whatever she wanted. Reporters were there taking pictures and recording the day's events. Jewel thought the reporters were there for their story that was to be published in Essence magazine but Sharese vetoed them replacing them with Bryson's crew to record for the adventure he planned. The real videographer was removed before the ceremony started. No other footage to be revealed until movie was released. They even forbid cell phones during the ceremony.

"Did anyone see Bryson yet? Has anyone seen Bryson?" Jewel was screaming out to her bridesmaids and anyone else that was in site.

"I saw him pull up with his brother about fifteen minutes ago. Will you relax everything is going to be wonderful. You just worry about looking beautiful and marrying your man." Jewel's sister was standing next to her fixing her dress. "Be still I almost have the last button. As much as this dress cost it should not be this hard to prepare."

"Thanks sis for being here." Jewel spoke softly.

"I wouldn't have missed it for anything in the world. There, I am all done. See how perfect and beautiful you look?" They stood together looking in the full length mirror at Jewel's complete look. Jewel was a beautiful bride.

Her sister had no clue what had been going on with her and Bryson. She didn't know of Jewel's sexual addictions. She kept that part of who she was away from her sister and everyone else who was close to her. Jewel put on a façade to everyone.

"Is everyone ready in here? Do we have our beautiful bride ready yet to walk down the aisle?" Said the wedding coordinator peeking in to make sure everyone was ready.

"Yes we are all ready." Jewel's sister said, still looking at Jewel in the mirror with a smile on her face.

"Alright I need my bridesmaids to line up and prepare to walk. Come on lets go. Now Jewel." She stopped and turned to Jewel. "Wow you are absolutely gorgeous. You have about ten minutes and you will be walking down to meet your groom."

"Okay. And thank you for helping make this day beautiful for me."

"That's my job and you are very welcome. Let me get these girls down the aisle to await the bride." With a smile on her face she turned and walked out the door to make sure everything was going to remain perfect.

You could hear the wedding song playing as the groomsmen escorted the bridesmaids down the aisle. You could see camera's flashing and see the video camera's set up to record the event. The place was packed wall to wall and everything was decorated very elegantly and expensively. Bryson and his brother Bradon stood still at the altar without an expression on their face. The moment has arrived for Jewel to walk down the aisle. Everyone in the church stood.

Bryson's parents were not there. He didn't want them to partake in any non sense, getting caught up in any of this mess. They knew what happened and he wanted to spare them from the details. He didn't care about people asking where his parents were. They would know why they were not in attendance soon enough.

Outside the church doors stood Jewel and her wedding coordinator. Her father was teary eyed looking at his beautiful daughter. Jewel stood there nervous and anxious to become Mrs. Bryson Mathews.

"I am so nervous and shaking. Is Bryson in there?"

"Yes he is waiting on you. Take a deep breath and try to relax. Everything is going smoothly and so will this part. In a few moments you will be standing next to your man and you will become his wife. Are you ready?"

"Okay, yes I am ready. Dad, are you ready?"

He nodded his head and took his daughters arm. Walking down the aisle Jewel was excited and relaxed when she saw Bryson standing there.

Bryson turned and looked at her and for a moment he forgot about everything she had done. She was stunning in her dress. Just as beautiful as he remembered her. At a moment's glance he looked backwards and saw Michael standing on one of the aisle's in the back trying not to be noticed. He immediately had flashbacks of that night. He could see Jewel with her legs spread wide open for that man. He tried to compose himself as she was given to him by her father.

Jewel turns and holds his hands squeezing them, whispering I am sorry. She whispers a little louder saying, "I missed you so much."

"Me too." Was all Bryson could say to her.

The preacher was about to start preaching but before he got started he turned looking at Bryson saying, "I believe your soon to be husband has a surprise for you before we begin the ceremony."

"Thank you sir. Yes I do have a surprise for my Jewel." He turned and looked up toward Kenneth who was in the video booth over top of the church. He nodded and at that moment the screens were on around the church and everyone's attention was there including Jewel. She was excited about the surprise.

There was a video playing of Bryson kissing Jewel good bye and admiring her beauty. You could hear the guest saying ahh how sweet. Then it went straight to playing the morning Jewel snuck into Bradon's room and seduced him trying to blackmail him afterwards. Everyone was shocked. Jewel was panicking and breathing hard. Tears were falling fast down her face. People were looking at her with an evil eye. Everyone was in shock. The preacher was screaming for someone to turn the video off. Kenneth locked the door before he left out so no one could get in to stop the video. Jewel turned to look at Bryson only to see the backside of him leaving out the side door. He turned back to look at her mouthing the words wedding off. He left her there with tears in her eyes.

The camera crew was flashing pictures like crazy at the screen and at Jewel and her family trying to console her. The wedding events were all being recorded by the film production team capturing every detail. Jewel's father ran up to the video booth kicked the door down and stopped the video blast. All he could see was his daughter hurt running down the aisle into hiding. He was so mad but couldn't believe what he saw and heard of his daughter trying to blackmail and manipulate a man all for money and sex.

Her father remembered all too well about the incident of the falsely accused black man. He was a participant in the march for justice for the young man. And now here he stands witness to his daughter attempting to do the same thing. He felt sorry for his daughter and at that point he knew that her sex addiction was still very much active. Her future has been ruined by this and he vowed to get her help. She lost a lifetime of happiness and has turned into a young woman that he doesn't even know anymore. He knew Bryson was a good man and hoped for a forever of happiness for his daughter. But at that moment he was very angry at what just happened and at Bryson. At the same time he was happy his daughter was exposed. Jewel was humiliated in front of everyone she knew and strangers that she did not. Sometimes God works like that, to humiliate people to help us when we don't know how to help ourselves.

CHAPTER 18
~KENNETH~
HOLDING IT DOWN

"Bryson are you alright man?" Kenneth walks into Bryson's office and can tell that his boy is hurting from the events that went down. Nothing could change what happened and he knew he needed time. He took off for a week and left him there to run the business. Kenneth held it down for the both of them. But he needed Bryson to close out on the major deal they had been working.

"Hey Kenny, yeah I'm good. Just thinking." He sits there in a daze. Loosing Jewel was hard but he knew it had to be done. She had an issue with men and sex and it hurt him to his core. Her being with his brother was the ultimate betrayal.

"Well it is good to see you back here in the office. I know this situation is still hard for you. Just glad you found out before saying I do." Kenneth sat in the seat across form Bryson. "Anything I can do for you right now?"

"No man, really I'm good. Let's talk about the business deal. We needed one more deal and they were pleased with what I presented. This fits perfectly for my mood and will help me in the process. I have prayed about it and God has placed this on my heart. So I am still planning for it one hundred percent. Me, Mr. Bryson Mathews will portray my life as a homeless man to see how the world treats me. I will need security disguised all around me of course just in case I get into an ordeal and need the help. But I want to live as if I have nothing so I can really see how people in general would treat me. See how women would act when I am in their presence thinking I had nothing. One of the richest men alive, living life as if he had nothing, seeing how society treats him. How they judge the cover not knowing the story." Bryson looked to Kenneth for confirmation to see what his thoughts were.

"Brys man, are you sure you are serious about this? I have never seen you dress or smell any kind of way but fresh and expensive. I mean, we have been boys since we were kids and not that I just smell you but you get what I'm saying. Are you sure you want to experience life in this manner?" His eyebrows were raised looking at Bryson for reassurance.

"Yes I'm sure. I will make this commitment and follow through. The producers are using the footage from the wedding. This will be a great story that people will love to watch. I will need you to be the main contact and run the business while I am on this mission. I say it should take no more than six weeks to get a good amount of footage to air. You never know what spin they may come up with. Who knows why God is leading me to do this documentary. Maybe I need this to cleanse my spirit. So, are you with me?"

"I'm with you. This is going to be interesting for sure. We will complete negotiations today and make sure you are covered all the way around. We can let the team know this afternoon during our meeting. You sure you are okay with this?"

"Yes, I am sure Kenny." Just then Bryson's phone buzzed from security. Bryson and Kenneth both looked puzzled. Security only buzzes when there is an emergency present.

"Mathews." Bryson said as he answered while on speaker phone so Kenneth could also hear.

"Mr. Mathews, I hate to bother you with this but we have a situation in the lobby. We were asked that Miss Jewel Taylor not be allowed on the premise and she has managed to get pass us and up the side stairs. She has badge access which we have our team on it now to see what access she has so that it can be disabled. She may reach your floor before security can get there."

At that moment Kenneth was up out of his seat and in the hall way to cut her off before getting to Bryson. He warned Mrs. Jackie of the situation and she too was on her guard to protect Bryson from this foolishness. Right as she busted through the door huffing and out of breath security had made it up the elevator and intercepted her before Kenneth had a chance to. They hemmed her up against the wall, found the badge she had and hand cuffed her. Jewel looked a mess. Her hair was not done and her clothes looked dirty. She was not even wearing makeup. The lifestyle Bryson gave her was abruptly taken away.

"Kenneth sir, what would you and Mr. Mathews like for us to do? Have her arrested?" The security guard asked.

"No, no need to do that. Jewel you are not welcomed here. If you come back to this building to bother Bryson again you will be arrested. Leave Bryson alone. You have caused enough harm to him as it is."

"Go to hell Kenneth. You don't know what the hell you are talking about. Bryson loves me. He has to still love me. I know he does. Please just let me see him and everything will be alright."

"Jewel do you have any idea how bad you have hurt that man? Do you?" Kenneth said in a stern voice.

"But I love him Kenneth and I am sorry. I won't do it anymore. I just need to talk to him and tell him that." Jewel had tears in her eyes and for a moment she thought she had Kenneth.

"Jewel, you don't get it do you. There is no undoing what you have done to Bryson. You don't get an opportunity to apologize to discuss it or explain anything. You cannot walk up in here and think you can see him, sweet talk him and everything will be okay. It's not going down like that."

"Kenneth please! If I can just see him for one moment. Can you go get him and tell him I'm out here? Please Kenneth." Jewel was begging with every word she spoke.

"Get her out of here." Kenneth watched as they put her in the elevator as she fought trying to get away.

Jewel was kicking and screaming and begging Kenneth to let her see Bryson. The security guards were earning their pay this day.

After Jewel was gone, Kenneth headed back to Bryson's office. He was sitting at his desk still deep in thought.

"Brys, are you alright man?" He could tell Bryson was not alright.

"Why did this happen to me? It's not even just about Jewel but the fact that I don't have the desires of my heart fulfilled of marriage and family." Bryson was choked up as he spoke.

Kenneth felt bad at that moment for his friend. He knew what Bryson was going through. He knew that Bryson didn't deserve this. So he told him the only thing that made sense to him at the time and that he knew would comfort his friend. "Bryson you right. This should have never happened to you. You are a good man and one day you will be a great husband to the right woman. Sometimes God allow what seems like bad things to happen to good people so that they will gain something better than what they had. God has a plan for you man. You will be over Jewel soon and have a new tender roni in your heart before you know it."

"You right man. I know God has not placed me here to hurt me. But right now I just don't understand. Thanks for being here. And thanks for handling that situation." Bryson stood up and walked to the window.

"That's what I do. We are partners and we are best friends. I'm going to always hold it down. Don't worry about security either. I sent an e-mail to the chief so we shouldn't have any more security breaches. I will follow up to make sure of that."

"Jewel will find a way in man if she wants to. I am sure she has made several friends and has a few tricks up her sleeve. She keeps calling my cell and all of my other lines as well. I am going to have them all changed except of course my business cell."

"I will get Mrs. Jackie to handle that for you. So are you ready for the meeting? Can you put your game face on for this man?" Kenneth looked to Bryson for reassurance.

"Yes I am ready, I can do this."

After the meeting Bryson and Kenneth were smiling. Kenneth more so than Bryson. They sealed the deal with Bryson taking on the journey. They liked the thought of playing on the idea of a wealthy man who couldn't buy love in search of something more. He wanted people to see him for who he was and not how much he was worth. His life as a homeless man would start the following Monday and he would give them a full six weeks of filming under their direction. This would be a challenge for Bryson being out of his elements. But feeling the way he did would help give him a change of scenery to escape reminders of pain. This would be Kenneth's first time running the business for this long but would give Bryson and Kenneth both a chance to see how Kenneth could handle running the business on his own.

CHAPTER 19
~BRYSON~
GOING HOMELESS

Sunday night Bryson was sitting at home with Bradon and Kenneth getting ready for his journey living his life momentarily as a homeless man. He hired costume professionals to come and make sure his wardrobe was believable, smell and look. He didn't want to smell breath taking stank, but he needed people to think he had been living on the streets. Musty masculine outdoor scent is what he was aiming for. He worked out the day before and didn't have a shower to freshen up. Bryson was shaking his head wondering what he had gotten himself into. He didn't like to be funky and this was going to be weeks of funk. He didn't know if he would be able to last without freshening up every now and then. Sunday he couldn't take it and jumped into the shower but decided to not put on deodorant, lotion or cologne.

"What did I sign up for? Kenny man why you didn't talk me out of this?" Bryson had his finger up to his nose trying not to inhale the scent the lady had for him to spray on his clothes the next day.

"Hey, I asked you if you were sure and you said you were positive. I tried to talk you out of it. Just think about the millions of dollars you will have afterwards to spend on the counseling you are going to need and to buy as much soap and cologne you want." Kenny and Bradon laughed but quickly stopped when Bryson sprayed the musty stink smell in their directions.

"Man that shit stank. That's what you gon smell like?" Bradon was frowning with his hand over his nose and mouth. He was looking at his brother with eye brows raised still frowning in disbelief.

"Yea man that stank for real. Don't waste that shit on us we don't mind you not sharing that at all." Kenneth choked a bit. "I think it got in my throat a bit man for real. Can you omit that spray and just not shower? That is going to drive everyone away from you." Kenneth was fanning the air.

Bryson was laughing out loud. Kenneth was a clean freak. He had to take a shower immediately after playing ball or working out and he didn't like for his hands or his face to be dirty, not even for a second. "Sorry man, I know how you are. You can shower upstairs if you need to Mr. clean."

"Fuck you man. Just don't spray that stank shit again. Hey little lady, can you bury that in the bottom of your bag please. He won't need that at all. Not showering should do the trick. Just go workout tonight and don't shower, that should do it." Kenneth was acting like he was about to pass out from the smell.

"Can you just lightly treat the clothes outside of course, and let them air out a bit so the smell won't be as strong? I have to ease into the smell. And it is a bit over bearing." Bryson handed the spray to the lady and she agreed with him taking the costume off him.

Bryson had been letting his hair grow out on his face and his head since the wedding day, anticipating this journey. He had a hairstylist there to make his hair look beaded as if he had not combed it in a while. They wanted his transformation to be as real as possible. They needed him to be unrecognizable as Bryson Mathews the millionaire. With his hair not cut and groomed, Bryson looked like a different person and nothing like the millionaire on the front of Essence magazine. He was ready for the challenge.

"Kenny, the company will be in your hands for the next few weeks. You can always call me if you need to. Or just shoot me an e-mail and I will respond. I will be wearing an ear piece so the producers will be able to talk to me as well. But we both know I will be limited to the amount of work I am able to do." Bryson was talking as he was getting his hair done.

"Bryson, I got this. We all know you are a workaholic and actually you are still working, but I think I can manage without you for a few weeks. I know where you will be. Under the bridge or on a park bench somewhere, I will find you." Kenneth was making jokes. He was happy to see that his friend had forgotten about Jewel for the moment.

"Yeah I know man. I guess I'm a bit nervous about how this is going to play out. I mean this will be a new experience for sure. But it will be good for people to see how a man like me is treated when no one knows who I am. I really am looking forward to see how women treat me in particular. I just hope one day I can find my Miss Right so I can have a family of my own and have that love like our parents have." He said looking at Bradon.

"Yeah, I feel you bro. Mom and dad have a one of a kind genuine love that we all want some day. One day I hope to have a love like theirs as well. They set the bar high as hell making it hard for women with their boys." Bradon chimed in.

"What about that girl that had your nose wide open at the club a few weeks ago Bradon. I heard you still kicking it with her. Is it serious?" Kenneth said.

"What's up, you holding out on your big brother? Are you in love Bradon?" Bryson said to Bradon.

"Well, I like her and we will see where it goes. She is cool peeps and she is hot. The girl I was talking to you about a few weeks ago Brys. I just don't know how she is going to react when I tell her this is really not my house. She's a bit high maintenance. Or should I say use to having nice things. She has a J O B and her own money. But a brother don't have a job. I am living off my big brother right now with limited funds."

"Is she a gold digger?" Kenneth asked.

"Naw, she's not like that but she comes from a family of money. She has never once asked me for anything or insinuated she wanted anything. Right now we are having fun, getting to know one another." Bradon was acting as if he was hiding something, leaving out some key details.

"That means he likes her and they have not had sex yet." Bryson said to Kenneth.

"Bradon you mean you didn't hit it the night after the club? You found someone who could resist your charm and flashy ways?" Kenneth said.

"Man, how did this turn into a session about me? We are talking about Bryson."

"He didn't hit." Bryson and Kenneth said in unison as they were laughing at Bradon.

Bryson stopped laughing momentarily. "Well, if you have not had sex with her and she is not asking for anything from you then you may have something genuine. She obviously has morals and standards so wine and dine her and treat her like a queen like daddy treats momma. See how she responds. If it's something you like then take it to the next step. You will be your own millionaire one day little brother but until then, you need to tell her the truth and don't string her along."

"I agree. You do need to tell her the truth. Tell her now. I am sure she is bragging to her friends and her family and if she thinks you are making a fool out of her it might not end how you want it to end." Kenneth added his advice as well.

"I will tell her. Honestly she just assumed this was my life. But I never corrected her. But I will tell her next opportunity I have. I think I am getting close to hitting it so I will be sure to tell her before then. Maybe after." Bradon said.

"How about before lil brother." Bryson said.

"You sure not after?" Kenneth chimed in trying to help Bradon out a bit.

"Yeah, you sure not after? Then she will see how good it is and it would be harder for her to walk away." Bradon added.

"That's up to you. But I am telling you, before is the best approach. She will appreciate you more for the honesty and it could make the sex part even better. That way she will know you are genuine and didn't tell her a lie just to get her in bed." Bryson was trying to give his brother good advice, hoping he would take it and put it to good use.

"I hear you brother. We will see how it plays out." Bradon wanted the attention off of his love life. "You just make sure you are careful out there in those streets. Security is on duty close by twenty four seven right?"

"Yes, we have that all lined up on our end and with the producers. He will be protected at all times." Kenneth said, in his businessman tone.

"Kenneth took care of all that and we had a meeting with security and the producers and everyone knows what to and not to do. We don't want to blow my cover at any time. Besides I can handle my own if someone wants to flex, but if we can avoid it we will. I know it can be an ugly world out there at times but we are prepared." Bryson said.

"Alright bro tomorrow is the day. I will be sure to take care of home and have a big party here while you are away." Bradon was worried but excited to have the house to his self.

"You know I don't mind about the parties. Help yourself." Bryson was not a materialistic person although he had plenty of nice things and plenty of money to buy what he wanted.

"Just make sure you invite me when you do Bradon." Kenneth said.

Bryson chatted with his best friend and brother for the remainder of the night and prepared his mind for his journey. The next morning will be the beginning of a very interesting adventure in his life. Humbling and a life lesson he would never forget.

Bright and early Monday morning, the sun not even peeking to rise, Bryson's production team was at his home going over his agenda of places he need to visit and things he should do. This was a reminder course of what they have been drilling in his head all week long. Bryson was ready. After much preparation and getting his mind set, he knew that he would survive. So he thought. He was about to adventure an entire new lifestyle and have an eye awaken realty check of how people live and survive on the streets.

He was dropped off on a corner close to an alley. He had security posted on top of buildings and dressed themselves as common people all around him. He was very well protected. He stood on the corner of the alley posted up against the building. His nerves kicked in and reality started to sink in regarding what he contracted to do.

"What the hell have I done? I am really out here on the corner in the middle of nowhere. Is this real?" Bryson had his hands over his face and immediately removed them when he was startled by someone talking to him.

"This may be nowhere to you but this is home to me and you are disturbing my beauty sleep. You don't have to leave but can you be quiet so I can sleep a little longer before the sun comes up, please sir?"

Bryson looked around trying to figure out who was talking and where they were sleeping. He looked over and saw a card board box moving with some feet hanging out from underneath. It was a lady beneath the box and she was repositioning herself. She was lying on the ground in the alley right by the corner where he was standing. Bryson was shocked. He didn't notice the lady there sleeping under a box. "Oh I am so sorry for disturbing you. I will be quiet."

He stood there for a moment longer wanting to talk to the lady but didn't want to disturb her. After about thirty minutes of waiting, a man walked by and threw some pennies at his feet. And said, let me see you pick the pennies up boy and I might give you some more change. Bryson didn't move and his jaws flinched. Being called boy struck a nerve in his body, and his mind went into defense mode. He didn't know if he should punch the man or stand there and take it. If he was any other place he would have punched him and made him eat his words.

"Leave him alone he doesn't want your pennies." The lady said raising the box from her face. "Go on and get now." She screamed.

"Yeah, whatever. Get a job bum." The man said walking away.

The man kept on moving. He was wearing a suit and headed towards the bus stop. He was very ugly with Bryson not knowing who he was and how much power he had. This was his first encounter with how cruel society could be. It was just about day light and the lady moved the box from around her. Bryson's heart sank when he saw that she had a baby and a toddler under the box with her. "You have kids?" He didn't know what to say.

"Yes, I have kids. Little Darla here is six months and Charles is three." She looked him up and down making sure he was of no threat to her. "You look like you could be trusted. I guess. So what are you doing out here? What happened to you?" She asked as she was preparing herself to feed her baby.

"I ran in to hard times and have no place to go so I ended up on the streets." He turned his head quickly when he saw her pull out her breast preparing to nurse her baby. "Oh, oh, yeah. So yeah, I just ran into hard times is all." He was a bit nervous. This lady pulled out her breast while talking to him and he had an eye full of her entire breast, nipple and all.

"What? Have you not ever seen a titty before or seen a woman nurse her baby?" She shot back at him.

"Oh sorry, I just wanted to give you a bit of privacy. It was unexpected. I think it is good that you are nursing your baby." His back was still turned to her.

"Well, don't turn around because I am nursing both of them now. Our food supply is limited so I have to feed them the best way I can." Her voice was low and sad even.

Bryson was touched and his heart was breaking seeing a woman with children on the streets. He heard the directors in his ear, "Find out what her story is. See how much she will tell you". He turned around more towards her but not looking directly at her. "So what is your story? Why are you out here in the streets with your babies?" His voice was very sincere and concerned. Even though the Director requested to find out this info, Bryson genuinely wanted to know why for his self.

"My story huh?" She paused looked up at Bryson. "Well I don't share much with strangers but you seem like a nice guy. To make it short, I was put out of my own home by my husband because he decided he didn't want to be with a good woman and his own kids. He wanted to be with his beautiful young secretary and every other woman who would have him. So he put me, his wife and his kids out with no money and no place else to go. His family wouldn't have us and the only family I have is a brother who is on drugs. I did have a car that we were sleeping in but my crack head brother stole that and what little we had in it and probably sold it to a chop shop for a quick fix. I reported it stolen but it's been a month and the police still have not found my car. So, that's my story. That's why me and my babies are out here sleeping on the streets." She was pulling up her clothes from feeding her children.

Bryson remembered he had food in his bag to eat on and he gave the lady all the food he had inside. "Oh, here I forgot that I had these snacks. A lady stopped and gave them to me yesterday on the street and you can have them for you and the kids." He handed her the bag and she hurriedly opened up bags of chips and packages of chicken salad mix in the can and started feeding her children and herself food. "What is your name?"

"My name is Ameila. Ameila Churchwell. Thank you so much for this food. We have not eaten in three days." She continued to eat and feed her babies. He even had bottled water and juice and they drunk that. "My milk supply has been running low because of my lack of nutrition. I could feel my body getting weak and I didn't want to lose my milk supply you know. My baby was born premature and she needs the breast milk. I try to stay in shelters but we have not been able to get into one in three days. They say they are all full." She ate some more food. "I don't give up though. My babies keep me going. I am going to find my way back soon. I have dreams and a purpose in life and I know God is going to bless us with a way."

Bryson was on the brink of tears watching what was happening in front of him and listening to this woman's story. She was beautiful and strong. She had a real struggle and didn't deserve the hand that was dealt her. For her to still have faith in God and believing that he was going to bless her let Bryson know that he was there at the right time at that moment to be a blessing to her. "God just sent you a blessing. I am going to help you but I need you to do me a favor okay."

At that moment Bryson heard the producer in his ear. "Bryson we just started and you are about to blow your cover with her aren't you?" The producers were even touched by this lady and were not about to try and stop Bryson or change his mind. They let him do what he felt lead to do for Ameila and her children.

"Yes, I am. Sorry. I just need to do this for her and her children. I get a free pass don't I?" He looked at the woman who was looking a bit confused at what appeared to be him talking to his self. Bryson had reached in his pockets for his cell phone.

"Ok. I thought you looked trust worthy but now I am beginning to think you are crazy, bipolar or something. And I don't do any 'favors' for strangers. If that's the type of favor you are insinuating. I don't get down like that and I am not that type of woman. I rather stay right here with my babies. No thank you." She started packing up her stuff.

Bryson was walking around to see if anyone was coming or near them. He pulled out his cell phone and put an ear piece in his ear. "Kenneth I need you to send a car to my location and pick up a lady name Ameila Churchwell and her children. Put them up in the hotel suite and give her anything she needs unlimited. And arrange for Dr. Zackary to come check her and the kids out. Give them whatever medical treatment they need. Take real good care of her okay." He closed his cell phone and looked over at the lady looking confused. She was trying to figure out what was happening.

"Are you okay? I am a bit confused here." She was holding on to her babies looking at Bryson.

"Sorry, yes I am fine. I'm not crazy at all. My friend Kenneth Cartwright is coming to pick you up and take you and your babies to the hotel I own. You will have everything you need all on me. Just take care of yourself and your babies and don't worry about anything. This is your blessing from God, I'm just a vessel. Try to get back on your feet. Whatever you need my friend will take care of for you so don't hesitate to let him know. My favor is for you to keep this a secret for me. What I am doing. I don' want to blow my cover. I'm doing a documentary on my life, a very rich man living as if he was homeless to see how people will treat me."

"So wait. Let me get this straight. You are rich and you choose to be out here? Yes. Now I really know that you are crazy." She looked at him with confusion still in her eyes.

"You are a funny lady you know. You speak your mind I like that." Bryson said.

She smiled back and asked. "Are you really going to help me out like that? Is this for real? Are you serious? I don't have time for no games."

"Yes I am serious. No games. You see that van across the street? They are watching and filming us. Somebody wave." Just then one of the guys leaned forward and waved.

"Oh my, will I be in your documentary?" She said smoothing out her hair.

"If you like. I think your story will make a great addition to my documentary." Bryson watched as she started to blush. "A car will be here in a few minutes to pick you up. My name is Bryson Mathews and I own Cole Estates. You don't need to be out here with these babies."

"Wow, God has blessed me. I knew he would. You are my Angel sent from heaven. Thank you Mr. Mathews, thank you so much!" With tears in her eyes, she grabbed Bryson by his face and kissed his cheek. And then apologized just as quick for invading his space.

He assured her that she was okay and didn't need to apologize. It made him feel good to be able to help her and seeing how grateful she was. She told him to sit with her so she could give him some advice about living on the streets. From that moment until the car arrived for her, she told him what he needed to know about being homeless. What not to do and how to survive. Her tips from her experiences with being homeless. Her stories she shared were very interesting and Bryson knew he had to share in his documentary.

Bryson never imagined meeting someone who would need his help. God works like that. He places people in places and situations to be a blessing to others and to receive a blessing. Helping this lady made Bryson feel like his journey was worth it. It gave him the mindset to stay focused and finish his journey. He said a prayer to God to give him strength and allow him to be a blessing to as many people as he could. He was touched. Although she called him her angel, she was really his angel. And he now knew that God has him on this journey for several reasons and to fulfill a purpose. To heal him of his heartbreak, touch his life in ways he didn't imagine, as well as be a blessing to other people. He had a purpose and a plan for his life and he was exactly where God intended him to be. So no matter how difficult the journey was, he knew that he had to continue.

The next couple days were challenging for him. This was a serious ordeal and he didn't wish this struggle on anyone. He encountered some very cruel people some nice and some that didn't want to be bothered or even acknowledge his presence. He took it all in and hoped this was a speedy journey. He wasn't sure how long he would be able to deal with everything going on, knowing he had a stress-free relaxing life compared to being homeless. He wasn't any better than the next man so quitting was not an option.

CHAPTER 20
~BRIELLE~
AT THE PARK

Brielle woke up Saturday morning bright and early. She worked out, showered and made the kid's breakfast. Her normal Saturday routine. The kids were awakened by the smell of bacon cooking. They got up and washed their face, brushed their teeth and made their beds before heading to the kitchen. The kitchen window was open and you could hear the birds chirping and singing. Brielle thought to herself this would be a great day to go to the park.

"Good morning my little angels."

"Good morning momma." They all said almost in unison. Olivia, Jayla and Carter were all sitting at the table in the same seats they always sit in. They were trying to wake up more than their sense of smell.

"Momma I could smell the bacon while I was asleep. That's what made me wake up." Jayla said.

"Yes momma that bacon woke me up too." Olivia said.

"It smells good momma, what else you cooking? Bacon is all I smell." Carter said.

"Well bacon does have a powerful aroma. I have French toast and cheese eggs as well." Brielle said.

"Mmmmm, that sounds good momma." Jayla said.

"Is it done yet momma?" Olivia asked.

"Almost baby. Give me one minute and I will make your plates. Can you get the syrup out of the pantry baby girl?" Brielle asked of Olivia.

"Yes ma'am." Olivia rose from the table to retrieve the syrup.

"Momma you want me to get the juice out and pour it?" Carter asked.

"That would be good baby."

"What about me mommy? What do you want me to do?" Jayla asked.

"Well everything else is done I think so how about you say grace and bless the food." Brielle said.

"Okay I will. Come on let's hold hands." They all gathered back at the table and held hands as she began to pray. "Dear God. Thank you for my beautiful mommy and my nice and pretty sister and my handsome funny brother. Thank you for my family and oh thank you for my granny and my paw-paw and my uncle Isaiah. Thank you for this food my mommy has cooked for us to feed our hungry bellies. In Jesus name, Amen."

"That was beautiful baby girl. Thank you." Brielle said hugging her four year old daughter. She handed them all their plates and they began to dig in. "So I was thinking today would be a good day to have lunch in the park and feed the ducks. How does that sound?"

"Yay. I am going to bring my fishing pole I made last time." Carter said.

"I can't wait to feed the duckies." Jayla said.

"Momma that's a good idea. We like the park." Olivia said.

"Okay, well finish your breakfast and we can clean our mess and head to the store. We have to go shopping for the bread." Brielle said as she sat down at the table with her children to enjoy breakfast.

Arriving at the park, there were quite a few people there. Brielle gathered the picnic basket, blanket and the kids and they found a spot near the water. She spread the blanket and placed the basket in the middle so it wouldn't blow away. The kids took their shoes off so they could play in the water and placed them on the corners of the blanket to hold it in place. Off to the water they went. Carter had his handmade fishing pole and his artificial bug bait. The water was cold and the girls were easing into the water to get use to the coldness.

"Be careful babies." Brielle shouted out. "Carter watch where you swing that fishing pole."

"Yes ma'am." They all said back to her.

Brielle sat there with her shoes off watching her kids play in the water. She looked to her left and saw a man walking in her direction. He appeared helpless and sad to her. She watched him for a moment trying not to stare. She saw him approach a lady and her son and it looked as if he asked for some bread. They were feeding the ducks and turned to him laughing and threw crumbs of the bread to his feet and told him to pick it up like the ducks do. They were laughing at him and her heart started to ache. She looked up and saw that her kids had witnessed this cruel act as well. She got up and walked over to where her children were to distract them.

"Carter, have you caught any fish yet?" She said in an attempt to bring his attention back to the water.

"No not yet momma." He looked up at her with worry in his eyes.

"Come here all of you. Give me a hug." She hugged them all together. I know you all witnessed that cruel act. Some people are different. Just know that God will take care of them. You just know that it is not right to mistreat people no matter what is going on with them or how they look."

"Yes ma'am." The children said.

"But momma is something wrong with him?" Her baby girl Jayla asked.

"I am sure he is just as normal as you and me. This water is cold." Brielle said as she walked into the water.

"It's not cold to me anymore. I am use to it." Carter said. Just then Brielle splashed some water onto her son and he jumped and tensed up because of the cold water. "Momma that is cold."

"Un huh, I thought you said it wasn't cold." Olivia said.

Brielle was giggling and she walked out further in the water until it was up to her knees. Her son was still fooling with his fishing pole he made. He tossed it again into the water and it got caught in his mom's hair.

"Momma watch out." He shouted. "I am so sorry momma. Are you okay?"

"Carter. You got it hooked in my hair baby. You could have really hurt someone." Brielle was walking out of the water as quickly as possible. "Come help me get this out. I am so glad this is not a real worm. Ewwww. Help me get this out of my hair." She was bending over so her son and daughter could help untangle the hook and bait from her hair.

"I can't get it momma. It is really tangled." Her son said.

Just then she heard a strong manly voice from behind. "Here allow me to help if you don't mind. I'm sure I can get it untangled."

Carter looked stunned. He realized this was the man that was being mistreated and here he was helping his mom. Brielle looked at him in his eyes and paused a few seconds before responding. His eyes were so peaceful and spoke to her soul. Her heart skipped a beat and then started beating rapidly. He was scruffy but amazingly handsome through the entire rough dingy look.

"Sorry, yes please can you help me get this out of my hair. My son loves to fish and he has made his own fishing pole. One of the joys of being a kid, they have a very imaginative mind." She felt like she was rambling from being nervous.

"Fishing is something you either love or don't care for and he seems to have a passion for the sport. There I got it out. It was wrapped in there pretty good. He must have a good swing." Bryson was so close to her. His eyes looked into her eyes and he was mesmerized by Brielle.

She smiled up at him. "Thank you so much for your help." She turned to look at her son as a distraction. "Carter you have to be more careful baby. You don't want to hurt anyone."

"Yes momma. Thank you sir for helping me get my fishing hook untangled without breaking it." Carter looked up at Bryson as he handed him his hook back.

"No problem son. You want me to show you a cool trick making your own fishing pole work like a store bought one?" Bryson asked. "If it's okay with your mom? Is it okay mom?"

At that moment they were both looking up at Brielle for permission. Brielle looked into Bryson's eyes. Their eyes were locked. Brielle had a good sense of people and she had an overwhelming feeling that he would never hurt them and could be trusted. "Sure that would be fine. If it's not a problem for you, I don't mind." She smiled.

"I would be honored. Thank you. Let me see your pole for a second son." Bryson had his attention on Carter and his fishing pole. He showed him how to turn his stick and string into a pole that would catch a fish. The girls were intrigued as well and watched and learned as Bryson taught him how to use the pole. After a few moments of trying and them being quiet Carter actually caught a fish. They all were excited as they jumped up and down screaming.

Carter brought the fish over to his mom. "Look momma. He helped me catch a fish. He said we should probably throw it back though because it's a baby."

"Wow, did you tell him thank you Carter?" Brielle was examining the fish on the hook as Carter held it up.

"Yes, he thanked me. Your children are very polite. You have taught them well." Bryson said.

"Momma his name is Matt." Jayla said. "I asked him his name and we told him ours. Was that okay momma?"

"Yes Jayla that is okay." Brielle looked up at Bryson. Matt was the name he was going by on his journey.

"Let me help you take it off the hook so you can release him back into the water. Hold him here so he won't flop away Carter." Bryson helped him place his hands on the fish to keep him in place.

The kids were all headed back to the water to release the fish. "Carter when you're done you all come back here so we can clean your hands and eat." She looked up at Bryson. "Would you like to join us for some lunch Mr. Matt?"

"Mr. sounds old. You can just call me Matt. I would love to join you but I don't want to intrude on your family time any longer than I already have." He said. He never took his eyes off Brielle and hoped she would insist.

Brielle was feeling so nervous and she didn't understand why. Her heart was pounding and her stomach was in knots. How could this be happening to her when in her mind she felt like she should have the power over this situation? "You know what. I won't take no for an answer. You helped me get a fish hook out of my hair and you just made my kids day helping them with their pole and actually catching a fish. That was priceless. So no is not an acceptable answer Matt. If that's okay with you?" She looked up smiling. Every time she locked eyes with him her heart started pounding faster. He never took his eyes from hers, even when she looked away.

"Thank you. I guess I will be joining you. May I ask you your name?" He asked her.

"Oh sorry. My name is Brielle." She reached her hand out to him to shake his.

He held her hand in his, heart beating and sparks flying and immediately bent over to kiss her hand. "Thank you for your kindness Brielle."

"You are welcome Matt." She was blushing and trying to hide any reaction. "Come on lets clean our hands so we can eat. Mr. Matt is going to be joining us for lunch kids." She pulled the hand sanitizer and wet wipes out and passed them to the kids to clean their hands.

Jayla had the hand sanitizer and was giving it to Bryson. She walked over to him and said, "You need a lot of hand sanitizer and wet wipes. You have a lot of dirt on you and you smell really bad. Momma doesn't like for us to be dirty at all when we eat."

"Jay-Jay. That's not nice to tell someone they stink baby. Matt I am so sorry. You know kids can sometimes say whatever comes to mind. Jay-Jay, tell him you're sorry." She looked at her daughter with embarrassment on her face.

"I'm sorry sir. It's okay if you stink I still like you."

If Brielle was any lighter she would turn red. "Matt I am sorry."

"You don't have to apologize. I do stink a little I guess. I am the one who is sorry for offending you all with my smell. So is it that bad Jayla? Did I get your name right?" He looked at Jayla.

Jayla looked at her mom for confirmation to answer. Once her mom gave her the ok she responded. "Yes, it is way bad."

Matt laughed. "Thank you for telling me the truth. I promise as soon as I can I will shower and wash my clothes." He looked up at Brielle knowing that she was embarrassed letting her know with his eyes it was ok.

"Do you have a shower that work at your house?" Jayla kept going.

"That's enough with the questions Jayla. Since you want to talk say grace. Better yet I will say grace." Brielle said

"I would love to say grace, if you don't mind. In my house growing up as a child the men always said grace. It just brings back memories." Bryson's eyes were again locked on Brielle's' eyes.

Brielle was amazed. She was also confused. He seemed to be a strong grounded man but didn't understand why he was what appeared to her as homeless, living on the streets. "Go right ahead, please." She said with a smile.

"Let's hold hands everybody." Jayla said.

Matt reached up for Brielle's hand. He was sitting across the picnic table from her. As she placed her hand in his he held it gently but tight. The connection was powerfully present between them. They all held hands, bowed their heads and he began to pray. "Dear Heavenly Father. We come before you at this moment heads bowed giving you the glory and the praise. Lord bless this beautiful family that has so kindly and open heartedly given of themselves to share their meal. Lord we ask that you bless this food and the hands that have prepared it. Thank you Lord for everything that you have done and will do. Things that are seen and those that are unseen for we know Lord that through prayer and faith all things are made possible through your son Jesus Christ. We thank you for your Mercy and we thank you for your blessings. In your name Heavenly Father and in your son Jesus Christ name we so humbly pray. Amen."

"Amen" They all said in unison.

At that moment, Brielle felt connected to him. She was not use to any man taking charge and praying besides her father. Here Bryson was a perfect stranger and he still knew how to lead being the man of the table. They all began to pull the food from the basket and pass it around. Bryson tried not to stare at Brielle but it was hard for him not too. They had sandwiches cut into four, pickles, cookies, plain chips and hot Cheetos for the kids and bottled water.

The kids were chatting away with each other as they were eating. They were acting normal as kids do and talking about the fish they were going to catch when they were done eating.

"So do you come to this park much?" Brielle asked in between bites of her sandwich.

"I just recently started. It's a nice park. It's very peaceful at night time." He said before stuffing his mouth. He was eating as if he was starving.

"When was the last time you ate anything?" She looked up at him with concern in her eyes but didn't want to cross any boundaries. "I'm sorry you don't have to answer me. You just appear to be eating really fast." She looked down at his food and then back at her food. She started to fidget with her fingers nervously.

"You can ask me anything you want. It's okay." Brielle looked up and he was staring at her looking into her eyes. "I don't know when the last time I had a complete meal. I am very grateful to you and your children. It's hard being a man who has fallen down on his luck. Shelters are hard to come by but they do provide a hot meal there. They normally place women and children first and then take whoever is next in line." He looked up to see her face and study her reaction. "I don't plan to stay down for long. I will bounce back on my feet soon. Just made some bad choices and lost some things I thought were important to me. But I eat when I can. I think too much about life to think about eating. But I find food."

"I am sorry to hear that. What about your family? You seem like a man who would have lots of friends, what about them?" Brielle stopped eating for the moment.

"I have a brother but he does his own thing and I don't bother him. The rest of my family does not live close most of my friends have their own families and I could never be a burden to anyone. My pride won't let me be a burden." He looked at Brielle and smiled at her. "You are a woman with a very big caring heart, I can tell. I have not smiled in a long time or felt any happy feelings and today you and your children gave me just that. So don't let my situation bring you down. You don't worry about me at all pretty lady." He took a bite of the kids flaming hot Cheetos as he saw a smile spread across Brielle's face. Not realizing they were hot he started choking and gasping from the heat. A few of the hot Cheetos went flying to the ground.

"Are you okay? We should have warned you those were hot." Rubbing him on the back Brielle reached for the bottled water. "Here drink this." She handed him the water and he downed half the bottle.

"Man you kids eating these like its candy. I would have never known they were hot. Unexpected I tell you."

The kids were giggling at Bryson.

"They not hot to us." Carter said.

Just then a duck walked up by their table and grabbed one of the hot Cheetos from the ground. He put it in his mouth and after a moment he started quacking loud and acting crazy. The hot Cheetos were burning the duck's mouth too. The kids were laughing and trying to give the duck some of their bottled water but it ran wild back to the water. The duck was quacking and ducking his head under water trying to cool his mouth.

"I feel your pain ducky. I feel your pain." Bryson said still clearing his throat and laughing.

"That was funny and bizarre all at the same time." Brielle said still watching the duck. She glanced down at the kids and she had to join in laughing with them and Bryson.

"I needed that laugh." Bryson said.

"Yes that was too funny." Jayla said still laughing.

"I wish I had my video camera for that one." Brielle said. "That was a priceless once in a lifetime moment. Both you and the duck." She looked over at Bryson and continued to laugh.

Bryson watched her laugh with a grin on his face adoring her glow. He could not believe that this beautiful lady and her kids were opening up their hearts and accepting him as he was. This touched his heart and his mind. He knew at that moment that God was at work in him and in his life. She had just been a blessing to him. He didn't know if she had a man or not but she was not wearing a wedding ring at all so he thought he would find her again after he was done with the documentary.

After the laughter ceased, Bryson watched the kids head back towards the water. They were full of energy and excitement to play. He turned back toward the table not really knowing what to do at this point. Then he heard Carter calling for him.

"Matt can you help us again with the fishing pole? We want to catch a big fish." Carter said.

"Sure thing my man." He said back to Carter. He turned to Brielle before heading toward the kids. "I don't want to over stay my welcome with you and the kids. I will help him with the fishing pole and head on my way. But thank you again Brielle. You have been so kind."

"Please, no need to thank me at all. We have enjoyed your company, really." Bryson was looking at her smiling. Brielle was a bit nervous. "If it's okay with you I would love to come back tomorrow and bring Sunday dinner to enjoy with you. I mean it's not much but at least you could have a really good home cooked meal. You have to eat right?"

"You are an angel you know that? I would love that." He was amazed by this woman. He looked up at the sky and thought to himself, *God you are up to something.*

"Well okay, tomorrow it is then. Oh, are you allergic to anything?"

"No not at all and I am not picky either. I am sure whatever you cook will be great." The both of them were staring into each other's eyes. They could not explain what was happening at the moment. Bryson looked toward the kids as Carter was calling him again. "I better go help him with his fishing pole." He smiled before turning away. Looking back at Brielle he smiled at her once more before turning his attention to her son.

Brielle did not understand what she was feeling. There was no way that God could be sending her a man who was homeless. But he sure was great with her kids. She looked at him in the same way she looked at a house. A really great house could have been torn up and dirty from a previous owner but once you moved in and add your loving touch it could look like a castle made for a princess. She was thinking about taking him home to meet mom and dad and how they all would look together in a family picture. He was very intriguing to her. He gave her a feeling of belonging.

Brielle joined them fishing and playing in the water. After about an hour and a half she knew it was time to go. Time had flown by and she didn't realize it was that late. She still had errands to run and had to meet her Realtor. She knew it was time for them to go. She broke the news to the kids and everyone was disappointed including Bryson.

"Matt are you going home now too?" Jayla asked.

"Jayla you asking Mr. Matt a lot of questions. Come on let's get your shoes on and you can help me with the blanket." Olivia said taking her little sisters hand.

"But does he have a home to go to? I don't want to leave him here alone." Jayla said to Olivia as she walked away.

"My kids have taken a liking to you. They witnessed those people being cruel to you earlier and at that moment they wanted to protect you." Brielle said.

"That is really sweet but it is the man who should be protecting the woman and children. Those people were idiots. They didn't hurt me at all. Some people try to hurt others in an attempt to cover up their own pain. But not all people are cruel." He glanced at the kids and smiled.

Brielle heard loud and clear him say the man should be the protector and that stood out. That was something she yearned for. To feel protected by a man other than her father. This was the reason she was afraid to open up to another relationship. But his physique screamed protection among other things. "Well I should be going. But thank you for everything with the kids and all."

"No thank you, very much."

"I will see you tomorrow about three?" She said.

"I will be here." He put his hands in his pockets. The urge to grab her and pull her to him was taking over his mind, his heart and his body. But he knew he would run her away and that this was not the time to be making a move on any woman. So he buried his hands and took a deep breath.

"Okay, see you then." She smiled and walked toward the kids to help carry the basket. "Let's go kids. Tell Mr. Matt good bye. We will see him tomorrow for dinner here at the park again."

"Bye Mr. Matt. See you tomorrow." Jayla said looking sad because she had to leave him. She never took her eyes from him until she reached the car.

"Bye. Thank you for teaching us how to fish with our poles." Carter said.

"Bye" Olivia said waving at him.

"Bye kids. Be good for your momma." He waved as they headed away. He watched as they loaded up her car and pulled away.

He listened to the producers in his ear but heard nothing they said. He was in a daze smiling. He just met an Angel that he wanted to get to know more. He didn't want Brielle or her kids to leave. He wanted to indulge in their company for a while longer. He felt connected and didn't want that feeling to ever end.

CHAPTER 21
~BRYSON~
THOUGHTS CONTINUE

Bryson could not stop thinking about Brielle. It was hard for him to concentrate on anything else for the rest of the night. He desperately wanted to shower and be more presentable when he saw her again the next day. Maintaining his rough look for now was very important in the role he was playing to disguise his identity. A couple of people that passed him told him he looked like the owner of Cole Enterprises but they didn't think more about his look due to him being homeless.

The producers allowed Bryson to stay in a nearby motel so that he could rest at night. It wasn't the best place to stay but it worked for Bryson considering the circumstance. Kenneth had access to the room and made sure he was well taken care of before he got there. Personal cleaners came to disinfect the room. He had a hot dinner there waiting on him. Kenneth even had a new mattress with new sheets and blankets. He knew it was hard enough for Bryson to be doing this documentary and going through the motions. So when he found out they were allowing him to stay at the motel he took care of him. He even left him a cell phone since they took the other one and a note.

Brys,
Hey man, hang in there you are doing well. Stinking I am sure, but you are doing well. I have been viewing the footage and it is some good stuff. I heard about the girl in the park today. You must fill me in. Call me when you get a moment. I left a cell phone for you in the drawer by the bed. Hope you like all the extras I had done for you. I even had new mattresses put on the bed and all new bedding for you. If you

*are planning to see the girl tomorrow please use the deodorant
I left and air out some of that funk. Dude really, it's been over
a week and I know you have fungus growing by now.
Enjoy.
Your boy Kenny*

Bryson looked under the top that covered his food. Steak,
potatoes, broccoli, rolls, a fruit salad and a bowl of banana pudding.
"My man. You have hooked your boy up for sure." Bryson looked in
the drawer and pulled out the cell phone Kenneth left for him and
dialed his number.

"What's up Brys man?"

"Kenny." He stretched out his name in excitement to hear his
friend's voice.

"How you holding up man? I know it has to be rough out
there."

"I'm holding up ok. Trying to hang in there. I am learning a
lot. Meeting some interesting people. But it is a challenge every
day."

"Yeah I'm sure it is a challenge. I was about to watch today's
footage because I keep hearing about this beautiful lady you met
today. What's up with that? Are you making love connections out
there?"

"So that is what everyone has been talking about huh."
Bryson was smiling from ear to ear eating on some of the fruit from
his plate.

"Yes. They are saying how beautiful she is and how she had
your nose wide open. I heard you could not stop staring at her and for
a moment they thought you two were going to kiss." Kenneth laughed.

"Is that what they are saying? I need to see that clip myself.
When you get it send me a copy of the footage to the phone so I can
watch." Bryson said. He couldn't stop grinning at the thought of his
encounter with Brielle.

"Okay you have not said one word to me about her, what's
up?"

"She is beautiful. I don't understand it myself what was
happening today. From that moment I laid eyes on her my heart
skipped a beat. I zoned out and all I saw was her standing there, well
she was sitting, but I was mesmerized by her smile and her beauty.

My spirit was touched and I had this unexplainable feeling like I was meant to be with her, her Adam you know."

"Dang, it was like that?"

"Yes, Kenny man. It was like that. I have never felt what I felt today ever before in my life. It wasn't a lust thing either. And then she embraced me looking like a fucking bum. Then her daughter told me I stink and that was hilarious."

"She has a daughter?"

"Yes. She has three kids I think. Two girls and a boy. I even helped them fish and they like me too."

"Wow man. So you were at the park like you were a part of her family. That's what they were saying. Did she know you were homeless?"

"Yes. Man I was funky, hell yeah she knew. And she didn't let that or me stinking run her away. Her daughter gave me a bunch of wet wipes and hand sanitizer." Bryson laughed at the thought. "She was so embarrassed but it was okay with me. They were accepting me for who I was and not what I have. I have to find her when I am done with this mission and see if I can make her mine. I really enjoyed her and those beautiful kids. It felt so natural to be there with them."

"Wow. Man you never know. God could have led you here to find her. She could be your soul mate for real."

"Well when you watch the footage let me know what you think afterwards."

"You know I will no doubt."

"Oh yeah, she said she is coming back tomorrow with dinner. Said she's going to cook and feed me." Bryson was smiling really big.

"Get out of here. She told you she was coming back tomorrow with dinner and your ass was stinking and looking like a bum?"

"Yes, she seems to have a big heart man. Not sure if she just feels bad for me or what. She did insinuate that shelters will let you shower even if they don't have a bed for you so I am sure that was a hint to freshen up." Bryson and Kenneth both laughed.

"You think she will show up tomorrow?" Kenneth laughed.

"I hope so man. I really hope so. She is all I have been thinking about since they left the park today. Send me a picture of her as soon as you get the footage before you start watching it. I can't wait to see her pretty angelic face again."

"Yeah you got it bad. You don't even know if she will show up tomorrow or not. I'm watching live taping myself tomorrow if she does. This is getting really good. If you end up making a love connection out of this it will be all worth it."

"That would be good. My only worry is if I am looked at as a liar. Nothing I am saying is or will be the truth about my life. At least certain details about who I really am and what I do for a living."

"If you find someone who loves you having nothing I am sure they will love you still if not more finding out you have so much more."

"Honestly man. I think if a woman was excited about the more part I would question that. That was my issue with Jewel. She loved the money and wasn't just satisfied with me. This girl seems special. So after tomorrow I hope to have enough information to find her again after this documentary is done."

"I feel you bro. But Jewel was a snake. She was so deceiving she could have bitten us all and we wouldn't have seen it coming."

"I'm just glad it was revealed to me before I married her. But meeting Brielle today has made the memories of her start to completely disappear." They both laughed.

"Yeah a new woman will help you forget about the last one." Kenneth was laughing with Bryson. "Man she is beautiful. I just pulled her picture from the footage and sending it to you now. Wow. I see why your nose is wide open over this girl. Stunning."

"I just got it man. Damn she is just as beautiful as I remember. She has that pretty honey smooth skin." Bryson was quiet looking at the picture and Kenneth was quiet watching the footage.

Kenneth broke the silence first. "Man Brys, watching this I see why everyone is talking about you and her. You may not like this but prepare yourself. They may try to push this into a love story. If they are seeing what I'm seeing, I know what they are already thinking."

"What do you mean turn it into a love story?"

"If she shows up tomorrow, then she is either crazy a bit or it's something there between you two that she feels just as much as you do. What I'm looking at is not just a woman being nice. You never know how God works man. Sometimes its situations you would have never expected for a miracle to come out of and it happens. Just like with Ameila. Look at where she was when you appeared and her life has been changed because you were placed right there in front of her. This may be your blessing in disguise. Your answered prayer."

Bryson was deep in thought. He knew that his contract was open to exploring how women would treat him. As much as he wanted to be with Brielle he doesn't want to ruin chances of being with her because of the lies he was living now. "How is Ameila doing man?"

"She's doing very well. You didn't realize that while you were blessing her, but she is becoming a great asset to our company as well. She is very smart and talented. I was talking to her and she is a writer. A damn good writer at that. You have to see when you come back some of the stuff she has done in just the few days she was here in the office helping out."

"You putting her to work in the office? She must be good then if you are putting her to work." Bryson was finishing his food on his plate.

"She is talented with words and has a very creative imagination. She makes you see what she sees in her mind. I gave her a manuscript to read when she asked if I had any work for her to do. I gave her one that was still in review and the next evening she was done. When I looked over her work she was on point with her review. So I brought her in and gave her an assistant job. When you get back man and see her work I was thinking of putting her on payroll permanently but you can make that decision. She's good though. And she writes novels. I haven't seen any of those because she said she had to get them back from her ex or something."

"Yeah she told me about that. I feel good about her. I have a good judge of character about people. How are her children doing?"

"Dr. Zackary had to tend to the baby for a few days but they are all doing great now. You did good helping this family. They are good people."

"Good. Tell her I said hello and I will meet with her about working for us when I get back to the office."

"Sure thing man. Do you need anything else?"

"Naw, I'm good. Thanks for the picture man. You can send me some more if you get them. Oh yeah check on Bradon for me will you."

"We played ball this morning and we missed you. Bradon and Andre tried to gang up on me on the court. Those boys are a fool. Always keeping me entertained."

"Keep the tradition going Kenny. Don't let them slack."

"For sure. Take care of yourself and hide the cell phone you know they don't want you to have it."

"I'm going to keep it on silent. Shoot me a text if you need anything. I will respond when I can."

They ended their conversation and Bryson took off his clothes exposing his bare naked ass and flexed his chest muscles before heading to the showers. The producers decided to allow him to take a shower but he had to use the soap in the motel and he couldn't wash his clothes. They didn't want him to stink too bad if he was to meet Brielle again tomorrow. But they didn't want him to be fresh and clean if she didn't show. The entire production team had bets going if Brielle would show up or not. They were watching the footage and determining what they wanted Bryson to do next on his journey. With the wedding footage and the week long recordings they nearly had enough to shoot a great documentary but Brielle had everyone's attention. She intrigued everyone and kept their interest as to what her next move would be. Bryson wrapped a towel around his waist and laid across the bed on his fresh smelling clean sheets. He wanted to enjoy that moment. Although clean sheets were simple, it's something ordinary people take for granted.

Hearing a knock at the door, Bryson assumed it was the producers. Wrapping the blanket around his now naked body he opened the door. He knew it had to be someone who worked with him because security was all around twenty-four-seven.

"Hey Sweetheart, sorry I mean Brielle, how did you find me?" Bryson said answering the door. He was in shock to see Brielle standing in front of him.

"I followed you here earlier today. I came back to the park looking for you and I saw you leaving. So I followed you. I took the kids to my mom so I could come back here alone. I needed to see you. I hope it's okay, I don't mean to intrude." She was looking down at her hands twiddling her fingers.

"Yeah, that's okay. Come in please. You are not intruding at all. It was a bit shocking as I wasn't expecting anyone. Sorry I'm not dressed. I just got out of the shower. Are you okay?" Bryson didn't want to grab the stinky clothes to put on so he stayed wrapped in the blanket.

"I couldn't stop thinking about you after we left today. I can't explain it but the attraction between us that I feel is exciting and powerful. And now, seeing you here out of those stinky clothes with your chest exposed showing your muscles, what definition. You appear to be so strong." Brielle shook her head to snap back to her reason for coming. "Sorry. Your body is very sexy. Do you work out? I'm sorry, again. I am rambling. I came here because I want you to come stay with me and the kids. I know we just met but I feel a strong connection between us. And...."

"I can't do that. I'm a man who needs to be able to provide for my family and move you and the kids in with me. Your way is backwards for me. I think I fell in love with you today but I can't move in. My father raised me to be a man and to be the provider. Boys shack, men build homes. That's what my father use to say to me." Bryson looked at Brielle with utter amazement in his eyes. She was beautiful to him inside and out.

Brielle looked down at her hands again as if she was just rejected and didn't know what to say or do. At that moment Bryson reached for her and with one hand on her neck he pulled her closer and kissed her. Passionately. Deep throat kissing. Tongues dancing, entangling together, kissing. Hearts pounding, panties getting wet, boxers expanding, kissing. He kissed her long and hard. Bryson forgot all about the blanket wrapped around his waist and it fell from his naked body as both hands were now on Brielle peeling away her clothes.

Brielle was moaning. As Bryson lifted her shirt above her head they immediately wasted no time to lock their lips back together. He moved from her lips to her neck. Biting her gently and hard, making her body tingle and her moans louder. He unfastened her bra and as it fell to the floor he moved backwards to the bed pulling her with him as he kissed her down the nape of her neck stroking her collar bone with his tongue. He moved to her breast flicking his tongue over her erect nipples. One hand was caressing her back as the other was unfastening her pants.

Brielle's moans were increasing and he was making her cum by sucking on her breast. His tongue was flickering fast and his hands touching her skin increased her arousal and she was experiencing her first orgasm with this man. As her pants fell below her waist and her thongs hung at her curves he caressed her butt squeezing as he worked his wet warm mouth back to her neck and back to her lips. He grabbed her by her thighs and with one swift motion Bryson lifted her up to meet his bare skin, turned her around and laid her on the bed. Brielle was experiencing a pleasure she had been yearning for.

Bryson kissed her neck again grabbing her breast in both of his hands. He started to work his way down planting kisses on her stomach. Brielle arched her back enjoying the pleasure. He lifted her legs in the air and buried his head in between her thighs. He inhaled the sweet scent of her flowing honey and licked the opening to savor her juices. He flicked his tongue over her warm opening to indulge in her taste. He worked his way to her clit, driving her crazy with his hands still caressing her thighs and caressing her breast. He sucked and licked and buzzed over her clit until he felt her juices flowing beneath his mouth. He was enjoying every moment making her cum.

He rose up to his knees and watched as her eyes were wide with amazement looking at his rock hard, long and thick erection saluting her with veins bulging and throbbing with an urgency of excitement. He fell gently atop of her, bracing his weight with his arms on the bed, kissing her passionately allowing her to taste the sweetness of her honey from his lips. "I need to make love to your insides right now." Bryson softly whispered in her ear. There was no hesitation from Brielle. He went back to sucking on her neck, caressing her warm body on his way down to her honey pot. Feeling all of her wetness, he guided his hard erection inside her pushing gently deeper and deeper until her body was moving with the sway of his movements.

He pushed in and out at a slow pace until he heard her say, "Give it to me baby, give me all of daddies dick, I can take it." Bryson was surely turned on hearing her demands and he picked up the pace and started stroking her faster. Moving in and out faster he went deeper with every stroke. Brielle held on to his neck and shoulders enjoying every thrust he gave in and out of her pulsating wet honey of loveliness. "Oh daddy, cum with me." He heard her say.

Bryson started moaning and making a weird noise while he was cummin. He heard another slow knock at the door and the handle turning. He jumped a bit. Startled that someone could be coming inside his room to interrupt this wonderful feeling only to realize he was dreaming. He just had a wet dream that included the beautiful Brielle. He heard the knock again and heard security through the door. "Mr. Mathews are you okay?" "Uh yes, I'm good." Not knowing what to say. He had cum all over his stomach and thighs, and all over the towel he had wrapped around his waist before he fell asleep. Then he started smiling, thinking, *Damn she even has an effect on me in my dreams. Only I won't be cummin that fast when I make love to her for the first time. Yeah she does have my nose wide open. I can't wait to see her tomorrow. Huh, I done made love to the woman in my dreams and actually had an orgasm. That's a first for me.*

CHAPTER 22
~BRIELLE~
THOUGHTS REMAIN

Brielle and her children were on their way home from the park and the ride home was all about Bryson, well Matt as they knew him. The kids were concerned that he did not have a place to sleep and no more food to eat. Jayla didn't understand why he had no home and wanted to take him home like a stray puppy. They all took a liking to him and felt safe around him. It was an instant attraction for Brielle and she didn't understand why.

Brielle knew that God would be sending her a man to protect, provide and prosper with her. She knew he would be a spiritual leader as well. The way that Bryson showed leadership in prayer over their meal sent chills through her body. She saw so many qualities in this man within minutes of being around him and talking with him. Surely God would not send her any junk she thought. How could she feel the way she does about a man she just met who appeared to not be what God has in his promises for her? What she imagined did not appear as what she assumed and she hoped that Pastor's sermon was right. All she could think about was not closing her heart to love and not judging him. Maybe he just needs someone to give him a second chance. Maybe she is his second chance. Brielle thought about what her Pastor said about everyone having a story and how God sends you blessings in ways you cannot even imagine. God sets your life up according to His plans. He positions you, allows things to happen so that in the end you can reap the benefits of His blessings.

Brielle was keeping an open mind and an open heart. Her heart was saying yes to allow this man in and she didn't even know him. But she also thought about wanting someone to take care of her for a change instead of always being the one who takes care of others. Although she never complains about being a blessing to others. When you are a blessing to others God is preparing your blessings even greater. Maybe God gave her a caring heart to lead her to this moment in her life.

"Mommy is Mr. Matt going to be okay? Does he have to sleep at the park?" Jayla asked.

"I'm not sure where he sleeps Jayla. He will be okay I am sure. God always takes care of his children and he seems to be a good God fearing man. So don't worry your pretty little self about Mr. Matt baby girl." Brielle surely hoped he would be okay and wondered herself where he sleeps. She had an idea of helping him if he would accept it from her. She knew how men could allow their pride to keep them from accepting help, especially from a woman.

Olivia was quiet for a moment deep in thought before speaking again. "Momma why does he have to fear God? You said God fearing why?"

"That's just a saying that people say sometimes Olivia." Her brother Carter said before his mom had a chance to respond.

"Well actually Carter, people allow fear to hold them back in life. Keep them from moving forward with their dreams, goals, relationships or anything. But when you trust and have your faith in God you don't have to fear anything or anyone but God. So to fear God is to know that God is the only one you have to answer to on judgment day. So they say that to let you know to live your life not in fear of anything but God so that people will live according to how God would want us to live." Brielle thought about her own words to her children. She needs to listen to them herself. She has allowed fear to hold her back from being in a relationship. Bryson has really impacted her life in this short period of time.

The kids were in the back seat chatting away. Brielle was thinking about helping Bryson and thought about allowing him to stay in her new home until her lease was up where she was currently living. She would know for sure after their dinner tomorrow her decision to help. She needed to sleep on it and pray about it.

When she stopped at the light she heard her phone ringing so Brielle reached over to answer. "Hello."

"Hey Brie." Her mom said.

"Hi Momma. Kids it's your granny."

"Hey granny." The kids yelled in unison.

"Tell my grand babies I said hello."

"Your granny said hello kids."

"What are you and the kids doing?"

"Oh nothing Ma, on our way home from the park."

"Oh that sounds like fun. Did the kids make their fishing poles again attempting to fish?"

"Of course mom. But this time there was a nice man there at the park that helped them make their fishing poles a little better. And he showed them how to catch a fish. Carter actually caught a fish."

"Wow that is awesome."

"They threw it back in the water because it was a baby but they were thrilled to have actually caught a fish."

"So this man, who was he?" Her curiosity was getting to her and the excitement that her daughter was actually allowing a man to come around her and the kids was showing in her tone.

"His name is Matt. We invited him to eat lunch with us after some people there at the park were being very mean to him." Whispering in the phone so the kids couldn't hear, "Mom I think he was homeless. But his spirit was pure and genuine. A very handsome man too mom, just down on his luck I guess. He said the economy caused his downfall."

"Well that don't mean he is a bad person though. If you were talking to him and say that his spirit was pure and genuine and you allowed him around you and my grand babies then he must be a good man. You know I can't say anything bad about anyone. You just have to trust your gut feeling at all times. I am excited because you were actually talking to a man. That's very hopeful." Brielle's mom was so excited and smiling that she even chuckled a bit.

"I know right. He even volunteered to pray over our lunch mom. I am trying to think of a way I can help him. Give him a second chance."

"Oh that would be good. I will look into a few things as well then for you. That's a good sign in a man who takes leadership and prays. I like this man already and don't even know him."

Brielle and her mom talked until she pulled up at her home. Jayla had fallen asleep in the car so she knew she would have to pick her up and carry her inside. She ended the phone call with her mom and gathered the children to go in the house. Once they were all in,

Brielle laid her baby girl in her bed to finish her nap. The other two kids went straight to watching TV and Brielle headed to unpack the picnic basket. She smiled really big pulling out the Cheetos to put them away, remembering Bryson. All she could do was think about him. She has never thought about a man this much before. She didn't know what it meant but she did know that she wanted and intended to see him again. She started making her grocery list for items to purchase for Sunday's dinner. She was excited and filled with butterflies anticipating her Sunday to be spent with Bryson. She sat there at her dining table with her elbows on the table and her hand resting under her chin in a daze.

It's something about his eyes that speak to my soul. I can't wait to see him tomorrow. I just wanted to kiss his juicy sexy lips. The way he took control and prayed for our family was amazing to me. What if he is just down on his luck and need a helping hand. The way he said he was brought up sounds like he understands what it means to be the man of the house. If he believes in God and prays freely like he did today surely he is a God fearing man who lives by the word. I need to talk to him more tomorrow about his story. Yeah that's what we will talk about our stories, well maybe hopefully not mine. Tomorrow can surely come a little bit faster. I don't know what this means but I am all smiles and I like it.

Brielle finished her list and got up to join her children in front of the TV before they went to the store. Family time was very important to her. She prayed that one day she could add her soul mate to complete her picture perfect family.

CHAPTER 23
~BRYSON~
I MET A GIRL

Kenneth called Bryson early the next morning before the producers were there to pick him up to start his day.

"Hello." Bryson said in a groggy sleepy voice.

"Okay, now this I am not use to. Me calling you and you're still asleep." Kenneth said.

"What time is it man?" He said reaching for the bedside clock.

"It's actually four thirty in the morning. Filling your shoes requires an early start." Kenneth chuckled a bit. "Naw, really man I have actually been up all night working at the office. I been watching the footage from this past week and I must say this is good stuff. It's going to be hard trying to keep your cover and be around this girl. I already know how you are."

"Yeah I will be okay. I wouldn't know how to explain what I am doing any how and expect her to see me in a different light. She would probably think I was schizophrenic or something. I can't believe I actually met a girl I feel so strongly about."

"Well I heard the producer say this could be a love story so this could be good in a way. Depending on what happens today. They could take the footage from the wedding and this could be your happy ever after." Kenneth was hoping that Bryson would have an out to his adventure if Brielle ended up being his angel in disguise. He thought he could woo her and end his contractual obligations at the same time still giving the producers a great story.

"Oh yeah I didn't think about that. We will see what happens today and maybe we could offer them that scenario. I thought about that girl all night man, even in my dreams. I surely hope she comes back today."

"You know I was laughing so hard when she was insinuating you stink without actually saying it. And then baby girl giving you all the wet wipes. That was funny as hell." Kenneth laughed out loud.

"Yeah get it all out now man." He listened as Kenneth laughed. "I took a shower when I got here but I have to put those funky clothes back on. You know how disgusting that is going to be for me?"

"Well I put some clean under clothes in the drawer in your room just in case you could use them."

"That's what's up." Bryson said jumping up from the bed to open the drawer. "I am so thankful for the little things in life." He said picking up the under clothes and kissing them. He looked at the size. "They are a size too small but shit I'm about to make this work. I can cut them a bit and they will be fine." He mumbled to himself. "Thanks Kenny man for looking out for your boy."

"No doubt. I looked your girl up online to try to see if I could figure out who she is. I found a Brielle Summers that looks very much like her but I am not one hundred percent sure it is her. There was a news article about her a little while back."

"Oh yeah? You found a picture?"

"Yes, but her hair was completely different and much longer."

"Okay well what did the article say?"

"Again, I am not sure if this is her or not but this girl was in an abusive relationship where the man almost killed her and he beat his own son pretty bad as well because he tried to save his mother from his own dad. Apparently a neighbor heard the chaos and called the cops who got there just in time to save them. The neighbor said she heard him abusing her all the time and that particular day it sounded worse than any other so she called the cops."

"Dang that's messed up. So did it say what happened to him?" Bryson said with rage coming over him. He despised men who felt a need to hit a woman or a child. His thoughts went straight to wanting to protect Brielle and her kids.

"Yes it does. I sent the article to your phone and you can compare the picture yourself."

"That may explain why her and the kids were hesitant a bit when I approached. I hope this is not the same person. She seems to be a free spirited wonderful young lady and a great mother to have deserved anything like that."

"Well I hope she shows today man. The two of you looked to have been in love from yesterday's footage. Oh yeah and really man? You choked on some hot Cheetos?" Laughing out loud a bit before he continued to speak. "That was funny. I spit my drink out and then when the duck ate one I almost fell out of my seat laughing."

"Yeah that was funny. I didn't expect to eat something hot at that moment. The duck stole the show and kept the attention from me being embarrassed. I was really choking." Bryson chuckled.

"Well let me know if you need anything. I will be watching today. I think we all are anxious to see if she shows up and how this day will go."

"I know, not as anxious as I am though. But thanks again man. I will talk to you a little later. Now that I am awake I will lay here for about another hour daydreaming about the famous Brielle." Bryson smiled and placed one arm behind his head while holding the phone with his other hand up to his ear. Stretched out in the bed with his chest exposed he looks at the ceiling thinking about Brielle.

"You do that and I will be watching and praying she is there. I'm just a phone call away if you need anything Brys."

"Alright Kenny man Thanks! I really hope she shows up." Bryson said with a smile.

"Anytime Brys. I'm sure she will show."

"I can't wait. I will talk to you later today. Send me footage of anything good with her in it after you watch today." Bryson said.

"I gotcha bro. I will talk with you later man." Kenny said before hanging up to get him some much needed sleep.

"Later Kenny." Bryson hung up the phone and before placing it on the table he viewed the picture of Brielle. It was her he was sure. Now he knew a bit more about her and had a picture to view when he wanted to see her pretty face beyond his memory. With both hands now behind his head he grins and closes his eyes. He drifts back to sleep for another hour before starting his day.

CHAPTER 24
~BRIELLE~
TWICE IS A GOOD SIGN

Sunday morning and Brielle woke up smiling. Her dreams were consumed with Bryson. He was stirring up emotions in her that she has never before felt. Her hormones were wide awake after the erotic dream of excitement she just had. It felt so real. She realized her panties were soaked of her sweet honey. As long as it has been since a man has touched her intimately, she knew something had to be done before she saw Bryson today. She wanted to act out every naughty intimate moment from her dream, scene by scene. But she knew that could not happen. She was a good girl saving the naughty girl for the man she would spend the rest of her life with.

Brielle went deep into her closet looking for her stash pillow. The pillow with the secret compartment filled with goodies that vibrate, move and stay hard. She opted for her water proof bullet and decided to please herself with a nice long clitoral tease and an enjoyable orgasm. She found her bullet and quickly put the bag and the rest of its secrets away. Turning it on the batteries were dead and she panicked. No woman wants to be horny and have dead batteries. She found some fresh batteries in her top drawer of her bedroom dresser and headed towards the bathroom.

"Please work." She said aloud as she put the batteries in the bullet. When she turned it on the bullet was fully powered and the vibration was fast and powerful. "Oh yes, we are in business now."

Brielle turned the shower on steaming hot and removed her thigh length night gown. She caressed her breast and ran the bullet over her fully erect nipples. The vibration sent a pleasurable sensation from her nipples all the way through to her orgasmic loveliness between her thighs. She stepped in to the shower and allowed the water to caress her caramel skin. Her thoughts immediately went to Bryson and the sexual desires she could not deny she had for him. She moved the bullet to her pulsating clit and massaged it with the vibrating bullet. With one hand holding the bullet in place she used the other to caress her breast. Grabbing them both going back and forth to each nipple pinching, squeezing and running the tips of her fingers over them in a fast paced motion. Brielle was in pure bliss.

The warm water was feeling good over her body. Light moans were being released as she started to pant at the onset of her orgasm. She held the bullet steady on her clit and used two of her fingers to move in and out of her honey pot hitting her g-spot. She gently bit down on her bottom lip. Squeezed roughly at her breast. Pressed the bullet hard to her clit. More light moans. Her body started to tense up and her breathing was now heavy. At the release of her orgasm she held her breathe and the pulsation was rapid. She was experiencing pure ecstasy at the mercy of her own hands. Sweet honey cum squirted from her loveliness, streaming down her legs. She had to compose herself realizing she missed the pleasurable feelings. She wasn't sure if this temporary relief made her desire Bryson more than before or if it really would calm her burning fire until the time was right. In her mind that time would be after she would say I do.

When she was done with her orgasm she leaned up against the shower wall for a few moments to exhale. She then grabbed her sponge soaped it up and wiped away the honey. Brielle felt renewed and sexually alive at that moment. She allowed the warm water to continue to caress her skin and mellow out the moment. She was relaxed and stress free and was ready to handle what the day threw at her, even if that meant fantasizing and wanting Bryson more. She finished her shower and put away her toys before waking the kids. It was time for them to get ready and head to church.

Church was good as always and Pastor Malone was on point with his message. "Receiving God's Blessings" was the sermon topic. She was starting to realize that Bryson could very well be her blessing. Before the message was over she had accepted just that and decided she would embrace him during their meeting for dinner that day. She said her silent prayer to God. *Dear Heavenly Father. You know my hearts desires and you know my thoughts and actions before they even happen. God I know that all things happen according to your Will and Lord I thank you for directing my path and guiding me along the way. Lord you know my venture for today and Lord if this man is not intended to be a blessing to me and my children then please allow your interventions to happen and give me the knowledge I need and the strength to walk away from this situation. But Lord, if you have intended for this man to be a part of my life for any reason or any season to be a blessing or part of a blessing according to your Will Lord then please let your Will be done. I thank you for your many blessings and the favor you give, I love you Lord. I have faith, believe and trust in you Lord and all that you have planned for my life. Thank you, in your son Jesus name I pray Heavenly Father, Amen.*

After church, Brielle and the kids were excited to get home and prepare dinner so they could go to the park to meet Bryson. She knew that she would be disappointed if he didn't show but she hoped for the kids' sake he would show so they would not be disappointed. She did not date nor has she had a man around her children since their dad so she didn't know what to expect. Bryson just kind of happened and quickly became a part of what her and her kids talked and thought about. He became a part of her family instantly and he didn't even know.

"Mommy, are we on our way home now to cook dinner? I can't wait to go to the park to see Mr. Matt today." Jayla said to her mother.

"Oh yeah, well we are headed home now to cook some lasagna and make salad. You think he will like that Jay-Jay?" Brielle asked.

"Mommy I think he will love anything that you cook. You are a great cook and we are always happy so I know Mr. Matt will be happy." Jayla said.

"Mommy's little angel is so sweet to me. Thank you baby girl." Brielle picked up Jayla and gave her a big hug. She said her goodbyes to her church family as they walked to the car to leave.

Brielle worked fast preparing the final touches for her meal. She was overcome with butterfly sensations, anxious to get to the park.

"Kids, are you ready? I need some help with the picnic basket." She yelled for the kids to come.

"Coming momma." Olivia said skipping into the kitchen. "Is our brownies ready we made for Mr. Matt?" The kids were so excited and they wanted to make something for him as well. Brownies were easy, quick and a lot of fun to make together.

"I took them out already. They are on the counter and should be cool by now. Get your brother to help and you both can cut them and put them in sandwich bags."

"Carter, come help me." Olivia said out loud.

"I'm right here sis. Ohh the brownies done!" Carter said heading straight for the brownies.

"Carter. Don't eat the brownies. Help your sister cut them and put them in bags. You can have as many as you like after dinner." Brielle knew her son loved sweets.

"Ok mom." Carter said with a smile. He grabbed a butter knife and started to cut the brownies into perfect squares.

"Momma I think Carter can't help it and he is going to eat some brownies cause he smiling and you know he loooves brownies momma." Jayla said when she came into the room.

"Where have you been lil momma?" Brielle said turning to Jayla giving her a kiss on her forehead.

"I made Mr. Matt a card. Olivia and Carter helped me. I had to finish coloring the pictures."

"Well that was very sweet of you all. I bet he will be surprised and happy." Brielle started packing the basket with Jayla's help.

Once they had everything together in a basket they loaded the car and were ready to head out to the park to meet Bryson, well Matt as they knew him.

Brielle had butterflies in her stomach thinking about seeing Bryson. She wondered what if he wasn't there or if he didn't like her cooking. She didn't want to have her hopes up but this man gave her hope. Hope is what she needed. Her faith in God to bring her a man made in his image of what a man should be gave her the hope she needed. She wasn't for sure of her purpose in meeting Bryson. She wondered if she was intended to bless him by helping him get on his feet or if God had a plan for her and him.

Brielle said a silent prayer before arriving at the park. She wanted to make sure God was involved in any decision she made. She knew she wanted to try and help him but didn't know what that help included just yet. Once at the park she said to herself in a whisper, "Brielle just take it step by step and let the conversation flow."

"Alright kids we are here, let's gather up everything and find us a spot in our normal area." Brielle had turned around talking to the kids in the back seat. Jayla had fallen asleep holding the card she made tightly in her arms. "Jayla we are here baby girl wake up."

Jayla wiped her eyes, stretched out long still holding on to the card then jumped up ready to get out of the car. "Momma where is Mr. Matt? Do you see him yet? Is he here waiting on us? You see him momma?" She was sleep one moment and the next full of energy and excitement.

Brielle's heart melted. She hoped he was there if for nothing else to see her baby happy. She didn't like for her children to feel any disappointment. As she was gathering stuff out of the car she heard Jayla giggling. Bryson had walked up behind them and signaled for the children to be quiet. "What's so funny Jay-Jay, huh?"

"Momma your panties are showing and I can't tell you the rest." She giggled some more. Carter and Olivia started giggling as well and that signaled Brielle to look up.

Her heart was beating fast and the butterfly feelings were now taking over her entire body. "Matt, hi. I didn't know you were standing there." She said as she stood up out of the car smoothing her hair behind her ear. "How are you?"

"Just fine now that I see you and the beautiful trio here."

"What's a trio? Does that mean three?" Jayla said.

"Jayla, the beautiful trio is you, your sister and brother." Bryson said looking down at Jayla smiling up at him. Her smile was priceless to him and reminded him of the family that he dreamed of having.

Seeing Jayla happy made Brielle happy and seeing Bryson standing in front of her made her very happy as well. "I was just getting the picnic basket and things out of the car." She said with a smile on her face.

"I saw you pull up and thought I would come up to see if you needed help with anything. I have been anticipating you all coming today since you left. Was kind of watching for you. I hope that doesn't sound stalkerish. I was just really happy when I saw you pull up."

"Is that right?" Brielle said trying not to blush but it was too late. Her face lit up giving Bryson the satisfaction of knowing she was happy to see him as well.

"Yes that's right." Bryson said with a smile on his face. "Can I carry anything for you?"

"Oh yeah thank you." Brielle said. She turned to get the basket from the car and noticed the kids watching her and Bryson interact with smiles on their face. "You can carry the basket it is a bit heavy but be careful not to tilt it."

"Yes ma'am." He said taking the basket from her hands. She gave the kids each an item to carry and she grabbed the blankets. After securing her car, they all walked to the same area where they were before.

Brielle spread the blankets on the ground and they all placed the items on the blanket leaving room to sit. "Kids lets go ahead and eat before you play while it's still warm okay."

"Yes ma'am." They all said in unison.

"Wow that looks great. Did you cook this lasagna Olivia?" Bryson looked over at her smiling. He knew she didn't make it but wanted to interact with the children as well.

"No my momma made it." She said with a smile on her face.

"Well it sure does look good. She must be a great cook. Is Lasagna your favorite Carter?"

"Yes sir. My mom makes the best lasagna in the entire world. She is an awesome cook." Carter said with a smirk on his face. He had a feeling of being respected and cared for by a man that he barely knew but he could definitely tell he was in the presence of a real man.

"I will bless the food today if that's okay with you Brielle." Bryson spoke to Brielle never taking his eyes from hers. He admired how beautiful she was. And seeing her smile made him smile and feel warm inside.

"But of course Matt, please lead us in prayer. We would love that." Brielle reached her hand out to him and he grabbed it gently holding on tight. She was enjoying the warmth and softness of his hand. She reached for the kids and they all joined hands as Bryson blessed the food, leading them in prayer.

As Bryson was blessing the food, Brielle said her own quiet prayer. Silently she asked God to reveal to her what her purpose was with Bryson. Her holding his hand was sending chills through her body and tingling sensations through her middle loveliness causing her heart to beat fast.

"Amen." Bryson said, followed by everyone else saying amen as well.

"We made you something Mr. Matt. Here you go." Jayla said handing Bryson the card. "We made it together just for you. Hope you like it."

Bryson was touched. He read the card and a tear came to his eyes. He wanted children around him to give him father's day cards, birthday cards and just because cards. "Thanks kids. This was very sweet and I love the card. I will cherish this forever." He sat there for a moment still reading the card before looking back up.

Brielle passed the sanitizer around and Olivia passed out the plates to everyone. Brielle served everyone lasagna and they helped themselves to the salad and garlic bread. Once their plates were made it was silent for a moment as everyone was enjoying their meal.

"How is it Matt?" Brielle said in between bits.

"Fantastic! This is the best lasagna I have ever had. And lasagna is my favorite. I would never tell my mom but it's even better than hers."

Brielle chuckled a bit. "Well good I'm glad you like it. Please have as much as you want Matt. There is plenty."

"Thank you, you all are too kind to me. I am glad you came back today. That makes me feel special." He said looking at them all before resting his eyes back on Brielle. He was mesmerized by her and the selfless acts of kindness touched his heart.

"The kids worked on your card by themselves. You really left an impression on them. They couldn't stop talking about you." Brielle said engaging in conversation. The kids were talking about catching fish and Brielle seized the opportunity to have one on one conversation with Bryson to get to know a bit more about him.

"Wow. Really?" He looked at Brielle nodding yes as he smiled. "They are some wonderful kids. I have grown quite fond of them since our fishing bonding moments." He said with a smile.

"I simply adore them. I always wanted a big family. Lots of kids. I ended up with three beautiful blessings. They are everything to me and more." She paused for a second thinking to herself. "So Matt, do you have kids or want kids?"

"No kids but I would love to have a house full running around some day. Children are a blessing and have their own unique personality that adds character to any home."

"Matt what is your story? I mean everyone has a story. And you seem to be a nice guy who may have fallen on bad times but I can only guess at your story. Do you mind sharing with me a little bit about who you are, your life story?" Brielle didn't know if she was asking too much of him or not but she did know she wanted to know more about who he was and why.

Bryson looked down at his plate knowing that he had to be careful of what he said and at the same time not blow his cover. He didn't want to lie but he didn't want to lose Brielle. He thought that this was an opportunity to see if Brielle would still like him for who he was as a man. "Wow, okay. I never had anyone to ask me about my story before."

"If it's too personal you don't have to share. I just wanted to know a little bit more about the man me and the kids talked about up until now. I must say you captured a piece of our hearts." Brielle said with a warm smile.

Bryson wanted to surrender to her and tell her everything at that moment. He was falling for this girl and her children. His heart was racing with excitement that started within his spirit. He was still getting over Jewel but Brielle was making him forget that she even existed. "I'm flattered Brielle. I don't mind sharing at all. I have my parents and a brother here. They don't know about any of this or they would try to come for me. I don't ever want to be a burden to anyone and I don't want my parents to know I have fallen to this point. They raised their boys to be providers, to be strong willed and to always protect the people around them, who depend on them and especially women and children. They raised us to be go getters, to put God first and family second and then career. My brother is still finding his way but he tries really hard. I lost some things in my life and I guess I let it get me down a bit and that's how I ended up here. My reason for fighting left me until now." Looking up at Brielle he smiled.

"Why now? What's different now?

"Seeing you and these kids reminded me of the family that I desire to have and I know God is going to bless me with. I just need to get back on my feet and be the man God intended for me to be so I can have that family I want. Your kids are wonderful, you should be proud." They both turned looking in the kid's direction. They were done eating and up playing by the water. This was a good distraction for Bryson. He wanted to reach for Brielle's lips and indulge in the sweetness of her kisses. He knew he needed to change the subject quickly. His nature was rising and he had to calm down.

"I am very proud of them. They are my reasoning for everything I do in life. They are my motivation and my inspiration to never fail."

"So what is your story Brielle? That is if you don't mind sharing with me." He asked knowing more about her then she was probably ready to share.

"Oh no, I don't mind. I actually never talk about my story. My Pastor just gave a sermon about sharing our stories. It actually got me to thinking about mine and what I would say."

"So you attend church?"

"Yes, the kids and I attend every Sunday and sometimes on Wednesday's for bible study. My mom instilled that in me and my brother growing up."

"What else you want to share? Is the kids father still around?" Bryson knew that he was reaching here and she would either feel comfortable enough with him to talk about it or will shy away from him and quickly change the subject. He was taking a chance.

"Well, actually he's not. I was in a 'not so healthy' relationship with him. He left some unpleasant memories for me and the kids. As of now, he is in jail and we don't see him or talk to him at all. I pray for us every day for peace about what happened during that relationship. He was very abusive. But me and the children have moved on from it and have tried to rebuild our lives to overcome that experience. I work every day and come home and be mommy to my kids. I enjoy being a mother. I have my parents and my brother. We have a tight loving family."

"You have a strong loving spirit Brielle. I don't see how any man couldn't and wouldn't love you for that. He wasn't a man to have abused such a delicate beautiful creation from God. Women are a reflection of who we are as a man and are intended to be treated like a queen." He said as he looked her in the eyes. Still his mind was taking him to places of him kissing her. He wanted to embrace her at that very moment, protect her and make her a part of his life.

He couldn't stop staring at her and Brielle was blushing uncontrollable. "Thanks Matt. It is very easy talking to you."

They talked more about their families and passions in life, enjoying each other's company. Bryson ate more lasagna before going to help the kids with their fishing poles again. This time Brielle joined them and Bryson helped her with baiting her own fishing pole hook. They were enjoying family time and Bryson fit right in as if he was right where he belonged. Time was passing and before they knew it the sun had gone down and night was setting in. Saying good bye to Bryson was hard for her and the kids. Brielle told him she would be back soon. That made Bryson happy and the kids were also excited. He walked them to the car and helped load the picnic basket. Bryson wanted to ask for her number but knew the position he was portraying to be in and didn't think it would be appropriate. He was happy that she was willing to come back in spite of him appearing to have nothing to offer her.

"You take care of yourself and those kids Brielle. And thanks again for dinner. Everything was amazing."

"Thank you. I am glad you enjoyed dinner. I will be back to see you soon, Saturday afternoon maybe."

"Saturday sound good to me." Bryson said with a smile. He wanted it to be sooner but would be patiently waiting.

"Take care of yourself Matt."

Getting into her car, Bryson closed Brielle's door before saying their final good-byes. Departing ways seemed weird for the both of them. The chemistry was obviously there. Neither of them spoke about the strong feelings they were having but they both knew they existed.

Brielle drove away thinking about how she could help him have a second chance in life, at the same time have him be a part of their life. Even if only as friends.

CHAPTER 25
~BRADON~
NEW LOVE

Bradon talks of his new love with Chantae while playing ball with his friend. He tells Andre about finding an amazing girl.

"I met this girl that I been kickin it with right."

"That you been smashin or like actually dating and going out?" Andre said cutting Bradon off.

"Both." Bradon said with a smile.

"What for real? You smashin and dating her? She must have some good..." Andre started to say before Bradon cut him off.

"Andre listen man, seriously. I never thought I would meet someone who meant so much to me. Someone that I could possibly spend the rest of my life with. She is amazing. I love everything about her. But I'm scared." He paused for a moment thinking about Chantae.

"What are you afraid of, love?"

"I wouldn't say that I am afraid of love but more so of her finding out that Bryson's house and life is not mine and possibly losing her."

"So she a gold digger?"

"Naw, its nothing like that. She sweet and down to earth and has a great personality."

"So she not a gold digger but you scared to tell her about material things not being yours?" Andre sarcastically said.

"You got jokes I see."

"Naw no jokes man. I just don't think you should be scared to tell no girl who you like that some things are not yours. Might as well get that out up front with no expectations. That way if they are there for you it's all good. If it's for the materials then get what you want and then you keep it moving. You feel me?"

"Yeah I feel you and I live by that as well but this girl is different and she special. The night we met I took her home with me against her will because I got her wasted and the chemistry between us was unexplainable. I didn't want to smash her I wanted to make love to her. I mean she said all the right things, she made me laugh and I actually fell for her and not just her sexy ass body."

"Are you going through a young midlife crisis Bradon? Cause you talking like you in love or done lost your damn mind. And when did you start talking about women like this Mr. Casanova?"

"When I met Chantae. You remember the girl I was talking to the night we went out with Kenny?"

"Yeah, is that who you are in love with? She was beautiful."

"Yeah that's Chantae."

"Aight so what you afraid of?"

"I never told her the place and things were Bryson's and I led her to believe that was my place. I plan to tell her the truth soon but if she walks away from me then I don't want to feel rejected. I don't want karma to come back on me you know."

"I feel you. I got it now"

"Although she has never said anything about any of the things, I know that because I presented it that her mind has already ran through scenarios of us being together and being in that house. She probably told her friends more. So I'm going to tell her after the party."

"You having a party? At Bryson's house?"

"Yes I just decided we are going to throw a party so call every one you can think of that should be there."

The guys played ball for a little while longer before calling it quits. Andre knew his friend was feeling some type of way about Chantae and he didn't want to discourage him with some of the advice he normal throws at him. So instead he kept his comments to his self and his opinions to a minimum.

"So what day we having this party?"

"This weekend sounds good to me. You think you can get a good crowd there?"

"Yes I think so. I have a lot of hotties that would cancel their plans if I said so just to come hang out with your boy. And my home boys will surely come through. Wouldn't miss a chance to party at Bryson's house."

"Aight cool. I'm going to call Yvette the event planner so she can pull her strings to get everything we need. You got the DJ right?"

"Yeah I am sure that money will talk and we will have the DJ we want. It's all good we got this. Friday night right? Cause you know how your brother is about partying and getting up the next day for church."

"Yeah Friday. He's not there so I am sure either day would be good. Bryson is working on some big project so we good. That's why Chantae think the place is mine. We have been there as if it was my place and no one else lives there except for the maid."

"Well is she coming to the party?

"Of course she is coming to the party. I will be sure to tell her about the party. Hopefully she will invite her beautiful friends."

"Okay, so this will be a true test for you and her. All those big booty half naked girls prancing around. If you get through the party still wanting only her then I will believe you and your feelings."

"I got this man. We are going to celebrate me hanging up my player card." Bradon laughed. Just hearing this didn't sound right but he knew he was falling hard for Chantae. She was everything he wanted in a woman.

Andre started choking on his spit when he heard Bradon say those words. Knowing his best friend since they were kids, this was something that Bradon never spoke of. "Man you made me choke. Did I just hear you right? Hang up your player card? You, Bradon Mathews?"

"Yeap. It didn't sound right with me saying this either but I think I have fallen in love with this girl. I think I fell in love with her the night I met her and now about two months later I am still feeling this way." Bradon was sprung. And he knew this was love without a doubt.

"Wow! Bradon said he was in love with someone other than himself. That's deep man. Am I being punked? Is there a camera somewhere?" Andre said looking around.

"I'm serious man."

"And the scary part is I believe you. I believe you are in love with this girl. Now I see why you are afraid to tell her. You are afraid of losing her because you love her."

"Yeah man. That's it. I am afraid to lose her because I love her."

"Aight. You have my support man. Now let's plan this party cause look like I am going to get first choice of all the ladies."

They both chuckled. They chatted a few moments more before ending their game and parting ways.

CHAPTER 26
~CHANTAE~
PARTE'

Chantae was hard at work when she received a text from Bradon. She was all smiles as she finished her task so she can check her phone. Typically she would stop immediately but she was working on time sensitive material and had to complete by her deadline approaching. She pulled her phone out with a big smile upon her face.

> *10:33 am*
> *Bradon Mathews Cutie Pie*
> *Hey beautiful I am planning a party at the house this Friday night so tell all your home girls to come out with you to kick it okay. Starting at 10pm but you have an open invitation no time limits. Can't wait to see you.*

She quickly responded to his earlier text.

> *10:58 am*
> *Miss Curvatious Chantae*
> *Hey baby I have been so busy today at work. I miss you. I'm about to tell all my girls about the party, you know I have to be the prettiest representing you boo. Muah!*
> *#ThickCurvatiousSuccessfulDiva*

> *10:59 am*
> *Bradon Mathews Cutie Pie*
> *Babe you will be I will make sure of that okay. Don't worry about that part at all. You will have my black card to shop*

and get what you like. I got you. Catching that sweet kiss and sending you one back. Muah!

10:59 am
Miss Curvatious Chantae
Okay baby. Black card wow! Thanks babe! Not worried I know you got me! I can't wait to see you today!
#ThickCurvatiousSuccessfulDiva

I am about to send out my invites to some of my hotties that need to be there. She thought to herself. When Chantae received a text message for the party she was excited to finally get her girls together so they could see the big mansion where her new man lived. It was a reflection of the type of lifestyle she was about to move up too. She started sending out text messages to all her friends she wanted to be there. She made sure to send a special note to her best friend Brielle to make sure she was going. Brielle didn't sit next to her anymore since her promotion that landed her in an office space.

10:35 am
Sharla, Mystic, Breanne, Natalie, Big Booty Cynthia, Shondra, Mary Ella, Nina, Candice, Cuz, Brielle...
Hey girlfriends, clear your schedules for Friday night we are going to a party at the Mansion of my new boyfriend. You do not want to miss this party. You might find you a keeper. Dress to impress and I will send you the address soon. Let me know if you are going.
#ThickCurvatiousSuccessfulDiva

She loved to be surrounded with pretty successful women, especially women who inspired her to want more from life. And her friends were just that, pretty and successful. "Now to send Brielle a personal e-mail. My best home girl has to be there." She said in a whisper at her desk.

To Brielle
From Chantae
Subject: Private Affairs

Brie you got to go to this party with me Bradon is having at his place Friday night. Please say your parents can watch the kids and you will go with me. I need you there with me okay girl! We have to dress to impress. I will help you find something but please say you will be there with me.

Chantae Reid
Sr. Financial Analyst
Desk: 615.444.7723/ EFax: 615.444.2369

Chantae was playing over in her mind what will be the perfect outfit to wear. She knew it would be a lot of beautiful bodacious women there so she had to make sure her man looked better than any other man did with her on his arm. She wanted to excite him as well in hopes of having a freaky fantastic ending to their night. She checked her computer to see a response back from Brielle. Hoping she would say she would go.

To Chantae
From Brielle
Subject: Private Affairs

Hey girl, I haven't been out with you in a while and I would love to see the mansion so count me in. I may have to come shop in your closet to see if you have a shirt or dress for me to wear. You know you have way more bottom assets but surely you have a top. I may not have time to go out shopping before Friday. I close on my house this week and will be putting time and energy into that. Looking forward to the party. :)

Brielle Summers
Financial Assessment Manager
Desk: 615.444.7723/ EFax: 615.444.2369

Chantae was excited and since Bradon was giving her his Black Card and told her to buy what she wanted. She thought she would do Brielle one better and find her something to wear when she looked for herself. She even thought about designing their outfits.

To Brielle
From Chantae
Subject: Private Affairs

I am too excited about your new home. I know you and the
kids are too. Don't worry about something to wear I got you
girl. I can't have you going with me looking all business
casual. Lol. Although you be cute and can't no body touch
your business and casual look, I will take over your partying
look. And don't worry it will be tasteful. I know you won't
wear it if it's not.

Chantae Reid
Sr. Financial Analyst
Desk: 615.444.7723/ EFax: 615.444.2369

Chantae knew that Brielle would be hesitant about her picking
out clothes for her. But Chantae had been working with a new stylist
who was teaching her how to have an eye for all types of style and to
dress anyone with class and style to fit their taste. This would be one
of her first challenges.

To Chantae
From Brielle
Subject: Private Affairs

Okay Bestie, I will let you do what you do best and give it a
shot to dress me. You already know what I won't wear so have
at it. I can meet you at your house around 7pm on Friday. Do
your thang girlfriend and make me beautiful. You can even do
my makeup and hair for me.

Brielle Summers
Financial Assessment Manager
Desk: 615.444.7723/ EFax: 615.444.2369

To Brielle
From Chantae

Subject: Private Affairs

You know I got you girl! I am excited that you are going with me! Yay!!!

Chantae Reid
Sr. Financial Analyst
Desk: 615.444.7723/ EFax: 615.444.2369

So Friday was planned and even if none of her other divas showed up she would have her best friend Brielle with her and that is what mattered the most.

CHAPTER 27
~BRYSON~
WHO IS SHE

Bryson wants to know who this girl is beyond the park visits. He wants to see more of her. But how can he do this without blowing his cover on his mission. "Why did I agree to a contract?" He said out loud to his self. Bryson was in the room he stayed in until morning and couldn't help but to wonder about Brielle. He decided to look her up on line to see if he could find out more about her.

"Let's see if she is on Facebook. Brielle Summers." He said as he was typing her name. He accessed his company site Facebook page to search for her but he couldn't find a Brielle Summers that looked familiar to his Brielle. "Hmmm, maybe she is not on Facebook. I got something better." He opened his cell phone back up and proceeded to call his assistant

"Hey Jackie, I know it's late to be calling you at home but I need a favor."

"Hey Mr. Mathews. It's not a problem at all. I have been missing you at the office what you need?"

"I will be back shortly but right now I need Mr. Maxx number, Roger Maxx. Can you access my contacts from home?"

"Sure I can, hold on for a second okay. Let me boot up the computer."

"Okay no problem." He sat there waiting for his assistant to come back on the phone. He decided to put her on speaker phone and do some pushups while he waits for her to return.

"I just about have it sir. Sorry it's taking so long I had to get my cake out of the oven."

"I'm asking a favor of you off the clock Mrs. Jackie so I can wait. Not a problem." He said coming up from a pushup. He got in about twenty more before she was ready to give him the number.

"Okay you ready sir?"

"Yes, I'm ready Jackie?" He wrote the number down as she spoke. "Thanks Jackie, I appreciate you as always." He said.

After ending the call he called Roger. He got his voicemail and decides to leave him a message. "Roger my man, I have another job for you. Her name is Brielle Summers, I will text you details. You won't be able to contact me but I will call you next week to get the information from you. Kenny will have your money so just go by the office. I will leave instructions for him to meet with you. And thanks again man." He left Roger a message and called Kenny to let him know details.

"Hey Brys."

"Hey Kenny everything good?"

"Yeah man I'm keeping everything together over here. Are you good?"

"Yeah man I wanted to let you know Roger will be coming by to see you. I have him working on something for me and I need you to pay him. Same as always."

"Okay I got you. Consider it handled."

"Thanks man."

"No problem. So does this work involve Brielle?"

Bryson laughed. "You think you know me don't you?"

"Brys, you know I know you. Don't even pretend like this has nothing to do with her."

"I got to know more man. I don't want any surprises."

"Understandable. I think this girl is different and I think you know that too. You can't let one bad experience scare you though. Embrace your blessing."

"I know man. I actually have my heart wide open to her for some reason she is in my spirit."

"That's God right there. He answering your prayers."

"I surely hope so man."

"Aight man I need to catch this line some of us are working."

Bryson laughed a bit. "Thanks for handling everything Kenny."

"Not a problem at all, we got each other's back! Talk to you soon Brys. Take care of yourself out there."

"Thanks Kenny."

They ended the call with Bryson thinking on Kenny's words. *That's God right there he answering your prayers.* Even though he knew that to be true, Bryson wanted to make sure she didn't have some secret double life. He was feeling love at first site and he wanted to make sure he wasn't setting himself up for failure and experiencing this because he got his heart broken.

He pulled out the article Kenneth sent him regarding the abuse Brielle went through. After reading about what happened he pulled resources to look into the legal files of her children father. Once he did he saw pictures that broke his heart. Swelling and cuts on Brielle and her son were photographed all over their bodies. This would be something he would never let Brielle know that he knew. This was enough to make Bryson want to hurt that man regardless of how long ago this happened.

He made a few more calls to ask for favors to make sure her kids father would not be getting out any time soon. This was his first attempt at protecting Brielle and her kids from a man that would never be a part of their life again. He hardly used his power to make something happen but this time he could and he did.

He really wanted to know more about her. He was anxious and couldn't get to her like he wanted too. He wanted to breathe the air she was breathing, wanted to be in the same space as she was and hold her tight in his arms. He was falling hard for Brielle and didn't realize at the moment what was happening, he was experiencing true love.

CHAPTER 28
~CHANTAE~
KICKING IT
LIKE A SUPERSTAR

Brielle dropped her kids off to her mom for the night. She arrived at Chantae's house at seven on the dot. She had a bag of options just in case she didn't like what Chantae picked out for her to wear.

"Hey girlfriend." Brielle said as she embraced Chantae before walking through her door.

"Hey Diva!" Embracing her back. "Are you ready to see what I got for you to wear tonight? You are going to love it!" Her confidence was high and she had a strong feeling that this outfit would be a winner with Brielle.

"Girl yes I am ready. I just hope I don't look like a hoochie momma. You doing my hair right?" She said following Chantae into her kitchen.

"Yes I got you babe. You just leave your over all look to your girl and I promise you will be the coldest bitch at the party tonight besides me of course." She said before laughing out loud.

"Okay heifer I'm trusting you to make me gorgeous." Looking at the glasses Chantae pulled from the cabinet, her eyes followed her movement to the fridge where she pulled out her favorite wine, Moscato Provincia Di Pavia Castello del Poggio. "Now that makes me happy! Pour my glass full none of that half full mess." She said smiling.

"I got this especially for you. I can't have you all tense when we get to this party. There will be some very rich and available fine men at this party and I don't want you scaring any of them off because you appear unapproachable." Chantae poured Brielle's glass full to the rim.

"Well dang, I am only unapproachable because men don't think they have at least a fifty percent chance with me and they don't want to be rejected. At least that's what my dad says anyhow."

"Well these men will have much confidence and you my dear will be a hot sexy beautiful target tonight." Chantae said before taking a sip of her wine. She picked up her glass and grabbed the bottle of wine as well and told Brielle, "Come on lets head to the dressing room also known as my bedroom."

Walking behind her, Brielle kept the conversation going. "Chantae you know just because a man has money that does not impress me. They have to have more than that for me to be interested."

"But money is a good thing when you are interested. I didn't know Bradon had money when I fell for him in the club that night, but girl it's a plus that he does. Let's me know that if something more does happen I don't have to work as hard all my life. And if nothing happens then I get to have fun with him in the process and portray as if I have money with him."

"You really like him don't you girl."

"Yes girl and I think he really likes me too. I can't explain it, it's like love at first sight but the feeling never goes away. He is so sweet to me and he treats me like I am his queen,"

"Love at first sight huh. Do you believe that really happens?" Brielle asked as she was thinking about her first meeting with Bryson and the feeling that still remains for him.

"Yes I believe in it. That's what happened to me and my Bradon. I didn't tell you but, I ended up at his home the first night we met I was so drunk but he didn't even try anything. He decided he just wanted to hold me and never let me go. He even cleaned me up after I puked all over myself and his bathroom." She was on Cloud nine walking into her bedroom.

"Oh wow, you didn't? On the first night?" She said laughing at the thought of Chantae's embarrassing night.

"Yes girl, but I don't remember being sick. I just remember waking up with those big giant arms and hands around me feeling something sticking me in my back." Raising her eyebrow to let Brielle know Bradon was very rich in his sexual parts as well.

"Ok girl. That's a double bonus." She said sitting on the edge of Chantae's bed.

"Then he made me breakfast and he was so sweet to me before taking me home."

"Wait, how did you end up at his house in the first place?"

"He was buying me drinks all night. I sent my girl on told her I was in good hands and I had planned to take a cab home but he insisted on taking me, which was cool. When I got in his car he said I passed out. So he took me back to his place."

"You sure he didn't try anything while you were asleep?"

"Well knowing what I know now I know for sure he didn't. I would have had after sex signs that he had been there for sure." She said laughing.

"Well I am happy for you and I can't wait to meet this lucky guy who has landed my bff."

"Ahhh thank you Brie! I am very happy. I haven't told anyone yet but he is going to help me launch my clothing line when I am ready. That's why I wanted to see if I could dress you tonight and you love it. If I can please you then I know I am going to be good." She said with a big grin on her face.

"Okay then let's see what you got. Let's dress me." She got up from the bed heading toward a rack of clothes up against the wall. Looking through the rack of clothes Brielle liked what she was seeing. "Are these some of your pieces?"

"Yes but they are not finished. I have to do some work on them all, I want this line to be flawless."

"Wow these are already fabulous and you still have work to do?"

"Yes a few flaws I need worked out so they can fit perfect and hug your body without your body hugging the material." Chantae was in her closet talking out and loud so Brielle could hear her.

"Ok I feel you. I am really feeling your line girlfriend. I love it. Okay where is my stuff?"

"Right here." She said pulling a garment bag out of her closet along with shoes and accessories. Unzipping the garment bag she revealed a beautiful knee length black and gold dress with a heart shape front and a low cut in the back with a double gold chain across the lower back. "Now before you say anything, the front has built in support and I have the magic strapless bra for you to wear as well so you will have the illusion of not wearing a bra for those big ole breasts you have." Looking at Brielle's reaction she couldn't quit read her expression.

"Chantae if I am wearing this then what are you wearing because this right here is a bad ass dress. I just might be the prettiest and the sexiest and the baddest chic there tonight wearing this dress. What the shoes look like?" She turned around to Chantae to see her holding the prettiest gold three inch pumps that laced up her legs and appeared to have diamonds everywhere.

"My dress is just as sexy girlfriend. These bitches at this party better step they game up cause we about to be flawless walking up in this mansion like we own the place."

"Chantae these shoes are absolutely gorgeous. Okay I am convinced you are going into the right business of fashion design and consulting. Flawless and Fine." She sat down on the edge of the bed and tried the shoes on her feet. They fit perfect.

"Oh great the shoes fit perfectly." She said looking down at Brielle feet. "And here is my dress." She pulled out a red dress that was mid-thigh and dipped in the front to show a bit of cleavage and also dipped low in the back down to her lower back. It had a diamond extender across her upper back and a diamond curvy stripe going from left hip of the dress to the hem bottom right. It was fitted to her curves and accentuated her big booty.

"Girl these are some bad dresses. Did you design these?"

"Okay you got me yes I did. I was going to shop for us some outfits but when Bradon said I could buy whatever I wanted on his black card I decided to pay one of the top designers in Atlanta to make these dresses I have been working on. And if Bradon likes these I am hoping he will be ready to invest in my business."

"Chantae these dresses are absolutely beautiful and he may not know much about fashion but when he see these dresses girl he is going to fall in love with the idea and for sure invest. I want to invest in your company as well. I may not have much but I will give something. I just want you to make clothes for me." She giggled at her bartering idea.

"Thanks girl that means a lot to me. Okay let's get our hair done and get dressed so we can get to this party and show these dresses off girlfriend."

"Okay, make sure my hair is just as cute as everything else I will be wearing. I'm ready where you want me?"

"Let's do it in the bathroom. You know I got you girl."

The girls were getting prepared so they could make their grand entrance.

CHAPTER 29
~BRIELLE~
PARTY WITH MY GIRL

When Brielle and Chantae pulled up at the house a valet driver opened their door and escorted the ladies through the front door of the home. They were beautiful to him. He figured the way they looked that they had to be someone famous. That and the fact that Bradon had a hummer limo pick them up to ride in to the party. Everyone outside was looking and whispering, wondering who these ladies were.

"Girl all eyes are on us. Go ahead and get use to this stardom treatment because this is just the beginning." Chantae said whispering to Brielle.

"Girl! You didn't tell me we were coming to the home of Bill Gates. This is beyond beautiful. I could live here for the rest of my life and do nothing more than sip wine, read romance and mystery novels and write stories of fantasies that do come true all in a different room for about 3 months straight." Brielle said admiring the fine architecture structure of the home.

"Well you will be pleased to know that Bradon designed this home. That's what he does, design fabulous artwork pieces from homes to furniture and anything else you can dream."

"Get out of here girl. Shut up, are you serious?" Brielle looked at Chantae surprised and pleased all at the same time.

"Yes, girl! I had the same reaction as you when he first told me." As they walked in to the party looking for Bradon they could hear people commenting about how fine they were even the women had to look at who would be stealing all the attention by their presences tonight?

"Damn, who are they?" One guy said as they passed.

"Oh Lord are we in Heaven?" Another commented.

After a few moments Chantae felt warm strong hands at her waist and heard a whisper in her ear. "You are absolutely gorgeous and I am the luckiest man alive." Turning her around to face him, Chantae was blushing and he kissed her on the side of her lips, on her forehead, on her nose and then on her lips. He marked her so that every man would know she was his and could tell the next man that doesn't know and so the women would know who had his heart.

"When you come up for air her best friend would like to meet this great guy I have heard so much about." Brielle spoke very softly.

At that moment Chantae started giggling. Bradon was smiling as he wiped the gloss from his lips he inherited from Chantae. They both turned towards Brielle. "Bradon, this is my best friend Brielle. Brielle this is my boo."

"Nice to finally meet you Brielle, I have heard a great deal about you." He took Brielle hand in his and kissed her hand.

"Such a gentleman. Girl I love him, do you have a brother?" Brielle said jokingly.

"Girl he is a keeper." Chantae said as she put her arms around him and kissed his cheek.

Hugging her back he turned and kissed her again saying, "I better be a keeper because I'm surely keeping you." He grabbed her by the hands to take a look at her dress. "Turn around and let me see your complete look with your sexy ass. Girl I'm going to have to have security watch you tonight from all the thirsty hounds in here."

"I think I can handle myself babe, this is all you." She said as she was spinning around.

"You two are too cute. Bradon where is your bathroom?" Brielle asked noticing men drooling as they were staring at her. Now that they knew she was the friend of Bradon's girl they assumed she was available.

"Actually the one here is occupied but you can use the one downstairs. My mom is down there somewhere. I don't want her to startle you but security will let you by. It's straight through there." He said pointing towards security leading down stairs.

"Come on girl I will go with you." Chantae said.

"Oh no stay I will find you. Bradon you have a beautiful home by the way. I love the detail of the stone and everything else about this home. It's very elegant and simply gorgeous. I am impressed."

"Thank you. I am proud of myself. It turned out better than I ever imagined, well as I imagined." He said as they all laughed. Bradon signaled for security to let Chantae through.

As Brielle turned to walk away she could hear Bradon tell Chantae he liked her that she seems sweet and pretty cool. And how beautiful she was that the guys would be all over her. She headed for the bathroom in the downstairs area and couldn't help but to be in awe of more fine designing. She wasn't ready to mingle and meet guys as she thought she would be. Her escape to the bathroom was an attempt to get her nerves together.

She was running her hands across the walls made of stones. She was at the bottom of the steps and realized it was like another home within a home at the bottom of the steps. She walked toward the living area touching the furniture, wall art, table statues and looking up to the ceiling and how it opened up to reveal the stars in the sky. Still looking up she said out loud to herself, "Wow this is beautiful, so peaceful. I could talk to God for hours laying here. Oh Lord one day I want a house like this." She looked away and turned towards the bathroom noticing someone standing close to her also looking up at the sky.

"You are right. I never noticed the view to be as beautiful as you just said it was. Talking to God does make it more appealing. I like you already and don't even know your name pretty lady." Bradon and Bryson's mom said to Brielle. She came up to visit her boys for the weekend not realizing Bradon was having a party. She agreed to stay downstairs out of their way.

Brielle had stopped in her steps looking at Mrs. Mathews smiling before looking back up to the sky. "My name is Brielle. I'm attending the party upstairs with my best friend Chantae. Bradon let me down to use the bathroom. I couldn't help but admire the beauty of his home."

"Yes that's one thing my son's take pride in is being the best at what they do. Let me show you another breath taking view. Come on, follow me." Mrs. Mathews walked over to the doors of the balcony and pushed them open. Pointing to a seat she told Brielle to have a seat. "Take a few moments and enjoy the cool air hitting your skin and look up at the sky. Now this is breathtaking beautiful. Every time I visit Bryson and Bradon I come out here to enjoy this view. When it's cold I use the climate control and make it warmer so I can sit out here."

"This is simply amazing. Thank you for sharing this with me. I just met Bradon, is Bryson your other son?"

"Yes he is my first born. This is his home that Bradon built. I always say it's both of theirs because Bradon lives here too. They are very big on family and taking care of one another. Bryson is working of course. He is always working. But I know God is preparing his wife just for him. He just went through a messy break up. That girl just wasn't right for him. But God is up to something marvelous just for him." At the moment she turned to Brielle and felt something come over her she couldn't explain. She felt the spirit of God all around her. "God I don't want to know but I know you are up to something, just have your way." She said looking at the sky. "Brielle do you cook?" Standing to her feet she asked.

"Yes I love to cook." She said with a smile.

"Are you married?"

"No ma'am, never have been. Waiting on God."

"Your friends are going to miss you upstairs at the party I am just taking you away from all the fun." She said to see how she would respond.

"Oh no, I am not missing anything! I am not a drinker except for wine occasionally and I don't really feel like being hit on by a bunch of thirsty hounds as your son called them." She said with a laugh. "I am enjoying being right here." She turned back looking towards the sky, closed her eyes and inhaled the fresh air. "This is heavenly."

"Well, I have a secret recipe that no one knows and right now I think I want to share it with you. It's my son Bryson's favorite. I was hoping he would be here tonight since Bradon was throwing a party. And if he does I want to have his favorite chocolate cake waiting on him." Mrs. Mathews already made a cake for Bryson but she wanted to spend a little more time with Brielle and teach her the secrets to making her famous cake that her son loves. She had a feeling that Brielle has already crossed paths with Bryson and she doesn't even know it.

"Oh that sounds like a great idea. I love baking sweets. And chocolate is my favorite. I always say chocolate has no calories and since I use apple juice instead of water when I mix my cakes I am getting a serving of fruit at the same time." She stopped in her tracks behind Mrs. Mathews stopping and turning.

"Oh yeah I like you chile. Yeap my son got to make him a chocolate cake. I use the apple juice and apple sauce. You know something about baking I see." She was pretty excited about having Brielle there with her at that moment.

"Yes ma'am and I'm always willing to learn more."

Brielle helped make the cake and bonded with Mrs. Mathews as if they have known each other for years. She thought her eyes looked familiar but figured it was because of Bradon's eyes. Security stuck his head down to check on the ladies and saw they were in the kitchen laughing and enjoying one another. He reported back to Bradon who in turn reported to Chantae. After the cake was placed in the oven the ladies sat back out on the balcony sipping on some homemade lemonade and enjoyed more of the breath taking view of the open sky filled with the moon and stars.

Brielle shared her story about what happened to her and why she has not been able to open up to people and especially men. She showed pictures of her children and even shared the story about meeting Matt.

Mrs. Mathews thought for a moment that she was describing her son. She knew he was on a mission to see how people would treat him not knowing who he was so she thought it to be possible seeing how she said Matt. That's the name he uses when he didn't want people to know who he was. By the sound of Brielle's voice it sounded like she was in love. "Sounds like love at first sight."

"I have never felt that feeling before but it was definitely real and different but it feels wonderful. Only God knows."

Mrs. Mathews started smiling and at that moment she knew Bryson was going to be ok. "God is up to something." She said under her breathe. The feeling she had was now confirmed and she knew for sure that Brielle was talking about her son.

Brielle pretty much missed the party but she was okay with that. She enjoyed her time making chocolate cake and indulging in two pieces with Mrs. Mathews. When she was done she decided to go up and say good bye to Chantae before having the driver take her home. Everyone was pretty wasted, some passed out, some dancing but the party was still live. Chantae and Bradon were very enthralled in one another. Her other friends were there and booed up with some of Bradon's friends. Bradon paused long enough to walk her out to the car making sure none of his drunken friends tried to push up on her.

"Thanks for hanging out with my mom. Chantae was a bit jealous. She has not met my mom yet. But mom must like you since she didn't send you running back upstairs." He said and laughed.

"She is a very lovely and smart woman. And she taught me her secret recipe for chocolate cake. Shhh don't tell anyone." She said with a wink before getting in the car. "Thanks for having me Bradon. Your home is very lovely. You have a very bright future ahead of you. Take care of my girl ok."

"Will do." Bradon looked shocked. He didn't understand why his mom would share her secret recipe with her. He dismissed the thought going back in to join Chantae.

Brielle enjoyed the peaceful ride home. She reflected on her conversation with Mrs. Mathews and realized that Chantae thought the house was Bradon's. But she knew at that moment that Bradon's life was merely his brothers, but she would never interfere and reveal that information. To her it was nothing. Material things would come and go but without love none of those things would be enjoyed. She now had her answer what she was going to do in the morning concerning Bryson.

CHAPTER 30
~BRYSON~
HOMELESS IS ROUGH

Bryson is still playing out the role of being homeless and realizing people can be so cruel when they think you have nothing. This experience was nothing what he imagined. Seeing Brielle today is what got him through the days of being dirty and treated less than favorable. On the evening before he encountered some people who had intentions of hurting him and his body guards had to intercept as innocent bystanders in an attempt to not blow his cover. The two weeks he had been on this journey were the hardest two weeks of his life. Brielle has been his peace in all of this and the anticipation of seeing her kept him going.

Early Saturday morning Bryson gets a call from Kenneth with some news that warms Bryson's heart. "Hey Kenny man what's going on? What time is it?" Bryson ask as he turns to sit up on the side of the bed and stretches.

"It's seven in the morning man. You sleeping well these days huh? I'm use to you being up before me every morning calling me at six being my alarm clock."

"Yeah. A lot of down time. Man I'm ready for this to be over. Being homeless is rough. It amazes me how cruel people can be. And then how they treat me when they know I have money. It has definitely been an experience."

"Well I got some news you are going to love hearing." Kenny said with a smile.

"Lay it on me. Besides the hope of seeing Brielle today I need some more good news." He got up to go to the bathroom anticipating what Kenny was going to tell him.

"Well this is news about the famous Brielle." He paused.

Bryson was aiming for the toilet and at the mentioning of Brielle name he straightens his body and his aim hits the wall and the back of the seat. Trying to concentrate to finish without making a bigger mess he asked, "What about her man? You said good news so what's the news?"

"Well you told me to keep an eye on Bradon and you know he had the party last night. Well I started watching the footage from last night and guess who walks in with Bradon's girlfriend?"

"Wait, the party was at my house. You mean to tell me she was in my house last night?"

"Yeap, she sure was."

"Damn, I know his friends were all over her."

"Yes and no."

"What does that mean Kenny?"

"Yes when she got there they were eyeing her and plotting but she wasn't even at the party twenty minutes. She looked very nervous and when she asked Bradon where the bathroom was he sent her down stairs because the other one was occupied."

"Ok, so what happened? You said good news." Bryson said anxious and nervous about where the story was going.

"Your mom was there and she was downstairs. To cut the story short, she spent all her time at the party down stairs talking to your mom. Your mom even had her baking a chocolate cake."

"Wait did momma show her how to make it or was she keeping her from seeing how she made it?"

"She showed her and had her right there helping."

"I see, what else man?" Bryson realized that his momma was a smart woman and God was busy at work preparing his future.

"So she told your mom stories about her life. One of the stories was about meeting Mr. Matt himself. And get this, your mom hung to her every word and told her it sounded like love at first sight."

"Mom said that to her?" He said with a big grin.

"Yes indeed. Brielle is feeling you man. And she is clueless about who you are. But be careful she may figure it out as her friend and Bradon are dating pretty seriously.

"My brother? Dating seriously? I have to see that for myself to believe that story."

"This is getting better and better. What time are you meeting Brielle today?"

"She said this afternoon. I am going to head that way about ten to make sure I don't miss her."

"Good, well I am watching today. Good luck, hopefully something exciting will happen today.

Bryson was now use to walking place to place and he ended up walking back to the park where he sees Brielle sitting on a blanket enjoying the cool breeze. She had on shorts that exposed her long beautiful legs and a sleeveless shirt exposing her toned arms. He watched her for a moment mesmerized enjoying having her that close to him. The wind blew her hair backwards exposing her naked neck. Bryson couldn't help but imagine kissing and sucking on the back of her neck. As he was standing there staring at her she turned and looked directly at him. Locking their eyes she smiled and motioned for him to come join her. He could see her excitement and the attempt to hide her smile. He walked over to join her looking around for the kids. She was alone with no kids and no food. At that moment he knew she was simply there for him. There were no other distractions.

She stood to her feet to greet him and when he approached she didn't reach out her hand instead reached and hugged him. He took that opportunity to feel her skin and to smell her hair before letting her go.

"Hey Matt how are you? How have you been?"

"I am good, even better now. I am ecstatic that you came back to see me."

"I am a lady of my word." She said smiling up at Bryson nervously. Without the kids with her there was nowhere to redirect the butterflies and the attraction she had for him.

"So, where are the kids? I didn't see them out here anywhere." Looking around to make sure he didn't miss them.

"They are with my parents I wanted to come alone today to talk to you by myself if that's okay."

"Oh yeah, that is definitely okay with me. Although I must say I am very fond of those kids. Hope I didn't do anything wrong last time they were here." He had a bit of concern on his face. Not knowing for sure why she wanted to come alone.

"Not at all. The kids love you. I had to promise them they would see you later. So speaking of my promise to them you determine if I keep my promise or not." Her heart was beating fast and he could see it through her shirt.

"How is that? I wouldn't want you to break your promise." He said with a smile.

"Okay great! So here goes. I have been thinking about you every day since I first met you. The kids can't stop talking about you. I have prayed and prayed and asked God to guide me so here goes."

"Wait you seem nervous. You don't have to be nervous with me at all. I am harmless. I'm a big man but harmless to the beautiful woman." He said seeing her blush.

"You are so sweet. I don't understand how, seeing who you are and feeling your spirit, you could be out her on the streets with no family and no one to love you and take care of you. I know you are a man who is very prideful and you don't want any handouts or anything like that but the kids and I want to be a blessing to you. I just had something happen for me that blessed us and now I need to share my blessing and be a blessing to you and offer you a place to stay for a few months free of charge until you can get a job and become stable. It would be your place no strings attached. Food and clothes and its furnished. Please let me do that for you." She watched as he turned away from her for a moment.

Choked up on emotions he didn't know what to say. He was the one always giving and here she is in front of him. She was beautiful and her spirit and her heart. His heart was overwhelmed with love he was feeling for her right now. "Wow Brielle. You are so beautiful inside and out."

The assistant producers was in his ear saying, "Take the offer Bryson. We all know you are a man of pride. She may be your God sent wife and you need to see where this goes, don't blow your cover. This is your chance to find love and you knowing in your heart it is love. I promise she will not be mad at you, I am a woman so trust me here."

"Thank you so is that a yes? I can take you there right now. I have a very tasty meal prepared for you waiting. It's a house I just purchased. I need to do a little work to it but its livable and it is yours for now, you could even help me fix it up if you want. My lease is not up for another four months where I am now but even then if you're not ready we can work some things out. Just please say yes. I was not prepared for you to say anything else but yes." Brielle started twiddling her fingers together.

Bryson knew she was nervous but at the same time he wanted to be closer to her every second he could. "Thanks Brielle. I can't let the kids down and have you break your promise to them now can I?" Bryson was trying very hard to swallow his pride. He knew the producer was right he just hope she was right about everything she said.

"Yes." She said with excitement. "I mean great. Thanks for taking me up on my offer. The kids will be excited to see you. Once you're settled and all."

"Looking forward to seeing them." Looking into her eyes he couldn't help but love her. Besides his mom no one else has ever offered to do anything for him to the extent as Brielle has offered.

"What? Why are you staring at me like that?"

"You are truly an angel you know that?" He watched as she smiled. "Are you always this happy and smiling?"

"I try to be. I try to live by let go and let God. I know that he shows favor and is protecting me and my children. Opening up to people has been a challenge for me and you have done so much in helping me do just that. So helping you is easy for me."

"Well that makes me happy. Maybe one day you will allow me to return the favor and be a blessing for you and your children."

"We will see. Come on let's get out of here. You are going to love the place. It's a cute little house. Quiet area. Needs some paint but won't take much to make it perfect."

They walked towards Brielle's car both feeling excited and anxious. The physical attraction was there and the genuine love they were feeling was exploding. Bryson could hear the producers scrambling to follow them. They all were excited about the direction of the story. But Brielle and Bryson were even more excited about the feeling of ordained love they did not speak of but could not deny.

CHAPTER 31
~BRIELLE~
EXCITED TO BE
IN HIS PRESENCE

Third time is a charm, Brielle thought to herself. She was enjoying being in Bryson's presence. She prayed about offering him a place to stay. Reality was Bryson is still a stranger to her and her children. Several men have crossed her path. Some wealthy, some very handsome. But Brielle didn't budge on her feelings or give them the time of day. Bryson was different. His spirit touched her spirit. Her soul was awakened just by being close to him. From day one of meeting Bryson her thoughts have been consumed of him.

"So do you have any items we need to pick up from anywhere?" She looked at him and smiled before turning back to the road.

"I saw that. You are always smiling. Is it me that brings that smile? I am starting to get the big head thinking it's me that make you smile."

"Well, I am very happy you said yes for one." She was still smiling.

"And for two?"

"Well for two." She said rolling her head still smiling. She was so nervous around him. "I like having you around. You are very good with the kids. They like you and my kids don't ever like men especially when they talk to their mom. And you are so easy to talk too. You being here feel natural, like we knew each other in another lifetime or something. You are good people and I like to surround myself with good people."

"Natural feeling." Bryson said out loud. He was thinking about the natural feeling of love and what he was feeling for Brielle in such a short period of time. His thoughts went back to the conversation he had with his mother and at that moment he knew what she said to be real and to be true.

Baby let me tell you. I prayed for you all last night and this morning all the way to your front porch. And son, God has a much greater plan for you. He has blessings far and beyond what you can even imagine. Blessings for you that money cannot buy. You may be feeling down and out and hurting over a love that you thought you had but when God created Adam he created him an Eve. Flesh of his flesh bone of his bone. And your Eve will be here right on time, when you don't even expect it. Not in your time, not when you think she should be here, but in God's time. He had to get rid of the mess that was in the way of your true blessings. This did not happen by chance. God was giving you signs from the very beginning but he needed a bigger distraction for you to see what he wanted you to see. To prepare you for the ultimate blessing of love that he has for you. You are being prepared in a way to receive the best blessing he can give you besides life and family. The blessing of true genuine love from someone who gives the same back to you. All things happen for a reason and your next actions will be preparing you for the rest of your life. So be prepared and get ready for it son. You keep your faith and you keep believing and don't close your heart to love… Your true love will find you in your rarest form and will fall in love with you, Bryson the man not the money or the fame but with whom God created you to be. You will know her when you see her. You won't be turned on by lust, her beauty will intrigue you. Not just the outer beauty but the inner beauty as well.

"Matt? You ok? You went silent on me…"

"Oh sorry. I'm wonderful actually. I was thinking of something my mom said to me just recently. I don't have anything to pick up. The things I do have I will get later." He too was smiling.

"What? Why are you smiling?" She said.

"No reason at all besides being happy."

"Happy is good. That makes me happy."

They found topics to talk about from the scenery and the kids and other general questions Bryson and Brielle both asked. Brielle was full of excitement. She had been preparing all night and morning getting the house ready for Bryson. She even went and bought paint in hopes of them painting together soon. They pulled up in front of her new home. Brielle was excited and her face lit up while admiring her new home.

"Home sweet home Matt. It's not much but its home. What do you think?"

Seeing the glow on Brielle's face was priceless. "It's perfect. Reminds me of home when I was growing up. And the smell. Is that coming from inside the house?"

"Yes I left lunch slow cooking in the oven. Come on lets go inside so I can show you around."

"Sounds good let's go."

They walk through the door and Bryson removes his shoes. The space is cozy and cool. Brielle had candles lit and the air up high enough to make sure he was able to cool down from the outside warmth. She walked him through the kitchen first so she could check on her meal she was preparing.

"Hope you like greens. I have been slow cooking them since early this morning. The chicken looks perfect. All I have left is to finish the mac n cheese and make fresh hot water cornbread."

"Girl you are spoiling me. It smells like when mom comes to cook or when I go back home to her." He had to remember what he was doing and not talk too much about his family. He wanted to tell Brielle who he really was but didn't want to blow his cover. When the time was right he would tell her all she needed to know even if it did mean breaking the rules of his contract.

"I got my cooking skills from my mother. She always cooked a full course meal for us when we were coming up. It was just me and my brother and my father. I stayed right there in the kitchen watching and helping." She started showing him where the food was in the kitchen and ensured him he had full access.

He followed her around the home as she showed him where everything was. The last place they ended up was in the bedroom where he would be sleeping, the master suit. "Brielle thank you so much for your kindness. It means the world to me. I promise I will spend a lifetime thanking you." He was looking into her eyes at that moment and wanted to kiss her lips. Being around her was hard knowing he wanted to make love to every inch of her body.

Nervous and fidgeting she was melting all over wanting to kiss his lips as well. Trying to keep her composure she quickly spoke and changed the subject. "Matt it's not a problem at all. I do want you to do me a favor right now. I have clean clothes here for you and I hope you can fit them but I would like for you to get cleaned up while I finish preparing your meal."

"Okay not a problem." He smiled. He couldn't wait to shower and be rid of those clothes.

"Okay great. Shower works by turning knob and pulling the round piece under faucet down. Towels and soap are in the closet in the bathroom as well as tooth brush, tooth paste, shaving stuff, lotion and anything else you may need. If it's something you are missing let me know okay."

"Thanks Brielle. I think you have me hooked up with everything. Can I hug you?" He said knowing he was reaching.

Shaking her head yes she allowed him to hug her smelliness and all. She welcomed his hug. He squeezed her tight picking her up from the floor. She laughed and held on to his arms as he turned her. She could feel his strength and definition of his muscular arms. She was sure to stop by the bathroom to wipe away the wetness of honey he has flowing between her thighs. "I can feel your thank you very tightly." He put her down slowly with her eyes never leaving his. The chemistry was flaming hot and before anything could transpire she spoke softly. "I think I better check on the food."

Putting her down to her feet right in front of him, he pulled his hands to his back in an attempt to tame himself. "Okay we don't want anything to burn. I will be down after my shower." He smiled at her.

Returning his smile she could only manage to say, "Ok" before leaving the room. She immediately went to the down stairs bathroom to compose herself. Her body was tingling nonstop and her panties were soaked with orgasmic honey. "Lord Jesus, stay with me here. I don't know what's happening nor can I explain these feelings but I like it. I hope that's a good thing Lord. Please don't let me get hurt and help me to make wise decisions you have led me this far Lord please continue to hold my hands." She said her prayer before finishing the meal. She set the table and thought she too was hungry. She decided to sit and join him instead of leaving as she planned.

Brielle called to check on the kids and chat with her mother before Bryson came down. Her mom was talking nonstop and Brielle didn't interrupt her until turning around and seeing Bryson standing there in too little clothes that she picked out for him. "Uh momma I have to call you back. Okay. Yeah. Love you too momma." She smirked and admired his body all at the same time. The funniness of the clothes being too little on his body kept her from being overly indulged in the handsomeness of his physique. "Bryson I am so sorry I got your sizes all wrong. I figured an extra-large would work but boy was I wrong." She laughed a little.

"What's wrong with my clothes? I think you did a great job." Teasing her a bit he thought he would make her laugh and show off his body at the same time. The tank top he had on was showing half of his muscular chest and every inch of his nice strong muscular arms. You could see the definition of his abs through the tightness of his shirt. The pants, well let's say it's a good thing they stretch. But there was no way he was going to hide any hard-ons she gave him so he was hoping to stay seated.

"Okay let me know your sizes and I will return the others for a much bigger size. Sorry never had to shop for a man before."

"So I'm your first?" He said as she turned to him quickly. "First experience with buying men clothes." He quickly added to his statement.

"Yes you are. Now my girl Chantae has an eye for fashion. She can look at you and design something that fits your body perfectly. She made me an amazing dress I wore to a party that was absolutely gorgeous and fit perfect."

He wanted to say that it was her that made the dress gorgeous and not solely the dress. He saw a piece of the tape from the party and she was breathtaking gorgeous. He could feel his nature rising again. As long as he was seated he didn't mind. "That's real talent if she does that. I hope she is taking her talents to the next business level."

Brielle was making their plates as they talked. "At first she did it as a way to make clothes that fit her curvy shape she has. Always been full of dreams though. Then she met this guy, a very nice guy who she fell kind of hard for. She really likes him a lot. He told her he wanted to invest in her dreams. I hope it all work out for her. She deserves to be happy."

"If she is friends with you she must be a wonderful person. People you have around you are a reflection of who you are or where you want to go." Using his business knowledge he engaged in intelligent conversation. Once again impressing Brielle. "Do you mind if I bless the food before we eat?"

"Please do Matt." She held her hands out for him to grab. His voice was so powerful and strong. He demanded attention when he spoke and praying blessings over them and the food was powerful, giving her chills. "Amen. Thanks Matt."

"A man should always take the lead and pray. My dad taught me and my brother to pray and take the lead and if we are among females to pray for our women. Habits that are unbreakable."

Our women. Ownership. I like the sound of that. Brielle slow down, pump your brakes. She was hanging on to his every word. "I like your father and I don't even know him. Maybe one day I could meet your parents."

Bryson thought to himself, *you already met my mom sweet Brielle.* "One day you will meet them both. The food is absolutely delicious. You got some serious skills in the kitchen."

Ummm that's not the only skills I have. Okay I have to get a grip on myself. "Thanks Matt. I am glad you like. I get it from my momma." She said in a silly way.

They talked for hours. Bryson ate two plates of food before he helped Brielle clean the table and wash the dishes. They talked about their dreams in life. Bryson's dreams being more of his reality, the only thing he was missing was his wife and children.

Before Brielle left she gave Bryson a cell phone to use with her number already programmed. A laptop with internet access and told him she would be back to help with his resume when he was ready. "You should have all the essentials to function. Just call me when it's okay for the kids to come by. I don't want to invade your space so if you ever want company I'm just a text or call away. And I will check on you."

"Thanks Brielle for everything. You are truly an angel."

"So sweet. Call me if you need me." *Please need me*, she thought to herself.

"Indeed I will. I'm sure I will need you." He said as if he was reading Brielle's thoughts. He walked Brielle to her car and stood in the driveway until she was gone and no longer in his sight.

Brielle could not wait to call Chantae. After calling her mom to let her know she was on her way she quickly dialed Chantae.

"Hey Diva how are you?" Chantae said answering the phone.

"Hey girl. I'm good you recuperating okay? You were pretty wasted last night."

"Yes girl I'm okay. Just getting up. Bradon just fixed breakfast for us. What happened to you last night? I didn't see you until you were about to leave. You get caught up with a cutie?" She said in between bites.

"Yeah I got caught up with a cutie but not at the party." Brielle said with a laugh.

"Oh do tell. You have my full attention Brie."

"You remember me telling you about the guy from the park who appeared to be homeless?"

"Yeah, the one you said was cute and you had a spiritual vibe, the kids like him and all that."

"Yeah that's him. Well last night when I went downstairs to the bathroom Bradon's mom was there and we ended up baking a cake and chatting the evening away."

"Oh I am so jealous. You spent time with moms and all I have had was a brief nice to meet you. How did that go?"

"It was a very nice evening. She is a spiritual woman very wise and full of great advice even when it's not directly to you."

"Wow. She really impressed you. When I have to be around her again you are definitely going to be with me." Chantae laughed.

"I gotcha girlfriend. I would love that!"

"Okay so the cutie, what's up with that?"

"Well after leaving the party yesterday I realized what I wanted to do to help the man from the park, Matt. So I invited him to stay at the house I just bought for a few months until he get on his feet."

Spitting her drink out, Chantae was in shocked regarding what she heard. "You did what Brie? With you and the kids?"

"You heard me right. And no, not with me and the kids. We will be at the apartment until my lease is up. I have been with him all morning and afternoon."

"Did you have sex with him?" She whispered.

"No Chantae, girl you know me better than that. But I am very attracted to him right or wrong I am."

"What? Well why is he homeless? What's his deal? I am trying to not judge him but I don't want him using you. You know your ass will give your last to even a dead man just because you so damn nice." She said sarcastically. She was still in disbelief Brielle moved a homeless man into her home.

"If you are in the room with him for even a few moments you would feel different. He feels well established and his body, oh my damn his body." Brielle said thinking about his body.

"Wait how in the hell did you see his body Brie? You are leaving some details out."

Laughing out loud at her friend, Brielle could tell she was getting an attitude. It's not too often Brielle has juicy details. "Girl I got him some clean clothes to wear after his shower and everything was like two sizes too small and I could see his nice body through them tightie whities. I'm telling you girl he don't seem like an average homeless person. He seems like a man who was just down on his luck. I know people and my spirit is telling me good things about him. He could be my future husband. I know God won't send me any junk and I know he will end up finding a good job. You never know, he could end up taking care of me and the kids. They say don't judge a book by its cover."

"Okay, well I see you have put a lot of thought into this so I'm with you one hundred percent girlfriend. And you are crushing on him too hard I can hear it through the phone."

"Girl I am. I just hope this is not a façade that I am missing somehow."

"Like you said, you know people. And I know you prayed about it before you made any moves so just let me know how the sex is because I know you will eventually do it."

"Whatever girl." They both laughed. "Although he is definitely a man who could venture down the naughty and oh so nice lane."

"Oooooh Brie girl, well I just hope it is good when you do. Bradon is back Brie, girl I will talk to you later okay."

"Okay girl, love you!"

"Love you back!"

Brielle turned the radio up singing aloud on her way to her mother's house. She was happy and feeling good about Bryson.

CHAPTER 32
~BRYSON~
AMAZING ANGEL

Bryson is amazed by Brielle's generosity and he realizes he is falling in love with her fast. She doesn't know who he is or how much he is worth. So if she falls for him, he knew it would be genuine true love.

He views the entire videotaping from the party his brother had and realizes that Brielle was in his home with his mom as if she has always been a part of their life. There was that natural feeling of Brielle belonging again. He calls his mom and talks about the young lady she was talking to at the party. The entire Brielle experience was just wowing him and he was falling hard in love with her. Even though he went through the breakup with Jewel, he knew in his heart that what he was experiencing with Brielle was real genuine love. He never wanted anything more in life than his desire to love Brielle and have her as his forever.

For his mom to spend time with Brielle lets him know there is something special about her and God has her close for a reason. He enjoyed seeing Brielle and his mom spend time together. He grabbed his cell phone to dial his mother. As he did he heard a knock at the door.

It was one of the technicians with the production crew. "Hi sir, is the home owner home at the moment?" He said to ensure it was a good time.

"We good man. Just not in the bedrooms okay?" Bryson said knowing he was installing cameras and microphones.

"I'm just hitting downstairs and the hallway upstairs. I will be done in about fifteen minutes."

"Cool", he said before talking with his mom. "Hey mom how are you?"

"Hey baby, your dad and I were just talking about you. Are you still on your journey?"

"Yes mother. I have about four weeks left. What are you and dad talking about?"

"About the young lady I met at your place last night. It's something special about her and I have a feeling you already know her, Mr. Matt." She said knowing that he was using that name on his journey.

"Kenny told me about her being in the house mom. She doesn't know who I am. Well she knows who I am but she knows me and not how society knows me. I was pretty excited when I found out you taught her how to make my favorite cake mom. You never give anyone that recipe. You must really think she is special."

"Son what I think is that you already know how special she is just for you. Just don't be afraid from past hurt. God is showing you favor son. He has put you in a situation that is out of your comfort zone to show you what he can do if you just turn it over to him. God knew your trust in women would be affected so he placed you in this situation for a reason. Not for work, but for you to trust him and trust your heart. If you would have been here last night with her, it may not have been the same connection the same feelings you currently have. Now you have the ability to trust your heart without any other distraction but true love."

"God has showed out with this one mom. Brielle is amazing. I just hope she is feeling me when I tell her who I am beyond who I have perceived her to believe I am. I love being with her mom."

"I can imagine. I enjoyed spending time with her myself. She is full of life and has a great spirit. I can tell she has alot of love to give. And she is if not already falling in love with you son. She chose hanging out with little ole me over partying and drinking with Bradon's friends. That said a lot. And when she told me the story about meeting Mr. Matt well I put it together what you were doing. Just be careful son. These are some deceptive lies that she is receiving and you can't let this drag out. You want her to be able to know what's real and what's not."

"Yes ma'am, I know. I am going to fight to keep her momma. I am working on getting around the contract terms dealing with her but for right now I am enjoying her affection towards me. I promise I won't let this drag out. I have four weeks left but I am planning to tell her before then."

"Okay son. I love you. Pray every day okay?"

"Yes momma, I will. I love you more mother dear."

"Bryson, Brielle has a place in her heart that is being healed by you. She may not know it yet but her children and her family and friends surely can see it and so can I. You make sure you protect her heart at all cost."

"Yes ma'am I promise to always do just that."

"Alright son. Call me later."

"Mom thanks for being so wonderful!"

"That's what mothers do baby."

After ending the conversation with his mom he called Kenneth.

"Hey Brys man." Kenneth said answering the phone.

"Hey Kenny, I know you know the story by now."

"Do I? Shit it took you long enough to call. I knew she was with you after the park but I have been dying to know what happened. No cameras just sound. So what happened?"

"She is amazing man. I want to make love to her and make her mine right now. It's very hard to resist wrapping her up in my arms. She cooked for me again while I showered and dressed in clothes she bought me." He paused and started laughing.

"What's funny what happened?"

"The clothes were about two sizes too small but I put them on anyhow to humor her and show off my guns and my eight pack."

"You are so wrong for that. What she do or say?"

"I could tell I caught her off guard but me being in those tight clothes she bought for me was so funny we both laughed. But it gave her the opportunity to check out my body see what she about to be working with." They both laughed. "Besides her nipples were hard and her chest was rising heavy so I know she was turned on just as I was."

"You both have an undeniable strong connection man. We all can see that. I am surprised with you both being all alone in that house nothing more happened. Nothing more happened did it Brys?" Kenny wanted to make sure his friend was not leaving any details out.

Laughing Bryson assured Kenny nothing more happened. "Nothing more yet. I am going to get you to leave a voicemail on this phone she gave me so I can get back into the office to work a little. Surely since the homeless part is done and the producers are focused on me finding true love this will be my way back in."

"I got you for sure text me the number. I will do that first thing Monday morning. I need you to fill out my application though and what position are you applying for? Gotta see if you qualify."

"You got jokes. Find me something good. When I tell her about the job I am going to hopefully land a kiss." Bryson started thinking about Brielle's lips.

"It's going down real soon. You two are in love already. Man what a great love story. You need me to do anything more?"

"Yeah I am going to text you a list of some things I need. Starting with some clothes that fit. Make sure I have a wardrobe in the office to change into when I get there as well. Plan for me to come in Monday about ten. I still want you to be point of contact and run everything for the next few weeks at least. We have these promising contracts in place bringing in a lot of money. You have ran the company for so long right beside me maybe it's time you take the lead at least fifty percent of the time so we both can have a life outside of the company. "

"No, we didn't lose 'Bryson the business man' I see. You are still focused and direct. I like your thoughts but we are better as a team but I like the idea of us having a life outside of work. Who knows, maybe I will find Mrs. Right for me."

"In due time my friend. Look at where we are. On top of the world living a good life. All we are missing is our soul mates to spend the rest of it with us."

"Well you have obviously found yours. Seeing you happy is making me want to step up and find her. I never tell people what I am worth. I always tell people I work for you. I have never had a problem being in the back ground in front of others. I am learning a lot watching your love story play out so hopefully I will have a few pointers to follow."

"You never did show up for photo shoots. I just accepted you wanted me to be the face of the company because I was better looking and had more swag."

"You funny. You sound like Bradon. I done told y'all I handle mines. So much swag and good looks. I just like being behind the scenes. You're not much of a front man either." Kenneth said.

"Yeah I know and I hear you. Thanks for everything man seriously. You are always there for me. But most of all thank you for not talking me out of going on this journey. One way or another I know I would have met Brielle but I'm not messed up it happened this way."

"Sure way of knowing if someone loves you is having them love you when you're at what appears to be your lowest point in life."

"Wow I am still amazed. Alright, I am going to send you the computer name and I want you to set me up a secure access so I can work. And thanks again Kenny for everything."

"I gotcha Brys. I will talk with you later. Let me know if you need anything."

Bryson ended the call and pulled out his phone and computer and started to work. His life has been changed. The way he views love has been forever altered. He pulled up footage of Brielle. He wished she was still there with him. He knew in his heart that God set him up for that very moment. Jewel was an experience Bryson had to have. He needed to go through the pain of heart break to appreciate true love.

He could still smell her sweet scent lingering in the air. He made a few more calls to business associates before exploring all the things he planned to do to get Brielle's home in tip top shape. He didn't plan for her to be living there long but it was still her home and he wanted to do something nice for her.

His next obstacle was telling Brielle who he was. Although it didn't seem like anything hard he didn't want to risk her believing he was using her for his journey. Reality was he had fallen in love with Brielle. And he knew she had fallen for him as well.

CHAPTER 33
~BRIELLE~
BRIELLE IS EXPERIENCING
TRUE LOVE

Chantae notices a glow on her friends face. After Brielle picked the kids up she went over to Chantae's home to discuss making a suit for Bryson. She wanted him to look impressive when he went on interviews. She also had Chantae help her pick out shoes. She looked inside the shoes he wore to the house while he was in the shower to see his shoe size and decided to go a size bigger.

"Do you think you could have me the suit ready tomorrow?" Brielle asked. "I will help you in any way possible and you know I will pay you and buy the material."

"Okay you're going to have me up all night I see. But I think I can, at least have it done by tomorrow evening. I have fabric already that I had shipped to me when I had Bradon's credit card so I'm good on the material. This will give me more practice with men clothing. You have to help me with his size though since I don't know what he look like."

"Okay not a problem. He is about Bradon size except he is about two inches taller and a bit thicker a little more muscular. His arms and legs may be an inch or two longer than Bradon's are. When he picked me up his arms were...."

"Wait he picked you up? What he pick you up for?" Chantae interrupted Brielle curious that Bryson picked her up.

"It wasn't nothing girl. He was just excited and anyways let me finish ok?"

"Ok, but we have some more detail talking to do. This is not over but carry on."

"As I was saying, when he innocently picked me up." She laughed a bit. "His arms wrapped around me extending to the opposite side like this." She demonstrated to Chantae and without my heels he is about this tall." She extended her hands to show how tall Bryson was compared to her height.

"Okay so compared to Bradon and what you are describing I think I have a pretty accurate idea. But if I am off don't blame me as I am doing this based on an idea not actual measurements."

"Okay I completely understand."

"Ok. One good thing about men if it's a little too big it doesn't matter much unless they are one of those finicky type. But men don't like tight fitting they like for their clothes to loosely hug their muscles and hang loose around their legs. We will be okay. I am going to start on him when I finish this shirt for Bradon."

"Yeah can you make two shirts?" She said laughing at her request for her friend. Chantae looked up at her friend with squinted eyes. "Practice my friend for when you get these large orders coming in before you get your very own manufacturing company." Brielle felt her phone buzzing and searched for it in her purse.

"Okay I here you Brie! I love the sound of that." Chantae was working as Brielle looked through her phone.

The kids were watching TV quietly and for the moment everyone was pre occupied. Brielle saw that the message was from Bryson.

4:27 pm
Brielle Summers
Hey Brielle, this is Matt. I wanted to make sure the numbers were connected and to thank you again for everything. You are my angel.
#Mr.TallDark&Handsome

Brielle was blushing and biting on her bottom lip excited to see that Bryson was reaching out to her so soon after she was just with him. She was also blushing because his signature she put in was popping up. She forgot she set that up in the phone before she gave it to Bryson.

4:28 pm
Matt 'Mr. Handsome' Cole
*Hey Matt. You are very welcome. No need to thank me
though. Being your angel is my pleasure. I have a surprise
for you. Hoping to come by tomorrow evening after church if
you will have us, me and the kids.*
#MissSophisticatedSummers

Brielle was blushing not knowing where the conversation was
going but at the same time flirting a bit with Bryson. She would
follow his lead. She was about to put her phone down when it buzzed
again.

4:29 pm
Brielle Summers
*Yes I will have you all tomorrow and anytime you decide to
come. You have an open invitation. You are full of surprises.
You are the type of lady that deserves and would be easy to
spoil. Always giving of yourself from the heart.*
#Mr.TallDark&Handsome

4:29 pm
Matt 'Mr. Handsome' Cole
*You are making me blush Mr. Matt! All that sweet talk. What
you trying to do to me? My cheeks are hurting.*
#MissSophisticatedSummers

"Brie you blushing too hard over there is that you know who
texting you?" Chantae asked Brielle.
Brielle was enthralled in her phone and didn't hear Chantae
talking to her.
"Brielle?" Chantae called again snapping her fingers.
"Oh huh? What you say girl?" Brielle said looking up and
smiling.
"I was asking you if that was you know who texting you but I
think I know the answer to that question now seeing the look on your
face." She said smiling back at Brielle

"Oh yeah, he just thanking me for everything and making sure he has the right number."

"Is that right? You can't fool me girlfriend. You two must be crazy about one another, yeah definitely. He texting you already." Chantae saw her reach for her buzzing phone again.

"I know right." Brielle said opening the text and completely dismissing Chantae questioning her. Her mind was focused on what Bryson was saying and thinking about her.

> *4:30 pm*
> *Brielle Summers*
> *Blushing huh? That's good. Angels should always smile. I can't wait to see you and the kids tomorrow. I notice a signature of #Mr.TallDark&Handsome in this phone, was that about me or just a default left behind?*
> *#Mr.TallDark&Handsome*

"Oh Crap! Chantae help, what do I say?"

"What girl? What he say?"

"I gave him a phone to use and when I was storing my number for him I was playing around and changed his text signature to Mr. Tall Dark and Handsome and he has found it."

"Either he has found it or someone else he texted has told him. Probably a man not wanting to see that." Chantae laughed.

"Oh my goodness. Okay I have to say something. But what? He gives me butterflies." Brielle was nervous but knew she had to respond.

"Tell him the first thoughts that come to your mind. Be honest what is the worst that can happen? He falls in love?"

"Okay okay, I got this."

> *4:32 pm*
> *Matt 'Mr. Handsome' Cole*
> *Sorry, I was playing around in your phone and that was my first thought of you so that's what I added as your signature. No default. That was for you. The kids are excited to see you tomorrow and so is their momma :)*
> *#MissSophisticatedSummers*

"Oh my goodness I'm not texting any more. I am officially flirting with this man." Brielle said falling back on the bed. They heard the kids snickering laughing at Brielle acting like a school girl who found her first crush except this was by far more than a crush.

Everyone was excited to see Brielle happy over a man. Even if it was Bryson under the circumstances of everyone knowing he was homeless. Brielle and the kids had firsthand experience with Bryson. Everyone else did not have the advantage of seeing how great of a man Brielle and the kids thought he was. Their perception was of him being homeless and not seeing through his kindred spirit and demeanor of strength and character, a genuine man of God.

"You are funny Brie. I am sure he is excited and experiencing the same butterflies you are."

"But I am not ready to be like that with him. At least I don't think I am ready." She said just as her phone buzzed again. She picked it up with the quickness to see his response.

"Oh you are ready. All of your actions and reactions are saying you are ready my friend." After that Brielle had zoned Chantae out again to text Bryson.

4:33 pm
Brielle Summers
Now I am blushing knowing that you think I am tall dark and handsome. The tall dark is a given but the handsome part even through the roughness is flattering. Now I am curious as to if you are attracted to me? Even a little bit?
#Mr.TallDark&Handsome

4:34 pm
Matt 'Mr. Handsome' Cole
Yes.
#MissSophisticatedSummers

Brielle gave a simple answer and bit her bottom lip. She thought about wiggling her way out of where the conversation was going. She had fear in a failed relationship, or being hurt again but felt different with Bryson and struggled to accept he was her blessing from God.

4:35 pm
Matt 'Mr. Handsome' Cole
Yes I am attracted to you a lot. But that's not why I offered to help. I helped because my spirit talks to me about you. You have been special to me since day 1 getting the fish hook from my hair, helping my babies' fish and eating hot Cheetos. ;) But yes I am attracted to you and your spirit.
#MissSophisticatedSummers

As soon as Brielle hit send she was receiving a message at the same time back from Bryson.

4:35 pm
Brielle Summers
Yes is good but is that all I get? I am very attracted to you. I feel like my spirit is connected to your spirit and it's a wonderful feeling that you give me. Since day 1 of meeting you I have felt this way. You have conquered my full attention.
#Mr.TallDark&Handsome

4:36 pm
Matt 'Mr. Handsome' Cole
Wow I guess we are connected. Both thinking and saying basically the exact same thing. So I have your full attention? Really? I am glad I met you Matt! I guess we were where God intended us to be. God amazes me sometimes but this time I am thankful for the amazement!!!
#MissSophisticatedSummers

4:36 pm
Brielle Summers
Yeap, I am convinced for sure now that we are connected. Sending the same message at the same time is a sure sign! I like that I am special to you and the kids. Allow me to make a promise to you. I would never intentionally hurt you or your kids. One day soon things will be different for you, meaning complete happiness. I am going to make sure of that. A promise I intend to keep.
#Mr.TallDark&Handsome

Brielle was enthralled in his every word. Blushing and bursting with happiness. She knew they were just chatting right now but believed his every word he said to her.

4:37 pm
Brielle Summers
I am glad we met as well Brielle. You are my Sunshine. Yes you have my full attention. You have given me a reason to want to live life to its fullest and be happy doing so. God has a funny way of bringing people together. At times least expected he shows up but he knows what he is doing. I am forever thankful to him for sending you to me.
#Mr.TallDark&Handsome

4:38 pm
Matt 'Mr. Handsome' Cole
You are too sweet. My girlfriend is teasing me because you have my cheeks on high beams right now. She said she can tell that we are crazy about each other.
#MissSophisticatedSummers

"You two are going to fall madly in love with one another. You are blushing too hard over there Brie." Chantae said watching Brielle's reactions.

"I know girl. I can't believe how everything is happening. You know I don't give men the time of day and I have been so careful and picky and not dealing with men. I'm just trying to make sense of everything that has happened to me up until this point. But I guess God's plan sometimes doesn't make sense." Brielle was still blushing. She was trying not to ignore Chantae at the same time not missing a beat with Bryson. "We are having a great conversation right now but when I see him I am going to be extremely nervous."

"You will be fine after the first few moments. I am sure he will make you feel comfortable Brie. Don't think too much about it. It's a part of the warm and fuzzy new beginning feelings. I still have those with Bradon." She said noticing Brielle turning her attention back to her phone.

4:39 pm
Brielle Summers
Your friend is wise and has pulled my card. I am indeed crazy
about you Brielle. Wish I could see you right now. I love
having you close to me. Hope that's okay.
#Mr.TallDark&Handsome

"He wishes I was with him right now. Girl I wish I was with him right now." She said in a whisper.

"Then go. The kids can stay here while momma run an errand they will be alright and so will momma."

"Girl are you crazy. I can't go over there alone. Not now." Brielle said both of the ladies still whispering.

"And why not? Nothing will happen unless you want it to happen. It sounds like you have him in the palm of your hands and I am sure he will be following your lead. So go hang out for a couple hours." Chantae was encouraging her friend.

"I don't know girl." Brielle was tapping her fingers and biting her bottom lip.

"Kids! Y'all want auntie Chantae to take you to the movies while mommy run a few errands?" She asked the kids.

"Yes." They all said together.

"Then we can all meet up at eight for dinner. That gives you time to spend and give you a getaway plan."

"Okay I see you have this all planned out for me. Let me mention it and see what he says."

"Girl he is going to say yes. Probably turning cart wheels when he reads your message." They both laughed as Brielle responded back.

4:45 pm
Matt 'Mr. Handsome' Cole
Well your wish could come true if you really want that.
Chantae just volunteered to take the kids to the movies before
dinner. I could visit for a couple hours if you like.
#MissSophisticatedSummers

4:46 pm
Brielle Summers

*Brielle I would be ecstatic for a couple hours of your time.
See you in a few. I promise I will be the perfect gentleman.
Please thank your friend Chantae for me.
#Mr.TallDark&Handsome*

"Oh crap, I'm so nervous. Okay get it together. You can do this just relax." Brielle was fanning herself with her hands and breathing in and out fast realizing what just happened. She agreed to go hang out with Bryson alone.

"Oh hell you talking to yourself, yes you are really nervous. Okay this is what we are going to do. Come on. Kids get your shoes on and stay here we will be right back."

Brielle followed Chantae into the kitchen. She watched as she pulls out a bottle of wine. "Wait you want me to take some wine with me?"

"No I want you to drink a glass while you get ready." She pours Brielle a half a glass of wine.

"So you want me to drink and drive?" She said looking at Chantae with a frown.

"Brielle you know this wine only has nine percent alcohol and it will only knock the nervous edge off a bit."

"Just give it to me." Brielle took the glass and drank half of what she poured at once.

"Well alright now. I know you are not planning on having sex with the man and not saying you stink but you still need to take a hoe bath. I have some fresh cleaning wipes and some smell goods you can put on before you go."

"Okay. Chantae thanks girl for being here and not judging the situation."

"Honey I know you all too well and if this was something other than what you have painted it to be, you would not be where you are with the situation. You are favored by God girlfriend. So I know it's all good."

"Thanks girl. You are on the outside looking in so that means a lot. Let's meet at Logan's at eight. If something happens where I need to meet earlier or later just let me know."

"I gotcha girl."

After Brielle was ready to go, she walked out with Chantae and the kids. She gave her babies kisses and hugs and thanked

Chantae again. She texted Bryson to let him know she was on her way.

> *4:45 pm*
> *Matt 'Mr. Handsome' Cole*
> *I am on my way see you in a few moments...*
> *#MissSophisticatedSummers*

CHAPTER 34
~BRYSON~
SHE IS ON HER WAY

Bryson received the text from Brielle saying she was on her way. He had never been nervous over a woman before now. He made sure he had on deodorant like five times. He made sure he brushed his teeth and his face was clean. He did a hundred pushups and a hundred sit-ups. He couldn't be still. He paused when he heard his phone buzz.

"Oh shoot the other phone." He quickly ran to answer it. "Hey Kenny what's up man?" He said as he looked out the window to ensure Brielle was not there yet.

"Brys man calm down. Take a deep breath and calm down. You are extremely nervous."

"Oh so you watching me too?"

"Yes! And I am sure your arms don't stink but smell sport fresh and your breath should be extra minty." He laughed.

"She likes me man. She likes Bryson the man. Her spirit, man she is the one. I can't believe this is happening to me." Bryson paused by the window speaking calmly thinking about Brielle.

"You deserve this man. I don't mean to bring her up but Jewel was just a place holder for you until you found your queen. It's expected to be anxious and excited when God blesses you with something as real as what is happening to you. Embrace it. Nothing to fear man this is real. I can see it and everyone else on the outside looking in can see."

"You're right man. Thanks Kenny. I needed that pep talk I am a nervous wreck."

"Yeah we all can see. But honestly we are biting our nails over here too. This is exciting."

"Okay so I don't know what's going to happen but promise me if any clothing of hers come off the cameras will be shut off."

"It's in your contract man, I made sure that was a given."

"Thanks man! Ok if at any time it feels like it will go there I will be sure to attempt to take it to the bedroom but just in case. I am not trying to be a porn star."

Laughing. "I got you man. I won't let that happen."

"Okay I am turning this phone off so I will talk to you later. I feel like I have to pray."

"That's better than running around like a crazy man. Call me later Brys when all is calm and Brielle is gone."

Bryson hid the phone upstairs to ensure it was out of sight. He said a prayer thanking God and asking him for guidance. When he heard a car pull up he rushed his prayer to an end saying Amen quickly before walking to the door to greet Brielle.

Walking to the door he could see her smile and tell she was nervous as well. Seeing her put him at ease and all he wanted to do was wrap her up in his arms assure her everything was alright.

"You are so beautiful Brielle." He said walking towards the car to walk with her from the drive way inside the home. He was the perfect gentleman.

"Thank you Matt. You are such a gentleman walking out here to meet me." She was still smiling.

As they walked in the door and he locked it behind him Brielle was so nervous she was shaking.

"Brielle, are you okay? You are shaking." He didn't know what to do knowing her history of abuse.

"Yeah, I'm sorry just nervous. I guess this is all happening so fast, not that I am not excited about it because I am, it's just my nerves." She looked down at her hands fidgeting.

Bryson walked over to Brielle touching her hands gently then pulling her close to him. He put her arms around his waist before gently caressing her face. At that moment everything stopped. Nothing else mattered. All they saw was one another. Looking into each other eyes they could feel love jumping from their spirits. With Brielle's lead, Bryson went towards her lips. He was close enough for her to feel his breath caressing her lips.

He ran his hands through her hair as she closed her eyes and melted in his touch he went in and kissed her lips gently. He kissed the sides of her lips taking his tongue and gently parting the crevices to taste her tongue. The kiss was sweeter than honey. Their tongues danced around in one another's warm wet mouth connecting and caressing and aggressively wanting more from one another. He picked Brielle up and walked towards the sofa. Making sure she can still trust him he spoke softly to her. "I have been waiting to kiss you since the day I first laid eyes on you. Can I just kiss you for a while? Nothing more just sharing in your sweet kisses?"

"Yes, you can kiss me." Her nerves were at ease. As she smiled looking up at Bryson he sat back on the sofa with her sitting across his lap.

He held her in his arms and softly kissed her exploring her mouth. Licking her lips around the outside and exploring her inner lips, her tongue, licking her teeth. He gently bit and sucked on her bottom lip then her top as her tongue entered his mouth he welcomed it as he caressed her tongue with his sucking as it entered his mouth aggressively. One of his hands were aggressively rubbing on her thigh and her lower butt.

Her body was in orgasmic mode. Her nipples were on high beams. Her chest was heaving up and down as her breathing was fast paced. Bryson went from exploring her mouth to her face. Kissing her eyes, her nose, her cheeks, and her ears inside and behind working his way to her neck. He aggressively sucked and bit and kissed as she scratched his back and held on tight to him.

"You okay?" Bryson whispered in her ear still kissing her neck.

"Unhuh." She said back panting her words. "I'm great."

"Good. I am enjoying this."

"Me too Matt." She said with her words barely coming out.

Bryson realized hearing her call him Matt that he was still in character. He wanted Brielle so bad he almost forgot where he was. "You want me to stop?"

"Never." She said. With her eyes still closed grabbing at his back and arms gripping him tight feeling like she needed to hold on to him forever.

"I could kiss you like this every day." He said lifting her body to reposition her legs so that she could be closer. She straddled his waist never once did the kisses stop. Her arms wrapped around his neck as his hands ventured down her back he grabbed her butt and squeezed pulling her hips in closer to him. There was warmth coming from in between her thighs. Bryson knew that if he wanted to make love to her right now he could but remembered she only had a couple hours and he would need more time than that. He didn't want to rush into anything but savor the passionate moment of intimacy.

"I love your kisses." She moaned. Her chest was pressed against his. Her legs spread across his body feeling his hardness pressed against his legs all the way up on his stomach. A smile appeared across her face knowing that this man was not all good looks and hard body but had a nice package to go with it.

Brielle was in a zone. Bryson was awakening all of her erotic places within her orgasmic zones. From her neck to feeling his legs and hardness beneath her she didn't want to appear easy but at that moment she was vulnerable and willing to allow him to make love to every inch of her body. "Matt." She said in a moan.

"Yes beautiful?" he responded still caressing her body and kissing her neck.

"I have to leave close to eight." She said moaning.

"In the morning?" He said becoming excited.

She giggled a bit at his excitement. "Tonight. I have to meet Chantae and the kids." She moaned louder as he aggressively kissed and bit her neck and pulled her in tighter.

"Okay can I keep kissing you until then?" He asked as Brielle phone was ringing.

"I'm so sorry. Because of the kids her call will be the only one I answer promise!"

"Oh of course. I'm going to grab us some water while you answer that." She eases out of his lap noticing the bulge in his pants.

Brielle tried to compose her voice before answering. "Hey girl what's wrong?" She said to Chantae.

"Oh yeah I already know what's happening by the sound of your voice. Brie did you answer in the middle of?" Chantae was chopping up her words due to the kids being in ear range.

"Oh no we were kissing girl that's all." She said in a whisper. Bryson was smiling hearing her whispered voice as he walked into the kitchen.

"Girl that leads to something else. Okay I'm not going to keep you just wanted to tell you we missed the first movie so we are going to Chucke' Cheese and then catching the eight thirty movie after that they want to help me finish Bryson suit. If it's okay with you, they want to spend the night and you can come get them in the morning before church?"

"Chantae are you sure?"

"Are you sure Brie? I mean this is a big step for you."

"I think I am I mean the kissing has me hotter than a fire cracker and I am about to explode."

"Ok I was talking about the kids but that's good too."

They both laughed.

"You tricked me. Girl yes I am okay with them staying with you. Let me talk to my babies. Put me on speaker phone."

"Okay but hey you have fun okay and enjoy yourself. I mean really enjoy yourself, like over indulge in some chocolate seriously."

"I plan too. And thanks girl. I owe you."

"Ok hold on. Kids your mother wants to make sure you okay with auntie Chantae say hi."

"Hey momma. Can we stay we are having fun." Her daughter asked.

"Hey babies. Do you want to stay?"

"Yes momma." Jayla said first with her siblings following.

"Okay, well mommy will come in the morning to get you for church okay."

"Yes ma'am. We love you. Thank you." They all were repeating one another." They were excited and having fun. They never sleep over anywhere besides their grandparents and with Chantae when their mom was there with them.

"I love my babies. See you in the morning okay."

"Ok momma we love you a whole bunch. Good-bye." Jayla said.

"Bye babies." Brielle hung up the phone turning to see Bryson standing behind her with water.

"Everything ok? You don't have to leave do you?"

"Everything is okay, and no I don't have to leave." She said looking up at Bryson.

"Good. That was a great hello." He said as he handed her the water. He wanted to make love to Brielle but figured she would want to wait. Her being with him at the moment meant a lot to him. Kissing her confirmed what he was feeling in his heart.

"That was a wonderful hello. You are a great kisser." She said with a smile. "I need to use the bathroom. I will be right back okay."

"I will be waiting." He said before he quickly pulled out his laptop while he was waiting to send Kenny a message. He used online texting to send a message without having his phone buzz. He didn't want to risk Brielle being suspicious of anything.

>*7:35pm*
>*Kenneth Cartwright*
>*Kenny man did you see what just happened? I think I am in love. What's your thought? Am I missing something? I am a semi porn star now huh.*
>*Brys*

Bryson was hoping he was indeed watching and could see that he was sending a message so that he could receive a quick reply before Brielle returned. He pulls up his resume to throw Brielle off if she does come back and see Kenny message pop up.

>*7:36*
>*Bryson Mathews*
>*We all are sitting here in awe of what just happened. Brys man you are thinking but we all know that you two are falling in love. A genuine real God Ordained love. And we all felt like we were watching a love story unfold with a pre porn show so is this going to be X-rated and taken upstairs?*
>*Kenneth Cartwright*

>*7:37 pm*
>*Kenneth Cartwright*
>*WOW okay and no nothing is happening like that tonight. I am not going to let it. I want her to fall in love with me first.*
>*Brys*

>*7:37 pm*
>*Bryson Mathews*

Oh and we could hear her conversation and she is available all night until morning.....
Kenneth Cartwright

Bryson was excited about that news that he could possibly have her all night. And he wishes he could use his money to buy a few things to enjoy the evening with. He had an idea that he hoped would work.

7:38 pm
Kenneth Cartwright
Kenny last text, I have an idea. Send a pretend neighbor with a welcome basket to the Mrs. and Mr. with some wine, wine glasses fruit and cheese. You know what I need playa so hook it up. Later...
Brys

Brielle was walking back and Bryson quickly hit send before exiting the application and pulled up his resume. "Hey beautiful everything okay?" He asked.

"Yes everything is great. What you doing over there?" She sat down next to him and leaned closer to see the computer.

"Working on my resume a bit. I want to make sure it is perfect so I can apply for a few positions tomorrow online."

"Oh yeah, I can help if you like." She started reading what he had listed and was impressed with his schooling and his job history.

Bryson didn't know how to down grade his resume so he did the best he knew how without making it too bad. Being a business man his mind was programmed to be the best at everything he did. Anything other than that was not in his mindset or acceptable to him.

For the next forty five minutes they sat there working on his resume and flirting with one another. They were enjoying being close to each other. When the door bell rung they both looked surprised.

"Are you expecting someone?" She looked at him.

"No not at all. Let's see who it could be." He motioned for her to join him at the door. They both got up and Brielle was right behind him headed to the door.

"Hello can we help you?" Bryson asked knowing why the lady was there.

"Hi I am your neighbor from four homes down and I saw your light on. Hope I am not imposing. I just wanted to welcome the new couple to the neighborhood with a gift." She handed Bryson the basket. "Okay you two have a great night and welcome to the neighborhood." She said and started to walk away. She didn't want to be questioned but to do the job Kenneth paid her to do.

"Thank you." Brielle and Bryson said together.

"That was nice. She didn't want to stay and chat either." Brielle said.

"No but this is a nice basket, check it out." He sat the basket on the table and started to open it up.

"This is a nice basket and appears to be very expensive. Now I feel bad we didn't even get her name to send a thank you card." Brielle said reaching for the card attached. "All this say is to the Mr. and Mrs. Welcome to the neighborhood. Enjoy!"

"Mr. and Mrs. So that would be me and you right?" He looked up at Brielle with a smile on his face.

"I guess so Mr." She said biting her bottom lip.

"Well Mrs., shall I grab some glasses for this wine?" He said as he brushed a piece of hair behind Brielle's ear.

"That would be nice Mr." She said smiling back at Bryson.

"How much longer do you have? I wouldn't want you tipsy leaving here and driving." Knowing she had all night he wanted to test and see if she too was enjoying their time not wanting to leave.

"Well the kids are staying the night with Chantae now until morning so I am not in a rush at all." Hoping he was not ready for her to leave.

"Okay well great then. I can enjoy more of you. I was not ready for you to leave. Now I don't have to beg you to stay." He said talking back from the kitchen.

Bryson returned with the wine glasses. Brielle pulled out the fruit and candles that were in the basket. Matches were even included. Bryson poured them both some wine before lighting the candles and turning down the lights. They sat there talking and eating the fruit and cheese. Bryson fed Brielle strawberries and grapes. The basket contained chocolate and pepperoni log as well that Bryson sliced for them to enjoy.

After drinking a bottle and a half of the two bottles of wine Brielle was pretty tipsy and bold. Bryson fed her another strawberry and after taking a bite he kissed her lips once more. Brielle was feeling good and turned on and wanted more of Bryson's sweet kisses. "Can you kiss me some more Matt? I love your kisses." She said in a flirtatious way.

"Come here and lay in my arms." He positioned himself on the sofa so that Brielle could lay with him. He was hoping after kissing for a few moments and soft pillow talk she would fall asleep in his arms so he could hold her all night. They kissed what seemed like an eternity of passion between them. Bryson held her close to him not wanting to ever let her go.

Brielle started talking soft and slow. "I trust you and I know God sent you to me. I'm happy." Was her last words before she drifted to sleep with her head nested in Bryson's neck. He kissed her forehead and held her close to him tightly in his arms. He was happy and in love with Brielle. Her actions spoke the same to him and he knew she was his Eve. He knew that he wanted her in his life forever and would make sure that happens.

CHAPTER 35
~CHANTAE~
PROUD MOMENT

Chantae was working on her designs when she received a call from Bradon. She wanted him to know how proud she was of what he does for a living, following his dreams and acquiring what he wants out of life. She wanted to know how he does it, and what exactly he does to gain his success. Bradon's pride is in the way and he doesn't want to let her down so he fabricates his story and tell Chantae what he thinks she wants to hear.

He was use to fabricating his story, telling women that everything that appears to be, which is his brother's life is really his life. It was easy to fall backwards to what he knew in fear of losing Chantae if she knew the truth.

"Hey boo." She spoke resting the phone on her cheek and shoulders to have her hands free.

"Hey baby girl you still working?"

"Yes. I don't have much left. I had Brielle's kids helping me which they were great help. They have passed out on me though watching cartoons. They had a long day."

"Oh yeah. Well what about my baby? Are you tired?"

"Just a little but I am okay. She needs the suit tomorrow so I will be up for a few more hours working."

"I am proud of you for working so hard on your passion. Your dreams will come true sooner than you think."

"I surely hope so and I do believe that to be true. Hold on baby let me put my ear piece in." She grabbed her ear piece so her hands could be free without using her shoulders. "Ok I'm back. Babe let me ask you a question."

"Okay sure anything."

"How do you do it? I know you have built your wealth over years of hard work but what is the secret to success?"

Bradon paused for a moment thinking about what to say to Chantae. He didn't want to lie but wasn't ready to tell the truth either. "I guess it is determination and focus. If you want to accomplish your dreams bad enough you have to stay focused and work hard daily. If you don't have self-motivation and believe in yourself then you cannot expect for someone else to believe in your dreams. Day by day you have to work on your goals. If you enjoy what you do then you will never view it as work. Instead you will just see it as enjoying what you do." He was speaking to himself.

"So when do you work? Or do you just always make yourself available to me? Is the hard part of what you have built over?"

Bradon was living off his brother. He made a lot of money building his brothers home but eventually that will run out. "No I have a lot of work ahead of me. I guess you can say I have been in relax-mode enjoying life."

"Well you deserve that. You are motivation for me. Because I have seen what you do and how hard you have worked, it has inspired me to launch my clothing line. Even if you don't think you have done anything please know that you have babe. I appreciate you, and I miss you." She said in a sexy voice.

Bradon was feeling bad for deceiving Chantae. He wanted to run and go back to his old ways but the love he had in his heart wouldn't allow him to run. "I miss you to Chantae. I am seeing you tomorrow right?"

"Yes, we are definitely seeing each other tomorrow babe. Brielle will pick the kids up in the morning then I am all yours. I should be finished with the suit by noon."

"Alright then baby. I can't wait to hold you in my arms with your clothes off and big daddy stroking that honey."

"You being a naughty boy. If these kids were not here you would be over here right now." She said blushing.

"Naughty all evening and all night tomorrow babe. I want you tonight but will let you work. I can't wait."

"I can't either babe. Make sure you here when you wake up and finish what you have to do okay." She blew him kisses through the phone.

"I caught them babe. Work hard but not too long babe."

"I will and I won't be too long babe. Talk to you tomorrow."

"Goodnight my love."

"Goodnight babe."

They finished their conversation with Chantae feeling good. She was smiling and motivated to accomplish her dreams. With Bradon beside her she knew anything was possible. She was on cloud nine and in love.

Bradon on the other hand was feeling down. He was living a lie and realized he had to grow up and be the man his father and brother taught him to be. He decided to write out his plan of action. He wanted to be the man Chantae was proud of but for all the right reasons.

CHAPTER 36
~BRIELLE~
THAT MAN IS AMAZING

Sunday morning Brielle awakened with a smile realizing where she was and what happened the evening before. Bryson was the perfect gentleman and at the same time expressed how much he was feeling her as well. He could have easily had her in his bed but he chose not to take advantage of her or the situation and treat her with respect as a queen should be treated. She laid there smiling thinking a bit more before waking him.

"Matt, are you awake?" She said, rubbing his chest looking up at him biting her bottom lip trying to mask her smile.

"I thought I was dreaming but glad to know I am really holding you tight." He said squeezing her in his arms. "Good morning Sweetheart, are you okay?"

"Yes I am better than ok."

"Oh yeah? How much better?"

"I am marvelously wonderful and still on cloud nine."

"Nice! Good to hear you have no regrets of staying the night with me."

"No regrets but I do want to make breakfast for you before I leave if that's okay?"

"Are you asking if you leaving is okay or the part about you making me breakfast?" He said with a smile.

"Breakfast." She said with a grin on her face. "What? You don't want me to leave or something?"

"I never ever want you to leave. I rather you stay forever." He said pulling her face toward his to kiss her lips. She was mesmerized by him and his kisses had her weakened and under his control. "I love your kisses. Breakfast would be good." She tried to get up and he pulled her in closer. "Are you still coming back this evening with the kids for dinner?"

"We wouldn't miss it for anything in the world. Besides that's all the kids been talking about and looking forward too. We will be here about four if that's ok?"

"Anytime you and the kids come is fine just as long as you do come back."

"Anytime huh, we just have an open invitation?"

"Yes, anytime!" He looked at her with a smile brushing her hair from her face with his hands.

She pulled herself up from the sofa kissing him once more before heading into the kitchen to prepare breakfast. She made him an omelet and fried up some bacon. She didn't mind doing anything for Bryson and treated him as if he was already her man. Not wanting to jump ahead she kept the idea open. He watched her every move in the kitchen keeping her company with more questions about her and her family.

"Breakfast is served darling." She said placing his plate in front of him with a glass of orange juice. She sat down to join him with her own plate with an omelet half the size of his and a glass of juice. She smiled as he took his first bite of omelet savoring the great flavorful taste.

"You are a great cook. I could eat anything you served me." Looking in her eyes he spoke again, "Literally eat anything you serve me." Licking his fingers still looking into her eyes.

"Is it hot in here? What is the air on? You hot Matt? Let me make sure this stove is off." She said fanning herself blushing.

"Brielle I want to make love to you with a passion. I know that's a given so I apologize for any comment I make that is inappropriate. If I had it my way you would have been my girl from the moment we were in diapers, seriously." He laughed out loud.

"Your words are beautiful music to my ears. You don't offend me but I do have to go." After finishing her juice she stood and wrapped her arms around his neck kissing him behind his ear and on his ear before saying, "Thanks for the compliment about my cooking and this won't be the last time I serve you food or dessert. I am hoping to fulfill your appetite completely in all aspects of anything you desire to eat, literally!" She kissed his cheeks before walking away.

She headed to the living room to put her shoes on and grab her things. She bent over in front of the sofa to get her shoes from under the table not knowing Bryson picked his plate up and followed her into the living room. As he was chewing he choked staring at her bottom in the air.

She jumped up and turned towards him. "Are you okay? I didn't know you were standing behind me." She came behind him patting his back.

"Oh yeah, I'm great. Just chewing and speaking at the same time." He said coughing in between his words. Catching his breath and clearing his throat he spoke some more. "Brielle you are a beautiful woman. I really appreciate everything you have done for me. You have cooked for me from day one. And you do everything with grace and a smile. I look forward to the day when I can give you all of the man I am, that you deserve to have in your life." He said wishing she knew his worth.

"What does that mean, all the man I am?" She looked at him with a smile.

He smiled at her caressing her face with the back of his hand. "There is so much more for you to know about who I am but I rather show you when the time is right. I promise you won't be disappointed!"

"Alright now. I think you want me to fall in love with you or something."

"Yes that would be my goal." He tilted his head still looking at her.

Her heart was skipping a beat as she looked into his eyes as if they were telling her his truth for her. Her heart was fluttering and she wanted to give him all of her, her love, her heart, her body, her everything. "Well you did say forever so I guess that's doable along the way huh." She was blushing and biting her bottom lip. "I better go get the kids so we can get to church and get back here."

He watched as she slipped her shoes on and grabbed her things. His food was gone and he placed his plate on the table picking up his orange juice. He downed it and as soon as Brielle stood to her feet he placed his glass down and grabbed her in his arms. "I need to hold you a few moments more before you leave."

She wrapped her arms around his neck as his arms were around her waist and back. As he lowered his head to kiss her she stood on her tip toes to meet him. His lips caressed her lips. With her eyes closed she allowed him to explore her mouth with his tongue as she slightly parted her lips for him to enter. His tongue danced with hers as he held her tight in his arms. He kissed her lips top and bottom and both sides and gently kissed her all over her face. Her eyes, her nose, her forehead, her cheeks, all before kissing her lips again. As she was coming down off her high she opened her eyes to see him looking at her.

"Hey beautiful." He said still holding on to her smiling.

"Hey." She said stretching out the word. "I better go. It's so hard to break away when you don't want me to leave and I don't want to leave. I would ask you to join us at church but don't think the tight fitted items I bought will work for church." They both chuckled.

"Okay I will see you all in a little while beautiful."

"Okay." She said kissing his lips one more time.

He walked her to her car kissing her once again before saying goodbye until later.

Brielle's drive to pick up the kids was spent telling Chantae about the wonderful evening she had and how she felt Bryson was meant to be for her. She was pushing for time trying to spend every moment possible with him so she had Chantae get the kids up brush their teeth and jump in the shower. She stopped and picked up their clothes from home getting herself showered and ready.

When she picked up the kids she peeked at the suit for Bryson and was very impressed at how expensive and stylish it looked. She knew Chantae would be very successful.

Once the kids were in the car they asked her all kinds of questions about seeing Bryson today.

"Momma are we still seeing Mr. Matt today?" Jayla said

"Are we going fishing today momma?" Carter asked.

"Is Mr. Matt still homeless momma?" Olivia said.

"We are going to see Mr. Matt today kids. You know how we were blessed with that money from that Dr.? Well momma thought since we were blessed we should bless someone else. I know you all are excited to move into our new home but momma thought it would be a great idea to let Mr. Matt live there for a few months until he get on his feet."

"That's a really great idea momma!" Jayla said with excitement.

"What you two think Olivia and Carter?" Brielle asked. She glanced into the back seat through her mirror.

"Well momma," Carter started with Olivia looking at him waiting for his response. "I think Mr. Matt is the kind of man who would appreciate you helping him but his pride wouldn't allow him to let you help him long and he would repay you as soon as he could. May not be in the form of money but surely in the form of loyalty and respect. And you two would be friends forever you know so I think it's a great idea too." Carter appeared to be deep in thought. Brielle could only imagine what he was thinking. She thought for sure he was happy at the thought of Bryson being around to protect them, especially his mom.

"Yeah me three momma." Olivia said in a soft voice. "We can wait to move a little bit longer. Besides that bad man won't be coming back for a long time and we could call Mr. Matt if he did. I know he would help us."

"Ahh Olivia, he is never coming back. I didn't think you all thought about him at all. I am so sorry I didn't know you all even thought about him possibly coming back. They wouldn't even let him into our building if he tried to come back. They all know what he look like and they know who comes to visit us and who would not be welcomed. Floyd would protect us like his family. Babies I promise momma will not let anyone harm you or me ever again. That's one reason why momma has been leery about people coming around us and particularly men. But yes I think Matt would protect us from anything. I don't believe he would ever hurt any of us. I don't know why I like him so much but I do, is that okay?"

"Yes." They all said in unison.

"We like him momma a lot." Olivia said.

"Yes we do momma, wish he was our dad. He reminds me of granddaddy how he naturally wants to take care of us."

"Oh yeah Carter? You have a lot of knowledge speaking like your granddaddy would. I love you three very much you know?"

"We love you very much too momma." Jayla said.

"Yes we love you a whole bunch momma. You are everything to us." Olivia said.

"We love you to the moon and back mom and then back to infinite and beyond." Carter said.

"You all are the sweetest. So, today we are going to the new house where Matt is now staying and we will be having dinner at his new place where he will be staying for a while."

The kids were all excited screaming, "yay", "he already moved in", "yes I knew it" and were bursting with excitement.

"Momma I thought we were going to church first." Jayla said.

"We are going to church baby and then we are going to see granny and granddaddy. We are going to make a chocolate cake before we go see Mr. Matt."

"Why we making it before we go over Mr. Matt's momma?" Jayla asked.

"It's a new recipe and I want to make sure it's perfect before we go so we will make two. One for your grandparents and one for Mr. Matt."

The kids were laughing in the back ground.

"But momma everything you make is always good except for that one time when you purposely messed up the…" Carter was saying before his momma interrupted him.

"Carter we said we would never speak of that now. Let's just stick to making everything good okay." She laughed and the kids laughed with her. He was speaking of a sabotage meal she made for their dad that made him very sick and the kids had to eat only what she gave them on their plate and not ask for any extra.

"Yes ma'am." He said snickering again.

They arrived at church, heard a wonderful sermon before heading to Brielle's mom house. She made the first cake and it was perfect just like the first time she tasted it at Bradon's party. So she made the second one to take to Bryson. Her parents loved the cake and her brother ate three pieces alone. He said that was his new favorite dessert and she had to make it for him often. They all laughed at him rubbing his full belly talking about the cake.

Brielle and the kids prepared the other cake to take with them to Bryson's house. When they packaged the cake for travel they said their farewells. When they arrived at Bryson's home he was excited to see them and they were jumping for joy very excited to see him.

Bryson and Brielle were both smiling from the evening before and the morning the spent together. Bryson surprised Brielle with dinner he prepared for them. Instead of her cooking he decided to be a show off and share his cooking skills he learned from his mom. She surprised him with the cake her and the kids made and the suit she had Chantae design just for him.

The cake had him. It tasted the same as when his mom makes it. He ate some of the cake before dinner and had to make himself stop because the kids were looking at him as if he was about to be in trouble for eating dessert before dinner. He opened the suit and was in love with the design. He kept talking about the suit and how it seemed perfect and looked like a million dollars. He was impressed with Chantae's work.

Just when he thought he was giving to Brielle he was yet again amazed of her loving giving heart. The love that they had for each other was instantly and naturally beautiful. The relationship Bryson and Brielle had established was growing quickly. And because of that, everyone including the children was happy.

CHAPTER 37
~BRADON~
CONFESSIONS TO CHANTAE

Bradon stayed up all night working on his business plan. The lifestyle he was living was based on his brother's success not his own and he was ready to change that. His brother had enough money to take care of him for the rest of his life, but Chantae has pulled the desire for more out of him. Not just for her but to prove to his self the type of man he can be and not just his brother's shadow.

He stayed up until four in the morning working. Staying up for business and not pleasure was new to him. He woke up four hours later, got dressed and left the house to run errands. He wanted to search for his own place and look for possible buildings to start his business. He hired a real estate broker to work for him and gave her a few leads that he was interested in purchasing. Now he had to fix things with Chantae. No more lies.

He picked up the phone to call her hoping she was awake. "Good morning handsome are you awake?" She said when she picked up the phone.

"Yes my love I have been up for hours taking care of business. You want to do lunch?"

"That sounds great babe but I am almost done with this suit. So can we do a late lunch? I need about an hour to finish then shower and get ready."

"No worries baby girl. Lunch is coming to you. I will be there in about an hour and a half ok."

"That sounds wonderful and I have dessert waiting for you."

"Umm I know you do. Can't wait to indulge."

"Can't wait to feed you." They both giggled.

"Hey thanks for being so beautiful inside and out Chantae"

"Ahhh thanks babe. Hurry here okay."

"I will see you soon babe."

After Brielle left with the kids that morning she laid back down. Being up all night working had her tired. Chantae finished up the suit within the hour and had it pressed and ready for Brielle to pick up. She had Brielle meet her in exactly an hour and a half after she hung up with Bradon. She didn't want any interruptions once Bradon was there. She planned to eat and have fun with her man. She finished with time to shower and throw on some clothes before Brielle called.

"Hey Diva you here?" Chantae said answering the phone.

"Yes I have the kids in the car can you bring it out for me and I have your money."

"Sure. Brie I didn't even tell you a price."

"I know my friend but I got you covered." She said looking behind her at the car pulling up. "Girl your boo here he just pulled up."

"Ohh lala, I am on my way out Brie."

Brielle got out of the car to greet Bradon. "Hey you, how are you?" She said as he greeted her with a hug.

"Well if it isn't Miss Brielle hear one moment gone the next. My friends won't stop asking me about you. They are still trying to find your glass slipper." He joked with Brielle.

"You got jokes I see. Well your mother entertained me that evening and I think she enjoyed my company as well. How is she doing?"

"Mom couldn't stop talking about you."

"Oh yeah, good things right?"

"Yeah good things. She adored you Brielle. And she taught you how to make my brothers favorite cake so you better watch out she will try to play match maker." Brielle laughed. "My brother would absolutely love you by the way. Maybe one day I will introduce you two.

"Maybe one day."

"Hey my two favorite people." Chantae said coming out the door. She had the suit in her arms and laid it on the hood of the car for Brielle and Bradon to look at.

"Hey baby." Bradon said kissing Chantae and wrapping his arms around her.

Brielle opened the garment bag and was very impressed at what she saw. "Girl this suit is nice and fancy. Looks very expensive. Matt is going to look like a million bucks."

"That is a nice suit. You paid attention to the details that men like in their suits and the colors are on point." Bradon felt the material of the shirt. "Oh yeah you on to something big baby girl. This is excellent work for sure." He kissed Chantae on the forehead.

"Thanks babe. I will be right there ok." She said as Bradon was walking towards the house.

"Okay y'all chat and do what girls do best." He took the food inside to prepare the plates.

"Girl that's my baby. So tell me what really happened last night did you get you some at any point? I gotta see your eyes when you tell me."

"Girl I was telling you the truth. I promise nothing more happened. We just kissed and he held me all night. After drinking that wine one of my neighbors brought over I went to sleep lying on his chest. And he held me all night."

"Okay I believe you. No need to rush into anything. I wish my neighbors would bring me wine."

"We were so close though girl. But he was respectful, such a gentleman. I have to go but here, take the check and use the difference of what I owe towards your business okay. I need to stop at my parents' house before we head over to Matt's. I'm cooking Sunday dinner for all of us." She said as she was zipping the suit up.

"Sunday dinner with the family I hear you girl. That's a good sign he likes the kids." She opened the check and saw the amount. "Brielle this say Seven Thousand Dollars are you crazy?"

"No not crazy just over excited and confident in your new business. Besides you made me a dress and a suit and bought me some shoes. Oh and I didn't plan on giving those back to you either."

"Thank you so much friend." She hugged Brielle. "I am going to make sure I take care of you and you know this right?"

"I know. Go on in there and take care of your man." She said winking.

"I'm going. You enjoy your man girl he going to be your husband watch."

"Okay! I would surely say I do. And Bradon is going to be your husband. I see the way he looks at you."

"And you know I would say I do. Be careful girl." She waved to the kids and Brielle as they were leaving.

She headed in the house to her man and some lunch.

"Now you are all mine and I am going to be greedy." Bradon said to Chantae.

"Be greedy babe. I want you all for myself as well. No phone, no kids, no interruptions. Just me and you." Chantae said as she straddled Bradon sitting across the sofa. Bradon kissed her lips seductively. Chantae couldn't help but smile. "You kissing my teeth babe I can't stop smiling."

"And why is that?" He asked kissing her face around her lips as he squeezed her bottom pulling her closer to him.

"Because I feel like the luckiest woman in the world having you." Her eyes were closed and she noticed his slight release of her.

"No I am the luckiest man." He said. "Come on let's eat I am starved."

"Ok." Chantae said feeling a bit confused. Bradon always take the opportunity to indulge in her loving. Never has he stopped to do anything else. "You alright?" She put the back of her hand on his forehead checking to see if he was running a fever.

He laughed as he pulled the food from the bag. "Yeah I'm good babe. Don't worry when we are done. I am just getting started and will have you all afternoon, evening and all night long."

"Alright now. That's what I'm talking about." She said smiling. "What we eating?"

"I got us some salad and some chicken and shrimp vegetable pasta. We are going to need the strength."

"Umm, is that garlic bread?"

Bradon was making their plates. "I couldn't leave the bread out babe. My mom prepared bread at just about every meal when we were growing up."

"I can't wait to officially meet your mom. I am a bit jealous that Brielle spent time with her." She said poking her pouty lip out.

"Don't worry my mom will love you."

"Well good. I surely hope so cause I have fallen in love with her son." She leaned in to kiss him.

"I love you sweetheart. I wanted to talk to you about some things."

"Uh oh, is this good or bad?"

"Not bad Chantae you are my diamond you are not going anywhere so don't even think that.

"Ok as long as we got that clear. I was nervous for a second. What's on your mind babe?"

"Okay I am just going to come out and say it okay. Do you know Bryson Mathews? What he does?" He asked looking into her eyes.

"That name sounds familiar but he is your brother right?" Chantae said confused at where he was going.

"Yes. He is also one of the richest men in this world. He owns everything that has Cole's Estate's in the name and countless other investments he is involved with."

"Well damn success runs through your family genes."

Bradon looked at Chantae with seriousness across his face. "Ok so the house that I live in is my brothers. The black card I carry is on my brother's account. Everything that I portray to have, the life I live is not mine it's all my brothers."

"Wait a minute. Do you think I am with you because of what you have portrayed to have?" She looked at him a bit confused.

"I think it has added to your happiness and this is what you have expected being with me would be like. I mean I'm not broke. I have money but it will soon run out. My brother could take care of me for the rest of my life and I could continue to live like this. But I can't take the credit for anything that I have. Up until now I have only worked when I wanted to like building the house I live in for my brother."

"So where is your brother? Why haven't I seen him at the house?" She asked trying to make sense of what Bradon was saying.

"He is always working and right now he is on a top secret project for a couple months or something so I have been there by myself. But I put together my business plan. I looked at a few buildings to start my own company and I am going to find my own place. You have motivated me in so many ways to grow up out of my brother's shadow and start being the man I am supposed to be."

"Let me say this Bradon. I am sorry that you thought your success influenced me to be with you because it did not. I fell for you the night I met you in the club and you took me home with you and took care of me without taking advantage of me. At that moment I knew nothing about you or what you had or where we were but I knew your heart and character. That's what made me fall hard for you. And over these last few months you have treated me like a queen. But the part that mattered the most did not include money or material things. It included quality time, conversations and text messages, holding my hand and treating me kind and like I was your most valuable possession, oh and the sex just sealed the deal." She said with a slick smile.

Before she could finish speaking Bradon went in to kiss her, and the flames were sparking. "I love you Chantae so much. I promise I'm going to make you happy and proud." He was indulging in her neck aggressively kissing and biting.

"I love you more. I am proud of you now babe. Oh that feels good." She said panting and moaning.

Bradon wanted to make love to her right then and there. He had her shirt off quickly releasing her bra. Their clothes went flying to the floor. Bradon picked her up in his arms and placed her back against the wall. She wrapped her legs around his body. He played with her clit from behind making sure she was good and wet ready to welcome him inside her loveliness. He penetrated her pushing deep inside while holding her in place. His body moved up and down while she held on to his back digging her nails into his skin. He sucked on her breast as he pushed inside her. He stayed in that same position until he felt her inner walls pulsating and flowing with honey. Her sweet orgasmic juices covered his manhood and the ride was slippery and wet.

"Baby you make me feel so good." Chantae said as Bradon carried her from the living room to the bedroom. He laid her on the bed pushing her legs in the air. He caressed her thighs teasing them with his kisses. His tongue explored her thighs until he met her honey flowing tasting the sweetness sharing the sweetness with his lips meeting her lips. He kissed her all over sucking on her bare caramel skin. He explored every inch of her body making her moan in pure blissful satisfaction.

Bradon made love to Chantae all evening and all night as if this was the first time he made love to her. The exhaustion from their love making was overlooked by pure ecstasy. The after sex was just as great as the first time that night. Bradon held Chantae in his arms. Their legs overlapping and tangled together. He caressed her hair and any other part of her body he could touch as they talked about future plans for them both individually and for them together as a couple.

Bradon noticed all of her sketches and models wearing clothes she designed. He was very impressed with the dresses she made for the party and with the suit she made for Brielle. He knew he would not only push his architecture business but help Chantae master her business with great success as well. They were in love and Bradon was ready to settle down and be a one woman man.

CHAPTER 38
~BRIELLE~
GIRLFRIENDS' MOMENT

Monday morning Brielle and Chantae both arrived to work with smiles on their face. The weekend was a success for both ladies with the men in their life. They met up in the break room to eat breakfast and catch up on the details of their weekend.

"Hey girlfriend, how are you this morning?" Brielle said to Chantae.

"Hey girlfriend. I'm wonderful this morning. Feel like a new woman."

"Ohh lala I know what that mean." She said raising her eyebrows.

She grinned nodding her head. "How are you Brie? How was dinner?" Chantae asked as they took their seats.

"Dinner was great girl. The kids loved seeing him again and we had a great time. Feels like a real family." She said gazing into day dream land.

"Brie you all are a real family, you are glowing something fierce. You're in love with that man already!"

Brielle was smiling. "It's just new feelings girl. I just can't believe that he was down like that Chantae. It's something about him that just doesn't say homeless. He is strong in his words and his character speaks volumes to me. He seems like the type of man that knows what he wants and knows how to get it. All he is missing is love."

"You are so in love and nothing you say will change my thoughts about that my friend."

"If you say so Chantae. You and Bradon are in love I know that. You lit up when you saw him Sunday. Just a blushing."

"Yes we are in love. That I won't deny but he dropped a bomb on me yesterday."

"Uh oh what do you mean?"

"He basically told me he was living in his brother's shadow."

"How so?" Brielle said raising her eyebrow. She already knew about the house belonging to his brother from the conversation with Bradon's mom.

"Well, you know that big house he lives in?"

"Yeah that big beautiful mansion."

"Well he did design it but he designed it for his brother. That house is his brother's home."

"No way? Did he tell you it was his house?"

"You know what Brie, I was thinking about that and he never told me it was his house. I just assumed because his room is a master suite that's enormous and beautiful I thought it was the main room in the home. And the fact that the maid took care of everything for him and he woke up to cook me breakfast and no one else was in that big ass house. I just thought it was his home."

"So where does his brother be at, why haven't you ever seen him there?"

"Bradon said he is always working and right now he is on some secret mission or something. But I do know he is very wealthy. Since my man is not and I am not giving him up because of that, I wish you could at least meet the brother. I mean if nothing happens with you and Matt."

"You know money and material things do not impress me at all girl. They are nice to have if love is first but not impressive to get me. But that house is immaculate. I would love to have a home like that."

"I know girl. He said he was looking for a place of his own just when I was envisioning myself living there."

"Well maybe he will design you a house just as magnificent."

"Oh I am sure he will. He said I have motivated him to become the man he was destined to be. This weekend he finished his business plan and started looking for a building."

"Well that's good. He doing his business and you doing yours and that equals great success. Girl shoot I think I want a house instead of clothes y'all are about to be rolling in money.

"I know right. It all sounds good Brie. Just pray for us that we do well in our business venture okay."

"Of course I got you girl. God has you both!"

"And thanks Brie for the generous check you wrote me. You are such a genuine great friend."

"You welcome girl. Thank you for the suit it was a huge hit!"

"My pleasure of course. I am glad he liked it."

"Girl he loved it. He praised your talents. Talking like he knew what fine clothing should look like. He said your suit was that fine quality."

"Wow! Ok I really like him now." She said as the ladies both giggled.

"So what about the black card? Is that his brothers as well?" Brielle asked.

"Girl yes! That was his brother's card. He has money but not that unlimited kind of money."

The ladies laughed and enjoyed the rest of their breakfast until it was time to go back to work. Their friendship was priceless. They talked about everything with one another. They shared personal stories and secrets. Chantae was like a sister to Brielle. They went through school together all through college and ended up working for the same company.

Chantae was there when Brielle went through her abuse. She made sure Brielle fought through that battle to recover for herself and her kids. She was mother to her kids when Brielle's mother wasn't there. Brielle was like a real sister to Chantae. Although they were different in many ways they shared the same loving heart. They didn't sugar coat advice telling one another what they wanted to hear but what they needed to hear.

No matter how many other friends came around the bond these ladies shared was undeniably inseparable. They shared a lifetime of friendship between the two ladies.

CHAPTER 39
~BRYSON~
SPENDING QUALITY TIME

After the heated evening and Sunday family time with Brielle and the kids, Bryson was determined to win her heart and make her his wife. His entire life was based on gaining success. Now he has more success than he has ever imagined and he was focused on finding true love, to raise a family and spend the rest of his life happy and in love. Brielle fulfilled every thought he envisioned that happiness would be and so much more. She gave him instant feelings of love that still lingered within his spirit long after she was gone.

He was experiencing the Naked Truth of Love. Just like when Adam and Eve met, the only thing Eve saw was the man naked, having nothing but his character, his words and his spirit. Eve fell in love instantly with the man God created and not the things man acquired. These are the feelings that Bryson hold dearly in his heart for Brielle. She loved him in his nakedness and there was no denying that she was falling in love with Bryson the man and not the lavish luxuries that he acquired.

A few days passed since their last encounter. They shared text messages and calls staying in touch and learning more about the other. Bryson shared the news of landing a job at Cole Estates as a business analyst. He told her he started the same day as his interview. He said the suit had a lot to do with it that he received several compliments. Brielle was excited for him. She knew from his character he was a go getter. The few weeks that they have been in one another's life were incredible for them both.

Brielle went to visit Bryson to see how he was settling in to his new space and his new job. She wanted to make sure he didn't need anything more. It made her feel good to realize she could help him get off the streets and have a warm safe place to rest. In spite of her attraction and the way he made her feel even when he was not around, she still wanted to help. As Brielle walked towards the house Bryson could see her through the window and met her at the door.

"Hello Brielle." Bryson spoke as he stood in the door way waiting for Brielle to approach. He had on grey cotton sweat pants, white socks and a black fitted t-shirt. And of course a big pretty smile across his face.

"Hey Matt, I hope you don't mind me stopping by. I wanted to see how you were settling in to the place and see if you needed anything." She noticed his nice physique screaming for her to caress. And his muscular arms were screaming 'let me lift you closer to me'. From the way his shirt laid on his chest and stomach she could tell he do sit-ups on a regular.

"I don't mind one bit. I was hoping to see you today." He grabbed her by the waist kissing her lips when she approached. "Where are the kids?"

"My mom gets them on Wednesday and takes them to church and dinner afterwards. I normally don't get off work until late, so I miss out on church and catch them for dinner sometimes. It's a way for my mom and dad to have some time with the kids and me to have a little time to myself. Actually they are out of school tomorrow and Friday for in-service or something so they are staying the night tonight. I took off Friday so we could have a full day of fun." She walked in and sat on the sofa.

"So I can have some of your time tonight?" He said sitting on the sofa kissing her again.

"Yes you can have all of my time tonight." She said smiling. She reached into her bag she had with her and pulled out a bottle of wine. "I have wine for us, would you like a glass?"

"I would rather have a glass of you. I would sip it slow to savor every ounce."

Brielle chuckled. "Is that right? A glass of me! Just a glass or the whole bottle? You know there is a difference." She said smiling.

"If I can have the whole bottle I will take the whole bottle. Girl you giving me chill's. I just want to embrace you and never let you go."

"Embrace me then. I would love that." She leaned towards him as he grabbed for her to come to him. He squeezed her tight and held onto her for a while. "I missed you not seeing you for a few days." She said inhaling his sweet scent.

"Yeah it was torture not being able to hold you or see you. It should be illegal for you to go an entire day without me seeing you."

Brielle turned to look at him and they both giggled. "That was sweet and you sounded so serious. How about we make it a must to see each other every day. Either at lunch time or we could all have dinner together or something. I mean if you are serious."

"As a heart attack, yes I am serious. I would love that Brielle. If I could I would give you everything in the world your heart desired. The moon, the stars, your own island. Anything and everything. You are that girl that deserves that and so much more. And yes I would make sure to be in your presence every day, every second I could." He kissed her forehead.

"Matt you are the sweetest. And I believe every word you say. But the only thing my heart desire is love. Pure genuine true love. I am not and never have been materialistic. I mean who wouldn't love nice things but that doesn't impress me. Those things are all replaceable. But love is something that is priceless and irreplaceable. It is ordained from God, it is nourished and groomed. Everything that the bible verse 1 Corinthians 13:4-8 says is what I want, what I desire."

"Do you know the verse by heart?"

"Yes of course, Love is patient, love is kind. It does not envy, it does not boast, it is not proud. It does not dishonor others, it is not self-seeking, it is not easily angered, it keeps no record of wrongs. Love does not delight in evil but rejoices with the truth. It always protects, always trust, always hopes, always perseveres. Love never fails."

"Love never fails." He said after her. "That is exactly what I want Brielle. My mom has always spoke those words over me and my brother. You are my angel. I must have done something right to have you here in my life just when I needed you."

"I'm sure you know how God works. Sometimes we go through bad things, rough patches in our life and that's his way of positioning us for the ultimate blessing. Getting us ready for that one thing we would have otherwise missed ourselves. Our setbacks will often be His comeback plan. God always has a plan."

"Brielle, I know with the situation I was in it may seem like I am just talking because I am grateful to you, kind of like how men do when they are in jail and then they get out and things are different. But every word I am saying to you, every emotion I am feeling is genuine. I would feel this way if I had nothing and I would feel this way if I had billions. I'm going to fix some things and in the next couple weeks I am going to ask you to be my girl, to be my everything. I don't want to ever lose you in my life. My spirit is saying you are my soul mate and I need you to trust me. I have to fix some things and make things right for you, me and those three blessings to be a family. And I promise to fill your heart's desire of that love you speak of. If you can't tell by now please know that I want you Brielle. God knows I want you from the first day I laid my eyes on you!"

Brielle had tears in her eyes. "Matt, I believe you. I believe every word you say. Your character and your spirit and everything that you say I believe." She reached up and kissed his lips.

"Brielle it is so easy to love you." He pulled her closer to him. She was sitting in his lap. "How long do I have you for tonight?"

"I would ask how long do you want me to stay but I think I know the answer so you can have me all night until I have to get up and go to work in the morning."

Kissing her with excitement he pulls back and say, "Really?"

"Yes really! And you can have the whole bottle." She said biting on her bottom lip grinning.

"Whole bottle huh?" He said with a big smile.

"Yes, but this bottle is very delicate and sensitive and needs caressing a lot. You need to give this bottle compliments on the shape of the bottle the contents of the bottle and how the bottle makes you feel, promise?" She was moving in his lap as she spoke ensuring he knew that bottle meant her.

"I promise! I want to make love to you so bad right now." He leaned in and kissed her aggressively. He grabbed at her body like he never wanted to let her go. She managed to run her hands under his shirt caressing his bare skin. She was exploring the hardness and the silky smoothness of his skin.

"Matt it's been a very long time for me. Like more than a couple years since I have been sexual in any kind of way with a man. But I think about making love to you, wondering what it would be like." She kissed his lips before he could respond.

Just moments later her phone rung with the ring tone of Michelle Williams 'When Jesus says yes' ringing in the air. They both smiled and didn't know what to think about that song playing at that moment. She answers, "Hey mom." Looking at Bryson with a smile and wide eyes. "Oh hey baby girl. Y'all having fun? Oh yeah?"

She talked to the kids and her mom for a few moments. She told her mom she was spending time with Bryson. Her mom wanted to meet him soon and told her to invite him over for Sunday dinner.

Bryson poured them some wine and when she finished talking to the kids and her mom it was back to the two of them. "Your kids love you so much."

"Yeah they my babies and they are surrounded with my love every day so they don't have a choice but to love they momma."

"Lucky kids, to be surrounded with your love every day." He took a sip of his wine never taking his eyes off Brielle. He loved to see her blush.

After a few more moments of talking and drinking wine Bryson grabbed Brielle by her hands and said, "Brielle, I don't want to make you uncomfortable. We can talk and kiss and I can hold you all night again. I don't want you to feel like I am rushing you into anything. I would wait forever to make love to you honestly. You are worth that." He leaned in kissing her slowly on her lips then pulled her in closer to him.

She leaned back slightly away from him and said, "Or you can make love to me right now!" The wine was making Brielle bold in her words and feeling at ease. She had been horny for Bryson since the first time she laid eyes on him so the feeling she had for him was not new. Their eyes were locked and Brielle took off her shirt in one swift motion revealing her yellow lacy Victoria Secret bra holding her voluptuous fully erect breast and a flat well-toned and defined stomach.

Bryson, forgetting for a moment about the cameras, was stunned by her sexiness she always covered up. She straddled him kissing him aggressively. With a feeling of urgency he remembered the cameras and stood to his feet with Brielle still straddling him. Wrapping her legs around his waist he headed up stairs to the bedroom, kissing her every step of the way.

"Oh yeah my parents want you to come over for dinner Sunday. We can talk more about details tomorrow ok." She said in between kisses.

"I'm there. Yeah let's talk about that tomorrow." Opening the door he took her to the bathroom never taking his lips from hers. He turned the shower on. Undressing the both of them quickly he picked her up in his arms and stepped into the shower. Kissing her every second. He washed her body caressing and touching and squeezing enjoying the moments of love making. He washed his body in between washing and exploring Brielle's body. When he was done washing he let the water run over their body as he kissed her skin, exploring her body with his lips. He explored her curves with his hands guiding her back up against the shower wall as he kneeled down and placed one of her legs around his neck and he tasted her honey spot gently licking her clit sucking on her lips and exploring her loveliness with his tongue. He was ready to dry her off and make love to her.

"You like my body?" Brielle asked.

"Love every inch of it. It's a master piece I can't wait to explore. Are you sure you are ready for this? We could stop here if you like and I can just hold you."

Looking down at his hard thick and long erection she said, "Yes I'm sure I am ready. I know I am in the best hands and you will take care of me." She said trying not to blush.

He picked her up and carried her to the bed kissing her every step of the way. He started with her neck, kissing her and biting gently. He grabbed at her breast and indulged each one brushing his face up against them both savoring the feeling of her bare skin against his. Her hands caressed his head pulling at his ears as she moaned in pleasure. He nibbled down her sides and along her abs rubbing on her legs. He lifted one of her legs and put her pretty manicured feet in his mouth sucking on her toes and nibbling on the arch of her foot. He worked his way up her leg, up to her thigh until his mouth covered her lips of her loveliness in between her thighs. He flicked his tongue like a butterflies wing until he made her cum sweet honey for him to taste. She moaned loudly as she squirted sweet milky honey in his mouth.

She had a grip on his shoulders squeezing as her nails nearly pierced his skin leaving passion marks. That didn't bother Bryson one bit. When he was done savoring Brielle's orgasmic sweet juices he went back up looking in her eyes confirming her satisfaction of her first orgasm of the night. He quickly indulged in her lips again kissing her passionately.

Their seductive kisses said I love you. Their touches said I love you. And the way he was making love to her body said I love you. Lying in between her legs kissing her she grabbed at his back wanting to feel him inside her. The anticipation for him was making her desire for him stronger. The hardness stroked her lips and grazed her honey pot until he was ready to enter and savor the sweetness he tasted. He worked his way up to entering the tightness of her loveliness until he was all the way inside her. He felt as if she was a virgin and he was her husband taking her virginity for the first time. He took his time making sure to be gentle enough but satisfying to her body. If she pulled at him he knew she wanted more. He went deeper inside and at a faster pace. He kept kissing her neck gently biting and sucking. He left no skin undiscovered. His in and out stroke drove Brielle crazy insane full of pleasure increasing her desire for his love. Her orgasmic juices were all over Bryson flowing from her warm walls of loveliness and that drove him crazy with passion. She moaned with his every stroke. He put her in positions he wanted her in with one motion. Her body was perfect for him and his was perfect for her. Their bodies were connected just like their souls.

He loved Brielle with every stroke and every kiss and every touch of his hands. Bryson made sure he took care of her to please every orgasmic spot she could imagine. He was gentle and he was rough when she desired it enjoying every moment of their love making.

Every time she started shaking and holding her breathe, he knew she was having an orgasm and he pulled out and put his mouth on her to taste all of her honey flowing. It was his way of having a part of her inside him. He made love to her body for six hours before he had his orgasm. He came inside her, something he has never done before. But Bryson was connected to Brielle and did not want to move. They were exhausted after making love and no one moved. They lay there in bed together cuddling as they fell fast asleep.

Embraced in each other's love making, sweat and cum, they were inseparable not once releasing their grasp from the other.

Four hours later Brielle awakened realizing she was in heaven lying in Bryson's arms but that she was also about to be late for work according to the time on the clock. She rolled over kissed Bryson and said, "We have jobs to get to babe. I need to jump in the shower can you grab the black bag out of my car, it's in the trunk." She said attempting to move from his tight grip.

"Okay sweetheart anything else you need?" He said with a smile on his face, slowly releasing her.

"No, and I apologize I won't be able to make you breakfast." She said walking into the bathroom.

"Don't apologize for that. You were very satisfying and filled my appetite just fine last night." He said to Brielle. When she was gone from hearing range he whispered under his voice, "I know I am in love, she is my queen."

When Brielle was showered and dressed she headed down stairs to see that Bryson had breakfast and juice ready for her to go. "Oh wow you are amazing fixing me breakfast." She said with a big smile.

"Damn!! You go to work looking this beautiful every day?" He said with a smile, wanting to grab her and head back upstairs.

"Thank you, I know heels and a skirt suit to work very business casual in my new manager role. Chantae designed this suit. She is amazing!"

"You are breath taking beautiful. I hope she plans to use you as a model when she launches."

"We will see, maybe. I need some more sweet kisses before I go." She said walking towards him. He placed her breakfast on the table before kissing her. She had on lipstick as well wanting to make sure she was sexy for him when she came down stairs. "I love your kisses. Thanks for a wonderful night together." She said wiping the lipstick from his lips.

"You are glowing and have a very happy spirit this morning." Kissing her again and squeezing her tight as she smiled. "Will I see you this evening after work?"

"Sure. We can have dinner together. I will pick the kids up when I get off work and we will be right over."

"Love it! I can't wait to see them." Kissing her again he pinned her up against the door kissing her all over her face and neck. She allowed him the few moments to say good bye with his kisses and enjoyed every moment of his lips caressing her skin.

All hot and bothered she was panting and didn't want him to stop but knew she was about to be late. Eyes closed she whispered through heavy breaths, "I love your kisses. You have an un-denying wonderful effect on me and I love it."

He came up to meet her eyes whispering, "I'm glad I do." He said and indulged in her lips once more. Brielle dropped her bags and wrapped her arms around his neck. "Ten minutes please?" He whispered in her ear.

"How could I say no I want you right here right now." She said holding on to him tight.

He picked her up in his arms and quickly headed to the bedroom. Removing her clothes quickly he was all over her body. Savoring her sweet honey before placing his hard erection in between her creamy warm thighs, she was eager to receive his thickness and feel him deep within her loveliness. For ten minutes he loved her body kissing her nonstop. They were in love and there was no denying it. The passionate love making they shared was yet another sign of the true love they were experiencing.

After they were finished she quickly washed up needing to leave for work. "That was so worth me being late for work." She said smiling back at him standing there watching her.

"You be sure to think of me while you are working and keep that smile on your face." He said following her down the steps.

"That is surely going to happen. Every second of my day until I am back in your arms." She said turning to kiss him again.

Not wanting to let her go he knew he needed to for now. But when she was his, he knew her having to punch a time card would no longer ne necessary. "You make it so hard to let you leave." He said pinning her against the wall.

"That's what got us in trouble moments ago." She whispered as he kissed her face.

"Okay I am forcing myself to stop. Until later." He said pulling back from her.

Gathering her composure she whispers, "Ok until later my love." She picks up her bag and grabs breakfast from the table.

"You have a good day beautiful. See you tonight."

"See you tonight." She said leaving out the door. "Don't be late to work you just started." She shouted back.

"I will be ready in five minutes don't worry Sweetheart."

Brielle headed to work while Bryson started dancing around the house excited. He started talking out loud to the producer, knowing they were watching and listening. "We need to discuss our contract so I can have an early out. I found love in these streets. Who would have thought living as if I had nothing I would find my everything. Brielle is my everything, she is my true love! She is my soulmate!" He thought for a moment about the words he spoke. "Yes my soulmate! Thank you God!" He was screaming. He started singing and couldn't stop smiling. He finished getting ready before heading out the door.

CHAPTER 40
~MRS. MARCELLA SUMMERS~
PRAYING FOR HER DAUGHTER

Late one evening getting ready for bed, Mrs. Marcella Summers and her husband were getting ready to call it a night. She finished talking to Brielle on the phone and couldn't stop thinking about her daughter and the new man in her life.

"Mitch baby. I told Brielle to bring that fella by for dinner Sunday. I sure hope he will come so we can finally meet him." Brielle's' mother said to her husband Mitchell.

"Did she invite him to church as well?"

"Knowing Brie I'm sure she will invite him to church. I know she is conscious of her decisions now but I hope she is being very careful with this situation."

"We are talking about Brie baby. I'm sure she is fine honey and everything is what she says it is with this man. He has to be someone special. It's been way too long with her being involved with a man to just be naïve all of a sudden. It's not like she's sleeping with him and their moving in together." He said dismissing the thought.

"I know but he is living in her new home and she was so excited about moving."

"Everything happens according to God's plan and she is favored by His Grace. I am sure there is a blessing coming out of this. God didn't have their paths cross for nothing. Trust me, you know we raised Brie right and this is nothing like the devil of a man she got caught up with before. But as bad as it was that situation has made her stronger and wiser and has helped get her to where she is today."

"You're right honey. We pray for her constantly and she is a Christian woman and prays herself. You are absolutely right she will be fine." Mrs. Summers was worried about Brielle. Although she teased her about finding a man because she wanted to be sure she was protected at all times, she still wanted to ensure she was safe. They were older and her husband almost killed Brielle's ex witnessing him hurting her and the kids and that's something she never wanted to happen again.

She heads to her bathroom to take a bath. As the water was running she kneels at the tub and prays for Brielle.

"Heavenly gracious Father, I come to you right now giving you all the glory and thanksgiving as we owe all thanks to you for your continued blessings and your continued covering and your favor you have bestowed upon us. Lord you have always been so good to us and the outcome in our life has already been determined. Even so, I'm asking you Lord to please continue to cover my daughter and her three beautiful children, my grandchildren. This new man she has in her space Lord, let him too know you and protect my daughter. Give her the grace and mercy and bless her with a loving husband and father for her children. We have raised our daughter with your help Lord to be a beautiful intelligent young lady and she deserves nothing but your great blessings. Heavenly Father, I thank you for all that you have done and all that you will continue to do in our lives. I thank you for favor in this situation and trust in my heart and know that you already have given my daughter the desires of her heart and your blessings will forever flow in her favor. Thank you Jesus! Thank you Heavenly Father. In your son Jesus name I thank you abundantly! Amen!"

Pausing for a moment before she got up she couldn't stop praying just yet. "My God I know you have my baby! I ain't gone worry no more! Just hope he comes around soon so we can all meet him and see and know for ourselves." She said out loud. She got up off her knees turned her bath water off and she then had calmness over her knowing that her baby girl will be just fine.

270 | **Donna Christopher**

CHAPTER 41
~BRYSON~
LET'S TALK BUSINESS

Bryson was sitting in his office after a wonderful night with Brielle waiting to talk to the producers. By now he figured they should have enough footage to tell the story of his adventure as a homeless man and the finding love part as a bonus. But he also knew if it was him he would not give an out until the contract ended. The story was unbelievable and too good to be true that even he felt like he could be dreaming at the possibility of the outcome being a fairytale ending. There was so much that could happen in the time that he had left that would add to the story being even better, and hopefully not worse.

As he waited he thought about Brielle. *This feels like a dream come true. A dream I will awaken from any second. A dream you never wanted to wake from. God I am the luckiest man in the world.* He thought.

He was in a daze, he didn't even notice Kenneth walking through the door. "You in a lovers daze aren't you Brys?" He said standing in front of him snapping his fingers laughing.

"Hey Kenny man. Thinking about my blessings."

"I see." He said walking over to have a seat in the chair in front of Bryson's desk.

"They are not going to let me out of this contract easily are they?" He asked Kenneth hoping he knew something.

"If they are smart, which we know they are, they won't. But you could still negotiate. They allowed you to come back to work seeing as how she wanted to help you get on your feet. Although it benefited them as well, it is a symbol of a hard worker and not a slacker wanting someone to take care of them. You show determination which makes the heart grow fonder. They see things as 'how will it benefit them'. This is a great story Brys and I think they will capitalize until the end. So be careful in your ask of them, try to prevent the obvious no." He said with a smile on his face.

"You right. Maybe they will take filming the wedding. Brielle may flip when she find out we were doing a film. And my name is not Matt. Well it was my nickname coming up and one of my alias but its deceiving to Brielle. I just hope she doesn't hate me once she finds out the truth. I don't even know how that conversation would go." He looked worried for a minute and then looked up at his friends smiling face. "What's that smirk about?"

"You know we saw your girl bra right? Not that we were trying she just took her shirt off so fast we were all stunned and couldn't find the off button quick enough." He said still smiling.

Bryson too started smiling remembering the wonderful night he had with Brielle. His eyes were glowing and you could see his beating heart through his shirt. "I had forgotten for a second about the cameras."

"Yes and then you jumped up taking her up stairs."

"Wait at what point did the cameras turn off?"

"Well we were all intrigued and once her shirt came off our mouths dropped and everyone was mesmerized by her and the situation so we forgot for a second. When you hopped up is when the camera went off. And that's the truth. We could only hear after that and everyone left except for the camera guy. He gets paid to stay so."

"Kenny, she is the one for me man. She is my better half, my souls mate."

"Soulmate or souls mate?

"Both. I'm in love with her. Last night was magical. We made love for hours before she fell asleep in my arms, then again this morning. I always want to be with her, I can't let her get away." He said smiling.

"Wait, this morning too? Yes the both of you are in love. I'm glad it happened this way so you both know that it's based on true genuine love and you will never have to guess if it was because of your status." Kenneth stood to his feet. "Tell me something. Did you ever think you would meet a girl while you were portraying your life having nothing but your character?" Kenneth asked.

Bryson shook his head. "Never. Sometimes I stop and think is this really real. Wondering was this set up by the producers. But no, I never thought I would meet anyone but glad I decided to take on the journey. My mom has said a numerous times how God orders our steps according to His plans for our life. It becomes more and more apparent that my mom was and still is the smartest woman in this world. Everything is aligning."

"Your mom is smart. She has spoken things over me before that have come to pass so any time she says anything I believe your moms."

"This is why I know everything will work itself out. I have faith that God didn't bring me this far, give me all the financial fulfillment and more that I desired. I'm successful, I'm brilliant, then he gives me what I thought was a dream girl take her away like he did to only present me with something more expensive than diamonds or gold but priceless. Brielle is my true love and I know God will work this out for me."

"Yes you are favored and I know that He will ensure that you are covered as always. I get it, it's scary. But the love between you two is like, wow so real. You don't see what we see when you two are together and even when you are not together. You light up literally as if Adam himself just met Eve. You got this! Trust your best friend on this one man!"

Just then the intercom on Bryson's phone buzzed. Jaqueline was informing him they had visitors waiting for them. Kenneth went out into the lobby and escorted the gentleman and his assistant inside. "Glad you could meet with me sir." Bryson stood to shake his hand. They all took a seat at the conference table in Bryson's office.

The producer started the conversation before Bryson even had a chance to say anything. "Mr. Mathews, Bryson or Matt, not sure what to call you anymore." He said with a smile. "I have heard so many names looking at the footage. Let me first say thank you! I know this is hard allowing someone to come into your space, watch and dictate your life."

"Yes sir it has been but a challenge well worth it." Bryson managed to get in a word.

"Well I know you wish to end the filming and inform the famous Brielle about who you really are and run off into the sun set and live happily ever after but it's not going to happen just like that. You have about 2 weeks left and I am willing to make a deal."

"Okay, I'm listening. What are you thinking?"

"This was all your idea from the beginning and I am assuming it all started over your former fiancée breaking your heart. We have all been there at some point in our lives. But you Mr. Mathews had a spiritual break to where you allowed God to lead you to a place that only he could cover you, protect you, heal you and show you his plan for your life. He led you to this place and you now have to trust that He will bring you out of this in a better place than where you started." The producer was shocking Bryson with his words.

"That sir I do believe. My concern is Brielle. I don't want to lose her to deception."

"Look at it this way, the deception is there, it exists. We all know this except for Brielle. I am surprise Brielle has not figured out who you are yet since her best friend is dating your brother. Brielle is a smart girl, very wise, although she is sheltered a bit. She doesn't pry into others affairs unless she is invited into their space. You have also been great for her and her kids. Me and my team of experts have analyzed the footage that we have so far and we all agree that love is a given factor here. But we also agree that we don't want to stretch this out another two weeks."

"Yes," Bryson said. "So you are letting me out of my contract early?"

"No not yet. We will film through the end of next week. Thursday we will release you from the contract and you have free range to tell her anything you like. We are giving you back eight days in exchange for her reaction to when you tell her your true identity and one day, a very important date, your wedding day. We want to have an exclusive look into your wedding day and be the first to air it when the documentary is released on the big screens." He paused and gave Bryson a chance to respond.

"Okay, next Thursday I can be released from the contract. you get the big reveal and an exclusive for the wedding. I love the sound of that! The wedding that is."

"Brys man it sounds good to me. What good would the story be if Brielle agrees and all if you don't tell people about the happy ending?" Turning towards the producer he asks, "But what if Brielle doesn't want to be with him after he tells her, and does not agree to have her face shown. What then?"

"Good Question. What happens then if she doesn't want to be with me?" Bryson had a disturbed look on his face.

"In the event she wants to stop everything, which no one believes that would happen, we all come back to the table to figure out how we construct the ending that is pleasing to everyone. We also would have to get her consent to have her included in the documentary. That would be the tricky part in putting this together, if she says no."

"We have a deal!" Bryson shook on it and agreed to the terms. It was exciting and scary to have one week left of deception. He had at least another week to enjoy Brielle completely in preparation for forever. Or, this would be his last week with her. Either way he planned to make the best of their time together.

After signing the amendment to the contract and seeing the producer out, Bryson chatted with Kenneth a bit more before getting some work done. He could not wait to see Brielle and the kids tonight. He paused thinking he needed to see Brielle for lunch and wanted to see if she was free.

> *10:15 am*
> *Brielle Summers*
> *Hey beautiful been busy here at work but I can't stop thinking about you. You busy for lunch? I would love to meet you if you can get away. I will be sad if you say no.*
> *#TallDark&Handsome*

As soon as Bryson laid his phone on the desk it buzzed with a message from Brielle. He was nervous and excited to see what her response would be.

> *10:16 am*
> *Matt 'Mr. Handsome' Cole*
> *Ohh lala lunch with a handsome man? Yes of course. I surely cannot and will not pass that up! What time and where? Don't want you to be sad.*
> *#MissSophisticatedSummers*

Bryson smiled and quickly replied back.

10:16 am
Brielle Summers
I can be there to pick you up at 11:30. My boss has me meeting a client to sign papers at 1:30 so I will have the company car. If that's ok?
#MrTallDark&Handsome

10:17 am
Matt 'Mr. Handsome' Cole
Yes that would be perfectly ok. I would love that. There is a place on West End called Black Diamond café, ever been?
#MissSophisticatedSummers

He knew exactly where that place was and knew he could not go there and risk seeing someone who may know him. That is a frequent meeting place for business lunches. It's very classy and rich feeling, great food and reasonable prices. It's a business casual favorite spot to enjoy and hang out during lunch. He had to rethink the lunch outing and think fast.

10:19 am
Brielle Summers
I was thinking something more personal and quiet so it can be me and you spending time together. What about the Frist Center? We can walk through and look at the art work before sitting down for lunch if that's ok with you?
#MrTallDark&Handsome

10:20 am
Matt 'Mr. Handsome' Cole
Frist Center sounds great. Can't wait to see you at 11:30. Thanks again for a wonderful night & morning. I enjoyed every moment until I had to leave this morning.
 # MissSophisticatedSummers

10:21 am
Brielle Summers

So did I! I wish we could have spent all day together. But I will gladly take lunch and dinner tonight. I can't wait to kiss your lips.
#MrTallDark&Handsome

10:22 am
Matt 'Mr. Handsome' Cole
Muah!!! You don't have to wait much longer Mr. Tall Dark and Handsome!! Your kisses are only an hour and 8 minutes away. I am blushing so hard anticipating your arrival.
#MissSophisticatedSummers

10:23 am
Brielle Summers
See you then beautiful!
#MrTallDark&Handsome

At eleven thirty exactly Bryson was waiting in front of Brielle's building. It was different for Bryson driving himself for a change. He normally had a driver for most places he went. This time he drove the company car for himself and had to figure out how to work the gadgets. He really didn't know as his driver did everything while he was in the backseat.

Brielle walked out the front door looking fabulous. Heads turning, catching eyes from all directions. But the one person she had her attention on was waiting by the car to open her door with roses in his hands.

"Thank you, they are beautiful. You are always full of surprises." She said taking the roses from Bryson.

Before she could dip inside the car Bryson pulled her close to him and kissed her lips. She wrapped her free hand around his neck and embraced his tongue with hers, kissing him back enjoying the sweetness of his breath.

"Wow, what a way to say I missed you and hello!" She said getting into the car. She waited for him to get in on the driver side and said. "This is a nice car."

"Yes it is but I have no idea how to work anything in here." He turned toward her before pulling off. "Can I kiss you again?"

Brielle leaned towards him saying, "Yes." Licking her lips, she met his lips. Their kisses were heated with passion and full of love. After a few moments Bryson's phone rang and they finally come up from air.

Noticing it was his brother he answers in a professional voice. "Hello."

"Hey bro have you picked up your girl for lunch already? I came to the bathroom to call you real quick."

"Yes I completed the task moments ago, is something wrong?"

"Naw, you good bro. Kenny called me said you were picking your girl up and he said he remembered in Rodgers report that her and Chantae work together so he called me to pick Chantae up early for lunch. And just as he thought, Brielle planned on allowing Chantae to meet you today. I don't think that would have been good."

"Good looking out I appreciate that." He said glancing over at Brielle trying to figure out the radio.

"I know you are with her now but did you know I met the girl already twice? I can't believe I didn't figure this out before now. Call me later when you are free." Bradon said.

Okay I have to be somewhere at one thirty and dropping my princess back off from lunch about one fifteen." He paused turning back to Brielle. "What time do you have to be back at work?"

"You can keep me until one fifteen I will let my boss know I am taking a longer lunch." She pulled out her phone to send an e-mail.

"Okay yes one fifteen I will drop her off and I will see you after that." Bryson said still talking in code.

"Oh I get it so I need to have Chantae back before then or after. I got you. Call me when you can."

"Hey thanks again, I owe you one!" He said hanging up the phone and turning to Brielle ready for her questions. But to his surprise she had none.

"I am so glad you decided on lunch. After a night and morning of passion, I don't think I would have been able to control myself in front of the kids seeing you tonight." She caressed his arm smiling back at him.

"Yeah that would have been hard for me to babe." He said smiling and amazed that he had Brielle in his life.

Bryson and Brielle enjoyed an afternoon of pure blissful happiness being together. They toured the art center admiring the wonderful unique pieces holding on to one another. Being together was their peace and their joy.

After lunch Bryson was a bit nervous taking Brielle back to work in fear of running into Chantae. Half way to her office he received a text from his brother saying all was good. Moments later, he pulls up in front of her building. "Stay here." He said as he ran around the car to open her door.

"Thank you sir." She said stepping out of the car to his awaiting arms. He embraced her close and passionately kissed Brielle not caring who saw him at that moment.

"Until later beautiful. I will be thinking about you." He said with a smile across his face.

"Until later Mr. Tall Dark and Handsome." Blushing she pulled away from him with their hands still locked together. As she walked their hands stretched out until she was far enough away. He blew her a kiss and watched as she walked into the building turning back smiling every second.

When he could no longer see her he got into his car to leave anticipating seeing her and the kids for dinner.

Another evening of dinner with Brielle and the kids felt so real and natural to Bryson. In his heart and mind they were already his family. He didn't meet them for a season, he met them for a lifetime and that is exactly what he desired and planned to have with Brielle and her children.

The kids adapted as if Bryson was naturally their father. Knowing that they were being raised without their father and only the love from their grandfather and uncle made it even easier for Bryson to want to love them as his own. He was hoping for a quick ending to the deception so he could have Brielle in his space to love him forever for who he is and has become. Loving her forever was a given for him. No doubts in his mind or his heart. She was destined to be his wife and he embraced the fact that she was his soulmate.

CHAPTER 42
~BRYSON~
ADMITTING HIS FEELINGS

Friday comes and Bryson wants to spend time with Brielle and her kids while they are hanging out. Brielle was off work and the kids were out of school. He thought this would be a perfect opportunity to take them out and show her how a man should treat a lady and to have a shot at being a father figure to the children. He decides to make up an excuse so he could work a half day in hopes of Brielle agreeing to him joining them. He was excited and prayed for a yes.

> *9:08 am*
> *Brielle Summers*
> *Hey Beautiful, just found out that every other Friday is half days and guess which Friday today is? Half day. I don't want to impose but I would love to spend time with you and the kids when I get off. What do you think?*
> *#MrTallDark&Handsome*

He sat there in his office grinning day dreaming about Brielle. He wanted to spend every moment with her that he could. He didn't see her as a rebound love from Jewel, he knew she was his Miss Right and he wanted to make her Mrs. Bryson Mathews, his wife. He was sure of that and would make sure to win her heart and fix the deception of who he really is, making a right out of his wrong. Just as he was about to start drooling at the mouth thinking about Brielle his phone buzzed signaling he had a message.

> *9:12 am*

Matt 'Mr. Handsome' Cole
I think that's a great idea. The kids and I would love to have
you hang out with us. We are going to the movies at 10:30
then bowling and ice skating at the family fun center before
grabbing dinner. What do you think? We could do something
different if you like.
#MissSophisticatedSummers

Bryson's smile was on high beam. He made sure to make a
mental note to have the option for half day Fridays or something
similar for his employees.

9:13 am
Brielle Summers
Bowling and ice skating sounds fun. I have not been bowling
in forever and ice skating would be new but you could teach
me. I still have the company car and can pick you and the kids
up after your movie. Just tell me where.
#MrTallDark&Handsome

Bryson was a bit nervous about ice skating. He didn't want to
fall and make a fool of himself but knew he would try anything for
Brielle to make her and the kids happy. Anything that made them
happy he would be happy doing.

9:14 am
Matt 'Mr. Handsome' Cole
This should be fun and interesting. I will teach you. Yes we
can ride with you and can meet you at your place after the
movies.
#MissSophisticatedSummers

They should be done with the movie about 12:30 and would be
at the house about one-ish. He thought. That gave him about three
solid hours to work before heading out. He was excited and nervous
all at the same time. This would be his first outing outside of the park
and the home and he was taking a chance on being recognized.

9:16am

Brielle Summers
Brielle I am counting down the moments until I am with you.
You all enjoy the movie and I will see you when you arrive at
the house. Be careful. Kisses!!!
#MrTallDark&Handsome

9:16 am
Matt 'Mr. Handsome' Cole
Smooches back at you lots of them, muuuaahhhh!!! See you
soon!
#MissSophisticatedSummers

At ten minutes until one, Brielle and the kids pulled into the driveway. Bryson was anxiously waiting. "Hey kids. How are my favorite people?"

The kids all said hello running to Bryson to give him hugs. "Are you really going to ice skate Matt?" Olivia said.

"Yes I am going to try but I will need you and your mom to teach me." He said, remembering he is going by Matt.

"Well, momma gonna have to teach you cause you too big for me to teach you Matt. If you fall I can't catch you and if I try you will make me fall so that's all momma. But if I fall you can catch me." Olivia said.

They all laughed at her comment.

"Well Brielle, I guess I have to lean on you to teach me the art of ice skating and catch Olivia when she falls."

"You can lean on me for sure. I will try not to let you fall or either I will fall with you trying to keep you up."

"Nice knowing you got me." He said looking in her eyes smiling.

"Yes I got you." She said smiling back at him blowing a quiet kiss.

"Alright. Does anyone need to use the bathroom before we leave?" Bryson asked the kids.

"No we ready." Carter said.

"I do." Olivia said. "We have a long drive to get to where we going."

"On that note I think we all should try to go after the soda we had at the movies." Brielle said.

After the bathroom break they headed to the Family Fun Center. When they arrived the kids did other activities before they started to ice skate. Meanwhile, Bryson and Brielle had a chance to talk to one another while the kids were enjoying themselves having a great time. Bryson decided to let Brielle know how he felt about her.

"Brielle I'm glad we have gotten to spend so much time together. In fact I am really happy I was able to fish with the kids the day in the park and have lunch with you all."

"Oh Matt I think we all are happy we met that day. You are not alone feeling that way."

"It wasn't just a day of me meeting a woman and her kids. That day I met my family, I met my future, my forever. That day I fell in love with an angel and you are my angel." He held onto her hands and her facial expression went from being happy in the moment of them being together to being happy in the moment realizing Bryson confirmed he was her forever. "Chantae was right when she said I was crazy about you. I fell hard in love with you from the moment I saw you. And I know there are so many things I have to tell you but please know when I tell you every word I say to you is from my heart and I mean every word of my truth to you."

"Matt you are too sweet to me and my kids. My truth to you is my love back. I have not opened up to any man in a long time and I have prayed to God to ease my pain from the past and allow my heart to be open just enough to know when my true love is revealed. And the day I met you. I tried to deny what I was feeling but I knew God was not sending me any junk that I would regret. But instead he would send me my king and give me a man like my father but better than I could ever imagine. I felt those sparks in my soul and from that moment our eyes locked you have consumed my every thought. Those feelings that have touched my spirit just won't go away and I don't want them too either. So I believe your truth and I want you to believe my truth just the same." She was squeezing his hands as he held on to hers tightly.

"God didn't send you no junk Brielle I promise you that. I can show you better than I can tell you and I plan to do just that. I love you from the bottom of my heart, deep within my spirit, and more than anything or anyone I have ever loved in my lifetime."

"Really Matt?" She said with tears in her eyes.

"Yes really. I can't lie on my heart and the feeling runs deep within my soul. I speak nothing but true feelings to you. And those tears I know are happy tears." He said as he wiped them away. "I promise to never intentionally hurt you or those kids. I love you Brielle!!"

"I love you too Matt." She wrapped her arms around his neck and they engaged in a passionate kiss.

"Ooohh momma. You and Mr. Matt are kissing." Olivia said as she approached, stretching her words.

They quickly separated and gave Olivia their attention. She was smiling at her momma being happy with Bryson. But at that moment she wanted nothing more than to get more tokens for games. As soon as she received the tokens she skipped back over to where her siblings were gathered.

"Those kids love you too. That warms my heart to know you also make them happy." Brielle said looking over at her children.

"Believe me when I tell you those kids make me happy as well." He said looking in the kid's direction.

"Hey why don't you join us for church Sunday? Come see where we worship, meet my Pastor who is also a close friend of the family. Then afterwards, dinner at my parents. My mom is a great cook and they are dying to meet you."

"That sounds like a plan to me. I would love to join you for church and meet your parents. I would be honored"

"Well it's a date then. A church and dinner date. I would ask you if you need more clothes but I think you have been managing very well. Your job definitely takes care of you. I am a bit jealous." She said sticking her lip out in an attempt to pout.

"Oh yeah? Why is that?" Bryson asked finding her pouty lips attractive.

"I want to be the one who takes care of your needs. Every last one of your needs." She said raising her eyebrows in a seductive way.

"I think you trying to get my man to stand at attention?" Looking down at his pants. "You know you do have his full attention and plenty of time to take care of my every need." He grabbed her hand locking it with his as she started to blush uncontrollably.

They both were blushing trying not to reveal the flustered erotic feelings they were sharing. Then they were saved by the kids. The subject was put on hold. They enjoyed the remainder of their time together as a family. Bryson treated them to dinner after leaving the Family Fun Center. He ran into a man in the restaurant who knew him calling him Bryson. The producers quickly intervened before his cover was blown. Bryson was a bit nervous realizing someone could recognize him and he didn't want Brielle to find out this way. He rushed dinner along and insisted they stay up watching movies at his place.

The kids were excited and Brielle and Bryson were excited. They were together happy as a family. They camped out in the living room watching movies. When the kids went to sleep Bryson covered them up. He and Brielle were up kissing and talking until Brielle fell asleep. Bryson was the last one to fall asleep. And he was happy knowing the kids were there and Brielle was in his arms tight.

CHAPTER 43
~BRIELLE~
PASTOR MALONE'S PERSPECTIVE

Brielle and the kids stayed with Bryson all weekend. They went back to the park Saturday to fish and enjoy the weather. They were so happy being together as a family and enjoyed every second possible. This was a true love story unfolding for the both of them. Brielle and Bryson didn't want to confuse the kids so they all slept in the living room together both nights, making pallets on the floor as if they were simply at a sleep over.

Sunday morning early after breakfast, Brielle and the kids went home to get cleaned and ready for church. Bryson stayed behind to get ready there. He would pick them up so they could all ride to church together. He spoke with his producers regarding the events happening that day. Today was the day he would meet Brielle's parents and share the intimacy of worship with her and the kids.

"I am excited you are attending church today with us." Brielle said on their way.

"Me too Mr. Matt." Olivia said.

"My granny and granddaddy wants to meet you. They will be there too." Jayla said.

"I'm excited too and looking forward to meeting your grandparents. Seeing how you all were raised I am sure they are pleasant people I will also love." He said looking over at Brielle for reassurance.

"Yes they are pleasant people. You will love my parents." She was blushing and biting her bottom lip.

Pulling up at the church butterflies consumed Brielle. Bryson could tell she was nervous and he held her hand to reassure her everything was fine. She had nothing to be nervous about. "I'm sorry I just hope everyone loves you just as we do." She said squeezing his hand.

"And if they don't that's okay too. It won't change a thing between us." He said reassuring her.

"And just like that you make all my fears disappear? I must warn you people may be talking as they have never seen me in church with a man or anywhere with a man. Now I walk in with an extremely handsome and very fine man they are sure to be anxious to say something or come up and meet you."

"Brielle, you are so beautiful. You and these kids are all that matter right now. After service we will deal with what comes our way." He didn't know if anyone would know his true identity. He was gambling and hoping that his security and broadcast team were close by to help him anyway possible. Meeting Brielle's parents and attending church together was important to her so it made it important to him. He was not acting with her but often forgot his true identity was still a mystery to Brielle.

As they entered the sanctuary Bryson could tell that people were looking and whispering. He thought it more so due to Brielle saying she has not been seen with a man more so than people recognizing him. As they approached their seat the choir started to sing. People all over the building were now standing and starting to worship God. They sat next to an older couple and Bryson was at ease. Jayla sat to his left with Brielle sitting on his right and the other two children on her right. The music was beautiful and heartfelt. It felt like Bryson's church his mom took them to coming up as boys. They sat through the service as a couple that was in love more so than friends. People were sure to question Brielle who this mystery man could be.

"My parents are smiling and looking back at you I think they are happy." Brielle whispered to Bryson pointing in their direction.

Bryson seeing where they were caught her mother and father's eye and waved as they discreetly waved at him. Her dad nodded his approval seeing him in church with his daughter. What father wouldn't approve of a man making his daughter happy and taking well to the kids as if he was their father?

"I think your dad likes me." Bryson whispered.

"You haven't been questioned by him yet." Brielle said smiling. He put his arm around Brielle hoping she wouldn't be uncomfortable. It felt natural for him and she immediately gravitated towards him and smiled.

As the Pastor stood at the podium motioning for everyone to stand the congregation stood to their feet. "Turn in your bibles to first Corinthians thirteen versus four through eight please. Those of you who do not have your bibles can follow along on the screen behind me. When you have it church, say Amen." The Pastor said. You could hear people saying amen at different times all around.

"What do you know my favorite scripture!" Brielle whispered opening her bible to the book marked page. She handed the bible to Bryson who reached to hold it for them.

"Our favorite scripture." He smiled and winked at her looking up at him.

"Alright, our favorite scripture." Her heart was warmed with love and care from this man.

"Let's read it together. Love is patient. Love is kind. Love does not envy, it does not boast, it is not proud. It does not dishonor others, it is not self-seeking, it is not easily angered, it keeps no records of wrongs. Love does not delight in evil but rejoices with the truth. It always protects, always trust, always hopes, always perseveres. Love never fails." He asked the church to bow their heads saying a prayer over the congregation. "You may be seated." Everyone took their seats and became quiet as the Pastor delivered the word.

"A few weeks ago I preached from Ephesians chapter one regarding Paul and his prayer that our eyes of understanding be flooded with light. That God's answer to his blessings are clear and understood. That our prayers are limitless and bold in asking of our hearts desire. That we understood what is of God and what is not of God. And that our God is love and love is of God. Today's message I want to talk about 'Love Never Fails'. Love Never Fails." He repeats what he said and waits as the videography team places the topic on the screen behind him.

"Four points I will be speaking on. God's love is true love. God's love is forgiving. God's love is undeniable. And last but definitely not least God's purpose for your life is to love and be loved."

The sermon flowed and kept Bryson's attention from the beginning. He noticed Brielle's parents praising and shouting. He watched as Brielle's hands went up to praise him and an occasional amen. This was home to him. Being with Brielle and the kids in the church gave him a confirmation of how real she was for him. He never doubted her being the woman of his dreams, his soul mate, his everything he ever wanted. All his life his mom brought him and his brother up in church, preached to him, spoke words over their life and prayed favor over them even for love. It was her way of covering them even when they didn't have time to completely give praise and thanks to God for everything they have and everything they have become. Bryson has always believed in God, and frequently would say, "Thank you God for...." At this moment he knew that Brielle and the kids were from God specifically for him. He has always honored God and given of his heart, done things Christ like. These things were natural to him in his spirit, that's how he was raised, that's all he knew.

"Sometimes in love you have to forgive and if the love is of God forgiving should come easy. Third point, God's love is undeniable. It is undeniable. There is no denying anything that is of God. If your prayer of God is to leave your heart open to love and God sends you that love there is no denying it is of God. I'm not speaking of the girl you see shaking her booty in the club and you think you are in love with her movements. That's not God's love. I'm not talking about the love of that man in that nice car, talking about oh girl he riding clean he got a Mercedes Benz oh I love him. That's not of God." The congregation laughed at the Pastor's joking point. "God's love is simply undeniable. I'm talking about that feeling when your spirit starts jumping and you don't know what's going on until your eyes meet and catch up with what your spirit already knows is from God. That feeling of wanting to spend the rest of your life with someone and you don't know anything about them, not even their name. They have never done a single thing for you. Their flaws are unseen, their bad habits do not exist, all you know is that feeling, that undeniable feeling that you have never felt before. It feels like the love you have for your parents but it's different. It feels like the love you have for your friends, your siblings, but it's different. The more and more you spend time getting to know that person you think 'how can I be in love with this person and I just met them'.

That's God's undeniable love. A baby is conceived. As soon as that mother finds out she is pregnant she instantly falls in love with that baby. She knows nothing about them but that she loves them. Because God gave that baby to them specifically, God ordained them. God has that one true love waiting on you to receive at the right time. God's love is undeniable. God's purpose for us all is to love and to be loved."

As he continued his preaching Bryson was touched and saw tears in Brielle's eyes. He gave her his handkerchief from his suit pocket and held her closer to him. He kissed her forehead and whispered, "Forever I promise."

As the Pastor was giving out confirmation of love looking in the direction of those who have been married for years he turned to look at Brielle and Bryson not even knowing Bryson but feeling God's confirmation and he passed the confirmation on to them. The old man next to Bryson placed his hand on Bryson's shoulder and also spoke the words "God's confirmation!"

After the service they sat there for a moment to wait on the crowd to dissipate a bit and the old man turned to speak to Brielle and Bryson. "Young man I don't know you from Adam but God do and his blessings are over you. You may experience something you don't understand but stand strong in the man God designed you to be for the blessings he is unfolding over your life. You are a good man, a loving man and your family here is priceless I know that myself. You take care of yourself and them as well young man. God bless you."

"Thank you sir, thank you. God bless you as well." He said shaking the old man's hand before he turned to leave. Bryson didn't understand what he meant by something you may not understand but he understood him calling Brielle and her kids his family so nothing else mattered.

"You ready here comes my mom and dad." Brielle turned to smile at Bryson.

"Of course. I am as ready as I will ever be." The kids were calling granny and granddad as they bombarded them with hugs. Brielle stood to the side of Bryson to introduce him to her parents.

"Mom and dad this is Matt the mystery man we have talked so much about."

"How you do sir." He said reaching his hand out to her father.

"How are you son? We have heard so much about you. Glad to finally meet you." Her father said.

"Likewise. Your daughter and the kids talk a lot about you all as well. It's obvious they truly adore you both." He said. When Mrs. Summers made it to him he spoke to her. "How are you ma'am?" Reaching out for her hand.

"No sir, I am a hugger. You better get over here and give me a hug." She paused briefly to hug Bryson. "Let me meet the man who has my daughter smiling."

"I like making her smile, plan to always make her smile if she lets me." He looked at Brielle blushing.

"You are doing a good job at that and we thank you." Her mom said. "You coming to the house for dinner right?"

"Yes ma'am. I wouldn't miss it for the world."

"Alright, I will have a spot waiting on you in the man cave while the women prepare the meal. I will see you in a few." Her father said to Bryson.

"Yes sir. I will be there." He said shaking his hand again before he left.

"I like that the man has a firm hand shake, good eye contact and he loves our daughter." Mr. Summers said to his wife as they walked away. The kids asked if they could ride with their grandparents and with a nod of approval they quickly followed them out.

"Yeap I think your parents like me." Bryson said smiling.

"I think so too. You even had them smiling. My dad is hard too. But you still have to venture into his man cave." She said laughing as she turned from him.

"Wait is that a bad thing? I thought an invitation into the man cave was good."

""Oh it is! But neither I nor the kids will be in there to save you from his questions or lectures. I am sure you can hold your own." She winked at him. "I want you to meet Pastor Malone before we leave."

Bryson heard someone talking saying that looks just like Bryson Mathews and as he looked up they took a picture. Just then someone was in front of them talking and Bryson quickly walked with Brielle out the door.

After meeting the Pastor and him welcoming him to the church Brielle and Bryson were out the door headed to the car, arm in arm. This was happy times for Brielle. Although they were not married or official she didn't care who saw them together as a couple.

Dinner at her mom's was going well. Bryson survived the man cave and her dad and brother loved him as if he had been a part of the family for years. Nothing he said was a lie except for being rich beyond means and owning the company he works for and several more. And the fact that his name is not completely his name. Her mom cooked fried chicken, turnip greens, mac and cheese, sweet potatoes, mashed potatoes, made a salad and some hot water corn bread. Everyone's eyes were wide in amazement. Even the Pastor who joined them for dinner was anticipating the full course meal before them. Everyone wanted to know about Bryson and confirm the happiness Brielle and the kids were feeling for themselves.

"Sweetheart you put your foot in this meal. Thank you for making all my favorites." Mr. Summers said to his wife. He knew she went over board for the sake of impressing Bryson. But he still had to make it feel like it was all about him.

"Yes mom. This is great. Dad's favorite and mine. Bryson you should join us for dinner more often." Isaiah said. He caught the squinted eye of his dad. But still felt the love in the room.

"Oh anything for you all, you know I enjoy cooking for my family."

"Thank you Mrs. Summers and you too Mr. Summers for allowing me to be a part of the family." The Pastor said.

"Any time you are always welcome. Especially after preaching a sermon like you did today." Mr. Summers said.

"Yes sir, that was indeed a great word today Pastor." Bryson said.

"Yes it was and it was received." Brielle said smiling at Bryson.

"Alright I am starving so everyone bow your heads so we can bless this food and eat. Thank you Heavenly Father for this food my lovely wife has prepared before us. Thank you for your blessings of love in our home that we use in our everyday life. Thank you for the new addition to our family and may you bless him and allow him to continue to be a blessing for my daughter and grandchildren. Father we thank you now and we thank you always for all things cometh from you. In Jesus name Amen."

"Amen." Everyone said,

"Now let's eat." Mr. Summers said grabbed the bowl of Chicken. Sunday dinner was quiet at first with everyone enjoying the good tasting food. But it was a success. The family loved and accepted Bryson and enjoyed his company. He was everything and more that Brielle made him out to be.

CHAPTER 44
~CHANTAE~
LOVE IS IN THE AIR

Monday morning Brielle and Chantae quickly met in the break room. Every time Chantae attempted to chat with Brielle she was occupied with Bryson and her family and did not want to interrupt their time. She had her own love nesting going on with Bradon anyhow. She waited until they both would be at work and could talk freely.

"Girl I know you have a mouth full after this long weekend you had with Matt. So you can go first and spill it." Chantae said smiling at Brielle.

"Well we had a great time I tell you that. Me and the kids stayed at his place Friday and Saturday and all day yesterday. He went to church with us and he met my parents, my brother and the Pastor and came over to my parents for dinner." Brielle said staring up at no particular space on the wall. She was smiling hard as if he was there with her at that moment. Chantae watched her until she sighed and snapped back to reality.

"Love is definitely in the air. Girlfriend that was brief but you said a mouth full. He went to church with you all and met your parents?" Chantae said as if she too was in a love daze.

"Yes he did! Girl it was amazing. Everything about this weekend was amazing!"

"Brie, you are truly in love. I may have been joking or assuming or not even sure before. But now I believe it when I say you are in love."

"I am Chantae. We even told one another we love each other Friday girl. Everything is amazing. I was nervous about everyone meeting him and liking him but it was just like when we met him for the first time. It was instant!"

"How can you not like a man who does this to you girl? I can't wait to meet him myself. We need to plan a double date or something."

"Yeah we do. I can't wait for you to meet him either girlfriend. And girl his job is going well. He has done really well since I initially helped him. I am impressed and very proud. He treated us to dinner. He pays for everything for us before I even get a chance too."

"I love him Brie and I don't even know him."

"It's funny we went to church Sunday and the message was all about True God ordained Love. And Matt would caress me, squeeze my hand, kiss my forehead or something all through service. It was if he was agreeing with every word Pastor Malone said."

"That is beautiful girl. I need Bradon to go to church with me. I want that same intimacy you experienced."

"Girl you crazy. How are you two doing anyhow?"

"We are good girl. He is helping me launch my clothing line. Pretty soon I won't be working an eight to five any more. I am excited about that. He is good to me honey. I am so lucky to have him in my life. Everything seems so much easier with him."

"Girl y'all should have been at church yesterday. I am going to have to get the CD for you both to listen to, it was that good. Oh he gave me his handkerchief in church. I was teary eyed and I didn't give it back to him. So now it's mine. I can smell his scent and keep him closer to me when he is away." Brielle pulled the handkerchief from her purse. "I keep trying to figure out what these initials stand for BCM." She said rubbing the stitching of the letters.

Chantae looked at the letters and thought they looked very familiar to her. "Yes get me the CD and we will listen to it together." She said not wanting to mention the familiarities of the initials.

"You know when you launch your line and have your fashion runway show I want to be a model. Don't forget about the little people out here ok." Brielle said.

"You my bff you know I can't forget about you ever. So I wanted to ask you what you thought about me and Bradon living together." Chantae dropped that question knowing Brielle would give an honest answer.

"Wow, okay well you know I am non-judgmental and my only advice would be to do what feels right to you and in your heart. If marriage is not an option right now then make sure it will be soon or eventual be an option that will happen and go for it. But do have that conversation. Have a plan."

"He said he doesn't want to wake up without me next to him ever again. We are always at each other's house so it's something I am considering."

"I support you no matter what. You have had your independence for so long are you sure you are ready to give up your space?"

"Girl the house he is about to build for us you can fit ten of my little house in that one and still have room. I am sure it will feel the same but better."

"Wait you didn't tell me he was building you all a place to stay."

"Yes he said it would be about a three month project. I could have my own design studio that would be bigger than any place I could imagine having. So I think I will nonchalantly bring up the marriage idea and see what he says. I don't want to be one of those girls who settle just to live together."

"Well if he is ready to build you a home he is ready to marry you I say. Both are huge commitments."

"Yeah you are right girl. I thought the house idea was huge when he mentioned it as an option."

"Come on girl let's get to work. I am happy for you two Chantae, you are going to be a beautiful bride one day." They headed back to their office space chatting along the way. Their sisterly love was priceless and even though neither of them had a biological sister they had each other and that was all the sisterhood they needed.

296 | **Donna Christopher**

CHAPTER 45
~JEWEL~
I WANT MY MAN BACK

Sitting in her one bedroom apartment, Jewel was looking at a picture of her and Bryson. She didn't come out of her apartment for anything besides trying to see Bryson. What she did to him was the worst thing she has ever done. She knew she had a serious problem and wanted to be back to normal again. The humiliation at the wedding broke her to pieces. Her father knew it would break her and he tried to console her the best way possible. What she did to Bradon could have sent an innocent man to prison. That was crossing the line even for her.

She sat there listening to her voicemail mostly from her dad and Michael.

"Jewel, this your dad again call me back sweetheart we need to talk." Beep.

"It's me again. I have been talking to Dr. Andrews and he said he could get you in right away. Call me back baby girl." Beep

"Jewel I am worried about you it's been weeks and you have not talked to anyone. You won't answer the door you won't answer the phone. At least let me know you are ok." Beep.

"Hey Sexy it's me. Call me. Wanted to see if we could hook up for old time's sake. I miss my sweet lips!" Beep.

At that moment she was crying. She was disgusted at herself for allowing another man to call her the very pet name Bryson gave to her. Just the thought of Michael disgusted her. She regretted ever meeting him. She could not change time and did not want to accept the fact that Bryson didn't love her anymore.

She vowed to get help for her addiction to prove to him she was a better person and did indeed love him. She decided to look up information herself about sex addiction and keep her dad's Dr. as an option. Pulling out her laptop she typed in Sex Addiction Treatment.

"Oh wow there is so much information online. So many different ways to deal with this. What the hell... Give up sex for a year? Hell naw! I can't do that. Damn this is a real serious addiction. I have hurt so many people around me. Wanting sex all day every day seems normal but I guess when you do things like hurt your fiancé by sleeping with his brother and blackmailing is a reason to get help. They didn't deserve this and my parents didn't raise a monster. I am sure they are ashamed and hurt by all of this as well. Why the hell would he do this to me? He was supposed to love me. I got to get him back. I love him I can fix this." She said talking to herself pacing back and forth.

She picked up the phone to call her dad. "Dad, I am sorry I hurt you again. I'm ready to get help."

"Okay baby that's the first step. Glad to hear you are okay I was worried sick about you."

"I'm sorry I have been locked up in this apartment sick at myself for all of this happening."

"Well that's a start to healing your addiction. Isolation. But you can't shut your family out. We love you and we want to help you."

She started crying and her dad told her he was on his way to get her. She showered and put on some clean clothes she knew her dad was taking her to see the Dr. Reading about the addiction and understanding it is a real problem, she knew she needed to fix whatever the real problem was. She did feel isolated from the world and when her father went to jail her mother went into a deep depression and lost everything causing the entire family to suffer. She was taken away from her mom and put into foster care until her dad was released. Once her mom was better their dad did everything he could to put their family back together. Things just weren't the same afterwards. She had already started seeking acceptance with men and they all wanted sex from her. This was the start of her addiction to sex.

When she was ready, she picked up the phone and called Michael. "Hey are you busy? Can you meet me?" And that quick she was out the door headed to meet Michael so he could satisfy her

298 | **Donna Christopher**

sexual urge. Just reading about sex made her want to put her healing on hold to satisfy her urge.

"When her dad pulled up she was gone. He knew the fight to save her was not over. He blamed himself for leaving and not addressing the issues when he returned. After years of his absence he wanted things to be back to normal when he returned without addressing anything as if nothing ever happened.

Jewel went to see Michael meeting him at the gym. He met her in the parking lot and they had sex in his truck. After five minutes of him getting what he wanted so he could get back to work he asked her to come by his house that night. As mad as she was she told him she would but only if he would redeem himself from the five minute joke he just gave her.

After leaving him she went to Bryson's job again in an attempt to plot how she was going to get through security. She called her so called friend Raquel at the front desk.

"Hey Raquel girl what you doing working?"

"Jewel is that you?" She sounded as if she heard a ghost.

"Yeah girl you don't know my voice anymore?" She said trying to feel her out.

"Yeah but I haven't heard from you in a while. What's going on? I heard about what happened to you and Bryson not getting married."

"Oh girl we fine we had a big misunderstanding we trying to work it out. I am going to stop by and bring you a gift. I know I missed your birthday. I have something for Officer Anderson too when does he work again?" Officer Anderson knew her well and would not let her into the building. He worked the front door where he would be the first person to see her.

"He here today but they are about to be off. And he doesn't come back until Wednesday."

"Well I was going to stop by tomorrow if that's okay?" Waiting for her response to see if she is still hot news on the do not allow to enter list.

"Okay girl yeah Jim will let you in I can't wait to see my gift." She was so clueless as to what her job was and the risk she was imposing allowing Jewel to enter the building. She doesn't know when Jewel is using her to pump her for information.

"Okay I got to go, see you tomorrow around lunch."

"Okay see you tomorrow."
Jewel was up to no good plotting to get to Bryson.

CHAPTER 46
~AMEILA~
GREAT BOOK BEFORE
THE MOVIE

Ameila Churchwell worked close with Kenneth in Bryson's absence. He tested her expertise to see how much creativity and knowledge she had. She was great help for Kenneth and a great new asset for the company. She watched the documentaries with him and one of the things she took upon herself to do was write Bryson's story. She wrote it as a tell all novel. She presented it to Kenneth thinking it may help the documentary. She wrote it more so as a don't judge before you know love story. The only thing missing was the ending.

"Good morning Kenneth. I see you are still hard at work." Ameila said walking into Kenneth's office.

"Yes, how are you this morning Ameila?" Kenneth said not even looking up from what he was doing.

"Oh, I am wonderful. Peachy. Better than I could ever imagine." She said sitting down in front of him smiling.

Looking up and leaning back in his seat Ameila now had his full attention. "Oh yeah? And what has you feeling this great this morning?"

"Well besides the fact that God has blessed me tremendously, life is great, my kids are great and I have something for you that I am very proud of." She said laying a stack of papers in front of him.

"What's this?" He said reading the first page. "All the riches in the world can't define a man. Riches only allow one to demonstrate more of whom he really is as a person, the good intentions or bad intentions that one tends to mask. A man is defined by his character and the love he holds in his heart for self and others. He is defined by the countless kind acts and God like love he gives to others in his lifetime. Who he is as a person in his nakedness having nothing more than his character and a prayer to God is who he is all the time. You take a man like Bryson Mathews who is all these things and more. Being a man to him is being just as God ordained him to be. Kind hearted loving and very giving. He is a generous fair man, one who does so much for others without even giving it a second thought. It's his nature of being. His down to earth caring and loving spirit and the things that make him a man that God himself is proud of, I'm sure is the reason he deserves so much genuine love around him. His circle is full of love from his best friend, his brother, his mother and father. But the love that he has always missed is the true love of his soul mate. God positioned him and broke him down to a state where he placed himself in a place of portrayed homelessness in an attempt to run from the pain and comfort of those close to him. This was his time with God and he didn't even know the magnitude of blessings that would come. He saved a woman and her children and changed their lives forever. He didn't even know how he would be blessing her by saving her children from starvation and brokenness and saving her life from depression and illness keeping her from raising her children. His blessing to her would be a blessing to him with her loyalty and debt to him that couldn't possibly ever be repaid. He has everything he ever wanted except true love. That is until God brought him to his knees and surrounded him with filth in a place unfamiliar to him to send him his Brielle. Her kindred spirit, her heart of gold, and the instant love connection between them was undeniable. That was God. His true love, his soul mate was now standing in front of him. He knew it. She knew it. Now his only flaw is life before her and this contract he was bond to. His loyalty has never been broken but he has never had to compete with loyalty and true love. Will he risk losing and breaking his loyalty for the sake of love? Or will he take the risk and trust that he can maintain his character and still have the girl of his dreams. Trusting that it will all work out in their favor of true love." Looking up at Ameila then back at the paper, he was quiet pondering on what he just read. He started flipping through the pages looking at the titles reading a paragraph here and there.

"So what do you think? You like it? I have two hundred and fifty pages of Bryson living his life on this journey and the love story unfolding." She had her hands locked together with a nervous smile on her face, waiting for him to respond.

"This is brilliant. I love it. Absolutely love it. This is like a tell all of why and how this happened to him. You write very well. I like your outline of events and how you explained why Bryson chose not to tell Brielle before the contract expired." He was still looking at the pages.

"I have not completed the book of course as it is still playing out but I took everything from the footage you gave me to look over. And I also have your information you asked for." She said giving him the documents.

"I think I am going to start reading your book tonight if that's ok. And then when I tell Bryson about it you will already have your first fan. This will be your project and we will pay you properly for your work and royalties for sales."

"This one is for Bryson. I couldn't ever repay him and you for what you both have done for me so this is on the house." She said with much gratitude in her voice.

"You said it yourself and you know Bryson would never hear of such a thing and neither will I. Now I want to see what else you have written and hiding from us."

"All my work was in the house when he put me out, there is no telling what he has done with my stuff. And my disk was broken when he dumped my purse on the ground." She looked down at the floor. That was years of hard work she put into her writing and it was destroyed.

"Oh I forgot about your disk." He got up from his seat to retrieve an envelope and a box of papers he received and sat to the side. "We have people for that too and all of your data on that disk was retrieved. They have it backed up and instructions on how to store your work properly to prevent this from happening again. We have cloud space here at Cole Estates free for you to use." He gave it to her smiling.

"You saved all of my documents, all of my work, everything?" She asked looking through the box of printed papers of her work. She was amazed that everything she had worked on was right in front of her. Tears fell from her eyes.

"Yeap. He said everything was there and recovered. I know those are happy tears. Where there is a way God is sure to have a will for those that belong to Him and you are now under the covering by default because of association even if you weren't before. Bryson's covering started with his mom. She is a constant for us all. The principals and values of God she instilled in him is a constant. He is not the holier than thou type but he demonstrates that blessing and covering every day. So for something to happen to him to hurt him we were all disturbed by that and now we all know why. It was God's way to set him up for his soulmate."

"I get it. I love it. I love you all, this entire company and what it was built on and stands for."

"And you my dear were in the right place at the right time where God needed you to be. You say you were blessed but really we are the ones blessed by you being here. Now that I think about it, I needed you to be here to help me during this time just to realize you were a missing piece for me and the company. You have a life long career here." He walked over to her to give her tissue.

"Sorry it just brought back the pain I endured from that man. I contacted the lawyer you referred me to help with the divorce. He had already filed and was about to go to court without me knowing to keep everything. Not that I need anything from him, but there is a few things in the house I want."

Lifting her chin to look at him Kenneth smiled and said, "Ameila, you are a beautiful woman. Very kind hearted and genuinely sweet. Trust me when I tell you he will regret ever hurting you. That pain is over. We got your back I promise."

She smiled realizing he just said she was beautiful and knowing he was right about her husband regretting he ever left her. She was about to be someone special and have way more than her husband ever had or gave her. She was right where she needed to be.

"Thank you Kenneth! I am surprised no woman has snatched you up yet. You have all of the right words of comfort." She said smiling.

He laughed. "They have tried but not the right one for me."

"In due time. You never know what God has for you. Could be closer than you think." She smiled as she started towards the door. "Thank you again for everything. I owe you big time."

"Anytime." Kenneth smiled and headed back to work. He used her more as his assistant now than he did his own assistant. It was a matter of time before he would eliminate the position and just hold on to Ameila.

CHAPTER 47
~BRYSON~
HEAVEN SENT

Bryson was sitting in his office thinking about the events that recently played out in his life. From Jewel causing him so much pain that led to him falling in love with Brielle. He heard the good news from Kenneth that a book about the journey was being written. He was excited and couldn't wait to read it in its entirety. God not only brought him Brielle but Ameila as well. She had a loving spirit and now has become a great asset for his company. You never know who you are meeting and how God packages his blessings for you.

Monday evening he was preparing to leave work and couldn't wait to see the love of his life. He was ready to walk out the door when his brother called him. "Hey Bradon what's up with you?" He said answering the phone.

"Hey Brys man, how are you?"

"Cloud nine Bro. I have my angel and in a week I will be sweeping her off her feet." He said about to walk out the door.

"Well I don't know any other way to say this but to say. Brielle's friend Chantae man I think she has figured out you are my brother. Apparently Brielle had a handkerchief from you that was monogramed and she remembered it from something at the house that was the same."

"Oh damn. Did she say something to Brielle?"

'No I don't think so. I told her we needed to talk about it together so I will try to diffuse the situation but can't make any promises."

"Okay do everything you can man without risking your relationship."

"I will. Maybe you need to tell her earlier than a week. Don't want you to lose her before you completely have her you know."

"It's going to all work itself out. I can't lose her she was heaven sent to me. Thanks for the heads up."

"It's all good. So you not out in the streets anymore right? You don't stink and stay out on the streets?

"Naw this is strictly a love story now. Boy meets girl, boy falls in love with girl."

"Yes you two are in love. Chantae even talks about y'all being in love and she has yet to meet you. She wants to double date too by the way. I will be glad when your journey is complete."

"In due time my brother. I will talk to you later. Keep me updated if you hear anything more and especially if she has said something to Brielle."

"Aight, you know I got your back." Bradon said before hanging up.

Bryson was now once more consumed in thought about Brielle and the kids. He did not want to lose them in his life. She was a gift from God. Heaven had blessed him and he would fight to keep her.

Bryson decided to call Brielle to see what she was doing and make sure everything was good.

"Hello there handsome how are you?" She said in her sweet Angelique voice.

At that moment Bryson knew everything was good and his heart beat slowed to a calmer rhythm. "Hi beautiful! I was just thinking about you. Are you still working?"

"Yeah, but it's close to quitting time. I miss you." You could hear her smile through the phone. Just the sound of their voice had a powerful effect on them both.

"I am sure I miss you more. I can't wait to see you tonight."

"Maybe just as much as I miss you. Looking forward to tonight. How would you like to come to our apartment instead of us coming over to the house? I mean you have never been there before. Or you could pick us up and just come up and check out the place."

"I would love to come into your space, see you in a more intimate comfort zone. I wanted to take you and the kids out tonight for Italian so I could just pick you up and check out the place then. I could be at your place about six."

"That sounds perfect. When you arrive just tell Mr. Floyd at the door you're coming to see us. I will let him know when I get there and he will buzz you up. We are on the sixth floor apartment sixty five."

"I will be there. Have those lips ready because I miss your kisses."

Blowing a kiss through the phone she couldn't wait to greet him. "These lips are always ready for your kisses."

"I will let you finish your work and I will see you soon."

"Okay handsome"

Bryson was always smiling after speaking with Brielle. That was just what he needed to calm him down. If she could leave work without Chantae saying anything to her they would be another day closer of her knowing the truth.

That evening Bryson was there exactly at six and the door man knew he had to be there for Brielle based on her description of him and the flowers he had in his hands.

"You must be Matt."

"Yes here for Brielle. It's that obvious? What gave me away the flowers?"

"The flowers and the very detailed description she gave of you sir. The kind of description of a woman who is in love if I may add. Hope those feelings are the same for you as well. I would hate it for anyone who would hurt that sweet lady and those kids."

"He smiled at the man and said you don't have to worry about that with me sir. Yes I too love her and those wonderful kids." He said with a smile and a nod of his head.

"Well carry on then. The elevator is to your right. I will send you up."

"Thank you sir. Glad to know she has someone looking out for her here." Bryson said as he walked away and the door man nodded and tilted his hat

He approached her door and knocked. When Brielle opened the door she was stunning. "You are the most beautiful woman in the entire world." He said with a smile pulling her closer to him.

"Thank you." She said smiling.

He planted a kiss on her lips. He kissed her in the center of her lips, then on both sides of her lips before kissing her full lips again. When he stopped kissing her he hugged her tight not wanting to let her go. When he let her go he gave her the flowers. "These are for you pretty lady."

"Thank you Matt. They are beautiful and my favorite. Come on in the kids are getting their shoes. While they are I will show you around." She held his hand walking him through her apartment. She stopped in the kitchen grabbing a vase to place the flowers in. "This is the kitchen of course. Can I get you anything to drink?" She politely asked.

"No thank you. I can wait until we get to the restaurant. Your home is lovely. Smells good and is very clean." He said loving the fact that he is in her space. She toured him around showing him every bedroom and bathroom. Her intentions were to let him see how clean she was and what her decorating tastes were. She loved the arts and exotic paintings and vases that were different and beautiful.

"Well this is where we live." She said.

"I love your home. You have great taste of art. I will be sure to add an art museum to one of the places I take you."

"That would be nice. I would love that. Looks like the kids are ready they are waiting by the door."

"Hey kids." He said walking towards them.

They ran up to him giving him a hug saying hello.

"Let me grab my purse and we can go. I love Italian. I am actually excited that's what you chose for tonight."

"You all will enjoy this place." Bryson had the owner close the restaurant for the evening to only serve him and his family. But Kenneth had people staged to look normal. Bryson didn't want to risk running into anyone else that may know who he was. This gave him a chance to be comfortable out and with Brielle and the kids and not have to rush.

Passing the door man they all spoke telling him bye. He was happy seeing Brielle and the kids happy. Knowing Brielle and how things were with her ex hurting her, he has never seen her happy and has never seen her with a man.

Dinner was wonderful and the food was perfect. He knew the kids had school the next day but he didn't want to leave Brielle. He walked them to the door and Brielle sent the kids to get ready for bed to give them a moment of alone time. "Thanks for dinner we enjoyed every moment."

"Anything to make you happy. This is the part that makes me unhappy, leaving you. But tomorrow will be here soon enough."

"Yes tomorrow will be here soon enough. But until then think of me." She said stepping a little closer.

Bryson leaned down and kissed her, tongue piercing her lips and his tongue dancing with her tongue. He picked her up off her feet. "I can't wait to make love to you again." He said.

"Ummmm. I love the sound of that." She moaned.

"I have an important meeting tomorrow morning, once I am done we will plan something so I can see you tomorrow ok." He said running his fingers through her hair still holding her.

"Sounds like a plan."

"I will call you when I get home that should give you time to get the kids and yourself ready for bed." Kissing her again before leaving it was hard to let her go. They held on to one another a little bit longer before Bryson headed for home.

CHAPTER 48
~BRYSON~
THE BUZZ
IS GOING AROUND

Tuesday morning Bryson walked into the office early to catch up on some work. Spending time with Brielle really had him thinking about giving more of the business responsibility to Kenneth. Now that he had a trustworthy assistant he could count on, he was empowered to do more. When Bryson walked out to his assistant he noticed people gathered around a desk. Once they saw him they walked off to get back to work and he thought that was weird of his employees. He asked his assistant Jaqueline, "What was that about?"

"I am not sure but I will surely find out give me a moment. Did you need me for something?" She asked.

"I have a client coming and I need to let them know downstairs to escort them up as soon as they get here. Here is the information." He said handing her a piece of paper. "And come in my office once you find out what that was about."

"Yes sir I'm on it. And I will take care of your guest." She said getting up from her desk.

Bryson looked back once more seeing eyes peering over desks and looking away quickly. His gut told him something was not right. Sitting in his office working Kenneth called his cell phone. "Hey Kenny."

"Brys man where are you?"

"Sitting in my office are you here? Hello?" He said into the receiver getting no answer.

"Yes I'm here. Sorry I didn't know you were here yet." Kenneth said as he entered Bryson's office. "The buzz is going around. Somehow a piece of the footage was leaked and I have no idea who would have leaked it." Kenneth said in a panicked tone.

Just then Jaqueline entered his office. "Sir, I'm sorry but they were watching a video clip of you and some woman at a park and you were wearing clothes looking a bit homeless." She said hysterical clueless to Bryson's journey.

"How could this happen Kenny? Who would have access to leak any parts of the video? This is not good!" Bryson rubbed his hand over his face in disbelief.

"Sir is there something I need to know? What was that about? Is it real? Is it true? You were homeless?" She wanted to put the pieces together.

"No Jaqueline, I was doing an experiment to see how people would treat me if they thought I had nothing. It's part of a documentary of my life that I am in the process of completing. Keep this to yourself and if you can get the video or find out how they got it then let me know. Call Roger Maxx for me. See how quickly he can get here." He was furious.

"This had to be someone from the production team or in our IT department who would have access to our computers. Dammit! It may be just that one piece and people are thinking you were really homeless."

"It doesn't matter, if they find out it has leaked this could be a breach in contract." Just then his phone buzzed. "Yes Jaqueline?"

"Sir Mr. Maxx said he was in the area he would be right over."

"Thank you send him in once he arrive." Bryson said.

"Yes sir." She said before hanging up.

"I know he will get to the bottom of this don't worry." Kenneth said.

Bryson walked out to the lady's desk who they were surrounding and asked her to come into his office and bring her laptop. He assured her she was not in trouble he just needed to find out where the source of the video came from. The girl was nervous and afraid she was about to lose her job. "Do you know where this video came from?" He asked once in his office.

"No sir. It looked like spam and I didn't intend to click on it but when I did and tried to click off I saw it was you. I only told my girlfriend to come see and everyone started surrounding my desk. I am so sorry sir."

"It's okay. You are not in trouble Mrs. Elaine. I just need to find the person who leaked the video. They are the ones who are in trouble." At that moment a member of HR and the head of IT came into the office. A few moments later Roger Maxx walked in.

"Now that the team is all here let's get to the bottom of this. Elaine was sent a video of footage from the taping of Bryson's mission. We need to find out who sent the link and how they got it and delete all traces of it." Kenneth said taking charge.

At that moment Bryson knew that Kenneth would be alright without him there full time. "I have already informed Mrs. Elaine that she is in no way in any kind of trouble and we appreciate her cooperation. There is no need to be afraid to speak freely to any of these people in the room. They are all to be trusted." Bryson said.

Roger started asking Elaine questions and the head of IT started looking and analyzing the e-mail. It took them a couple hours to figure out where the source came from and start to recall every e-mail sent out. It was an employee in the IT department that likes to joke around but was a computer whiz at everything even hacking. Bryson wanted him fired. HR and the head of IT along with security headed to speak with him and escort him away from the building.

"Thanks again Roger for your help. I am going to have to put you on payroll permanently." Bryson said. "Let me walk with you." Bryson and Kenneth headed to the lobby area with Roger to talk more about the incident and what more they needed done. When they got to the lobby no one was prepared for what they saw.

CHAPTER 49
~JEWEL~
ONE MORE ATTEMPT TO WIN

Jewel found her way into the lobby area to talk to Raquel. Her attempt was to get information out of her and see if she could catch Bryson around lunch time coming or going. She made sure she was looking sexy in a mini dress and top that revealed plenty of cleavage. Her hair was flowing down her back bone straight. She wrapped one of her old purses for Raquel's gift she promised her. That made Raquel very happy and enough for her to open up and run her mouth like a faucet.

As she was talking to Raquel she told her about the video. "Girl there is a video going around of Bryson and he looks bad but he talking to another woman and seem like he like her but it isn't you. Are you sure y'all trying to work it out. I mean rumor is this is just an act but this looks like real life stuff and he got caught on camera." She said in a ghetto fabulous way.

"What video let me see girl." Jewel's heart was beating fast. The thought of Bryson with another woman hurt her. She kept her cool and tried to brace herself for what she was about to see. It was about three minutes of clip chopped and pieced together. It was clear that Bryson looked homeless and that he was feeling the girl in the video, Brielle. "Oh wow. I knew he was going to do a film of some sort but I didn't know it was like this. Girl he acting we are in love." Her heart was beating fast and she wanted to break down and cry. The way he looked at Brielle he has never looked at her. It was the look of a man who was truly in love.

"Oh okay that make sense but why he dressed like that. I mean what kind of film is this?" She said admiring her purse some more.

"I don't ask him too many questions about his business girl I just love him. Have you seen him today?" Jewel asked. She wanted to run up the elevator to see him but wanted to be patient, knowing she didn't have badge access for the elevators.

"He here today. I had to buzz a man up this morning to see him. Something big is going on. It look like this purse has been used but shoot I don't care its fye. I like it." At that moment Raquel looked up at the lady coming through the door, then opened the video back up and glanced again. "Girl that is her, the girl from the video."

"Where girl?" Jewel looked with panic.

"Right there." She said pointing in Brielle's direction walking towards the desk. She was looking up at the building's design admiring the art work.

"Oh shit! I am about to mess with her big time." Jewel thought she would seize the opportunity to ruin any possible relationship the lady had with Bryson.

"Girl you know Bryson don't like no mess in this lobby you better be on chill mode." Raquel said.

Jewel's heart was beating fast. She couldn't believe this girl was standing in front of her and she thought briefly maybe Bryson was on his way down to meet her. She didn't want to look like a fool. "I am not starting any mess girl."

"Excuse me. This is a very nice building." Brielle said.

"Yeah girl the owner has excellent taste. How can I help you?" She said in her own fabulous way.

I'm looking for Mr. Matt Cole. He is a business analyst here with the company." Brielle said to Raquel.

Jewel started laughing. Raquel tried to hush her. Brielle turned to look at her but didn't understand what was so funny.

"I'm sorry. Please don't pay her no mind. You must be talking about Bryson Mathew's right?" Raquel said looking at her confused.

"Oh no ma'am he started about a month ago his name is Matt Cole." She said glancing at Jewel once more.

"Is that the name Bryson gave you? I'm so sorry he led you on for his own selfishness. You even brought him lunch in a cute little picnic basket." Jewel said now mocking Brielle.

"Excuse me who are you? And what are you talking about?" Brielle was confused.

"Jewel shut up girl! You are so out of line here. That's why I never tell you anything."

"What does this have to do with me? Can you just tell me how to find Matt Cole please?" Brielle said a bit irritated.

"Look sweetie. The name of the company is Cole Estates that's where Cole comes from. His last name is Mathews and he goes by Matt from time to time when he doesn't want to reveal his true identity. He owns this company and several more. He is rich beyond rich. It is obvious he was only using you if you don't know who he is." Jewel said in a nasty jealous tone.

"I still don't understand why you think I am talking about another man." Brielle said.

"Bryson Mathews is my fiancé sweetie and he has no intentions with you but for his film production. The picnic is sweet but is not necessary. That's where I need to draw the line." Raquel answered a call and Jewel leans over the counter and turns Raquel's monitor around so Brielle could see the clip. "This is you right here right?" The video was playing of Brielle and Bryson at the park. Jewel was smiling as Brielle had tears in her eyes. "My man was only using you for his film he is making. He is nowhere near homeless." Jewel said smiling, knowing Brielle was hurt and humiliated.

"Jewel I am going to have to ask you to leave girl. If Bryson finds out this video was watched from my computer I am going to get fired. And you are starting mess. Ma'am I am so sorry you had to see this and didn't know. I will see if Mr. Mathews is available." Raquel said.

"Raquel. I am waiting on my soon to be husband Bryson "Matt" Mathews. We are headed out to lunch at an expensive restaurant not to eat picnic food." Jewel said and laughed.

Brielle started to back up from the desk thinking about the monogram on the handkerchief and how someone approached him in the restaurant and he was nervous when they thought he was someone else. She thought about her kids how hurt they would be. She introduced him to her family. He went to church with her and the kids, been to her apartment. She had a rush of hurt and confusion. She didn't understand how or why, it didn't make any sense but it hurt deeply. The video of her at the park hurt. Jewel saying she was his fiancée. She looked up as the elevator opened seeing Bryson and two men walking out talking. Bryson locked eyes with her immediately smiling happy to see her but he quickly felt something was wrong.

"There is my baby right there." Jewel said as she rushed over to Bryson with Brielle watching.

Bryson looked up at Jewel with a frown on his face and immediately turned to Brielle and knew Jewel had already done damage. He watched as Brielle dropped the basket she was holding and all the food in it tumbled to the ground as she ran out the door. "Brielle wait!" He shouted as he headed towards her. Jewel embraced him stopping him in his tracks. He pushed her back away from him with Kenneth catching her fall and holding on to her. "What did you do?" Bryson yelled at Jewel.

Brielle was out the door fast running into a moving car that had to stop abruptly to keep from hitting her. She saw Bryson behind her with tears in her eyes she was in the car speeding off before he caught her. This was an unbearable hurt for her to endure.

Bryson watched as she sped off recklessly in the other direction. "I had three more days and I could tell you everything. Damn! God I need you right now!" He said to himself. He looked up to the sky and said a quick prayer for her safety. He looked up and Rodger was right behind him.

"Anything I can do?" Rodger asked.

"Yes, find out where she's going, make sure she is safe. I need to know she's safe. She did not look good driving away."

"I'm on it. Call you when I know more." Rodger said.

At that moment Bryson noticed that cameras where everywhere and the producers were coming towards him. The moment they saw Brielle and Jewel in the same space they knew they needed this footage to close out the filming. Hurt and disgusted he headed back into the building to try to figure out what just happened.

CHAPTER 50
~BRYSON/KENNETH~
HANDLING BUSINESS IN
THE LOBBY

Kenneth was talking with security as they had Jewel in handcuffs. Bryson walked into the building and straight to Raquel and the security guard working the door. "How did she get in here again?"

"Sir I am sorry. This is my first week and I wasn't left the list of who was not to enter. I did however get confirmation from Raquel that the young lady was okay to enter. I figured she would know and not steer me wrong but I myself was wrong. For my misjudgment I apologize sir." The security officer said.

"Raquel what happened with the young lady? What did Jewel say to her?" He looked at Raquel for an answer.

As she looked spooked and started to tremble she spoke even though she knew she was about to be fired. "Sir, Jewel told her she was engaged to you and she also showed her the video of you two in a park when you were dressed homeless looking. She told her you were using her. She called you Matt Cole and Jewel told her your real name. I am so sorry, I shouldn't have let her in but she said you two were working things out."

"How did Jewel get the video?" Bryson asked.

"She saw it on my computer and when I was on the phone she turned the monitor around for that sweet lady to see and that's when you were getting off the elevator." Raquel was hoping her job was safe.

"Okay, new guy time to redeem yourself. I need two things from you. I need the video of the incident that happened here in the lobby. You personally bring it to my office. Do that after you escort Raquel out of the building. Raquel you are no longer employed here at Cole Estate's. Please pack your personal belongings and leave the premises. This is our HR rep and she will answer questions about your final pay. You have five minutes to be gone." He turned to walk away even though Raquel was talking.

"But sir I need my job. Please sir. She tricked me. Ah damn I am going to hurt that bitch. She is fucking with my money now. I will see you on the streets bitch you best believe that." She yelled directed at Jewel. She was mad but could only blame herself for being so naïve.

Bryson walked over to Jewel. "What the hell are you doing here Jewel?"

"I wanted to see you. I love you Bryson. I am getting help for my problems. Please just talk to me in private please." She said with a sad look.

"I can't believe you. You don't fuck somebodies brother try to blackmail them with rape and do the other awful things you did to me and expect me to do what? Forgive you? Forget? Get it through your head we will never be back together ever. There is nothing you need to say to me." Bryson said furious.

"Sir, are you pressing charges? We can charge her for trespassing." The officer on site asked.

Jewel was crying. "Please don't send me to jail Bryson. I won't come back here I promise. I know you will eventually come around and you will find me please."

"Get her out of here." Bryson said.

"No, stop. Get your damn hands off me." Jewel said as she kicked and fought the security officers. She was hurting. With everything she did to hurt the people around her she never stopped to think about the pain she would be causing herself.

Bryson spoke with the head of his security team and immediately wanted a replacement at the front desk for Raquel with a thorough background check. He wanted to increase security check points and make it impossible for her to return.

With all of the commotion that was going on it brought unwanted attention to Bryson's building. A nearby news reporter saw what was happening and starting filming the commotion. When Jewel was released to her car the reporter tried to interview her. After being cursed out the reporter attempted to get inside the building to speak with Bryson. She was turned away.

Just as she started recording her take on the event that took place, Jewel came from nowhere and ran her car into the lobby of Bryson's building. Everyone tried to get out of the way in a hurry. Jewel tried to back up to make an escape but with so much debris falling behind the car she had nowhere to go. She got out of the car looked at Bryson. "All I wanted to do was love you. You didn't have to leave me at the altar like you did. We are supposed to be married right now." With tears in her eyes she searched for some type of sympathy from Bryson and received nothing.

Jaws clenched and furious he looked at security and said "Get her out of here now. And yes we are pressing charges." Kenneth said to the officers rushing towards Jewel. Everyone was stunned and shook up at what just happened. More police arrived and news reporters.

Bryson knew this was about to be all over the news. All he wanted was to get to Brielle. He turned towards the elevators when his phone rung. It was Roger calling to report on Brielle. "Hey man, please tell me you found her?"

"Yes. I am sitting in the parking lot. She came to the church she attends. She looks pretty upset still."

"Church is good. Thank you Rodger. You are not going to believe what just happened here."

"I am seeing the breaking news now. You have a car in your lobby, wow!"

"Damn. This is not the type of publicity I like or need right now. I am letting Kenny handle this one I need to get to Brielle." He was headed to his office to get his car keys. He wanted to be where Brielle was.

"Bryson, she is leaving the church. I will follow her. Call me when you are driving I will inform you of our whereabouts."

"Thanks Rodger." He said. Before leaving the lobby he turned to Kenneth letting him know he was out and that he needed him to handle the situation.

Maintenance crew and repair men were on the scene and everyone was taking care of what needed to be done to secure the building and ensure everyone's safety. Bryson felt comfortable enough to leave him in charge knowing everything would be handled.

When he called Rodger back, he informed him she was at an apartment building parking in a secure garage. He would wait outside until he arrived.

Bryson tried to get pass the doorman. He was denied access and scolded for doing the one thing he was instructed not to do. Brielle called down and told Floyd absolutely no visitors. After pleading his case he was still denied access and asked to leave the building. His power was not working at that moment. Although he could overtake the man he wouldn't. That was not his character and besides that would only hurt Brielle even more. The doorman was like family to her and the kids. He watched over them to ensure no one would harm them, and for that Bryson gave him mad respect.

Bryson was devastated. He called a hundred times with no answer. He sat outside her building for hours hoping she would come out. After several attempts and no luck getting in or her coming out he headed back to his office to see how well things were cleaned up.

Kenneth met him in the garage. "Were you able to see her Bryson? How is she?"

"Rodger saw her. She was upset as she should be under the circumstances. I couldn't get passed the doorman and she wouldn't come out or answer my calls. This is bad. If I lose her..." He stopped getting choked up. He couldn't hold back the tears.

Kenneth went over to hug him seeing he was breaking again but this time was different. He had pain of possibly losing the true love of his life. He caught Bryson as his knees buckled from up under him. "Remember you have favor. She is hurting because she doesn't know. You will figure this out and you will mend the situation because the one thing that is evident to us all is the fact that you both are in love. It's more than a puppy love it's a forever kind of love and she will let you in. You just need to find your way to her. Be patient. God has not taken you through all of this to take her from you."

Straightening his face he gathered his composure. "You are right man. I can't and I won't lose her. I can't lose her and those kids." Tears were still flowing out of his control. The pain was real and unbearable.

"Bryson you are not losing them. It will work itself out, you will see."

"What's going on down stairs?"

"That's all under control. It's secure and Bradon is coming with his crew first thing in the morning to start on the redesign. We needed a makeover anyhow." He said joking.

"He is the man to get the job done. Thanks Kenny." He headed to his office to be alone. He tried calling Brielle again with no answer. He was determined to fix everything and make her his wife. He left voicemails hoping she would listen to them.

CHAPTER 51
~BRADON~
IT'S ALL OVER THE NEWS

Bradon **was at** home waiting for Chantae to arrive. He wanted to talk to her about what was going on with Bryson and Brielle, make sure they were okay and see if she had talked to her friend. The television was on and every news channel was talking about the incident that happened today. "We have scenes from earlier today of the woman driving her car through the Coles Estate building. She was irate earlier when asked to leave and apparently what ever made her mad it was enough for her to risk her life and the lives of others. The building is boarded up at the moment as you can see behind me, and one of the owners stated the building is indeed safe. Normal business operations will resume tomorrow morning."

The news reporter played back the car running into the building and Kenneth's statement. She was the first on the scene and had more footage than other news reporters. She even had Bradon as he worked with the crew to secure the building. Just then Chantae arrived and joined him in the living room and began to watch the news. "Have you seen what's been going on?"

"No I don't watch the news much what happened?" She asked as she was watching the news.

He turned the volume up so she could listen and hear for herself. "This is my brother Bryson's company. All this started because his ex, the one I told you about was at his building today when Brielle came to see my brother for lunch."

"Wait. Why was Brielle there to see your brother?" She looked a bit confused.

"I wanted to tell you but couldn't and when you called me yesterday about the monogram on the handkerchief I thought you figured it out."

"Wait, figured what out?" Chantae asked still confused.

"My brother Bryson and Brielle's Matt is the same person. This journey he was on was for one reason only to see how people treat him not knowing who he was. He never intended to meet Brielle and fall in love with her but he did. He was under contract with the producers and Bryson is a very loyal dedicated person in all things he does. That's just who he is, a part of his character."

"Matt is your brother?" She asked trying to digest what Bradon said.

"Yes. Matt and Bryson are one and the same. He wanted to tell Brielle who he really was, or who the world see him as but he loved being just Bryson in the sight of Brielle and her kids without emphasis on his wealth. But treating him just as they did without knowing his status in Corporate America."

"Brielle is not that girl." She said wondering if her friend was ok. "So how does what happened today at the building have anything to do with Brielle?"

"His ex, Jewel, was there when Brielle came today and a video was leaked of Bryson's first encounter with Brielle and her kids. Jewel told her Bryson was her fiancé and they were getting married and he was only using Brielle. She showed her the video."

"Oh shit! I should have figured this out before now. She hasn't called me. I need to call her right now." Chantae was on her feet pacing back and forth calling Brielle. On her fourth attempt of no answer she left her a message. "Brielle you know you are going to have to talk to me. Call me right back tell me where you are so I can come to you." She hung up the phone still pacing. "She is not answering Bradon. What the hell is really going on? Is Bryson getting married to someone else?"

"Chantae, Jewel is the girl I told you tried to blackmail me and broke Bryson's heart. The girl he left standing at the altar. He will never marry her, be back with her or anything like that. He doesn't want to ever see her again. She ran her car through his building because she knows Bryson is in love with Brielle. And he put her out of his building placing a restraining order against her. But now she is facing jail time."

"So Bryson or Matt or whatever his name is loves Brielle? For real for real?"

"Yes he is in love with her." At that moment he heard a panic knock at the door. It was Bryson hoping Chantae was there just as Bradon told him she would be. "Hey brother how you holding up?" Bradon said answering the door.

"Not good man. I cannot find Brielle to talk to her I was hoping Chantae has seen her."

"She is in the living room come on." They headed to join Chantae in the living room still watching the playback of the incident on the news. "Chantae this is my brother."

"Damn you two look a lot alike. So what do I call you Matt or Bryson because at this point you are two different people to me?"

"Hi Chantae. My name is Bryson Mathews. Matt is a nickname I used growing up and the name I used when I met Brielle. I really need to speak with her to explain everything. Have you talked to her at all?" Bryson asked.

"I just found out about everything that went on today just moments ago. But she is not answering my calls. She didn't come back to work after lunch and now I know why. Last I heard she was surprising Matt for lunch, well you of course. How do I know you are seriously in love with her and not out to hurt her or really using her? Bradon, is this a brother thing were you in on this?"

"No. I didn't start putting it together until I saw my brother wearing the suit you gave Brielle for 'Matt'. And then when you said he was homeless but she said he didn't seem homeless I just started to put it all together. And my mom said that his new girl was in our home, I really knew then before even talking to Bryson."

"Chantae I need you to believe me. This was no setup. All this was God's planning, him positioning me where I needed to be to meet my soulmate. I love her and those kids and I am going to marry her first chance I get. If you can help me at all please do."

"You do sound convincing. I can see why she fell so hard for you. You better not be running game. I will try to see if Mr. Floyd her doorman will let me up to her apartment. He don't play any games when it comes to her."

"I know I already been to her apartment. I couldn't get passed him. This is not a game. I am truly in love with Brielle."

"Ok, I guess I believe you. Seeing how she never lets her guards down with a man and you had her glowing. Even if you did get pass Mr. Floyd he would have stopped you in the elevator and called the police. As big as you are you could have but you have to get through him period."

"Do we even know if she is at home?" Bradon asked.

"I had Roger find her and follow her to see where she was going. I needed to make sure she was at least ok while driving." He looked up at Chantae.

"Wait a minute. You had her followed? So you know she is at her apartment because you had her followed."

"Yes. And I sat outside the building for hours hoping she would come out."

"Oh well if you know she is there she has her shield up. Let me call her brother so he can meet me there. This must be bad. Tell me what happened to her again?"

"Babe I told you that Jewel girl…"

Chantae stopped him mid-sentence. "No I want your brother to tell me." Her hands were on her hips. Her sister defense was in full effect.

"Chantae I know you love your friend like a sister. She talks about you a lot. You are very talented. The suit you made for me was perfect in more ways than one and you didn't even measure me so that alone tells me a little about your character. So let me be straight with you. I was going to marry Jewel but had doubts and God showed me things about her and that relationship died the moment those things were revealed. She loved my lifestyle. And I took that all away from her. She wants that back not me. Anyone could see by looking at that video that Brielle and I have something special between us from day one of meeting. Jewel saw it. She was in a jealous rage knowing that any hope she did have was shattered. She knows how I love and how loyal I am to those I love. I don't love Jewel. I love Brielle. She is the life of my spirit. The beat of my heart and every breath I take I want to be breathing the same air as she. I need to be with her right now to fix this."

"Damn that's sweet." She said mesmerized by his words.

"Brielle is my soul mate and I love her in ways I never thought I could love any being. I have to find her and hold her and show her this was no joke to me, that all of this was real. More so than anything in my life. Please Chantae. I need Brielle. I can't lose her."

"I'm going to have to suck some toes and woo my girl after all this love talk. Damn bro. They are really in love Chantae, if there is anything you can do to help you won't be making a mistake I promise you."

"Alright I'm going. Hopefully she has not sheltered herself from all visitors."

Chantae grabbed her purse and walked out the door calling Isaiah on the phone. If Brielle would see anyone it would be them.

CHAPTER 52
~BRIELLE~
GOD THIS CAN'T BE HAPPENING

"God I know you love me and I have favor. This right here I don't understand. Why God? How do I go all of this time without seeing a man, no sex, no nothing just healing my heart, giving myself to you Lord and not looking back allowing my past to hold on to me? This hurts so bad, really bad Lord. What did I do in my former life to deserve this pain? I take care of my kids, I am good to people. Why do bad things happen to me when it comes to men? Lord I can't stop crying and I don't understand." Brielle was on her knees praying in her home. She then stood to her feet and started yelling still praying.

"God you said if I do right by you, Your Will for my life will be done. You would pour out that abundance of love. That you would protect my heart and protect my family. This can't be happening to me Lord. Please take this pain away Lord. I can't deal with this, it hurts. Please Lord take this pain away. How could I not see the deception? Oh he was good, he was real good Lord. Or either I was real stupid to not see the foolishness right before my eyes. God this hurts." She fell to her knees crying her eyes out. "Why me Lord?"

She made herself stop crying went to the kitchen and poured a glass of water. She looked in the cabinet over the stove and pulled out a bottle of sleeping pills. Instead of taking the recommended one she took two and downed the water. Then she poured a glass of wine, grabbed her cell phone and went into her bedroom. She changed her clothes into some oversized pajamas and dialed her mother's number.

"Mom I don't feel too hot. I need to lay down. Can the kids stay over tonight?"

"Of course sweetheart do you need me to do anything for you at all? You need to go to the hospital?

"No ma'am, I will be ok. I just need you and dad to watch the kids for me. I know they are staying tomorrow too but I just need to rest. I am going to take the migraine medicine the doctor gave me and sleep. I won't be at work tomorrow. I think I just need to rest."

"You sure you don't need me? Your dad can watch the kids. You don't sound good at all."

"Momma. It's quiet here and I don't need anything just to rest." Brielle started to cry trying not to let her mom hear her. Her heart was aching and her head was hurting. She didn't lie to her mom just didn't tell her the entire truth.

"Okay you call me if you need anything. We will take care of the kids."

"Thank you momma. I love you and tell my babies I love them too. I will talk to you soon when I wake."

"Love you too baby. Get you some rest."

She ended the call with her mom and the tears were flowing. She sipped on her wine and dialed the front desk of her apartment building. "Floyd no visitors okay. I am about to rest."

"Yes ma'am. You had a visitor earlier and I turned him away. The gentleman from earlier in the week."

"Thank you Floyd. Absolutely no visitors okay."

"Yes ma'am Brielle. I'm here if you need me ok."

"I know Floyd. I took a sleeping pill to relax and help me sleep. Can you stick your head in before you leave make sure I am sleeping and ok, that's all just real quick and only you ok.

"Yes ma'am. Consider it done. Get some rest dear."

"Thank you!" She knew she could trust Floyd.

She sent an e-mail to her boss letting him know she will be out for the rest of the week her doctors' orders and she will be back in the office Monday morning.

Brielle turned on some jazz music to play softly as she slept. She turned her phone on silent and got up under the covers holding onto her pillow tight. "Lord, please heal my aching heart." As the sleeping pills and wine relaxed her and she started to drift to sleep she could hear sweet sounds of Bryson playing back over in her mind.

Every word I am saying to you, every emotion I am feeling is genuine. I would feel this way if I had nothing and I would feel this way if I had billions.

"Was he trying to tell me something? What did I miss?" She said mumbling falling asleep. More sounds playing back in her mind. *I don't want to ever lose you in my life... My spirit is saying you are my soul mate... I need you to trust me... I have to fix some things and make things right for you, me and those three blessings to be a family... I promise to fill your heart's desire of that love you speak of... If you can't tell by now please know that I want you Brielle... God knows I want you from the first day I laid my eyes on you...Brielle it is so easy to love you... I promise! I want to make love to you so bad right now... When Jesus says yes... You are breath taking beautiful.... When Jesus says yes... When Jesus says yes..."*

She fell into a deep sleep and the only other sound that was there was God's voice. She couldn't hear him but he was healing her heart and speaking to her spirit so she would be able to feel his covering. *"My child, my words to you are always true. These things that are happening are not only for you. You are just one of my faithful servants being used to touch and save lives, to heal and save souls. You don't understand and my intentions are never to bring you pain. You are covered. You will soon have your happiness back. I need you to rest now so your pain will cease, I am working on your behalf to fix things for you. All will be renewed soon. You are my faithful loving child, how can I not bless you with the desires of your heart. It's already done. Rest my child..."*

CHAPTER 53
~CHANTAE~
IT'S GOING TO BE ALRIGHT

Chantae had Isaiah to meet her at Brielle's apartment. Chantae had a key she just needed to get pass Mr. Floyd. "Hey thanks for meeting me. You didn't tell your parents did you?"

"You know me better than that Chantae. We need to see what's going on with her first. Assess the situation from Brielle before my parents react in their own way. We both know how protective they are of us." Isaiah said embracing Chantae kissing her cheek. "I'm just glad you called me. Now tell me what's going on. You rushed through when you called, something about Jewel telling Brielle something and a car running into the building. Who is Jewel and what building? What's going on?"

"Ok you know she was seeing a guy name Matt right? I think you met him already."

"Yes, nice guy. Go on."

"His real name is Bryson Mathews. Apparently he was supposed to marry Jewel, some bull shit happened with that and he humiliated her at the altar and never wanted to see the chick again. She has been trying to get him back. Well Matt, or Bryson or whatever the hell his name is, was doing a documentary on his life but living as if he was homeless, had nothing. See where I am going with this?"

"That's when he and Brielle met and he gave her a different name. Ex girl finds an opportunity to come back and try to mess things up. Typical scenario."

"Wait how do you know he was sincere with Brielle, that he wasn't using her?"

"Have you been around them together?" Isaiah asked.

"No not yet and it's probably because I am dating his brother. Didn't know they were brothers until today. It's a lot going on I swear!" She said shaking her head.

"If you are around those two it's obvious that they are in love. There is no acting when it comes to true love. He was even in church with her. That is not an action of a man who is about to get married or has another girl. You know how many people attend our church?"

"I guess you are right. He sounded convincing to me as well so if you say he is the real deal then lets fix this or at least try."

"Let's just hope Mr. Floyd let us up."

They headed to the door and Floyd greeted them cheerfully. They tried to plead their case as to why he needs to let them up. "I understand she is your sister and your best friend but I have strict orders. I spoke with her and she is ok, she is resting. Let her rest. If you went upstairs now you would only be disturbing her. Sometimes that's how God work by allowing you to rest. She will be fine."

"We can't even just peek in at her?" Chantae said.

"Those batting eyelashes won't work here sweetheart. You know I'm old school. My word and my loyalty is bond. After what happened to her it's my duty to protect her."

"What if she overdosed or something. Not saying she is suicidal but you never know how much one can take." Isaiah said.

"We both know Brielle is strong and loves those children more than her life itself. She would never be that selfish." Mr. Floyd said. "If it makes you feel any better at the end of my shift I will check on her and call you afterwards. That's all I can do."

"Okay we tried. Thanks Mr. Floyd. Here is my card call me when you check on her." Isaiah said.

"Yes call me too. Let me write my number on the back of his card. He all fancy with business cards. Look at you Isaiah being a boss." Chantae said.

"You know me, low profile and about my business." Isaiah said.

Chantae wrote her number on the back of his card and handed it back to Mr. Floyd. "Thank you Floyd. Don't forget to call us as soon as you go up."

"I won't. You two have a good evening." He said giving them the cue to leave.

"Give me one of your business cards Isaiah. Those are nice. I need to have some made for my clothing line."

"Let me know when you are ready. I will make it happen no problem. I am worried about Brielle. Shutting everyone out is not a good thing. She must really be hurting."

"You know that's what she does when something is bothering her. But rest is good for her. When she talks to Bryson she will be okay."

"I thought he looked familiar when I met him. That dude is rich beyond rich. He owns several companies. I am sure he is a billionaire or close to it." Isaiah said.

"Damn! He got it like that? No wonder Bradon has a black card that is unlimited."

"Yeah, I understand why he loves my sister so much. Besides her genuinely being a sweet good hearted human being and being beautiful she loved him in rare form without knowing. She never has been materialistic and now she is about to be Queen B."

"Queen B?"

"Yes Queen Baller." He said laughing.

"I'm so jealous. She better forgive him and marry that man. For love not his money."

"See that's why he didn't marry that other girl."

"I'm just playing big brother. Call me if you hear from her before I do and I will do the same okay."

"Will do. Be careful out here and keep trying to call her." Isaiah said hugging Chante good bye.

"Yes of course I will." Chantae said stepping into her car.

Isaiah closed her door and before Chantae pulled off she decided to call Brielle one more time. She didn't answer so she left her a voicemail. "Hey girl. Me and your brother just tried to come up and check on you but you know how Floyd is so protective over you. That's a good thing but bad for us. We are worried about you. I heard from Bradon and met Mr. Wonderful today. Look, I know things look bad to you right now but I don't believe things are what they appeared to be. That man loves you I mean he convinced me and your brother is convinced as well. He is looking for you and came to me for help. Girl he is handsome. I can't believe I didn't put everything together but please call me. I know everything is going to be alright."

She paused for a moment sitting in her car to really think about all the revelation she had in just a short period of time. She didn't doubt Bradon's love for her and started to think about Bryson and Brielle and how that love story unfolded. It made somewhat of sense to her but she still had some missing pieces that she had to figure out.

CHAPTER 54
~BRADON/BRYSON~
I KNOW HOW TO
GET TO HER

Wednesday morning things were quiet. No one was talking much about the incident from the day before. Bradon flipped through every channel. He figured Bryson made some calls and had the topic ceased with all networks. He hardly ever used his power to make things happen but this was a good call. Bryson didn't like to be exposed and his business being talked about. He called Bryson to check on him. "Hey, good morning how are you holding up?" He asked.

"Not so well Bradon. I didn't sleep at all last night and now I am sitting outside her building waiting to see if she is going to work."

"You know we can take the doorman and get you up there to her apartment." Bradon said.

"I still would need to know the elevator code and then have access to get into her apartment. I have been there and she has extra locks only accessible from inside. I'm sure she has them all secure."

"Damn, is she afraid of something or someone? What's up with all the locks?"

"Another story another time little brother. Has Chantae talked to her at all?"

"No. She tried to get the door man to let her in with no luck and has called numerous times, all night actually. She even left messages."

"Are you two ok?"

"Oh yeah we are great. She is just worried about her friend."

"Good. I didn't want to interfere. You two are cute together and I am proud of you. She is actually good for you. She has you focused on your priorities. She a little feisty too."

"Yes she is a keeper. We are lucky and Brielle will forgive you and still love you so don't you worry about that. Just stay focused and try to find her. That's all you need is to see her and talk to her. Then she will know all of this was real between the two of you.

"I hope so Bradon. I can't lose her.

"You won't lose her. Hey I have an idea. She attends church sometimes on Wednesday evenings and if she didn't see her children yesterday surely she will see them tonight and go to church with her family. Chantae said she is very religious so maybe she will be at church tonight. We could all go for support and to let her know we love her too because you love her."

"That's a good idea. Tell Chantae to come and I will let Kenny know. I wish momma was here to fix this for me. She always knows the answer. Only this time I couldn't bear to hear her say move on."

"Bryson, I doubt momma would say move on this time. She spent the entire evening with Brielle the day I had the party so momma likes her. Maybe you should call her and at least tell her what's going on so she can pray about it on your behalf."

"I think I will do that. As soon as we hang up. Listen, I will really need everyone's support today. I am willing to marry her right then and there if she let me."

"Damn are you serious?"

"Yes, I am so serious. Bradon I really love this girl. All signs point to forever with her. I need her back." Bryson said being so sure about his words he spoke.

"Okay I feel you. Marriage is serious you know. Momma and daddy married at a very young age and they are still together, still happy. And if that's what you think you have then by all means bro marry the girl. You have my blessings!"

"Thanks Bradon. I have that and so much more with her."

"Alright then. I will see you at the church tonight."

"I hope she is there."

"If not then when the timing is right you will see her eventually and things will be right." Bradon said encouraging his brother.

"Thanks bro." Bryson ended the call and called his mom. He didn't want to hear her say anything that would suggest Brielle was not right for him. But instead she was saying the complete opposite. Letting him know that he caused the temporary heart ache not God but that this will pass and God's promise is his promise. She was praying for him regarding the situation right then at that moment. Bryson started crying. Her words stood out and ringed in his ear. "God's promise to you will not return void. Your patience and determination is needed in all of this. God brought her to you in a most painful trying time of your life. Love never fails my son. It's in the bible. God is Love and Love never fails. It's a beautiful thing to have love and know it is sent from God. It's up to you to protect that love. The same girl I spoke with spoke in a way that you could tell she was experiencing God sent love and I knew it was love for my son. That one is worth fighting for. You find her and you make it right. God has you both covered. You say your prayers and your momma will continue to pray. You hear me?"

"Yes momma. I love you so much! Thank you always." He said grateful to have a prayer warrior for a mom who loved her boys dearly.

He headed to his office to tell Kenneth he wanted him at the church that evening. He asked Ameila to join them as well.

Bradon met up with Chantae for lunch and she informed him that Brielle called out for the rest of the week sick. "That's not a good sign. We may need to call her parents. She has shut everyone out." She said worried.

"We are hoping she will be at church this evening and Bryson wants us all to be there." Bradon said.

"Do you know how long it has been since I have been at church?"

"It's been a minute for me too but I am not a stranger to church. My mom raised me and my brother up in church. So I am actually looking forward to it. Bryson said it has a feeling of back home when we use to attend with momma."

"I hope I can officially meet your mom soon." She threw that in as a spur of the moment thought.

"It is time for my mom to meet my future wife. We will make that happen as soon as Bryson and Brielle are ok. I promise." He said looking into her eyes.

"Really Bradon? I don't mean to sound selfish." She was happy and excited hearing him call her his future wife.

"You are not being selfish. Yes really."

"Wait! You said future wife. Did I hear you correctly?

Bradon smiled and replied, "Yes, you heard me correctly. The day I propose you will know how serious I am." He didn't want her to think that was his proposal.

"I love you Bradon Mathews."

"I love you too my queen." They embraced with a kiss. Forgetting about everyone else for a moment and remembering their love.

Evening approached and everyone met in the church parking lot. No signs of Brielle. With a few minutes to seven they decided to go in and take their seats. The choir was standing as the band started playing and they started to sing. Ameila sat next to Kenneth, Bradon and Chantae sat behind them. Bryson was on the same seat as Bradon but quickly moved when he saw Brielle's children. He sat on the pew behind them. Jayla, and Carter were excited to see him. Jayla stood on the pew and reached for him to sit next to him. Brielle's father asked him to stay for a second when service was done and he agreed.

Olivia asked if she could go back and sit with them as well and he gave her permission. Carter reached back to give him a hand shake as Olivia took her seat next to him. The affection from the kids warmed his heart. He had both of the girls in his arms and felt the closeness of Brielle. They were his family. If her father had to help him get to Brielle then that's where he would turn for help.

He looked over at Bradon and Chantae and smiled at the love they displayed. The message was based around love again. He didn't mind at all as it seemed to bring people closer together. He thought Kenneth may have a thing for Ameila but just didn't say anything. He knew Kenneth wouldn't impose knowing she was still married. Ameila had tears in her eyes and Kenneth pulled her closer to him. The Pastor had a way of touching hearts and touching lives. He had not seen his brother in church since they were younger and could see the childhood memories flooding back.

Maybe this too was all a part of God's plan. Brielle has five souls being touched by God. He turned to look back and saw Roger sitting in the very back. He wasn't for sure if he was there for him or if he actually attended the church. He nodded letting him know he was there on business.

Bryson also noticed the producers there as well. He assumed with everything going on that they had stopped but he didn't pay any attention that they were still around. Saturday was to be his last day and he wasn't about to lie to Brielle anymore. He was telling her the truth about everything. He was starting with her father.

Everyone enjoyed service. When it was done Bryson didn't move. He stayed seated with the kids and waited on Brielle's dad to return. "How is your mom? Is she working late again today?" He asked the kids.

"Momma doesn't feel good. Probably her migraines again. Granddaddy taking us to school tomorrow." Jayla said.

"She probably sleeping. Her medicine makes her sleepy." Olivia said.

"Granny talked to her earlier today and she sound sleepy. We told her we loved her and hope she feel better soon but we didn't talk to her long. We are letting her rest." Carter said.

"We supposed to go to the park Saturday to feed the ducks. That's what she said. If she feeling better." Jayla said.

"Okay we all are going to pray that she feels better soon. I miss her and I know you all miss her." Bryson said.

"Yes we do." They all said.

"Give me a hug your grandmother is calling for you." They all gave him a big hug, even Carter before heading to leave with their grandmother. Bryson saw Rodger meeting with Kenneth and giving him an envelope. He hoped it was good news. Kenneth waited for him in the back. "How are you sir?" He said to Mr. Summers.

"I'm good son, how are you?" Mr. Summers asked.

"Not so good. I have not heard from Brielle and I really need to speak with her." He said looking her father in the eye sincerely. He needed for him to believe every word he says.

"Isaiah already filled me in on everything so no need to explain. Have a seat. My Brielle is the sweetest most loving young lady I know. A few years ago something bad happened to her and we thought we would lose her. Ever since then she avoided men and clung to me and her brother and was all about her children." He put his face in the palm of his hands and wiped his face. "Listen son. She most likely has her defenses up and fear has set in. She is not really stubborn but will close down and shut the world out. I just found out everything right before service but first thing tomorrow after getting these kids to school me and the Pastor are going to see her."

"I tried. The doorman Mr. Floyd won't let me in."

"I'm not worried about him. He is an old friend of mine and he knows how I am about my daughter. Her mom talked to her earlier and she has not done anything crazy but we both knew something else was going on. She has migraines but something always triggers them when they are this bad. And now I know what. Don't worry she will be alright."

"That's all I have been doing is worrying. I truly love her sir. I want her to be my wife."

"You are a good man Bryson. It didn't feel right calling you Matt. It didn't fit you but I like Bryson." Bryson smiled at him. "You coming here tonight say a lot. The kids were happy to see you and they needed that just as much as you did. You will marry Brie if she says yes and my gut feeling tells me she will." He stood to his feet. "I need to get my family home but I will be in touch."

Bryson stood to his feet and reached to shake his hand. "Your words mean a lot to me sir. Thank you!"

"You're welcome son." He spoke to everyone on his way out who was with Bryson.

"What did Rodger say Kenny?" Bryson asked.

"He tapped into her phone somehow and heard a conversation between her and a doctor. It's on the flash drive. But he said she sound tired but well."

"Okay thank you man. I will hook it up in the car. Thank you all for coming to support me." He said to everyone who came to support him.

Bryson thanked Kenneth for the flash drive before leaving and they all said their good byes.

Once in the car Bryson hooked up the flash drive to hear the call. He couldn't hit play quick enough.

"Dr. Vanessa Carols office how may I help you?

"May I speak with Dr. Carols please? Tell her it's Brielle Summers."

"One moment please."

"Hey Brielle are you okay?"

"Hey Vanessa, no I'm not okay. I think I have the flu or something and I need to come see you quick so I can get some medicine girl I feel bad."

"Okay well can you be here in the morning at eight am?"

"Yes I will be there."

"You have someone to bring you? You sound awful girlfriend?"

"No. I will be fine. My parents have the kids I will pull it together to come in the morning."

"Okay, answer your phone in about an hour I am going to call you back when I finish up here. Turn your phone on, knowing you it's on silent."

"Okay I am doing it right now. And thank you my friend."

Bryson was happy to have heard her voice but hated that she was now sick. He figured that she knew this Doctor Carols personally and was glad she had yet another person to look after her. He would be sure to be at her place in the morning to try to catch her as she was leaving. He wanted to take care of her. Protect her and provide whatever her heart desired. He was determined to make this right.

CHAPTER 55
~BRIELLE~
DOCTOR DADDY
AND THE PASTOR

After bible study Mr. Summers spoke with Pastor Malone and they decided to pay a visit to Brielle that night and not wait until morning. Her father had a feeling that she needed him even if she said she was ok. When he arrived to her apartment Mr. Floyd greeted him and without question he allowed him to pass. He asked about the other gentleman who looked like a Pastor but allowed him to go up with him. Floyd knew Mitchell Summers was not going to negotiate about his daughter.

When he arrived to her door a woman who he remembered as a child opened the door. "Hello Mr. Summers. How are you?" She said hugging him at the door.

"I remember you but you were a little girl."

"Vanessa. Yes it's been a while. I moved out of state but came back to start my practice. I'm a doctor now. All grown up and educated." She said smiling at him.

"Yeah I remember you. Mr. Carols is your father. How is he?" He said walking into the apartment.

"Yes sir. He is well. Him and my mother just retired a couple years ago and I moved back to help them out."

"That is wonderful! Tell them I said hello." He said looking around for Brielle.

"Will do sir. This is Dr. Greenbrier. A friend of mine." She introduced the gentleman standing close to her.

"How do you do sir?" He shook his hand.

"Hello. Is my daughter okay? Two doctors in her home is a bit disturbing." He said with a worried look on his face.

"Yes sir she will be just fine. Brielle is in the bed. We were about to leave but I will fill you in if you like." Vanessa said.

"Yes please do."

"She called me earlier this afternoon wanting to come see me in the morning. I have been training with Dr. Greenbrier so he suggested we not wait and check on her tonight. You know just in case. Gives me experience out of office like old days when you made house calls. Since Brielle is a friend and was indeed sick we came to her. But she is fine. She has a touch of the flu it appears but we won't know for sure until morning. We took some blood and urine and cultured her throat. We gave her something that is safe no matter what's wrong with her but will help her sleep through the night. Depending what's wrong according to our test I will have a prescription ready for her first thing in the morning."

"So she is okay. Possibly the flu?" Mr. Summers asked.

"Yes sir. She is still awake if you want to go in and sit with her. She seems fine just tired and queasy with very low grade temp. But the medicine we gave her will start to work soon and she will be out."

"Thank you so much for coming to see her and thank you too Dr. Greenbrier."

"It's the least I could do when I found out who the patient was. I also heard about her migraines. I want her to come see me when she is feeling better. I am sure I have a solution for that as well. I am a neurologist but I also teach Colleagues to help them gain a better understanding of patients with issues such as migraines. A lot of times they are just misdiagnosed. A way of making great doctors greater."

"I like you. So do you know my daughter as well?"

"I met her a few months ago. I was in need and she was my angel, it saved my sons life."

"You are the man that blessed her and sent that check." He looked him in the eyes.

"Sir she was more of a blessing to me that no amount of money could repay. She saved my son's life and gave us all last moments with my dying father. She doesn't even know."

"Wow. Yes that's my Brie. An angel to us all. So you can fix her migraine issues? She has been dealing with those for a long time."

"I'm sure I can. But she doesn't seem to be having one at the moment which is surprising. It's like she has a covering over her. She is not sedated but she is in a calm state. It's like God is close and healing her and or protecting her from something. I don't question God's work."

"My God, my God. Yes, the power of the almighty!" The Pastor said and started speaking in tongues.

Everyone was smiling and nodding in agreeance.

"Thank you for covering God! Yes!" Vanessa said. "We are going to leave you two to attend to Brielle before she drifts off into lala land. Good seeing you again Mr. Summers. Pastor, have a good evening."

They said their good byes and the two gentlemen headed to Brielle's room.

"Hey dad, I thought that was your voice." She said sounding sleepy.

"Hey my princess. Vanessa told me you may have the flu."

"Yeah, I feel pretty sick. How are my babies?"

"I could tell they miss you. But they are good. They were excited to see Bryson today at church. That perked them up quite a bit." He said caressing her face.

"So you have heard about that huh." She said closing her eyes.

"Your brother told me. He was worried especially since no one has seen you. Floyd is tough."

"Yeah he is like you daddy, very protective over me. So what did you say to Matt? Or Bryson?" She said rolling her eyes.

"Hey Brielle. Hope you don't mind I tagged along with your father to check on you."

"I don't mind Pastor. I probably need you here too. I am so lost with that situation. I thought I knew and now my heart wont stopping loving him and then on top of that I feel awful."

"Sometimes we don't understand the things that happen to us. We are not supposed to understand because God has all understanding and allow things to happen according to His Will. Sometimes we see things and assume we know the answers and what we saw was only an illusion to get us to react a certain way so God can intervene to show up and mend what was never broken."

"Pastor what does that mean?"

"If you would have never experienced what you did and have so many people around you worried about you they all would not have been in church tonight feeling the presence of God for starters. If Bryson would not have been on the journey he was on he would not have helped the woman with two kids who were abandon and hungry needing medical attention. He would have not met you and those kids. Any other scene it probably would have been a hit and miss. Your heart was closed and aching for love but you wouldn't allow anyone in outside your family."

"But daddy he was making a film and using me and my kids. He deceived me. Why didn't he just tell me who he really was? I gave him my home when me and my children could have been living in that home."

"If he would have told you he had all the money in the world would you have given him a chance or thought he was buying your love?" He paused and she was silent. "I know you too well my child. If he would have approached you any other way or it was some other man that day in the park. The outcome would have been different. You opened up became alive again. You were happy and the kids were happy."

"I know daddy but how do I know if it's real or not. That girl said they were about to get married."

"I take it you didn't watch the news at all. That girl ended up in jail for running a car through the building. Bryson left running after you and she was so upset she tried to hurt him."

"Oh no is he okay?" She said.

"And that my dear is a sign of a caring heart of a woman who is in love." Pastor Malone said. "Love is undeniable. When that man showed up at church today with your friend and his friends and sat next to those children, he didn't have a care in the world. He was connected to you through them. He was in church looking for you."

"Nothing happened to him that day just a bruised heart. He really loves you Brie and I think it's genuine." Her father said.

"I think he has everyone fooled and I don't want to be hurt any more than what I am. Dad I need to rest. This medicine is working." Brielle said closing her eyes.

"Alright you rest dear. I really needed to see you for myself, make sure you were okay. I love you daughter."

"I love you too daddy." The medicine was working and her eyes remained closed."

"Mitchell, allow me to pray over her before we leave." Pastor said. As they stood to their feet, her father stood at the side of her bed and Pastor Malone prayed healing and blessings over Brielle. When they were done, they locked up leaving Brielle safe in her home to rest.

She slept through the night and through the next day. She got up only to drink a smoothie she had and some water and got back in bed. She saw she had several messages but didn't have the strength to check. Her doctor friend called her back several times and she knew over half the messages were from Bryson. Floyd came by that evening with some soup and crackers and a sprite. He sat there with her no questions asked made her smile and locked the door behind him when she laid back down.

CHAPTER 56
~BRIELLE~
FRIDAY'S HEAVY HEART

Friday morning Brielle woke up early after sleeping for so long. She decided to be the first person in line at the doctor's office. She was nauseas and threw up barely making it to the toilet. She showered and left Vanessa a message letting her know she was on her way to her office. When she arrived it was six forty five. She missed rush hour traffic and arrived before any of the staff. She lay back in her seat and closed her eyes for a moment. She was awakened by a tap on the window.

"Brielle, come on sweetie follow me into the office." Vanessa said seeing her sleep in the car.

"Startled she got herself together grabbing her purse and followed Vanessa into her office.

"Put your belongings there. Pee in this cup for me again and we will start there." She handed her the cup and retrieved Brielle's file of her test results.

Brielle didn't think she had any fluids in her to pee but managed to produce some urine. She felt nauseated and threw up again. Coming out she handed Vanessa the cup. "I am so sick."

"I know sweetie but you will be ok. I need to draw your blood again I want to test your HCG levels."

"Okay what's that for?" Brielle asked sitting in the chair to have her blood drawn.

Vanessa tested her pee smiling she turned back to Brielle. "Well after I left you Wednesday night I came back to the lab to test everything. You didn't have the flu, no signs of any viral infection but something was off. So I decided to test your pee and you had a

UTI. That didn't explain all of your symptoms so I took a pregnancy test." She said as she was drawing her blood. She got up to put the blood in a machine to test the hcg levels.

"A pregnancy test because I have a UTI?"

"Yes. That's often a sign of a possible pregnancy. With your symptoms and no other confirmed diagnosis." She said looking in her microscope and reading the results. "And you my dear are definitely pregnant. You have been so sleepy and sick because of it. Your HCG levels are very high. And this indicates that you are further along than expected for someone who didn't know they were pregnant or that you are having multiple births."

"I'm pregnant?" She asked again in disbelief.

"Yes sweetheart you are pregnant.   I want to perform and ultrasound to see how far along and if it's more than one is that ok?"

"Vanessa I can't be pregnant. How did this happen?"

"Are you seeing someone?"

"I was but..." She paused thinking about Bryson and their night of passion. How wonderful it was and how real it felt.

"Are you okay Brielle? I am sorry if I upset you. I assumed you were in a relationship. I mean you are beautiful, every man's dream girl."

"I don't know if it was real Vanessa and now I am pregnant by this man."

"I have a couple hours before I open let's chat. Let me help you like old times. I could use a break from my busy life. No judgment no pressure."

Brielle filled her in about Greg and she told her about Bryson. She told her how she let her guard down and that she now feels confused. She told her all the details of Bryson and her with Vanessa holding on to every word.

"Brielle based on what you have told me you are in love. Sounds like to me he wanted to tell you but enjoyed being just a man in love no other stipulations or interferences.   Men are simple girlfriend. I have read all about Bryson Mathews. His character does not scream use and abuse but he is a giver, he is kind and we both know how handsome and fine he is." They both giggled. "There is that smile. And guess what girlfriend? He is choosing love. He is choosing you and those kids. I read an article on him one day. Everyone knew his brother and his business partner but no one knew who he was until one day his business partners gave him a surprise party and the media got in and found out who this multimillion entrepreneur was. His picture was everywhere. But somehow he made it all disappear. No more magazines or newspapers to buy. If you didn't get one as soon as they hit the stands that morning you didn't know. He donated a large amount of money to our foundation here for our medical studies. Anonymously but we all know it was him from our sources."

"If he has all of this money why was he at the park looking like he was homeless?" Brielle asked.

"Not sure what that was about. But there were rumors that he left his fiancé at the altar because she slept with his brother when he was drunk and passed out and threatened him to scream rape if he said anything. Maybe he was heartbroken."

"Really?" Brielle started to think about everything. Wondering if all of this was true why was he using her. She heard Vanessa talking but didn't hear her words. Her heart softened thinking about Bryson hurting. "Okay let's do this ultra sound."

"Okay come on. But did you hear what I said?" Vanessa asked.

"Oh sorry I must have tuned out for a second."

"I have a colleague, who works with him, anything he needs he goes to take care of him and his people. I can ask him if he knows of any reason why he would appear to be homeless."

"Yes okay that would be fine." She laid on the table as Vanessa prepared her ultrasound equipment. "I guess this explains why I have been so tired."

"Yes it does. And why we thought you had the flu. Your hormones are not balanced and look at here." She said pointing to the screen. "It looks like we have two babies growing."

"Wow Vanessa are you sure? What am I going to do with two babies?"

"You are going to get married to Mr. Mathews right away and pretend you got pregnant on your wedding day. You are going to have these babies and the both of you are going to love them. You are about four weeks, conceiving about 2 weeks ago, still early so you have time. Then you and your husband will love these babies forever." She explained to her what the four weeks pregnant and two weeks ago conception meant.

Brielle was smiling. Vanessa was just what the doctor ordered for her. "You are what I needed right now. Thank you so much! I am going to pick up my babies early from school and take them to the park and relax. I told them I would take them tomorrow if I was feeling better but today would be better. Then I can think and take this all in. Wait what about the sick feeling, I really feel sick."

"I am going to give you a pill here and call you in a prescription to pick up from your pharmacy. I want you to get your prenatal vitamins started and take these pills at night. Don't want you being sick all day. Take them with dinner. Eat small meals. Stay away from soda and coffee or anything with caffeine. I am going to refer you to a Doctor to see on a regular basis for your prenatal care."

"You are not going to be my doctor?"

"I am not that kind of doctor and you need to be under an obstetrician. He is in this building though. But please feel free to call me regarding anything. I am always here for you."

"Thank you Vanessa for everything. You are my angel."

"An angel for an angel." Patients were coming in to the office and she knew that meant back to work.

Brielle went to pick up her prescriptions. She didn't know what to do about Bryson and now that she was having his babies she knew she had to face him to find out the truth.

After picking up her prescriptions she went to see her mom and pick up Jayla before getting the older kids from school. After about thirty minutes of her mom making sure she was okay she headed to get the older kids. She picked up bread and let them get whatever junk they wanted and grabbed some sub sandwiches for them to eat on. "I missed my babies so much."

"You feel better momma?" Carter asked,

"Yes baby I had some type of stomach bug but I feel a lot better."

"Momma we saw Mr. Matt at church he said he missed you too." Jayla said.

"He did?" Brielle was sad she missed him too and wanted things to be normal again. Especially now that she was pregnant.

"Yeap. And we were all worried about you momma. Glad you feel better." Olivia said.

"Thanks babies. Help me unload the car. I have a blanket in the back." They headed to their spot by the lake and placed everything out. Brielle sat down on the blanket. She wanted to lay down but knew that wasn't going to happen. "I'm going to bless the food before you all go to play so momma can go ahead and eat okay." She had not eaten in a while and was starving now that she had medicine to make her feel better.

They all bowed their heads and held hands as Brielle blessed the food and gave thanks for her children. When they were done she prepared her sandwich to eat as she watched the kids play. She looked to her left and a beautiful lady was standing close by watching her own children play with the help of what appeared to be a nanny.

"You have a beautiful family." She said to Brielle.

She turned in her direction trying to hurry and swallow before responding. "Thank you. Your babies are beautiful as well."

"They are my angels. Thank you."

"I know the feeling. My children are my everything. Would you like to join me? There is plenty of room on the blanket." Brielle said offering her a seat.

"I would love too." She walked over and joined Brielle on the blanket. "My name is Ameila Churchwell, nice to meet you."

"Brielle Summers. And those are my three little angels by the water." She said pointing in their direction.

"I only have the two and that's a co-worker helping me for a moment with the kids. I don't have family here just friends and my new work family."

"Oh okay. You can't deny your family and blood don't always bond you."

"That's true. I just recently got a divorce. My husband put me and his own kids out on the streets with no money and nowhere to go. I was homeless for a couple months."

"Sometimes men have no clue and can be so cruel to the ones they should love. Looks like you all are doing well now." Brielle was wondering why this stranger was telling her business to her. But she decided to listen anyhow.

"Yes thanks to this wonderful man who saved us. I wanted to keep my mouth shut that day and not help him but instead I spoke up not realizing he was helping me. You see, sometimes things are not always what they appear. You know how they say don't judge a book by its cover?" Ameila said, attempting to make a point with her story.

"Yeah I know that saying." Not sure where this lady was going with her story but Brielle was intrigued.

"My baby would have died, I probably would have died. We were homeless, hungry and sick. And God sent that man at the right time. You can take everything away from a man but you can never take away his spirit and his character. No matter how much they have or how little, a man is who God intended him to be."

"Did your husband come back for you?" Brielle asked now thinking about the story her pastor told her about Bryson helping the woman and her kids.

"Honey no. He is somewhere miserable wishing he would have kept me as his wife instead of the hoe's who took all of his money and left him diseased."

"Oh wow." Brielle's eyes were widened.

"Now I work for the man who saved me. Him and his cute partner that I am crushing on." She said smiling. "I do a number of things for them that I enjoy but the one thing I am very proud of is writing the love story that is unfolding. You see he too appeared to be homeless when I met him but he wasn't. And while he was pretending to see how people would treat him not knowing who he was he met a girl. She touched his soul and his spirit and his heart fell in love with her instantly. His every thought was of her. His every breath he wanted to be breathing the same air that she was breathing. And everything he did started revolving around her. She healed his broken heart and showed him the power of God. His only fault was the deception of who he was to society but he never deceived her of who he was as a man or how he felt about her. He never lied to her about his love or his feelings. Everything he said, all his actions were real."

"How do you know they were real?" At this point Brielle knew that this woman worked for Bryson. That she was the woman he saved. Her heart was beating fast.

"There was no denying it. Anyone that had the pleasure of seeing these two together felt their love. She was God sent to him at a time he was down. As we watched him interact with her and seeing how much in love he was when he wasn't with her even a blind man could see the true love between them. We described it as ordained from God himself. No games, no pretending. Nothing but true love. I have had the pleasure of writing the story from the documentary that was being put together. One of his strengths is loyalty which was also his weakness in this case."

"So how does the story end?"

"I haven't finished it yet. It is still unfolding." She turned to Brielle and smiled.

"Why?"

"Some unforeseen things happened that appeared to be one thing but was misread to be something more than what it really was. The girl was hurt and the man was hurt seeing her hurt. The girl shut everyone out and then became sick and the man also sick but was love sick desperately trying to get to the girl to proclaim his true love and promise to never heart her again. To tell her of his hearts desires, to love her forever and make her his wife, her children his children. It's up to her when and how I finish writing their story." She looked over and saw tears in Brielle's eyes. "Do you remember giving the homeless lady and her children breakfast from McDonalds one morning?"

Brielle turned to Ameila to study her face realizing it was her. "That was you?"

"Funny how God works. I was at a breaking point and was ready to give up on life. And when I pulled the food out of the bag a note you wrote for me fell out." She pulled the note from her pocket. "And it read, 'God loves you and he has not forgotten about you. This is just a small blessing but God has a greater blessing coming to you. Keep your faith and keep praying to God he hears you and he is going to answer your prayers. Stay strong my sister, the answer may not be clear but the blessing will be real. God will make a way out of no way. You will be in my prayers. God bless you and your babies.' And from that moment on I prayed for you as well. You were a blessing to me, then Bryson was the blessing I never expected to see and now it is your turn to receive God's blessing of love for you. It is real true love waiting for you to embrace." She said wrapping her arms around Brielle as tears fell from her eyes.

"Is he here?" Knowing the story she told was about Bryson and herself.

"Yes, he is standing right behind you."

Brielle froze trying to dry her face. She watched as Ameila stood to her feet and looked towards Bryson with a smile. Brielle turned to see Bryson. Looking up at Ameila before she walked away she said, "Thank you Ameila."

"Thanks for allowing me to join you. It was an honor to be in your presence." She said before she turned and walked towards the kids all playing together.

CHAPTER 57
~BRYSON~
FILLING IN THE PIECES
WHO HE REALLY IS

Brielle stood to her feet and turned to face Bryson.

"Brielle I have missed you so much and I am so sorry for everything. I never wanted to hurt you. Everything I said to you is true. I love you so much please give me a second chance let me make everything right? My real name is Bryson Mathews. I own Cole Estates Enterprise and numerous other companies. I am a very wealthy man. That doesn't change anything about how I feel about you. When I met you I instantly fell in love with you and your children. I want to marry you, adopt your kids and take care of you forever."

"You're not getting married?"

"Only to you if you allow me too."

"What about the cameras that are still filming." She said looking around.

"None of this will air if you chose for it not to. Today was the last day of my contract with them. They only wanted to see the ending of true love happening in a time when no one expected love to be a factor. Tell our story to the world. But if you say no it all goes away. Me finding you is worth losing any and everything else. I don't care about defaulting on the contract or anything that happens as long as I have you. Brielle I love you. I miss you and those kids and I love you so much please give me a second chance. Marry me be my wife."

Brielle started crying. No one understood why. She slowly walked to him with open arms and he ran to sweep her off her feet. Embracing her tight and kissing her for an eternity. When they come up for air Bryson placed her to her feet. Brielle looked up and saw her mom and dad, Chantae, Bradon, her brother Isaiah and several other people she had yet to meet all coming closer to her. Pastor Malone was even there.

Turning back to Bryson he was on one knee with an exotic expensive ring with an enormous diamond holding Brielle's hand. The kids were now by their side. "Brielle Summers will you do me the honor of being my wife, allow me to protect you and your kids, provide for you and the kids, care for and love you and these kids forever and always? Will you marry me?"

"Yes I will marry you." She said with tears in her eyes.

He picked her up spinning her around. She felt nauseated and tried to hide it. The kids were jumping and screaming and excited as well.

"We have Pastor Malone here. I have someone here from Justice of Peace that has a marriage license we will need to sign. If you agree we can be married right now and have a ceremony planned out to your liking as soon as possible."

"Right here right now?" Brielle asked.

"Yes this is where God brought us together, where my greatest blessing was given to me. Yes right here right now. My parents are here, my brother. You have your parent's your brother our family and friends here yes marry me right now."

"Wait is that your mom? I met her at your brothers party which is actually your home isn't it?"

"Yes my mom. And yes our home now."

"This has got to be a dream." She said and immediately Bryson kissed her embracing her in his arms. When he pulled his lips from hers he looked into her eyes. "Yes, let's get married right now." She said.

They signed the marriage certificate and gave it to Pastor Malone. He pulled out his bible and stood in front of them. "God has blessed us all on this day by allowing us to witness the true greatness of his love between Bryson and Brielle…"

They were married in the park where they met in front of their family and friends. Everyone who followed Bryson's journey of love was there to witness his happiness. Happy tears flowed and hearts were touched and forever changed. Bryson had a ring for him and her that matched. He wanted them to be bonded together with feelings, actions, rings, certificates and witnesses. He was in heaven having Brielle as his wife.

He promised her she would have the ceremony of her choosing when she wanted it to happen. Dress, bridesmaid's flower girls and all. He needed to prove to her that he was serious about loving her. That she would be his forever. He paid top dollar to get the justice of peace to come out. He didn't want to waste another day without Brielle as his wife. This day was the beginning of their happy life together.

CHAPTER 58
~BRYSON~
SHE SAID YES

Bryson invited everyone back to his home after the events in the park. He wanted to celebrate Brielle, and have everyone there with them. They were officially married and this was the happiest day of his life. A line of limousines were waiting to take everyone to Bryson's home. Some drove their own car and everyone else rode in class. The kids rode with their grandparents to give Bryson and Brielle some much needed alone time.

"You are my wife Brielle and I am the happiest man in the world."

"You are amazing. How did you know I would be at the park?" She asked Bryson.

"Well Jayla told me you were taking them Saturday if you felt better. Your dad told me you had the flu so I didn't think you would feel better by then. But then I get a call from Dr. Zackery. Apparently we have friends who are friends and he knows Dr. Carols. She asked him about me and told him that you wanted to know more about me from another perspective. She mentioned that she would call you after your outing with the kids at the park. I put it all together and thought I would hang out here until you did show. And Ameila found you first. Not sure what all she said to you but it must have been good."

"It was heartfelt. Very sweet of her to say the things she did and what you did for her."

"Yes she is very sweet and I think Kenny likes her. I have to formally introduce you to him when we get to our home."

"Yes I want to meet everyone. It's crazy one minute my heart is ripped out and the next I am back in your arms like nothing has changed except for the fact that now I am your wife." Brielle said admiring her ring.

"That's a good thing. I didn't know how you would react to knowing who I was after deceiving you. I wasn't really homeless but I met you and your kindness and loving heart. I know our spirits danced but you looked beyond any faults I had and loved me when it appeared I had nothing. And to give me your home you just purchased was priceless."

"I fell in love with you at that moment I saw you and I couldn't run away from it. But you having money does not make me love you more. I love you simply because my heart won't allow me to stop and I don't want to stop."

"I know. You are my forever and I thank God you are still in my life. I promise to make you the happiest woman and proud to be my wife."

"Oh I am already proud to be your wife. I am Mrs. Brielle Mathews now. I just met you and married you all in the same day. Just kidding." She looked at his smiling face and caressed his head. "So how did everyone else know I was there?"

"I was hoping you would say yes to marry me at the park and I wanted everyone who was important to us to be there. I don't want to deprive you of a wedding day so we will plan it still but I couldn't live another day without you being Mrs. Brielle Mathews." He caressed her face as he held her in his arms.

"That means you are my husband. I am married." She said looking at her fabulous ring.

He laughed out loud grabbing her closer. "Yes you are married and you are married to me." He kissed her lips, her nose, and her eye lids. "I love you Brielle!"

"I love you too Bryson very much. I need to tell you something."

"Okay anything. What's on your mind?"

"I didn't have the flu. I went to Vanessa, I mean Dr. Carols office this morning so she could give me medicine and tell me my results from her visit Wednesday and it wasn't the flu."

"What was wrong? We can handle anything so just tell me. Don't be afraid." He could sense her tenseness.

"I am pregnant." She said looking into his eyes.

Bryson smiled. He was happy that was her problem and that they were going to have a baby. "That is great. We are about to have a baby." He said hugging her tight.

"You're not mad?"

"No I am ecstatic about the news." He said hugging her again.

"Ok great, but that's not all." She said. "I was sick because the HCG hormone levels were really high because we are having two babies instead of one."

"Twins? We are having twins?" He asked as Brielle nodded yes. "Woohoo! A double blessing." Bryson was really happy. "Don't you worry sweetheart we will make sure you have the best care and all the help you need before and after the babies come." He pulled her close to kiss her more. They embraced and she pulled herself up in his lap to straddle him.

"You are my King. My breath of fresh air and I am so glad the other day was a misunderstanding. That was the worse feeling ever thinking I lost you."

"You will never lose me Brielle. I am yours forever. Is it ok if I have movers pack up your apartment? I don't want you to lift a finger. But more so I don't want you to be away from me any longer than you have to be."

She thought for a moment about some personal things she would like to gather herself. "I have some things I would need to get myself first is that okay? I don't want movers touching or seeing these things?" She said biting on her bottom lip.

Bryson wondering what those things could be and he wanted to know. "I am curious at what those things are. Can I go with you and help you?"

"Uhmm. Well. Okay yes. That's fine." She said blushing. "Let's go now and that way I can say good bye to Floyd and he will know I am in safe hands."

"Driver. Take us to Brielle's old apartment same place we were this morning." He said to the driver. "And yesterday morning and the morning before that." He said looking at Brielle.

"You were stalking me?" She said kissing his lips.

"I needed you. And I was going to get to you anyway possible." His eyes were closed enjoying her kisses.

"You want to make love to me?" The window separating their space from the drivers went up.

"Yes with a passion. I can make love to you at your place since we will be alone." Still kissing her.

"What about a sample before we get there?" She said rocking her hips back and forth.

"You want to do it in the limo?" He said nibbling on her neck.

"We are married. It doesn't matter where we make love. No one can see us. The window is up."

"You can have me wherever you desire sweetheart."

"The doctor said my hormone levels were high and if it didn't make me sick it may make me extremely horny. Hope that's okay." She said as her breathing became intense from every kiss he landed on her neck, squeezing at her breast. She had her arms wrapped around his neck caressing his head.

"I got you sweetheart. I am going to make love to you every day, every chance I can."

She pulled her dress up and out of the way and reached for his pants. He was rock hard as she released his manhood. "I love you Bryson. I need to feel you inside me." She raised her hips high enough to straddle his manhood.

"I missed feeling your honey wet loveliness all over me Brielle. Oh you feel so good."

She moaned as he held her tight in his arms moving his hips to go in and out of her warm honey filled walls in a slow motion. "You feel, oh yes, you feel wonderful." She moaned and managed to say.

"We are stopping sweetheart. Can I lay you down and make love to you upstairs?"

She smiled as she stopped moving her hips breathing heavily. "Yes you can but don't move yet. You feel that?" She asked as her loveliness walls were contracting from her having an orgasm.

"Yes I feel it." He said pushing further inside her kissing her neck. After a moment longer and he realized she was coming down off her orgasmic high he asked, "Are you ready to go upstairs now?"

"Yes my husband I am." She moved from his lap and waiting as he put his lovely package away and fixed his clothes. Do we have people waiting on us at your place?"

"At our home? Yes we do. But they have plenty of entertainment and food to keep them company until we get there. I hired a catering service and a DJ. I am sure my mom is showing the kids around so they can pick out their rooms."

"They are going to love that." The driver opened the door for Bryson and he held Brielle's hand as she got out as well. "How did he know we were decent?" She asked whispering in his ear.

"There is a button when I am ready to get out I press it and he knows to open the door."

"Oh okay." As they entered the building Floyd was all smiles seeing Brielle feeling better. "Hi Floyd." She said embracing him.

"Hello dear. Mr. Mathews." He said nodding his head.

"Hi Floyd." He said smiling. No words needed to be said.

"Floyd I am moving. Me and the kids are moving with my new husband." She said all gitty showing him the ring.

"Congratulations. Good to see you are happy and that the Mr. is making you happy." He looked up at Bryson.

"That I will always do sir. Make her happy. Mr. Floyd that is a promise I do intend to keep."

"I believe you. I admire your strength and persistence for love. Shows good character."

"Thank you sir." Bryson said.

"Floyd we are going to get a few things and then someone will be coming to pack up and take my belongings and clean the apartment for me."

"Sounds good to me. Just call and let me know details."

"Actually, Bryson will be calling you on my behalf if that's okay." She turned to him rising up on her tip toes leaning towards Bryson for a kiss.

"Not a problem. You two love birds go on up now. I'm sure you two have some things you need to handle." He said winking at Bryson.

Brielle blushed. Thank you Floyd for everything. I will be sure you get an invitation to the actual wedding ceremony. Make sure you come."

"Wouldn't miss it for the world."

They headed to the elevator. As soon as the doors closed they were all over each other kissing and touching. The elevator doors opened and he picked her up off her feet. Taking her key he opened her apartment door. Locking it behind him. They headed to the bedroom and he proceeded to undress her kissing every inch of her body. Stopping at her belly he paused. "I am so happy you are having my babies. I hope we have a boy and a girl. Then we will have five bundles of joy."

"I am excited as well to be having your babies. Especially now that we are married. Can we keep it between us for now and announce it in a month or so?"

"Absolutely sweetheart. Whatever you want is fine with me." He kissed her stomach and moved his way to her thighs. Kissing her love pot and tasting her honey. "I am going to enjoy tasting you every day."

"You promise?"

"Promise." He removed all of his clothes and the rest of Brielle's. He treated her delicately thinking about her being pregnant. This was the happiest moment for them both. With every stroke he loved her more. With every kiss he loved her more. He explored her body all over again cherishing the fact that she was now his wife.

He made love to her body for over an hour. They both knew they needed to leave but couldn't help to indulge in the love they shared and missed so much. A lot had happened with the hurt and distance between them and her marrying him that afternoon. Life at that moment was worth every second of his journey.

When they were up and ready to leave she grabbed a carry along bag and went to her closet. She loaded the bag with her good panties and her sexual toys. Bryson watched her every move as she blushed and bit her bottom lip. "Toys huh?"

"Sorry I didn't want those to be seen by anyone. I dated them during my drought. You know dated the toys." She made googly eyes.

He laughed. "They are okay with me Brielle if you want to keep them you can."

"But I don't need them anymore now that I have you. Well maybe I will keep the vibrating wands I have. I love those."

"If you like. Come on let me get you home. I have plans for you tonight." He said taking her bag and smacking her on the butt. They headed towards the door saying goodbye to Floyd on their way out. His driver was patiently waiting to take them home.

CHAPTER 59
~BRYSON~
THIS IS YOUR HOME

Bryson and Brielle arrived at Bryson's home, now their home and were welcomed by everyone there. Their friends and family, coworkers and staff were all excitedly waiting with smiles on their face. When the two of them stepped out of the limo they were greeted with horns and confetti all coming their way. Chantae embraced her friend in a happy hug followed by her father and a few other friends and family. Bryson was greeted with handshakes from Kenneth, Bradon and others.

The kids were excited and it warmed Brielle's heart to see them amongst all these good people happy and smiling.

"Mommy you got to see my new room. This house is a princess castle." Jayla said running up to her mom hugging her.

"Yeah mom this house is a mansion. Granny said we are moving in are we really?" Olivia said.

"Mom, Bradon has a room full of all kinds of video games and he said it was all mine now. It has everything. We played Madden and I beat him." Carter said.

The kids were all excited and surrounding Brielle. "So you all like the house I take it?"

"Yes ma'am we do." Carter said.

"We love it momma." Olivia said.

"Can we really live here momma?" Jayla asked.

"This is your home you can live here forever if you like or if your mom wants we can get Bradon to build us a new home." Bryson said to them all.

Looking up at the outside of the home during the day Brielle could see more details of the design work than she could at night when she came to Bradon's party. She was in awe of the beauty of the home. "I think we can live here for now." She said with a smile. Turning toward Bryson to mouth, *"this home is beautiful."*

Bryson wrapped his arm around Brielle standing there with the kids. They were now a family just as they both wanted to happen. "Come on let's get inside and show your mom your rooms." Bryson said grabbing Jayla's hand. Olivia ran up to grab his other hand as they all walked into the home. Chantae embraced Brielle's arm walking into the home. "I am so happy for you girlfriend. Are you feeling better? Girl Floyd is a trip not letting us up to you."

"I know girl. I'm sorry about that I was not feeling well at all. I missed my friend though. How are you?" Brielle asked.

"Girl life is good. I put in my two week notice today. Me and Bradon are moving in together and he told me not to worry about anything but starting my business. Girl life couldn't be better for the both of us. Blessed!"

"Truly blessed girlfriend. I am so happy with this man. God showed out this time didn't he?"

"Yes he did!" Chantae said walking with Brielle, Bryson and the kids.

Bradon was right behind his brother. "I am proud of you big brother. Your determination always pays off. And you are setting a great example for your little brother. Mom and dad are happy especially momma. She always wanted her boys to find true happiness."

"I am proud of you too Bradon. I must say I knew you would figure it out one day and Chantae made that day come sooner for you. True love has a way of changing your life forever. Now all you need to do is make things right for you and Chantae and you know what I am talking about." Bryson said and they both looked in Chantae's direction.

The kids were showing their mom their rooms. The rooms were huge and Bryson already had Jayla's room decorated like a princess room. The kids never imagined living in a home this big having their own rooms that were five times the size of their previous bedrooms.

Bryson and Brielle headed to their room and Bradon and Chantae stayed with the kids. They passed their guest having a good time in the living area ensuring them they will be right back. Bryson walked her to their bedroom and she was amazed at how beautiful it was. "I took some of your style from your home and incorporated it into our bedroom. The bed is brand new. Bradon designed it just for us. I have not even slept in it yet, waiting on you." Bryson was looking into her eyes standing at the end of the bed post. The bed was a California King with wooden bed posts. Heavy, thick and fit for a king and his queen. The head board was magnificent and the cuts were perfect with diamond reflections that Brielle loved. She took her shoes off and climbed up into the middle of the bed to run her hands over the design. "Bradon is excellent at what he does. He needs to start multiple companies including a furniture store. He could brand his designs and make millions selling to high class people and celebrities alone. This is something rich people would rush to buy to own." She turned to Bryson standing up in the bed and walking to him. "I forgot you are rich." She said smiling walking into his arms.

"No we are rich. Everything I have, every dime is ours. No limits, no boundaries."

"No limits? So I can go out and buy an expensive car a new wardrobe, a closet full of shoes and you wouldn't care?"

"Nope not at all. Whatever you want you will have. Come with me I want to show you something." He walked her into what she thought was another room. "These things are yours. I had my designer go out and get you a starter wardrobe. All the shoes are yours. This section is full of panties, bras, lingerie gowns. She had no limits only instructions to go all out for you."

"This looks like a store all these clothes and an entire wall of shoes. Bryson this is too much."

"Nothing is too much for you. You will be treated like the queen you are Brielle."

"This is all real, I'm not dreaming?" She turned to him with tears in her eyes.

"No dream sweetheart. This is all real. I'm real and our love is real. I have no doubts in my heart or mind about you about us. This is all real sweetheart." He watched her as she looked at her things he had purchased for her.

"And the lingerie is beautiful. But admit it. These things were meant for you right?"

"Beautiful pieces for a beautiful woman. And yes I can't wait to see you in them at least until I take them off of you." He said grinning.

"This look like a department store with all my sizes. Thank you Bryson." She said walking towards him to kiss him.

"No need to thank me. The kids each have their own wardrobe. And whatever you don't like you don't have to keep and we will get more." He held her in his arms tight.

"We are so lucky to have you." She kissed his lips.

"I am the lucky one. God showed out when he blessed me with you."

"Yes he did show out this time. I am happy Bryson. And I know the kids are happy."

"My mom loves you."

"I met her here at Bradon's party did you know that?"

"Yes. She knew you were talking about me and she fell in love with you that day. She said God told her you were my wife that day."

"Really? Wow!"

"Yes. I watched the video as well. I have cameras in every room except ours just so you know. It was more so for Bradon's protection bringing people in and out but they did come in handy to save his ass."

"I am looking forward to forever with you Bryson. I hope we have boys by the way."

"That will be fine with me. Come on let's get to our guest. I will give you a complete tour tomorrow."

"Yes I need something on my stomach I am feeling a bit queasy."

"Let's get you fed then." Holding hands they left the sanctuary of their bedroom and headed to their guest.

"There goes the two love birds." Mitchell Summers said.

"Everyone get a glass so we can toast to the newlyweds." Mr. Mathews said.

Chantae was handing Brielle a glass when she said, "No I will have ginger ale my stomach is still upset." She waited as the waiter poured her some ginger ale in her champagne glass.

Chantae was curious at that point if there was more to her reason for not having champagne. She would make a mental note to inquire about it later.

"To the newlyweds Bryson and Brielle. May God bless you both forever drenched in love and happiness. May he bring you nothing but joy and protect your marriage from any storm or turmoil. We all know this marriage is based on true love and we vow to protect you both as well as family and friends who love you dear. To Bryson and Brielle and a marriage of true love." Mr. Mathews toasted.

"Cheers." Everyone said as glasses clinked together.

Bryson kissed his wife and embraced his dad. "Thanks dad. I love you always."

Everyone celebrated this joyous occasion throughout the evening. Brielle started to feel sick again and Bryson excused them so he could take care of her. Bradon and Chantae as well as Bryson and Brielle's parents all stayed and helped with the children getting settled.

"We can rest and I can hold you all night. You tell me what you need and I will take care of you." Bryson said holding Brielle's hair back as she threw up over the toilet.

When she was done he handed her a wash cloth. "This bathroom is amazing Bryson. I absolutely love this house. It is perfect. It's like it was made especially for me."

"Well it's yours and maybe that was in God's plans too."

"After I brush my teeth can we take a bath together and then you make love to me for a while?" She said looking at him leaning against the sink.

"If you are sure I will make love to you all night until you tell me to stop, after our bath."

"Promise?"

"Always."

She brushed her teeth and he ran them some warm bubble bath in the enormous garden marble tub. She leaned up against him in the water secure in his embrace. They talked about thirty minutes before he picked her up out of the tub to make love to her. He dried her body kissing her in all her intimate spots. He watched as she blushed enjoying every moment of passion. He made love to her body for hours until they both were exhausted and he held her naked body in

his arms as they both fell asleep with smiles on their face, as Mr. &
Mrs. Bryson Mathews..

CHAPTER 60
~JEWEL~
I'M HAVING YOUR BABY

Jewel was in jail without bond waiting for her court date. She wasn't eating and barely drinking. She had made a mess of her life. *How can I be so stupid and drive a car through that man's building. I totaled my car and landed myself in jail where the guards want to take sex from me. I never thought I could feel so disgusted about sex and with myself.* She thought with tears in her eyes. She felt nauseated and started throwing up.

"What is wrong with you chile?" A lady guard asked.

"I don't know. I feel sick."

"Come on let's take you to the clinic get you checked out." She opened her cell and helped her out. She walked her to the clinic and told the doctor of her throwing up. "She probably knocked up."

Jewel knew that meant pregnant. It never crossed her mind to be pregnant as she never wanted kids. She thought her body was too flawless to allow a child to mess it up. "I am not knocked up." She said to the guard and doctor.

"Here." He said handing her a cup. "Go in there and pee in the cup and bring the pee in the cup back to me."

"Yeah okay." She said walking into the bathroom. She was feeling her stomach. *I have gained some weight. Maybe I am pregnant and maybe it is Bryson's baby and he will take me back and get me out of here if I am pregnant. It would have to be his baby. Michael is snipped. He can't have kids and I used protection with almost everyone else.* She thought to herself.

She handed the cup to the doctor who tested her pee. He turned to Jewel saying, "Lay here on the table and raise your shirt."

He took the ultrasound machine and put the device on her belly to look.

"What are you doing? Aren't you suppose to tell me what you are doing?" She asked in a smart way.

"You my dear are pregnant and by the looks of it you are very pregnant. She will need to be moved to the maternity ward can you call it up, I will write up the paperwork." The doctor said to Jewel and then the guard.

Jewel thought about Bryson and then thought about her body. *If he doesn't take me back I will be stuck with a messed up body and a baby to raise.* "What about an abortion?" She asked the doctor.

"You don't have that choice while you are here but you are too far along for an abortion. You are about thirteen weeks pregnant by the looks of things."

"How the hell I not know I was pregnant for thirteen weeks? How many months is that?"

"Three months. Sometimes women have no symptoms. Every woman is different. Or maybe you had symptoms and you decided to ignore them. Either way you are having a baby."

"Shit!" She said out loud. "Will they let me out of jail?"

"Girl naw! You will still do your time. You will have to give the baby to his daddy, family member or adoption. Otherwise he will be in foster care until you get out." The guard said. "I have a pregnant one coming to the unit." She called in to the guards working that area.

"Damn this is fucked up. Can I use your phone?" She asked the doctor.

"If you are calling the daddy then yes. But make it quick."

It was six fifteen in the morning she knew Bryson would be up. She dialed his number from memory. He picked up on the third ring. She could hear a woman's voice in the background. As bad as she wanted to say something else she bit her tongue trying to stay focused. "Bryson I am pregnant. We are having a baby please get me out of here."

"What the hell?" He thought that had to be impossible wiping the sleep from his eyes. "Call Michael and tell him the news not me."

"Michael can't have kids he got snipped fixed or whatever it is you do to not be able to have babies. Please come get me."

I will have my people do the necessary test and take it from there. Please don't ever dial my number again. I am married and happy now." He said and hung up the phone.

Those last words sounded over and over in her head. *Married and happy now. How the...When the hell did all this happen?* She started crying. She tried to call her dad but the guard stopped her.

"One call sweetie. Did the daddy say it wasn't his? That's how it always happens. I hear that story all the time. Come on so you can see your new home." The guard grabbed her by the arm to escort her out.

Jewel was silent. She didn't want to have a baby if she couldn't have Bryson. She was diagnosed as being suicidal and dangerous to her baby so she ended up in restraints and having to be force fed until she would eat.

She was devastated she didn't have Bryson. He went and married someone else. Now she was in jail pregnant and didn't know who her baby daddy was.

CHAPTER 61
~MRS. MATHEWS~
MOMMA'S FINAL THOUGHTS

I have lived long enough and experienced a lot in my lifetime to know a thing or two about some things. One thing I do know is the power of God and his love never fails. All things happen according to his Will. We make choices, some good some bad, but God already knows what we or someone else is going to do and yet he still directs our path down the road for us to ultimately get to our destiny. The destiny we are all born with.

I have been married forty two years and some change. I raised two young men, Bryson and Bradon and that was sometimes hard. Two different personalities and demeanors. Both determined. Both good boys who made me proud. Bryson on the other hand was a go getter from the time he was born everything had to be perfect. This is why I didn't understand how he got mixed up with Jewel. I knew in my heart she was not a part of his destiny. But maybe she was. Maybe he had to see what he didn't want, to know what he did want when he met his future. Jewel was beautiful, her body was lovely and her confidence was cocky. She will be another man's future when God is done preparing her. She is young and still learning.

Bryson on the other hand had years of grooming and struggled with how to know if a woman will love him and not just be in love with everything he acquired. Funny how God works. Taking you out of your comfort zones of life and changing your elements to allow you to see and feel and simply just know. There was no doubt of God's love for him. After all, my boys have a prayer warrior for a mother.

I learned from having a husband who had problems in the beginning of our marriage. I knew he was for me and I was for him.

Our journey was one God intended for us to have to give us our foundation to stand on for forty two years and counting. I prayed and begged God to give me the power I needed through prayer and understanding and he did just that. I was able to cover my husband and our boys through prayer. I knew God could hear me and he answered because he healed my husband from the alcoholic disease that had him bond. God is real and faith in him, praying a specific prayer and trusting that he will, makes all the difference in life. My boys will be okay. I know that now. Bryson has Brielle and that true love has been ordained by God and is forever. They are not done having tests and trials come their way but nothing that my God can't handle.

Bradon has come a long way from hiding in the shadows of his brother. He is a man of many talents with his hands. I knew this when he wanted me to buy him wood and art supplies when he was a little boy and would come showing me a master piece that no four year old should have made. His drawing was magnificent and his teachers wanted him to enter in every art show possible. His science projects were never simple and when he had to build a map for geography well let's just say his teacher has it in a glass exhibit case for all to see. I knew he was fine. His side jobs were not normal side jobs. They brought him in plenty of money. Even though his brother was his number one customer he was also his number one fan.

He had to figure it out on his own though. Chantae comes along and shares her dreams making him realize that dreams are real and it takes dedication and commitment and someone else to love what you do to sometimes give you that spark you need. Chantae was his spark. Not only did he find his spark, he found true love as well. His passion and desire to finish making his dreams a reality is now on its way. Sometimes that's all we need is a push or that someone special to believe in us to share our passion with us.

Let's not forget about Kenny. He was raised under my covering as well. Him, Bryson and Bradon grew up as brothers. Bryson and Kenny were inseparable and always had each other's back. That loyalty is powerful and bonded these two for life. Bryson not only found Brielle, he found Ameila too not knowing that she was meant for Kenny. First time Kenny has shown affection for a woman and everyone else has noticed this as well but Kenny himself. His morals are in play right now making sure her divorce is final and her heart is healing. He plans to help her along the way.

My boys will be just fine. No weapon formed against them shall prosper. No obstacle or trial is too great to overcome. Not even a baby by Jewel. God has them covered. And there mom will continue to pray. Thank you Jesus! And thank you Heavenly Father. God is Love and Love never fails!

I will continue to seduce your soul with my words
Unspoken and those spoken with my eyes
wanting your hearts flame to only burn for me
For the moment...

Feast your eyes upon the beauty they desire
Study the curves and desires your mind wants to explore
Reach if you dare to feel what you hunger
Longer than a moment...

Be prepared for my response, my reaction to your touch
Caressing you, allowing you to indulge the craving that lingers within
To taste the sweetness of my lips
To be memorized long after I am gone
Felt even when I am not there
And Fantasies the desires that were meant
To be for a lifetime...

But for the moment
Live with no regrets to fulfill desires
Seducing you
Reaching for that satisfying touch
Caress all the desires outside and inner wetness
Kiss passionately allowing your tongue to dance freely
Ignite the flames and allow them to be tamed
Enjoy the moments...
Seduce and be seduced

I will continue to seduce your soul with my words
Unspoken and those spoken with my eyes
Wanting your hearts flame to only burn for me
For the moment...
Feast your eyes upon the beauty they desire
Study the curves and places your hands want to explore
Reach if you dare to feel what you hunger for
Longer than a moment...
Be prepared for my response, my reaction to your touch
Caressing you, allowing you to indulge the craving that lingers
Flaming deep within your erotic nature
To taste the sweetness of my lips
To be remembered long after I am gone
Felt even when I am not there
And fantasize the desires that were meant
To be for a lifetime...
But for the moment
Live with no regrets to fulfill desires
Seducing you
Reach if you dare for that satisfying touch
And caress all the desires outside
Expecting the inner wetness inside the sweet honey spot
Kiss passionately allowing your tongue to dance freely
Igniting the flames and allow them to be tamed
Enjoy the careless moments...
Passionate moments of love
Love shared with the desires of your mind
Seduce and allow yourself to be seduced
Love like there is no tomorrow
Embrace the love burning between warm thighs
Enjoy the seduction of art controlled by the mind
Tantalizing...Teasing...Seduce...Arouse and be Aroused
Embrace the erotic orgasmic nature taking over
Your body waiting to explode shiver and shake
Causing a seductive natural high…

www.ingramcontent.com/pod-product-compliance
Lightning Source LLC
Chambersburg PA
CBHW051520250626
47156CB00001B/169